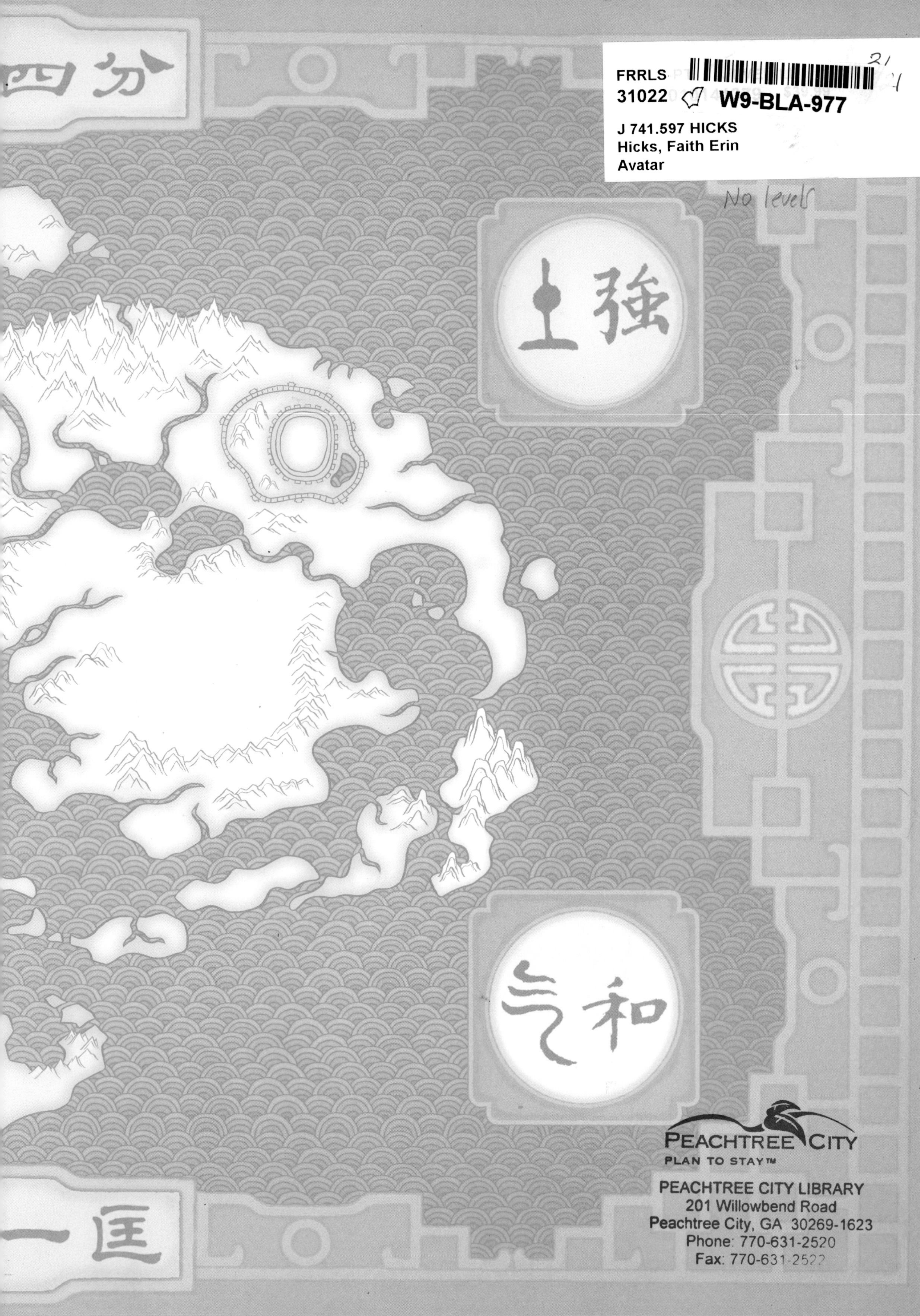
四分
土強
气和
一匡

AVATAR

THE LAST AIRBENDER

Created by

BRYAN KONIETZKO

MICHAEL DANTE DiMARTINO

nickelodeon™

降击神通

AVATAR
THE LAST AIRBENDER™

IMBALANCE

**FAITH ERIN
HICKS**
Script

**PETER
WARTMAN**
Art

**RYAN
HILL**
*Parts 1–3 cover colors,
Part 1 interior colors*

**ADELE
MATERA**
*Library Edition cover colors,
Parts 2–3 interior colors*

**RICHARD STARKINGS
& COMICRAFT'S
JIMMY BETANCOURT**
Lettering

DARK HORSE BOOKS

MIKE RICHARDSON
Publisher

DAVE MARSHALL AND RACHEL ROBERTS
Editors

JENNY BLENK
Assistant Editor

BRENNAN THOME
Collection Designer

CHRISTIANNE GILLENARDO-GOUDREAU AND SAMANTHA HUMMER
Digital Art Technicians

TODD BALTHAZOR
Martial Arts Consultant and Model

Special thanks to LINDA LEE,
JOAN HILTY, *and* JAMES SALERNO *at* Nickelodeon,
to DAVE MARSHALL *at* Dark Horse,
and to BRYAN KONIETZKO, MICHAEL DANTE DIMARTINO, *and* TIM HEDRICK.

5 7 9 10 8 6

ISBN 978-1-50670-812-6 Nick.com DarkHorse.com First edition: May 2020

Published by **DARK HORSE BOOKS**, a division of Dark Horse Comics LLC, 10956 SE Main Street, Milwaukie, OR 97222

To find a comics shop in your area, visit comicshoplocator.com

This book collects *Avatar: The Last Airbender—Imbalance* Parts 1 through 3.

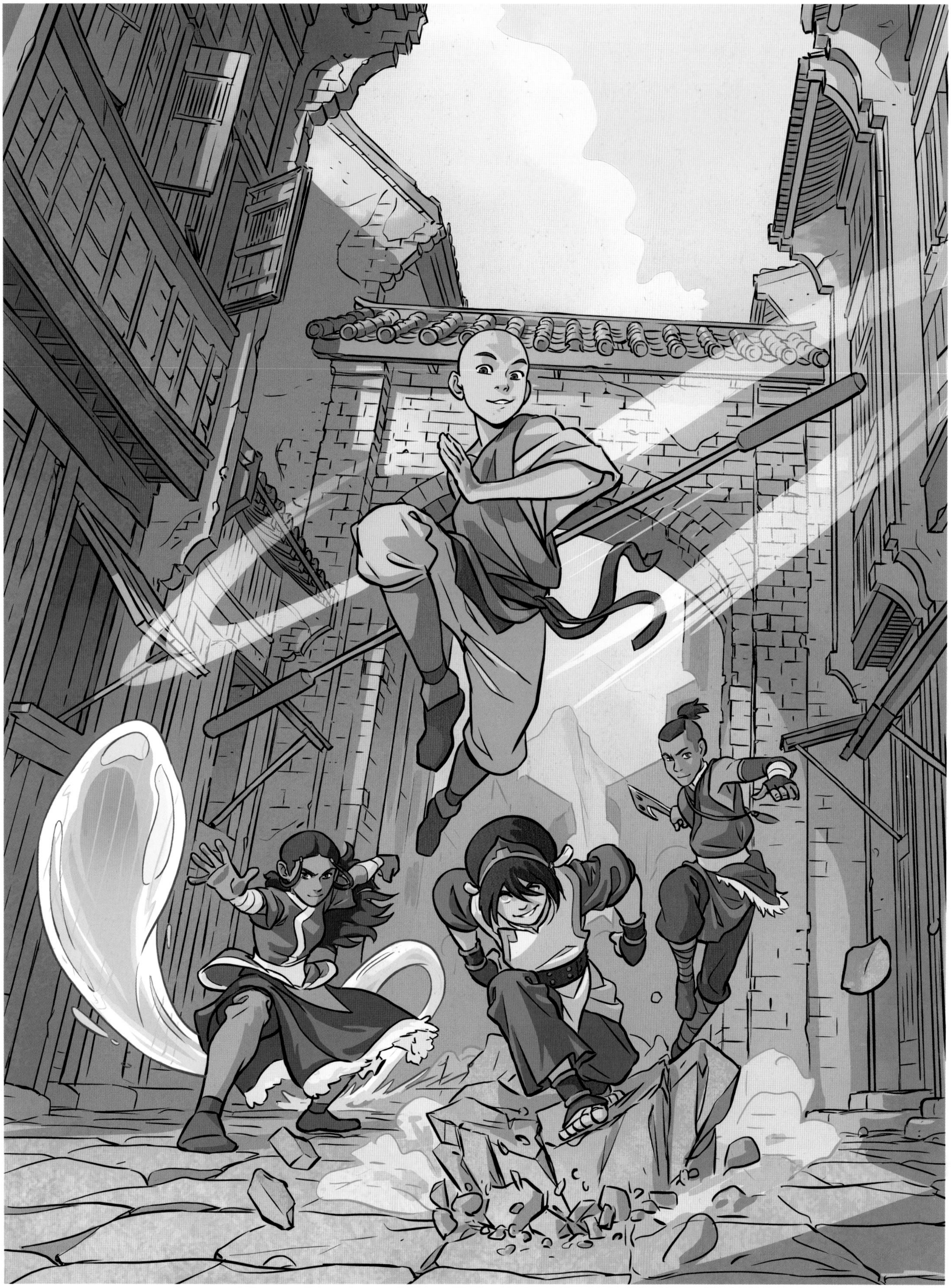

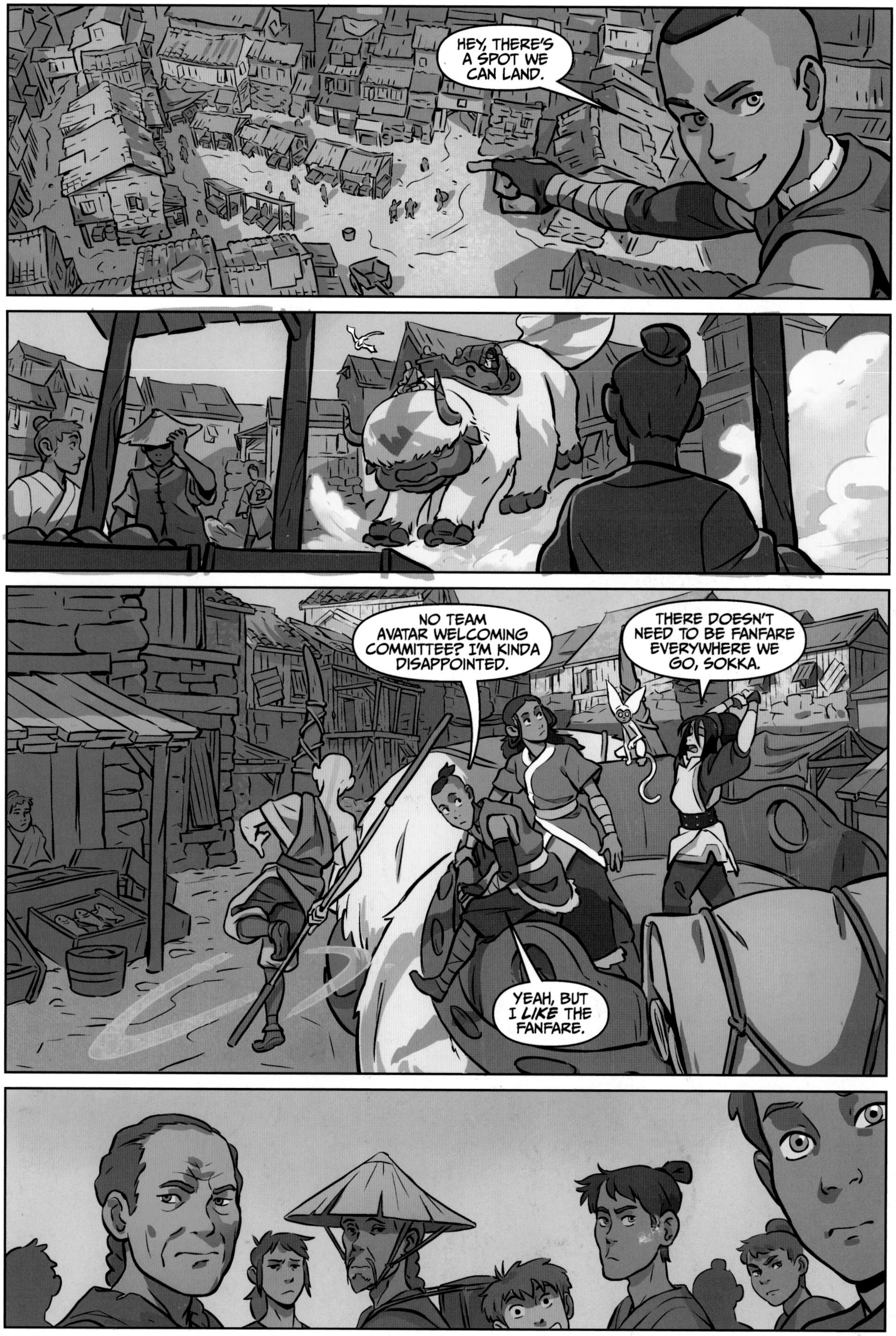
HEY, THERE'S A SPOT WE CAN LAND.
NO TEAM AVATAR WELCOMING COMMITTEE? I'M KINDA DISAPPOINTED.
THERE DOESN'T NEED TO BE FANFARE EVERYWHERE WE GO, SOKKA.
YEAH, BUT I *LIKE* THE FANFARE.

PW: *Massive amounts of rooftops will be a thing in this story. That's something Faith and I have in common: sticking lots of rooftops in our comics.*

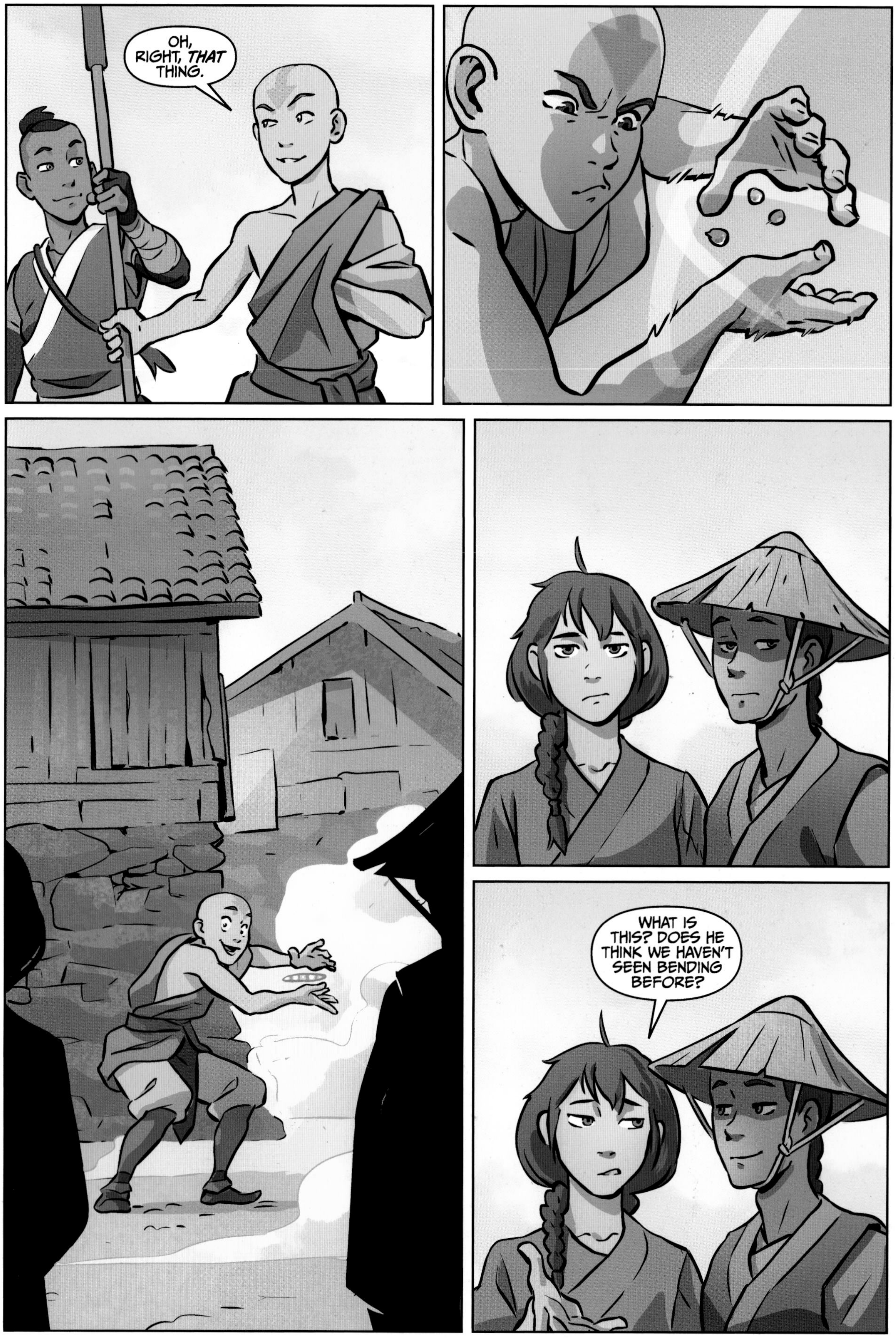
OH, RIGHT, *THAT* THING.
WHAT IS THIS? DOES HE THINK WE HAVEN'T SEEN BENDING BEFORE?

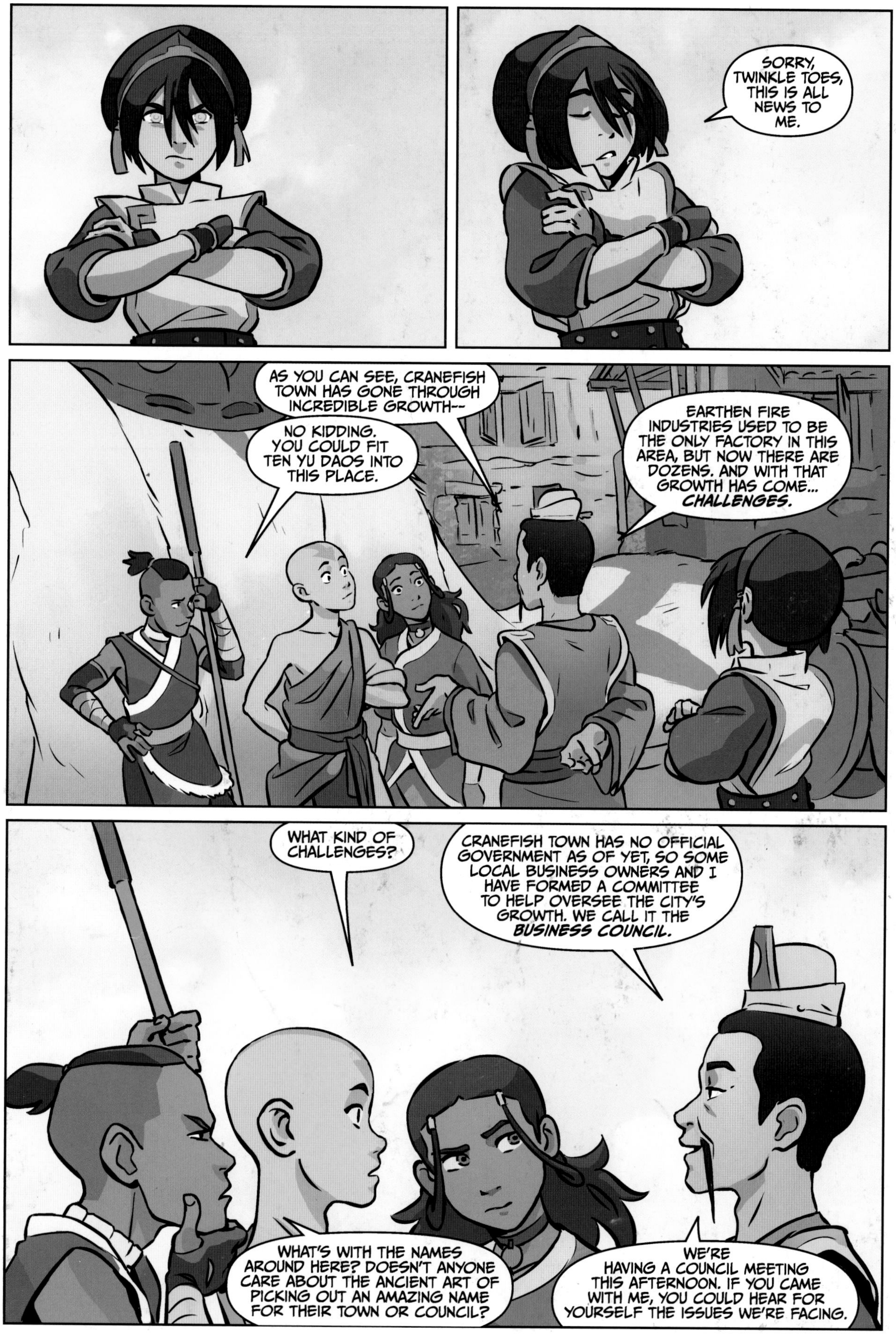
SORRY, TWINKLE TOES, THIS IS ALL NEWS TO ME.
AS YOU CAN SEE, CRANEFISH TOWN HAS GONE THROUGH INCREDIBLE GROWTH--
NO KIDDING. YOU COULD FIT TEN YU DAOS INTO THIS PLACE.
EARTHEN FIRE INDUSTRIES USED TO BE THE ONLY FACTORY IN THIS AREA, BUT NOW THERE ARE DOZENS. AND WITH THAT GROWTH HAS COME... CHALLENGES.
WHAT KIND OF CHALLENGES?
CRANEFISH TOWN HAS NO OFFICIAL GOVERNMENT AS OF YET, SO SOME LOCAL BUSINESS OWNERS AND I HAVE FORMED A COMMITTEE TO HELP OVERSEE THE CITY'S GROWTH. WE CALL IT THE BUSINESS COUNCIL.
WHAT'S WITH THE NAMES AROUND HERE? DOESN'T ANYONE CARE ABOUT THE ANCIENT ART OF PICKING OUT AN AMAZING NAME FOR THEIR TOWN OR COUNCIL?
WE'RE HAVING A COUNCIL MEETING THIS AFTERNOON. IF YOU CAME WITH ME, YOU COULD HEAR FOR YOURSELF THE ISSUES WE'RE FACING.

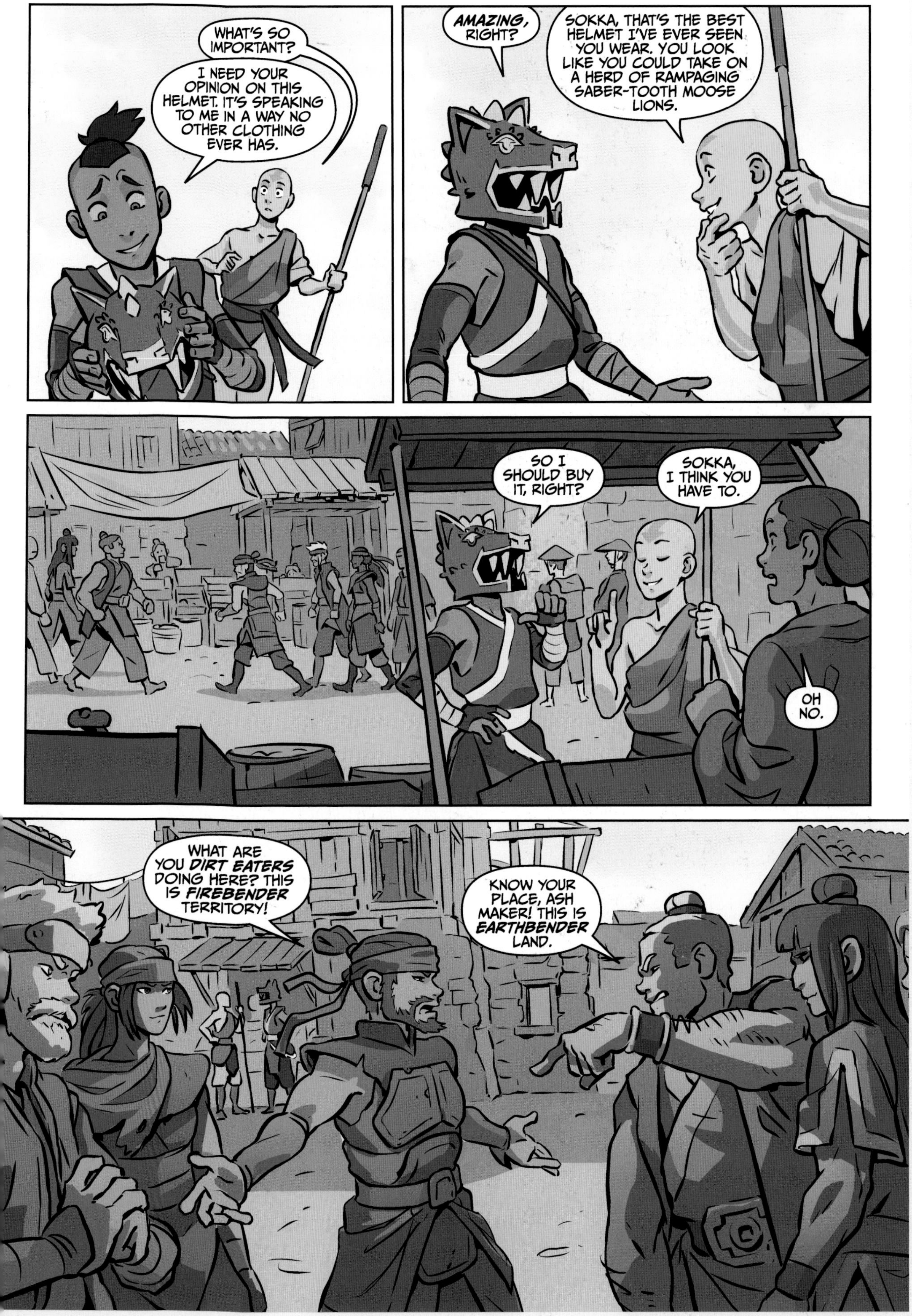
WHAT'S SO IMPORTANT?
I NEED YOUR OPINION ON THIS HELMET. IT'S SPEAKING TO ME IN A WAY NO OTHER CLOTHING EVER HAS.
AMAZING, RIGHT?
SOKKA, THAT'S THE BEST HELMET I'VE EVER SEEN YOU WEAR. YOU LOOK LIKE YOU COULD TAKE ON A HERD OF RAMPAGING SABER-TOOTH MOOSE LIONS.
SO I SHOULD BUY IT, RIGHT?
SOKKA, I THINK YOU HAVE TO.
OH NO.
WHAT ARE YOU DIRT EATERS DOING HERE? THIS IS FIREBENDER TERRITORY!
KNOW YOUR PLACE, ASH MAKER! THIS IS EARTHBENDER LAND.

PW: *I'm still pretty happy with Aang and Sokka's acting here. I'm less sure about Sokka's taste in headgear.*

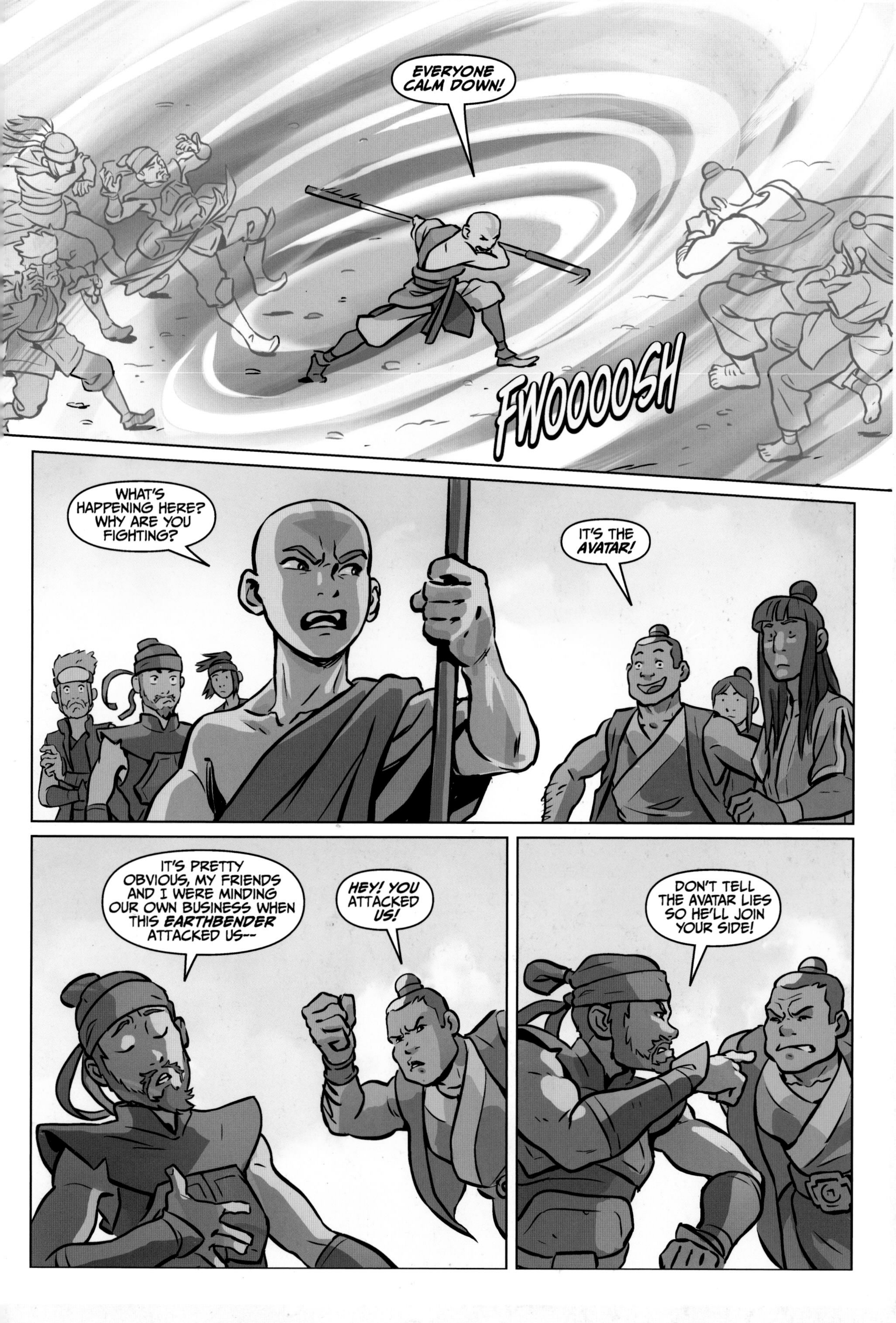
EVERYONE CALM DOWN!
FWOOOOSH
WHAT'S HAPPENING HERE? WHY ARE YOU FIGHTING?
IT'S THE AVATAR!
IT'S PRETTY OBVIOUS, MY FRIENDS AND I WERE MINDING OUR OWN BUSINESS WHEN THIS EARTHBENDER ATTACKED US--
HEY! YOU ATTACKED US!
DON'T TELL THE AVATAR LIES SO HE'LL JOIN YOUR SIDE!

PW: *I had fun designing these rival gangs.*

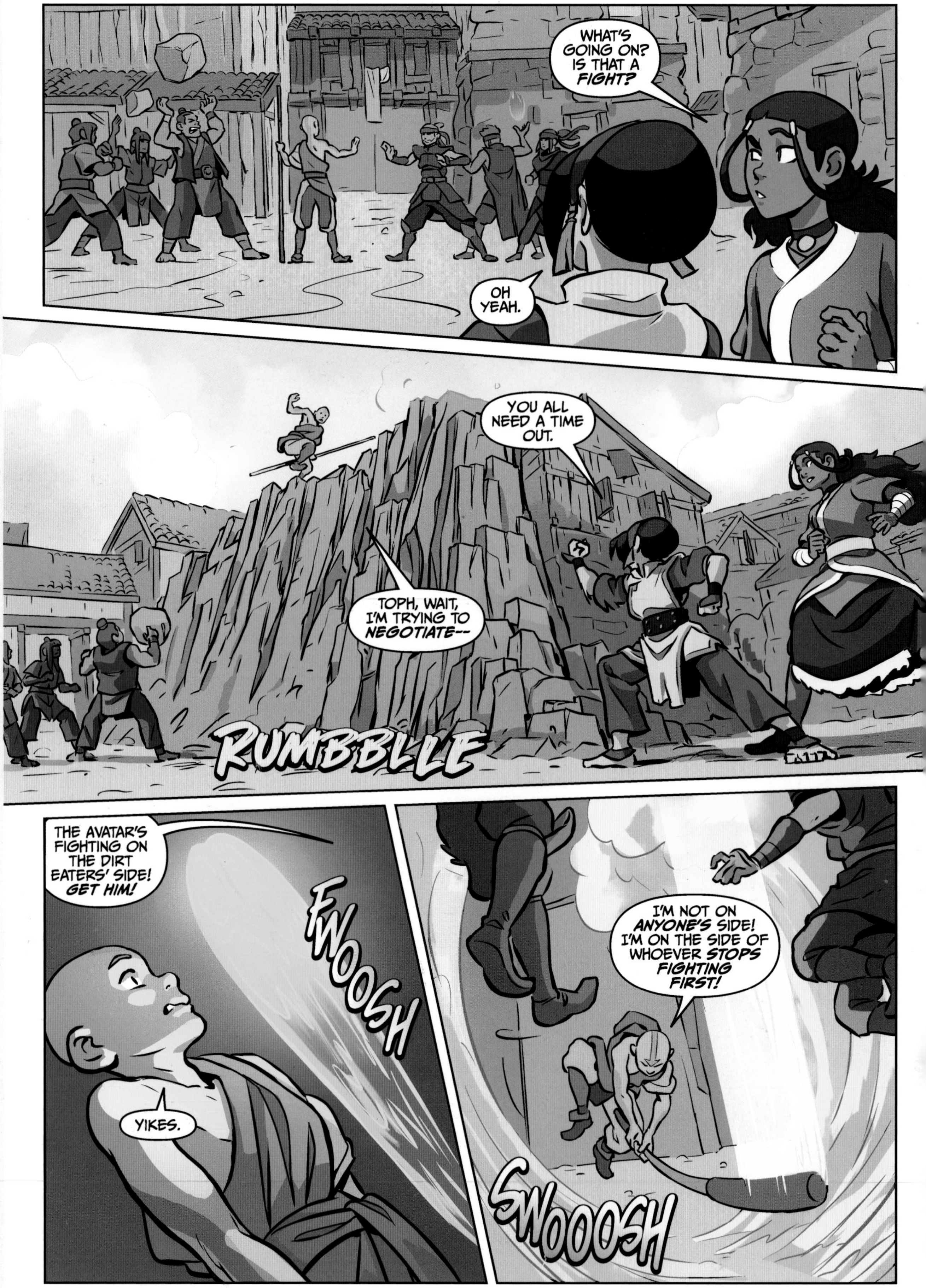
WHAT'S GOING ON? IS THAT A FIGHT?
OH YEAH.
YOU ALL NEED A TIME OUT.
TOPH, WAIT, I'M TRYING TO NEGOTIATE--
RUMBBLLE
THE AVATAR'S FIGHTING ON THE DIRT EATERS' SIDE! GET HIM!
FWOOOSH
YIKES.
I'M NOT ON ANYONE'S SIDE! I'M ON THE SIDE OF WHOEVER STOPS FIGHTING FIRST!
SNOOOSH

PW: *Toph has a very practical approach to problem-solving.*

FEH: *I'm absolutely with Sokka here. Getting in the middle of a bender fight if you're not a bender seems super dangerous!*

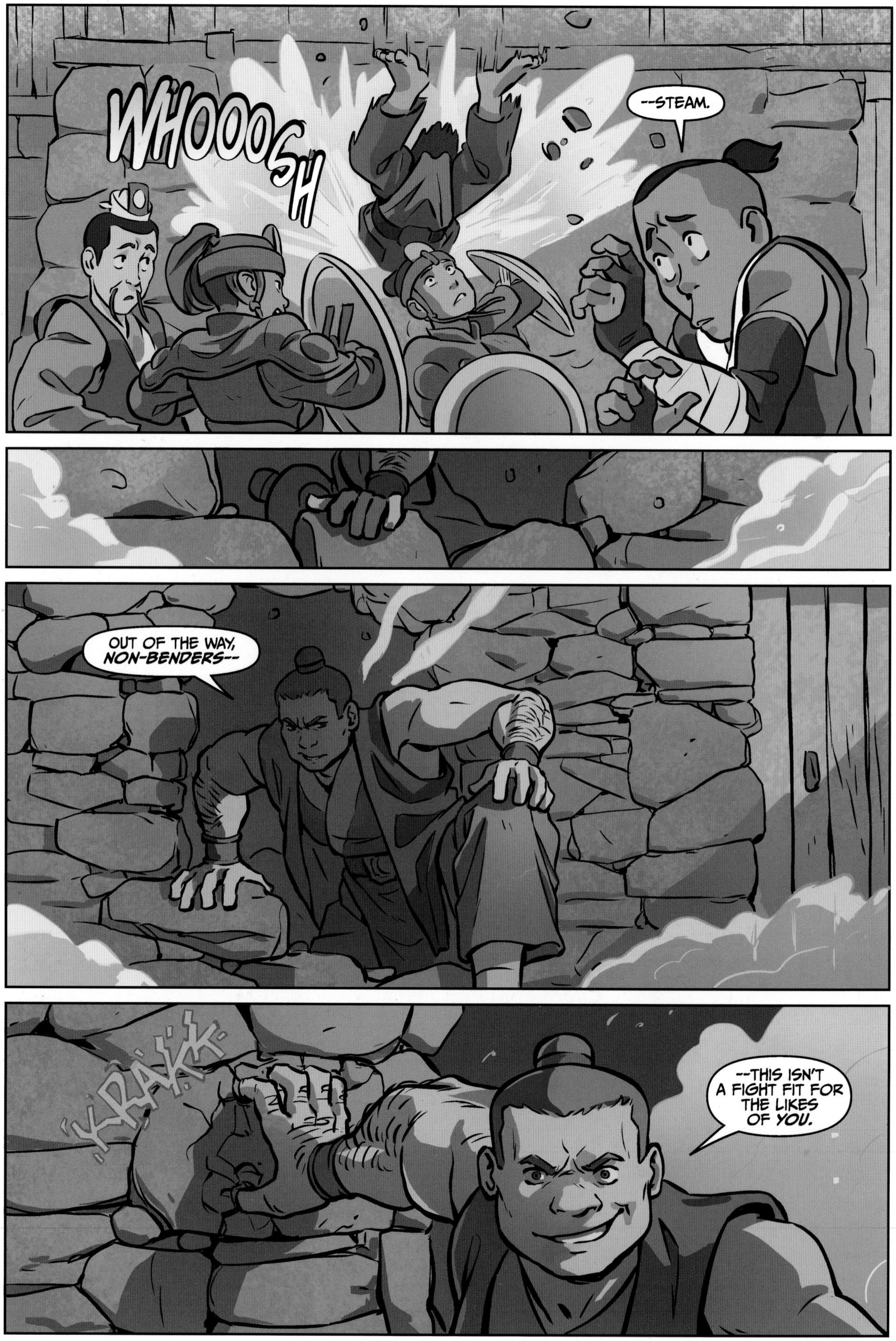
WHOOOOSH
--STEAM.
OUT OF THE WAY, NON-BENDERS--
KRAKK
--THIS ISN'T A FIGHT FIT FOR THE LIKES OF YOU.

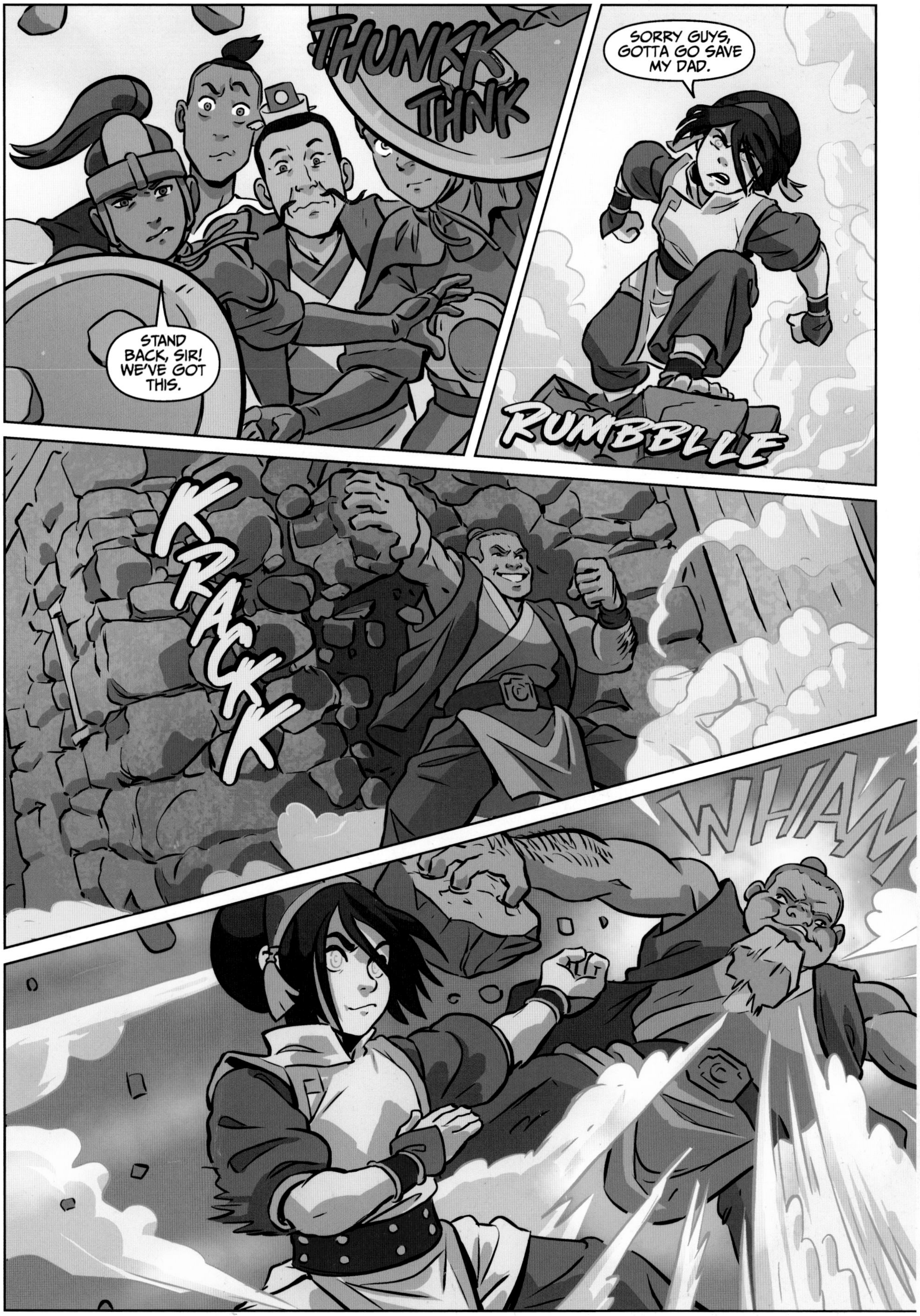
THUNKK
THNK
STAND BACK, SIR! WE'VE GOT THIS.
SORRY GUYS, GOTTA GO SAVE MY DAD.
RUMBBLLE
KRACKK
WHAM

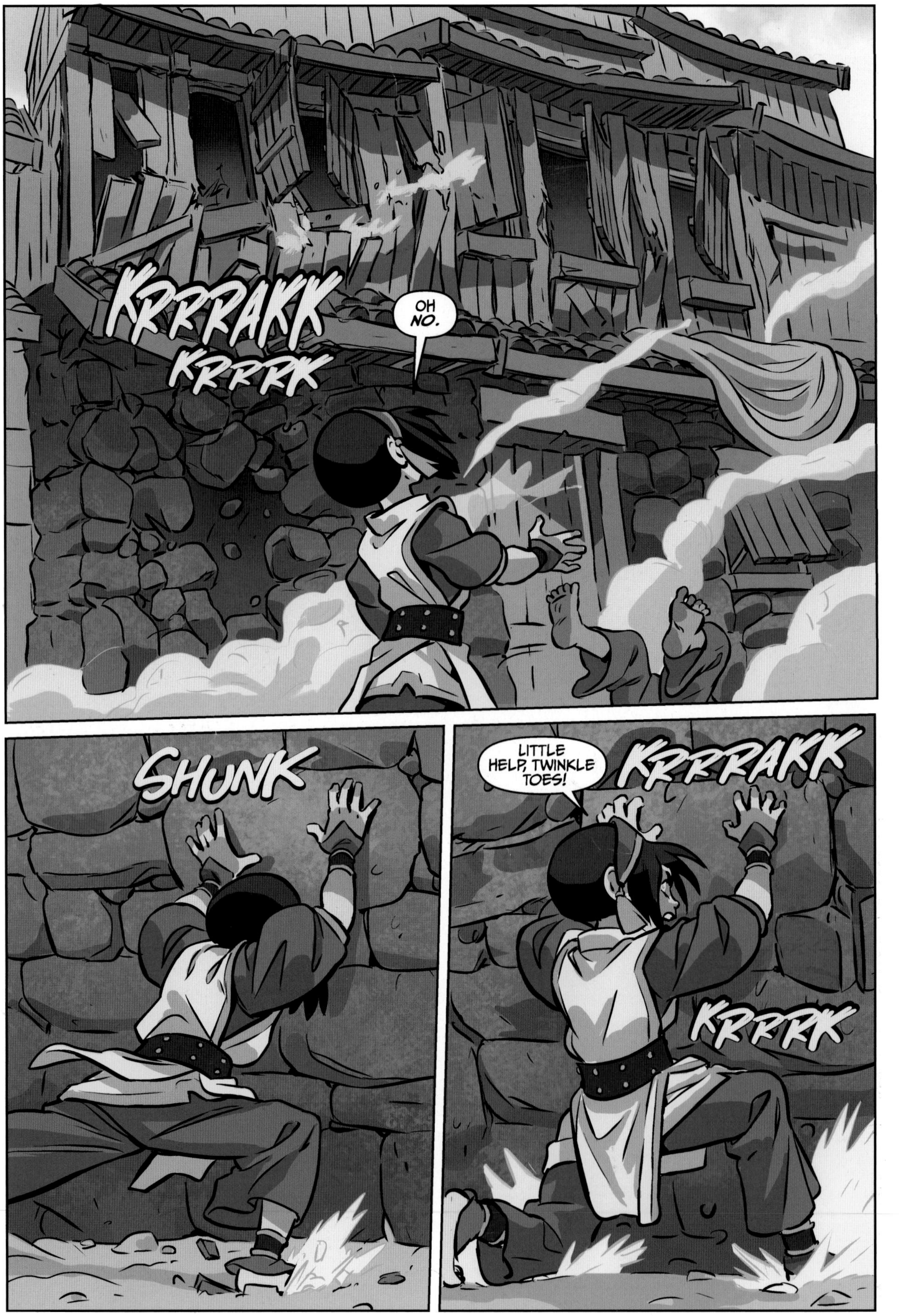
KRRRAKK
KRRRK
OH NO.
SHUNK
LITTLE HELP, TWINKLE TOES!
KRRRAKK
KRRRK

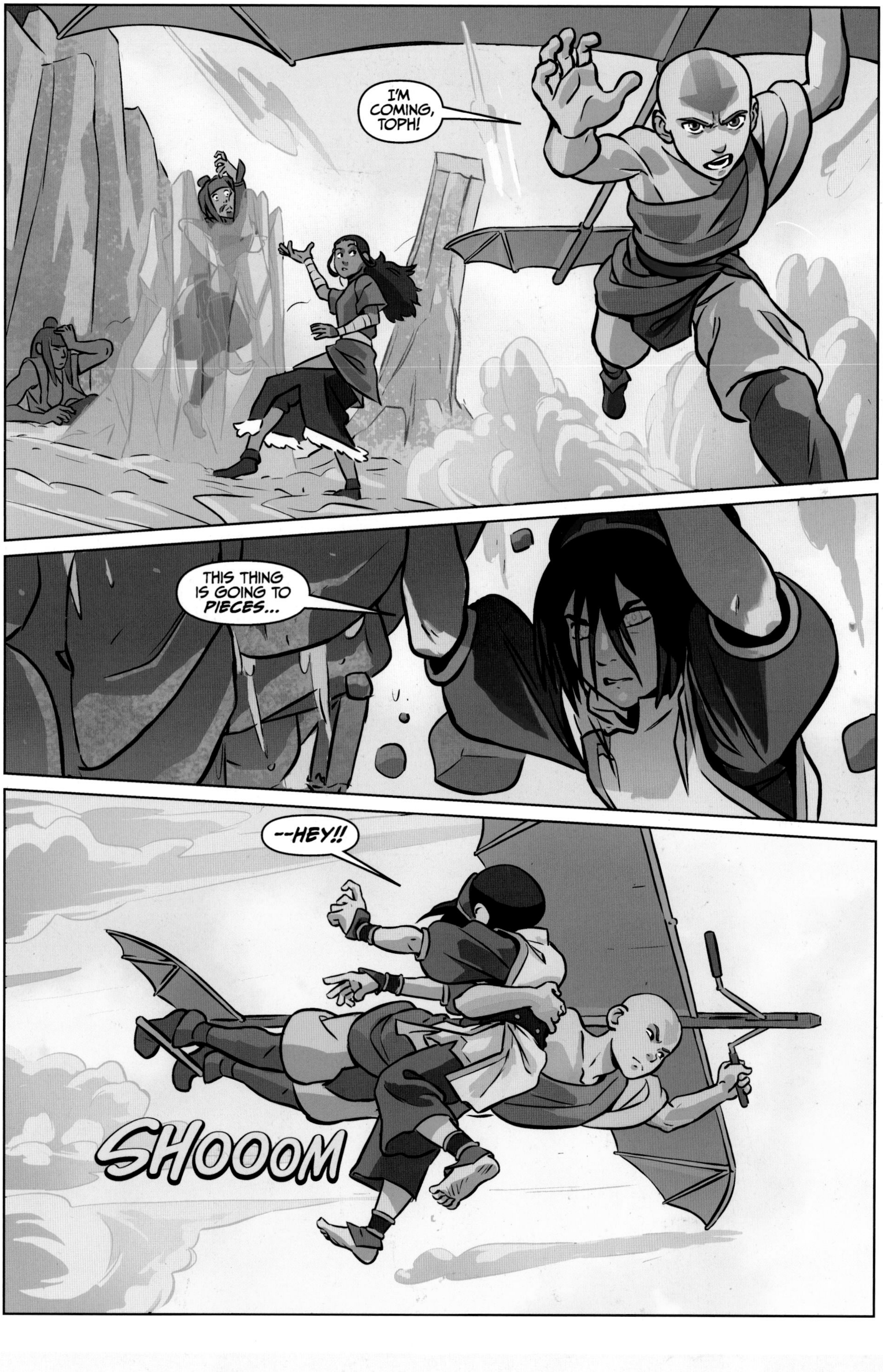
I'M COMING, TOPH!
THIS THING IS GOING TO *PIECES...*
--HEY!!
SHOOOM

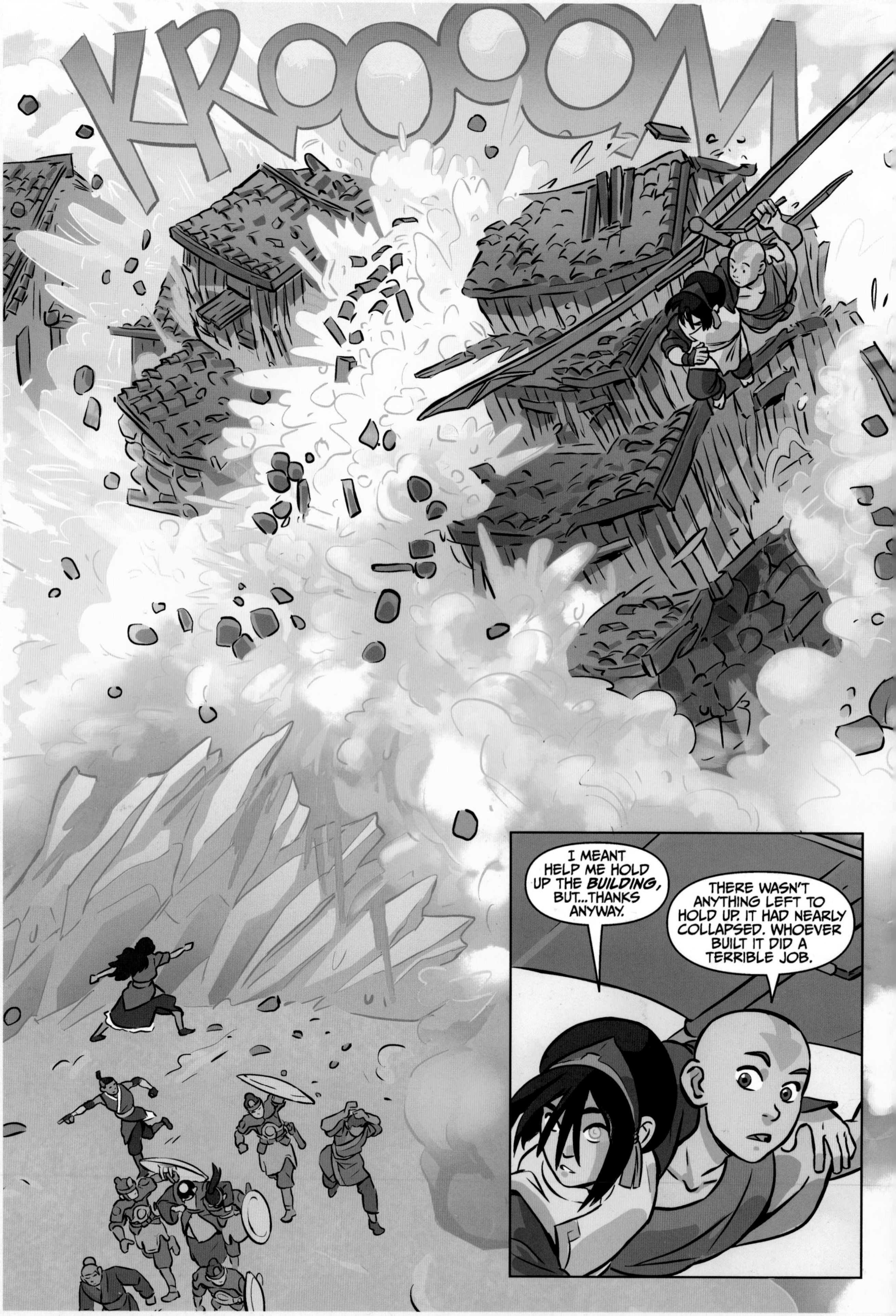
KROOOOM
I MEANT HELP ME HOLD UP THE *BUILDING*, BUT...THANKS ANYWAY.
THERE WASN'T ANYTHING LEFT TO HOLD UP. IT HAD NEARLY COLLAPSED. WHOEVER BUILT IT DID A TERRIBLE JOB.

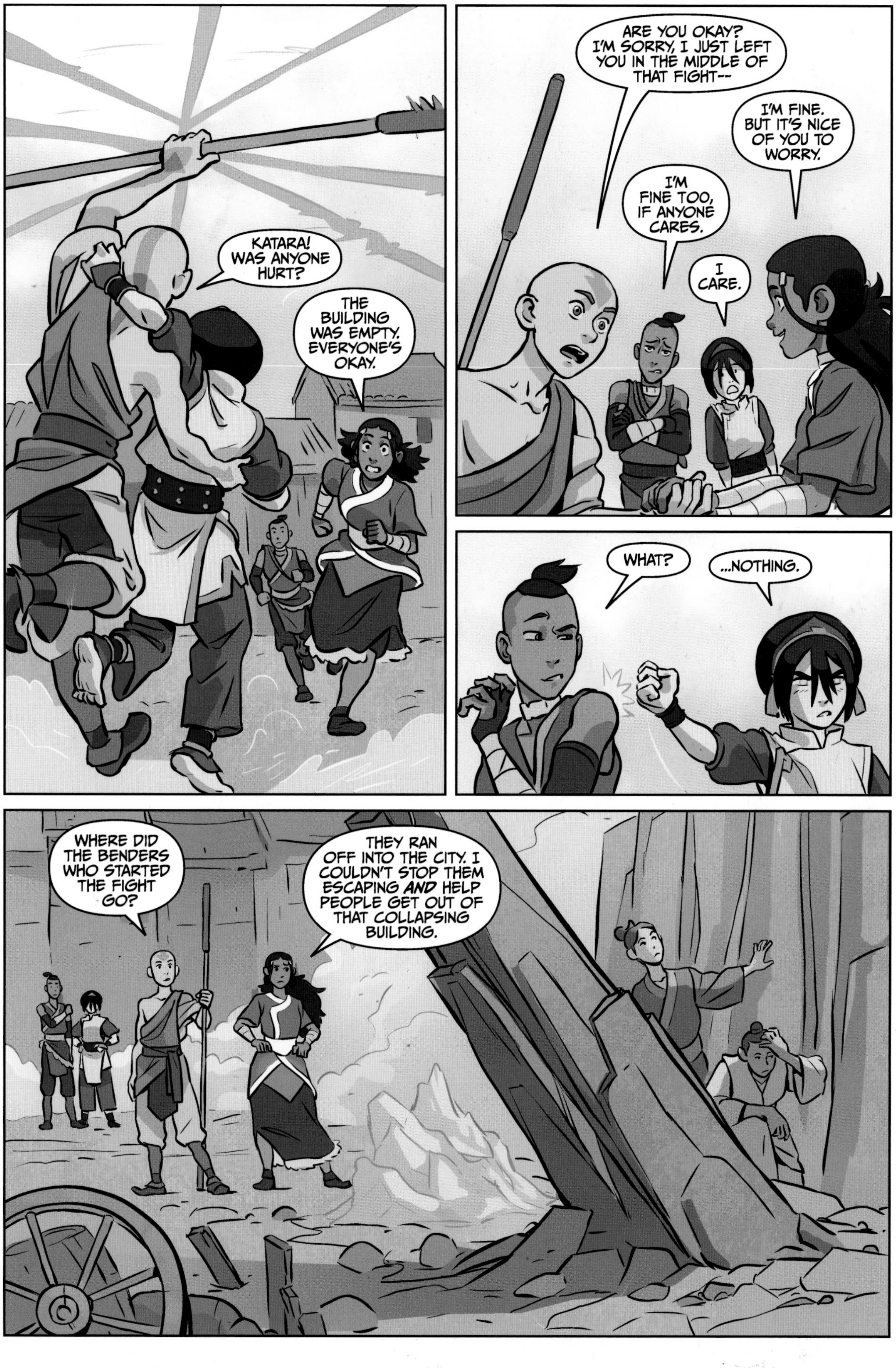
KATARA! WAS ANYONE HURT?
THE BUILDING WAS EMPTY. EVERYONE'S OKAY.
ARE YOU OKAY? I'M SORRY, I JUST LEFT YOU IN THE MIDDLE OF THAT FIGHT--
I'M FINE. BUT IT'S NICE OF YOU TO WORRY.
I'M FINE TOO, IF ANYONE CARES.
I CARE.
WHAT?
...NOTHING.
WHERE DID THE BENDERS WHO STARTED THE FIGHT GO?
THEY RAN OFF INTO THE CITY. I COULDN'T STOP THEM ESCAPING *AND* HELP PEOPLE GET OUT OF THAT COLLAPSING BUILDING.

FEH: *Toph expresses unspoken affection through punching! Aw.*

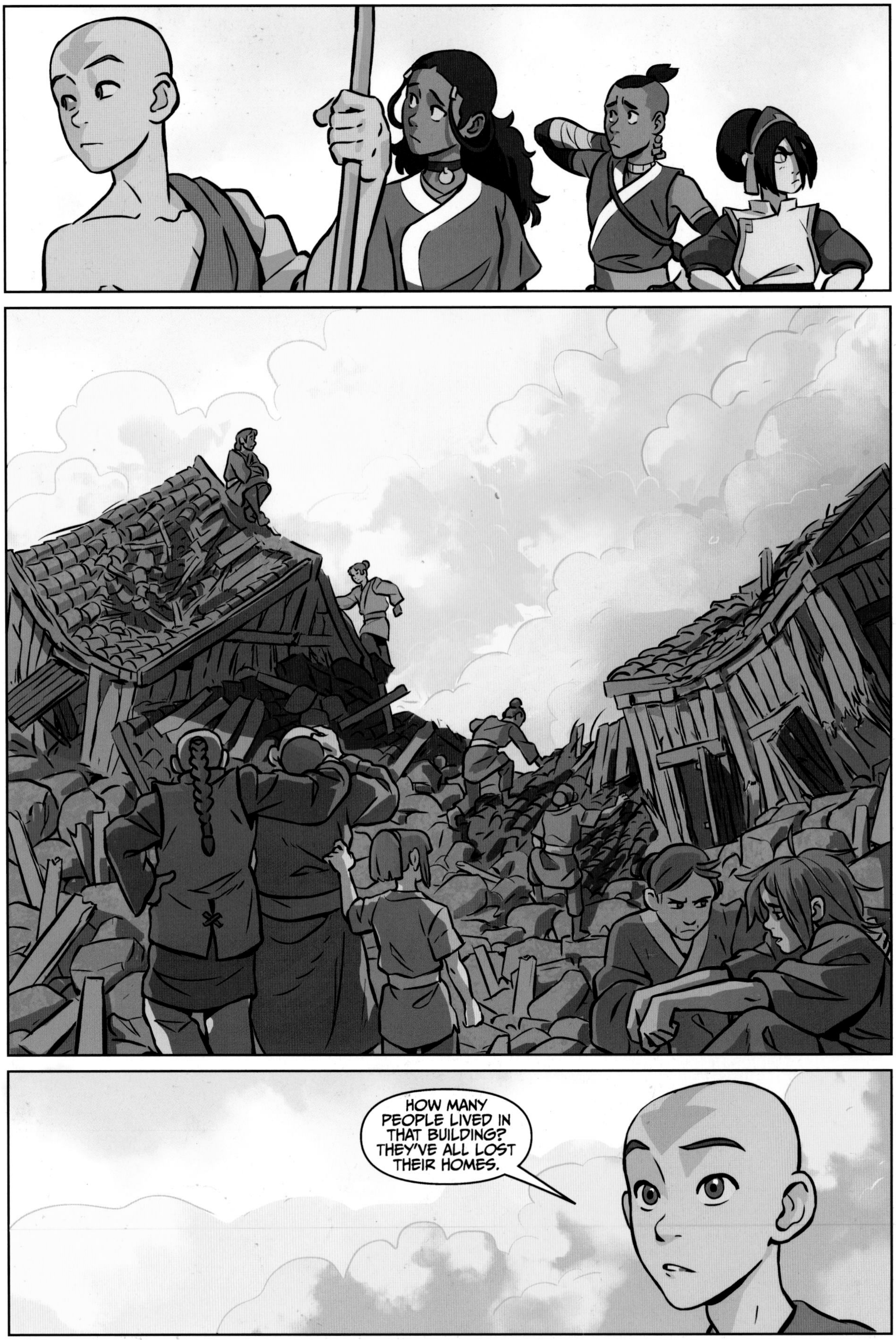
HOW MANY PEOPLE LIVED IN THAT BUILDING? THEY'VE ALL LOST THEIR HOMES.

PW: *Something I really liked about Faith's script is how we immediately see some of the downsides of bending here. There are consequences to having cool, scenery-destroying fights in the middle of a place people live.*

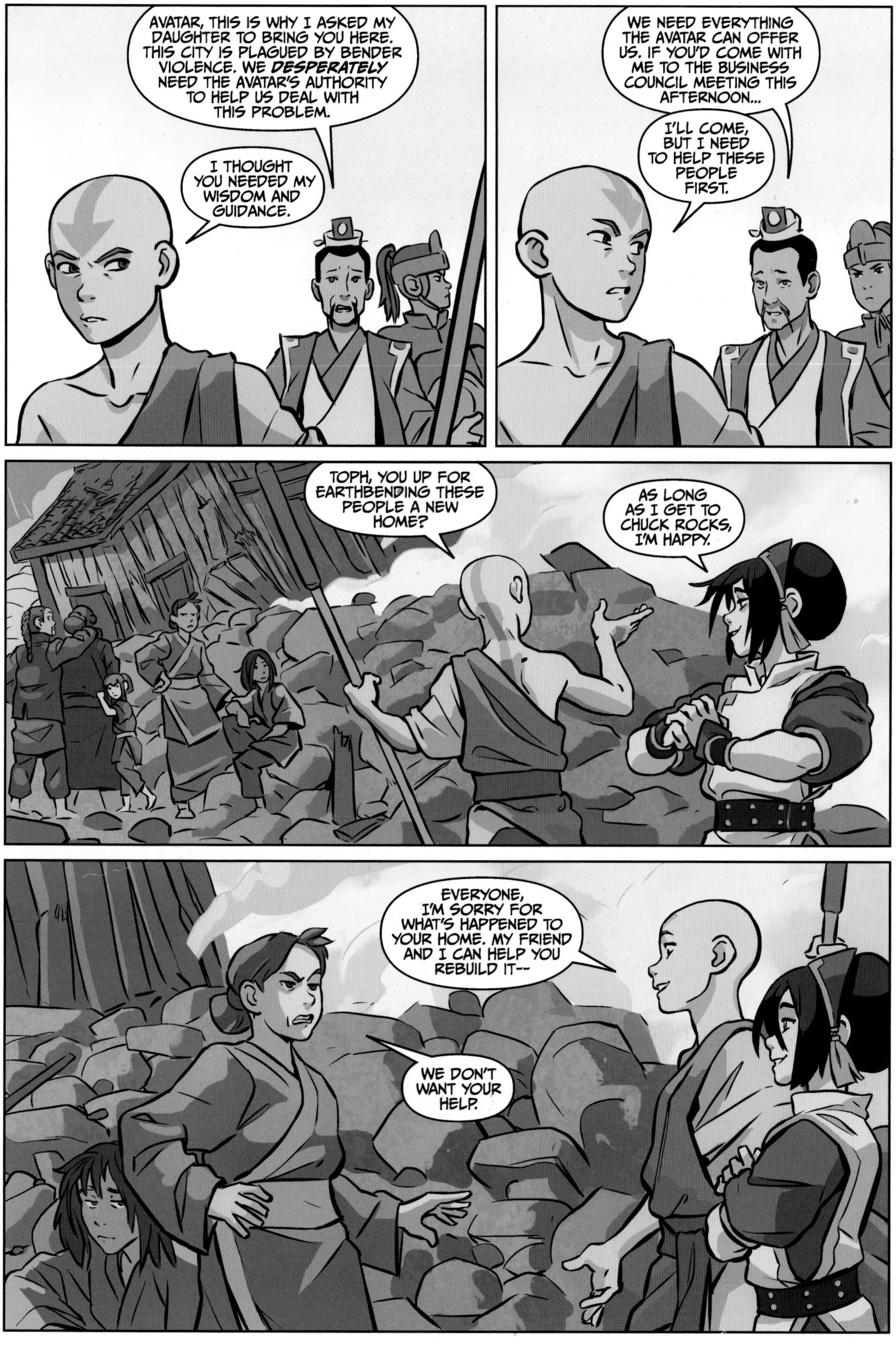
AVATAR, THIS IS WHY I ASKED MY DAUGHTER TO BRING YOU HERE. THIS CITY IS PLAGUED BY BENDER VIOLENCE. WE *DESPERATELY* NEED THE AVATAR'S AUTHORITY TO HELP US DEAL WITH THIS PROBLEM.
I THOUGHT YOU NEEDED MY WISDOM AND GUIDANCE.
WE NEED EVERYTHING THE AVATAR CAN OFFER US. IF YOU'D COME WITH ME TO THE BUSINESS COUNCIL MEETING THIS AFTERNOON...
I'LL COME, BUT I NEED TO HELP THESE PEOPLE FIRST.
TOPH, YOU UP FOR EARTHBENDING THESE PEOPLE A NEW HOME?
AS LONG AS I GET TO CHUCK ROCKS, I'M HAPPY.
EVERYONE, I'M SORRY FOR WHAT'S HAPPENED TO YOUR HOME. MY FRIEND AND I CAN HELP YOU REBUILD IT--
WE DON'T WANT YOUR HELP.

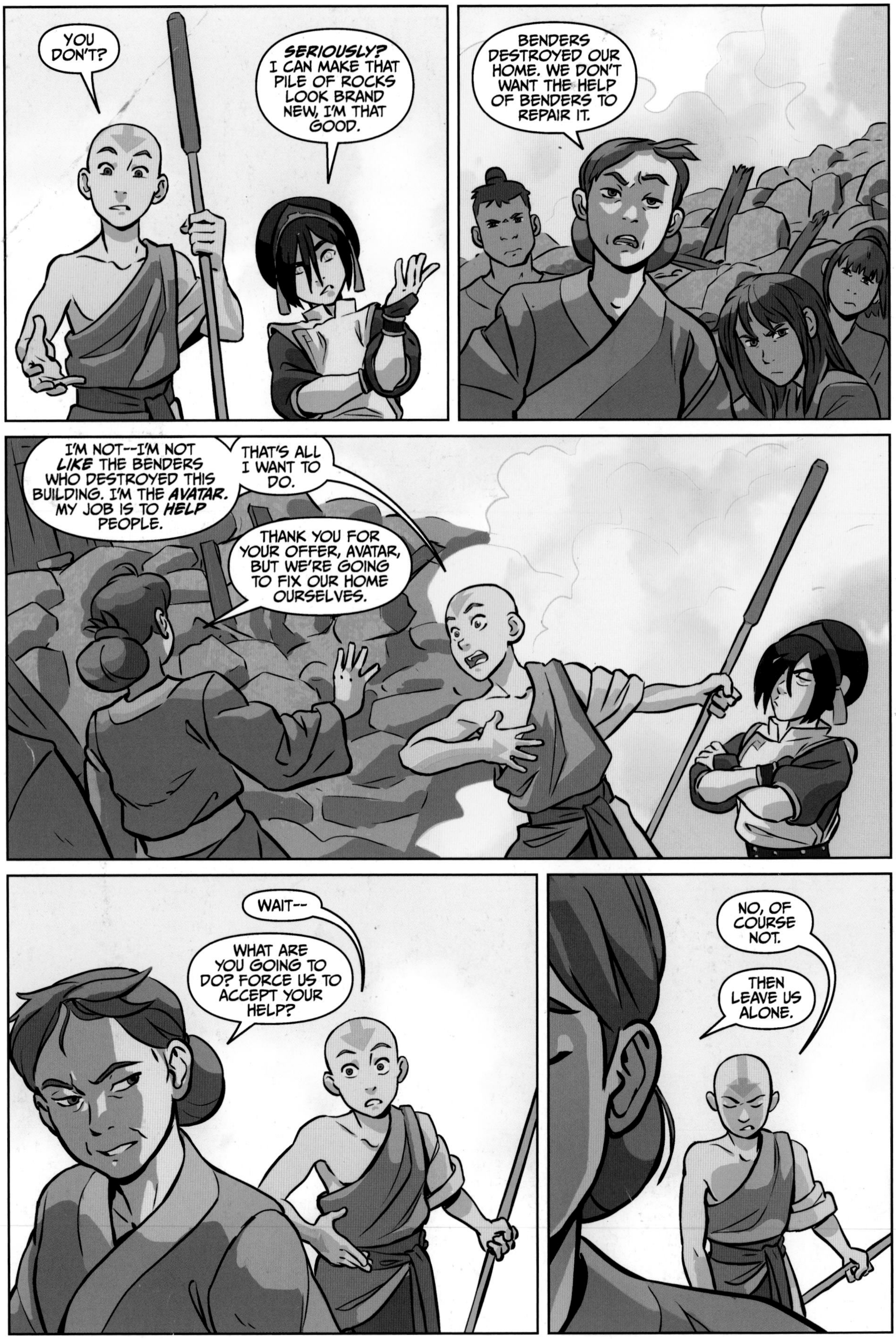
YOU DON'T?
SERIOUSLY? I CAN MAKE THAT PILE OF ROCKS LOOK BRAND NEW, I'M THAT GOOD.
BENDERS DESTROYED OUR HOME. WE DON'T WANT THE HELP OF BENDERS TO REPAIR IT.
I'M NOT--I'M NOT LIKE THE BENDERS WHO DESTROYED THIS BUILDING. I'M THE AVATAR. MY JOB IS TO HELP PEOPLE.
THAT'S ALL I WANT TO DO.
THANK YOU FOR YOUR OFFER, AVATAR, BUT WE'RE GOING TO FIX OUR HOME OURSELVES.
WAIT--
WHAT ARE YOU GOING TO DO? FORCE US TO ACCEPT YOUR HELP?
NO, OF COURSE NOT.
THEN LEAVE US ALONE.

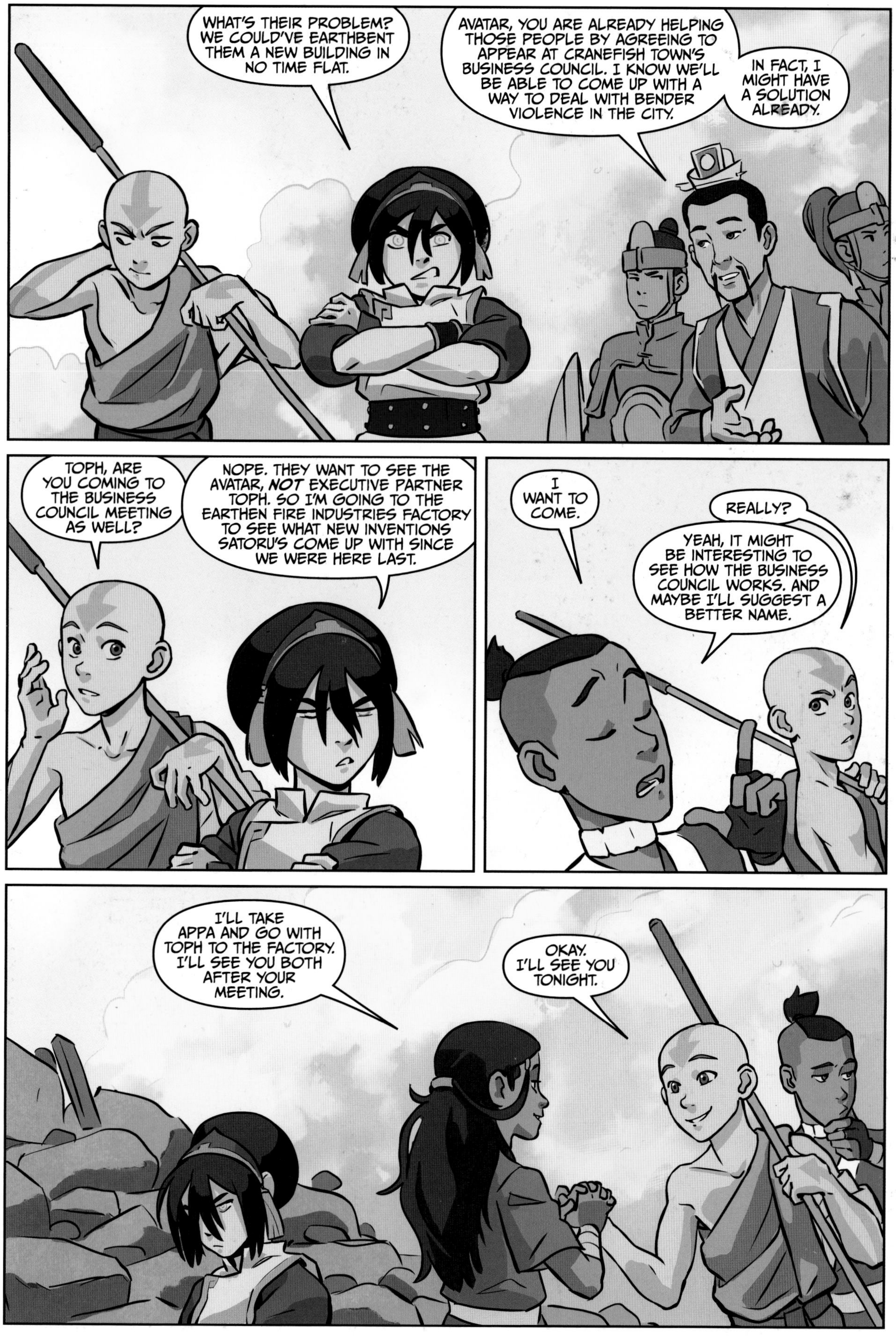
WHAT'S THEIR PROBLEM? WE COULD'VE EARTHBENT THEM A NEW BUILDING IN NO TIME FLAT.
AVATAR, YOU ARE ALREADY HELPING THOSE PEOPLE BY AGREEING TO APPEAR AT CRANEFISH TOWN'S BUSINESS COUNCIL. I KNOW WE'LL BE ABLE TO COME UP WITH A WAY TO DEAL WITH BENDER VIOLENCE IN THE CITY.
IN FACT, I MIGHT HAVE A SOLUTION ALREADY.
TOPH, ARE YOU COMING TO THE BUSINESS COUNCIL MEETING AS WELL?
NOPE. THEY WANT TO SEE THE AVATAR, NOT EXECUTIVE PARTNER TOPH. SO I'M GOING TO THE EARTHEN FIRE INDUSTRIES FACTORY TO SEE WHAT NEW INVENTIONS SATORU'S COME UP WITH SINCE WE WERE HERE LAST.
I WANT TO COME.
REALLY?
YEAH, IT MIGHT BE INTERESTING TO SEE HOW THE BUSINESS COUNCIL WORKS. AND MAYBE I'LL SUGGEST A BETTER NAME.
I'LL TAKE APPA AND GO WITH TOPH TO THE FACTORY. I'LL SEE YOU BOTH AFTER YOUR MEETING.
OKAY. I'LL SEE YOU TONIGHT.

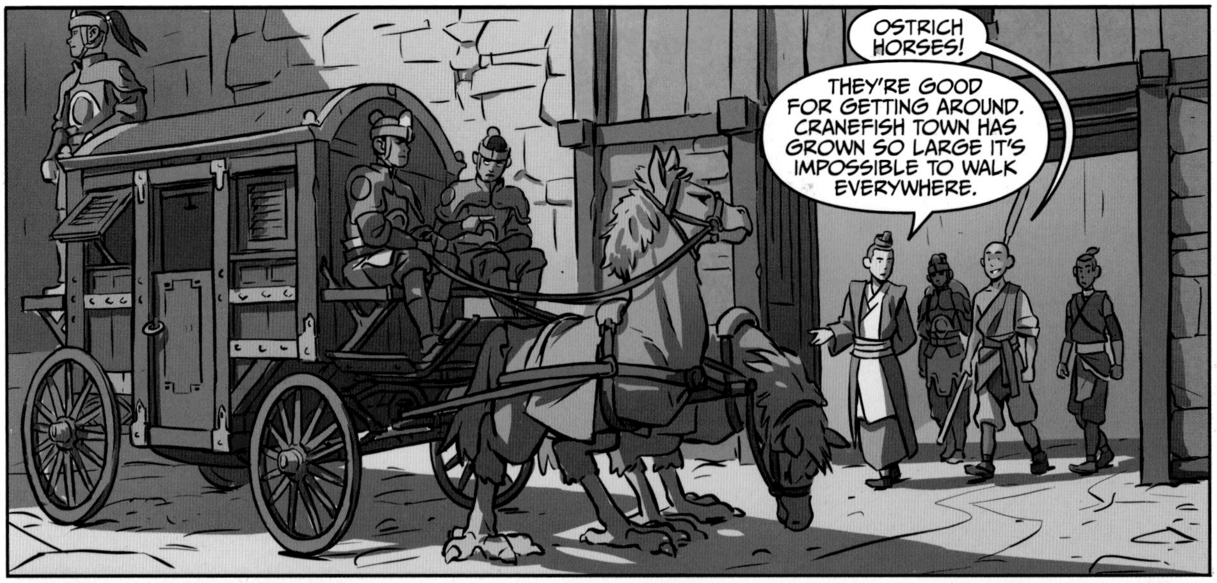
OSTRICH HORSES!
THEY'RE GOOD FOR GETTING AROUND. CRANEFISH TOWN HAS GROWN SO LARGE IT'S IMPOSSIBLE TO WALK EVERYWHERE.

FEH: *All the city backgrounds are wonderful here. Drawing comic book backgrounds is more than just putting a few buildings behind the characters; it's about creating a living, breathing world.*

PW: *Ostrich horses! So much better to draw than regular horses.*

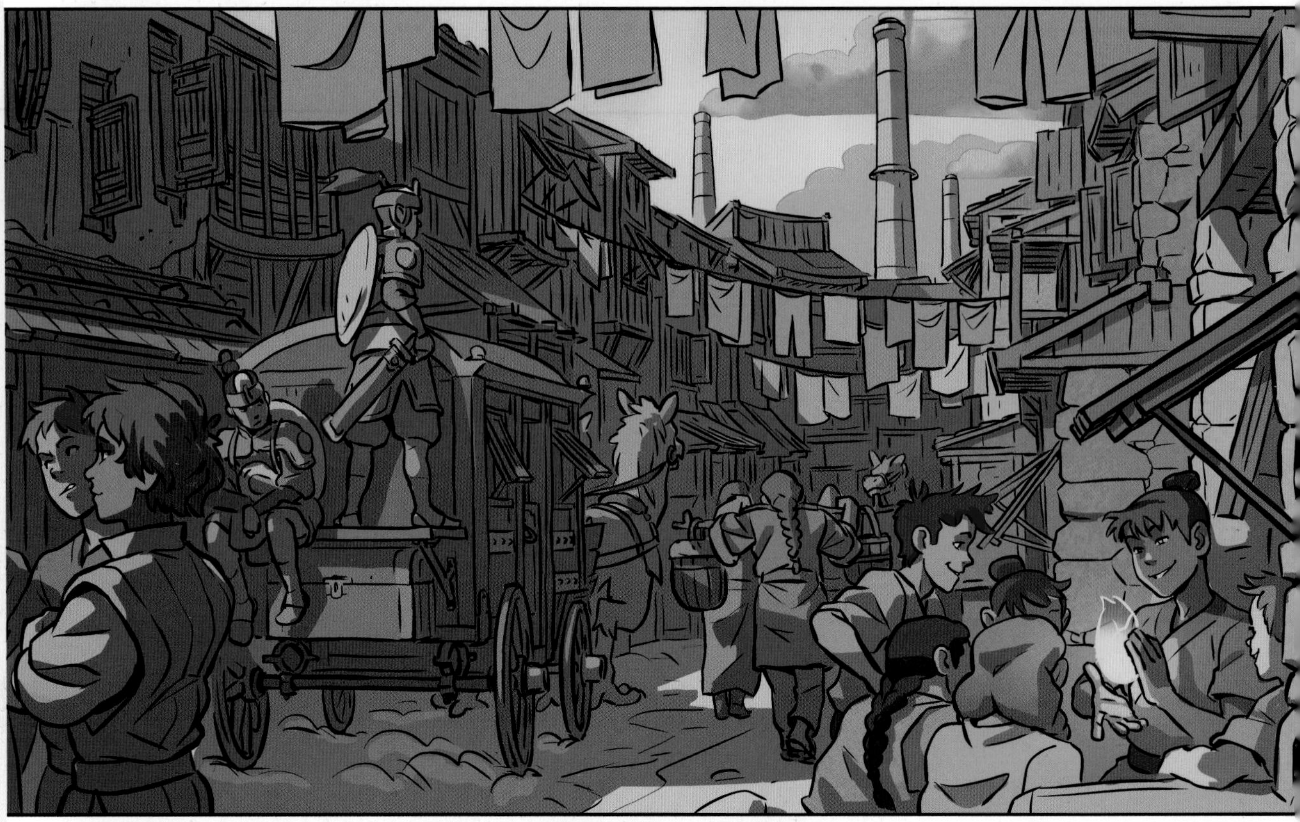

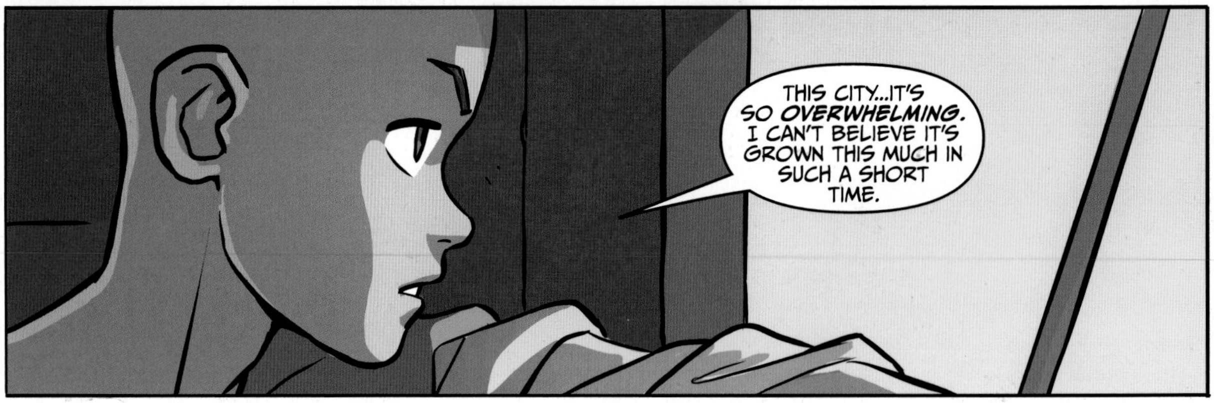
THIS CITY...IT'S SO ***OVERWHELMING.*** I CAN'T BELIEVE IT'S GROWN THIS MUCH IN SUCH A SHORT TIME.

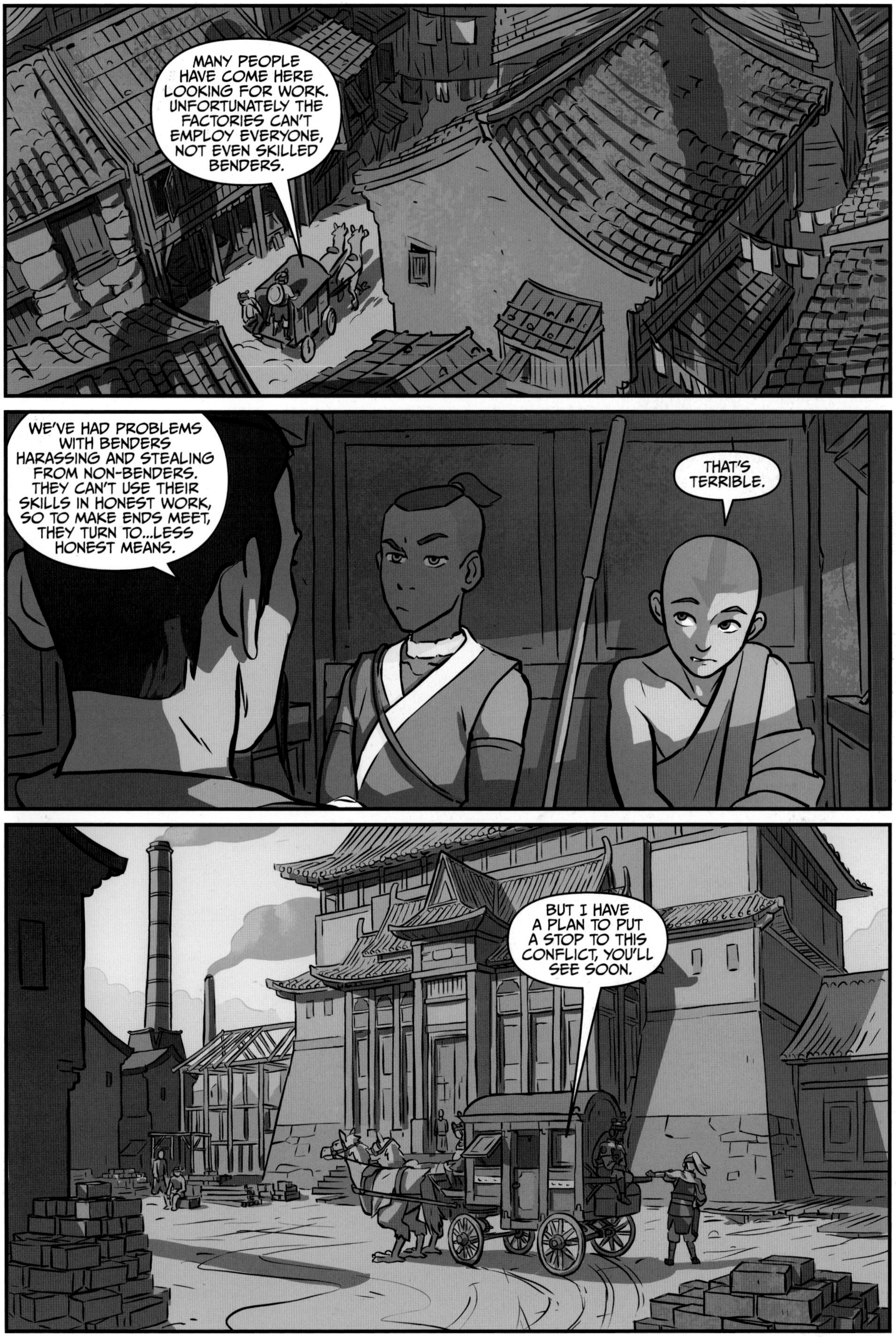
MANY PEOPLE HAVE COME HERE LOOKING FOR WORK. UNFORTUNATELY THE FACTORIES CAN'T EMPLOY EVERYONE, NOT EVEN SKILLED BENDERS.
WE'VE HAD PROBLEMS WITH BENDERS HARASSING AND STEALING FROM NON-BENDERS. THEY CAN'T USE THEIR SKILLS IN HONEST WORK, SO TO MAKE ENDS MEET, THEY TURN TO...LESS HONEST MEANS.
THAT'S TERRIBLE.
BUT I HAVE A PLAN TO PUT A STOP TO THIS CONFLICT, YOU'LL SEE SOON.

PW: *I rather like the lighting Ryan used in the Council scene— it feels ominous.*

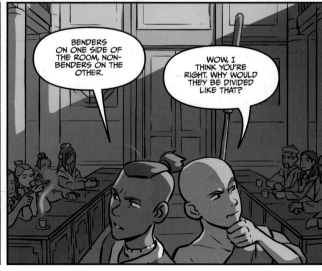

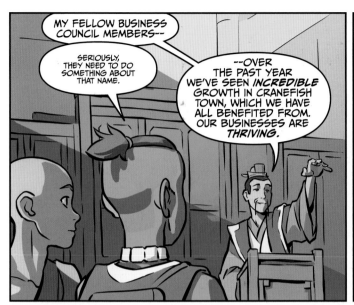

MY FELLOW BUSINESS COUNCIL MEMBERS--

SERIOUSLY, THEY NEED TO DO SOMETHING ABOUT THAT NAME.

--OVER THE PAST YEAR WE'VE SEEN *INCREDIBLE* GROWTH IN CRANEFISH TOWN, WHICH WE HAVE ALL BENEFITED FROM. OUR BUSINESSES ARE *THRIVING.*

HOWEVER, OUR CITY'S GROWTH HAS ALSO BROUGHT... *CHALLENGES.*

OUR HOME IS PLAGUED BY VIOLENCE, ESPECIALLY *BENDER* VIOLENCE. OUR FACTORY EMPLOYEES ARE AFRAID TO WALK TO WORK FOR FEAR OF BEING ATTACKED.

I WANT TO PROPOSE SOMETHING. *WE* ARE CRANEFISH TOWN'S COMMUNITY LEADERS. IT'S UP TO *US* TO FIND A WAY TO DEAL WITH THE ISSUES OUR CITY IS FACING.

I PROPOSE THAT BENDING BE *BANNED* ON PUBLIC STREETS. THIS WILL HELP PREVENT THE BENDER VIOLENCE THAT IS CAUSING SO MANY PROBLEMS.

BAN BENDING...?

FEH: *I wanted to play up the tension between the bender and non-bender communities in Cranefish Town. They're forced to work together because they share the same city, but there are unresolved issues between the two groups. Eventually we see those issues become the Equalist Movement from season one of* The Legend of Korra, *but* Imbalance *is about what happens before that.*

36

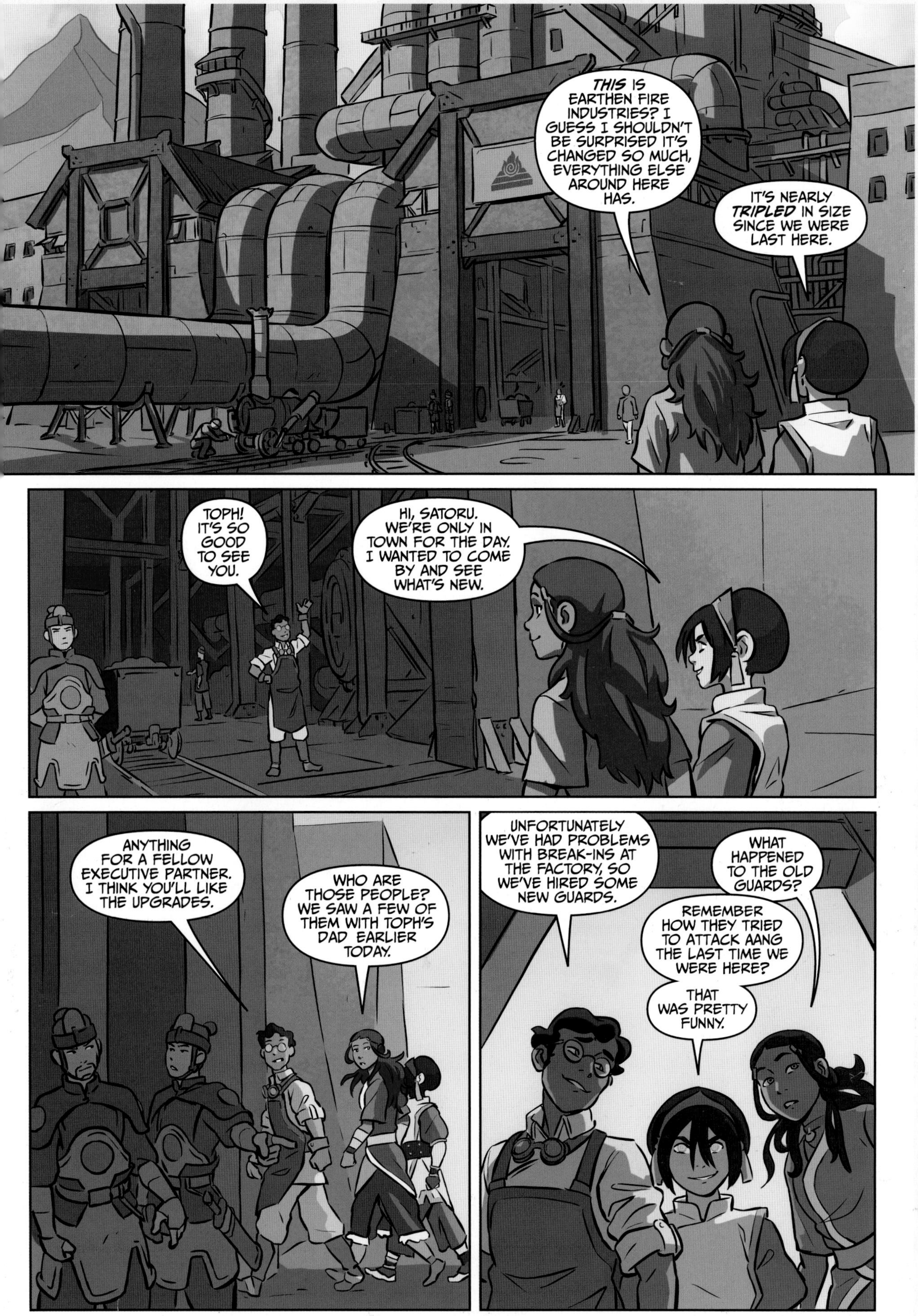
THIS IS EARTHEN FIRE INDUSTRIES? I GUESS I SHOULDN'T BE SURPRISED IT'S CHANGED SO MUCH, EVERYTHING ELSE AROUND HERE HAS.
IT'S NEARLY TRIPLED IN SIZE SINCE WE WERE LAST HERE.
TOPH! IT'S SO GOOD TO SEE YOU.
HI, SATORU. WE'RE ONLY IN TOWN FOR THE DAY. I WANTED TO COME BY AND SEE WHAT'S NEW.
ANYTHING FOR A FELLOW EXECUTIVE PARTNER. I THINK YOU'LL LIKE THE UPGRADES.
WHO ARE THOSE PEOPLE? WE SAW A FEW OF THEM WITH TOPH'S DAD EARLIER TODAY.
UNFORTUNATELY WE'VE HAD PROBLEMS WITH BREAK-INS AT THE FACTORY, SO WE'VE HIRED SOME NEW GUARDS.
WHAT HAPPENED TO THE OLD GUARDS?
REMEMBER HOW THEY TRIED TO ATTACK AANG THE LAST TIME WE WERE HERE?
THAT WAS PRETTY FUNNY.

FEH: *It's Satoru! We first saw him in* The Rift, *and now he's been promoted to Executive Partner at Earthen Fire Industries. I think Peter draws him really cute.*

PW: *The factory! I didn't know it would become such an important location when I drew it here, but I'm still pretty happy with how it turned out. I tried to keep some of the design from the previous books but, you know, added some really big pipes. I'm pretty sure that's how technological progress works.*

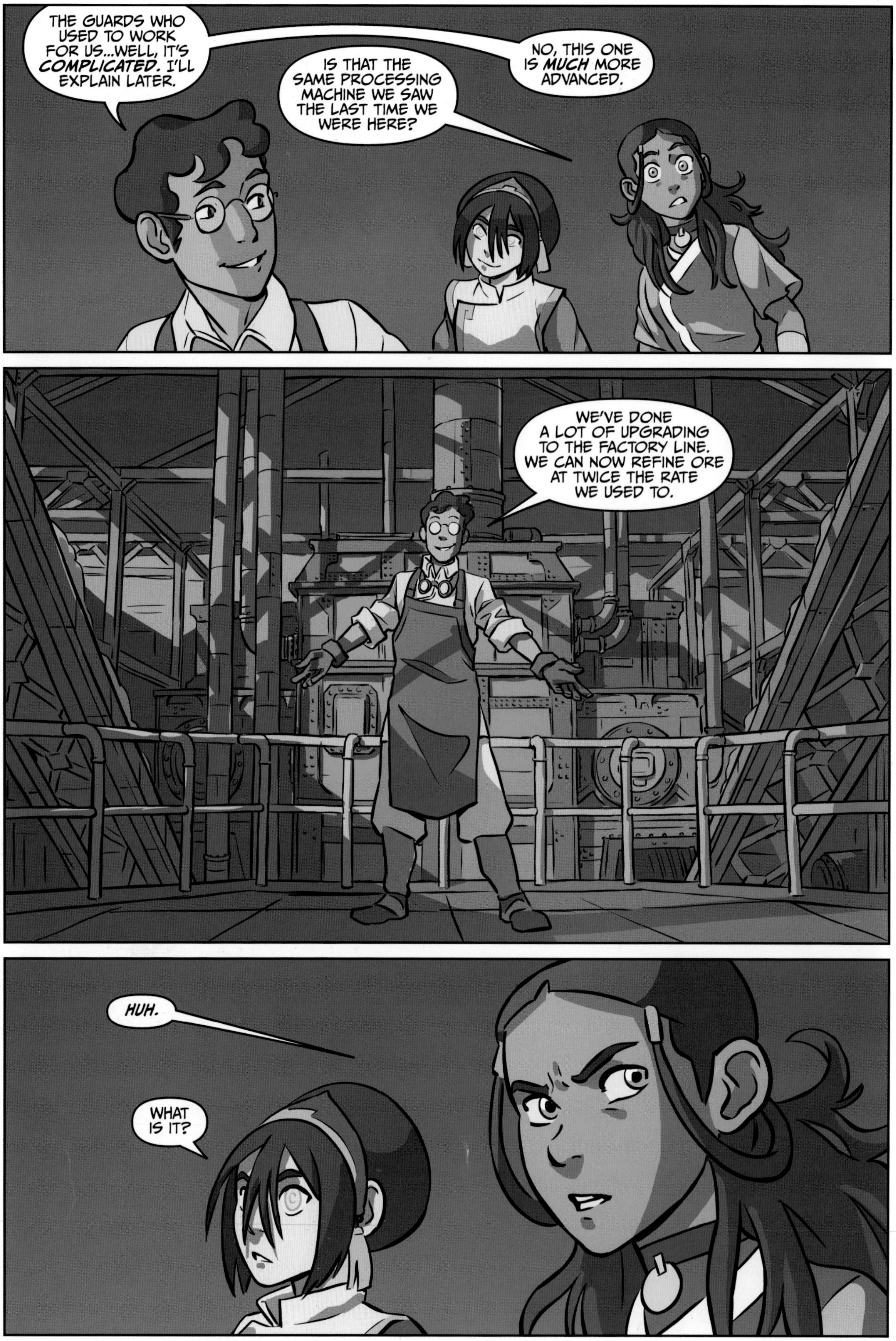
THE GUARDS WHO USED TO WORK FOR US...WELL, IT'S *COMPLICATED.* I'LL EXPLAIN LATER.
IS THAT THE SAME PROCESSING MACHINE WE SAW THE LAST TIME WE WERE HERE?
NO, THIS ONE IS *MUCH* MORE ADVANCED.
WE'VE DONE A LOT OF UPGRADING TO THE FACTORY LINE. WE CAN NOW REFINE ORE AT TWICE THE RATE WE USED TO.
HUH.
WHAT IS IT?

PW: *I have zero idea how the machine in the background works, but it's probably super dangerous.*

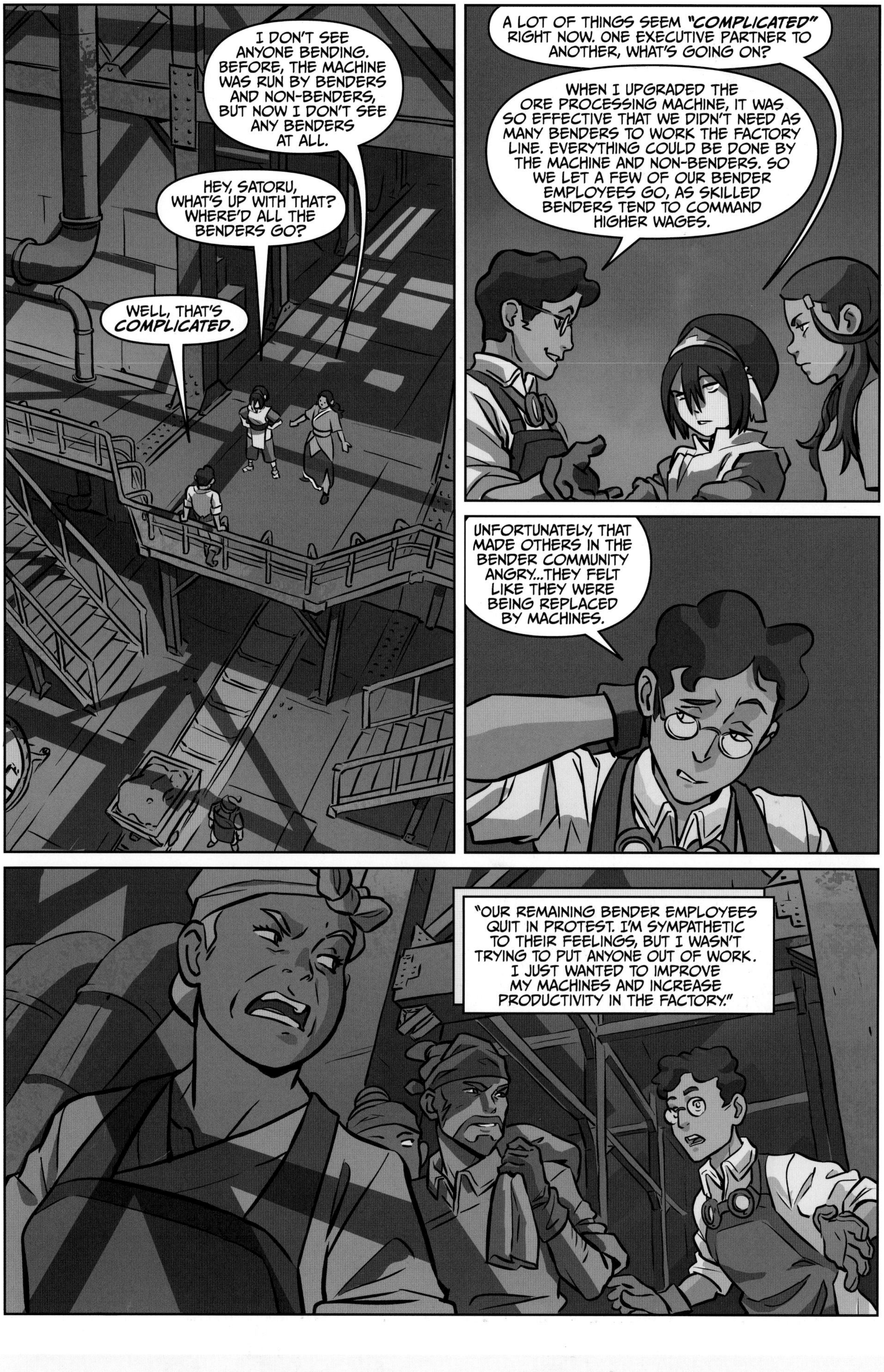
I DON'T SEE ANYONE BENDING. BEFORE, THE MACHINE WAS RUN BY BENDERS AND NON-BENDERS, BUT NOW I DON'T SEE ANY BENDERS AT ALL.
HEY, SATORU, WHAT'S UP WITH THAT? WHERE'D ALL THE BENDERS GO?
WELL, THAT'S *COMPLICATED.*
A LOT OF THINGS SEEM *"COMPLICATED"* RIGHT NOW. ONE EXECUTIVE PARTNER TO ANOTHER, WHAT'S GOING ON?
WHEN I UPGRADED THE ORE PROCESSING MACHINE, IT WAS SO EFFECTIVE THAT WE DIDN'T NEED AS MANY BENDERS TO WORK THE FACTORY LINE. EVERYTHING COULD BE DONE BY THE MACHINE AND NON-BENDERS. SO WE LET A FEW OF OUR BENDER EMPLOYEES GO, AS SKILLED BENDERS TEND TO COMMAND HIGHER WAGES.
UNFORTUNATELY, THAT MADE OTHERS IN THE BENDER COMMUNITY ANGRY...THEY FELT LIKE THEY WERE BEING REPLACED BY MACHINES.
"OUR REMAINING BENDER EMPLOYEES QUIT IN PROTEST. I'M SYMPATHETIC TO THEIR FEELINGS, BUT I WASN'T TRYING TO PUT ANYONE OUT OF WORK. I JUST WANTED TO IMPROVE MY MACHINES AND INCREASE PRODUCTIVITY IN THE FACTORY."

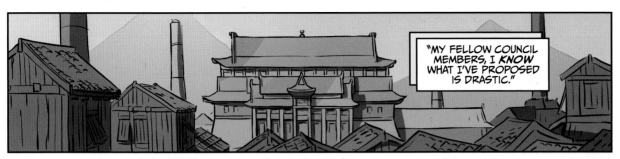

"MY FELLOW COUNCIL MEMBERS, I *KNOW* WHAT I'VE PROPOSED IS DRASTIC."

THAT'S WHY I'VE ASKED THE AVATAR TO JOIN US. HE'LL BE ABLE TO GUIDE US.

AVATAR...

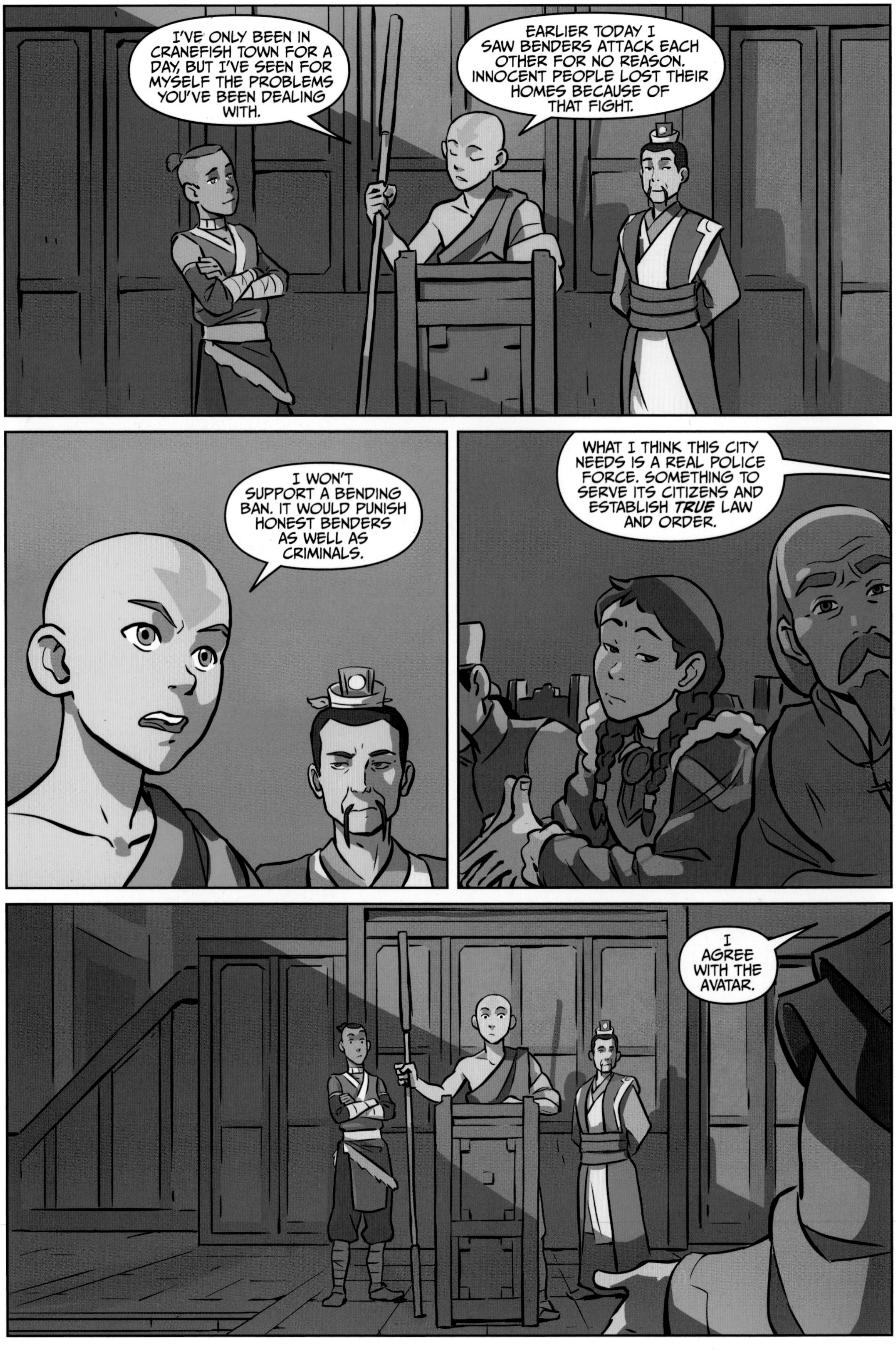
I'VE ONLY BEEN IN CRANEFISH TOWN FOR A DAY, BUT I'VE SEEN FOR MYSELF THE PROBLEMS YOU'VE BEEN DEALING WITH.
EARLIER TODAY I SAW BENDERS ATTACK EACH OTHER FOR NO REASON. INNOCENT PEOPLE LOST THEIR HOMES BECAUSE OF THAT FIGHT.
I WON'T SUPPORT A BENDING BAN. IT WOULD PUNISH HONEST BENDERS AS WELL AS CRIMINALS.
WHAT I THINK THIS CITY NEEDS IS A REAL POLICE FORCE. SOMETHING TO SERVE ITS CITIZENS AND ESTABLISH *TRUE* LAW AND ORDER.
I AGREE WITH THE AVATAR.

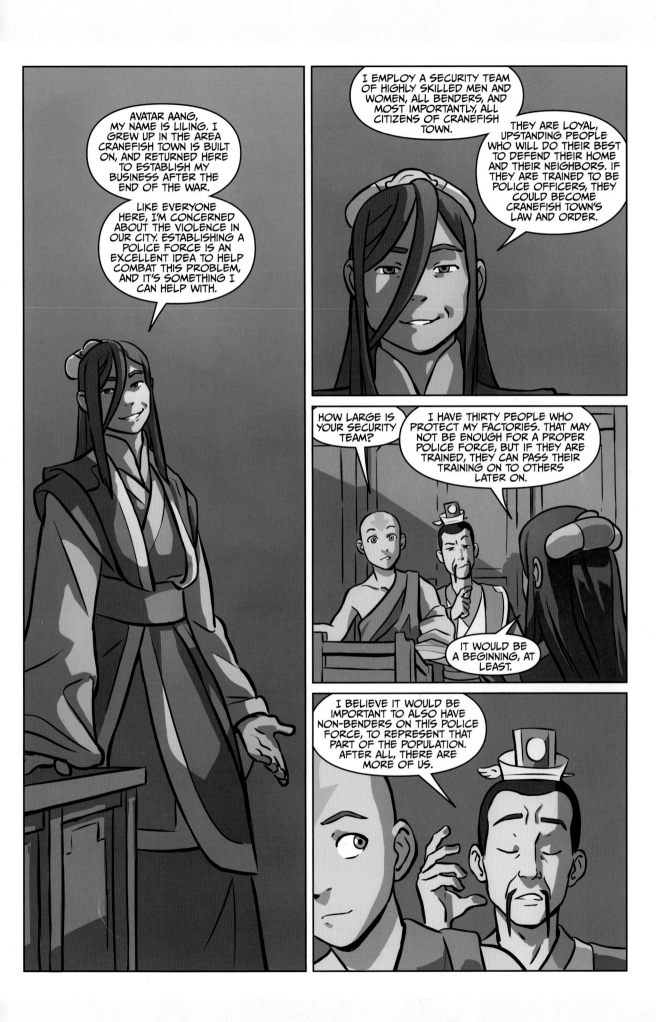

AVATAR AANG, MY NAME IS LILING. I GREW UP IN THE AREA CRANEFISH TOWN IS BUILT ON, AND RETURNED HERE TO ESTABLISH MY BUSINESS AFTER THE END OF THE WAR.

LIKE EVERYONE HERE, I'M CONCERNED ABOUT THE VIOLENCE IN OUR CITY. ESTABLISHING A POLICE FORCE IS AN EXCELLENT IDEA TO HELP COMBAT THIS PROBLEM, AND IT'S SOMETHING I CAN HELP WITH.

I EMPLOY A SECURITY TEAM OF HIGHLY SKILLED MEN AND WOMEN, ALL BENDERS, AND MOST IMPORTANTLY, ALL CITIZENS OF CRANEFISH TOWN.

THEY ARE LOYAL, UPSTANDING PEOPLE WHO WILL DO THEIR BEST TO DEFEND THEIR HOME AND THEIR NEIGHBORS. IF THEY ARE TRAINED TO BE POLICE OFFICERS, THEY COULD BECOME CRANEFISH TOWN'S LAW AND ORDER.

HOW LARGE IS YOUR SECURITY TEAM?

I HAVE THIRTY PEOPLE WHO PROTECT MY FACTORIES. THAT MAY NOT BE ENOUGH FOR A PROPER POLICE FORCE, BUT IF THEY ARE TRAINED, THEY CAN PASS THEIR TRAINING ON TO OTHERS LATER ON.

IT WOULD BE A BEGINNING, AT LEAST.

I BELIEVE IT WOULD BE IMPORTANT TO ALSO HAVE NON-BENDERS ON THIS POLICE FORCE, TO REPRESENT THAT PART OF THE POPULATION. AFTER ALL, THERE ARE MORE OF US.

FEH: *Liling appears! I love Peter's design for her.*

43

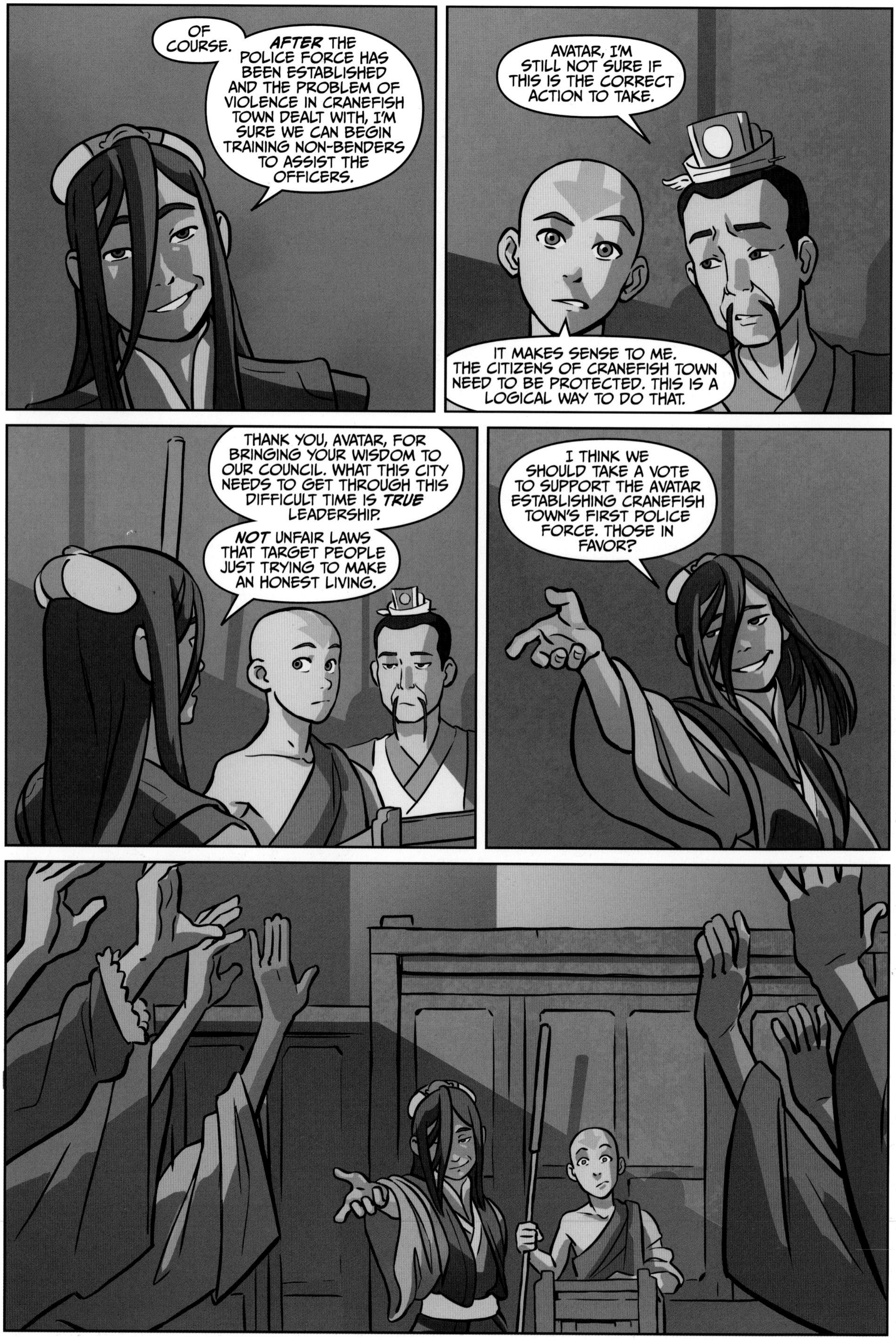
OF COURSE.
AFTER THE POLICE FORCE HAS BEEN ESTABLISHED AND THE PROBLEM OF VIOLENCE IN CRANEFISH TOWN DEALT WITH, I'M SURE WE CAN BEGIN TRAINING NON-BENDERS TO ASSIST THE OFFICERS.
AVATAR, I'M STILL NOT SURE IF THIS IS THE CORRECT ACTION TO TAKE.
IT MAKES SENSE TO ME. THE CITIZENS OF CRANEFISH TOWN NEED TO BE PROTECTED. THIS IS A LOGICAL WAY TO DO THAT.
THANK YOU, AVATAR, FOR BRINGING YOUR WISDOM TO OUR COUNCIL. WHAT THIS CITY NEEDS TO GET THROUGH THIS DIFFICULT TIME IS TRUE LEADERSHIP.
NOT UNFAIR LAWS THAT TARGET PEOPLE JUST TRYING TO MAKE AN HONEST LIVING.
I THINK WE SHOULD TAKE A VOTE TO SUPPORT THE AVATAR ESTABLISHING CRANEFISH TOWN'S FIRST POLICE FORCE. THOSE IN FAVOR?

WE *BELIEVE* IN YOU, AVATAR.

THAT COUNCIL LADY SEEMED ALL RIGHT, VOLUNTEERING HER OWN SECURITY TEAM TO HELP CLEAN UP CRANEFISH TOWN'S STREETS.

YES, EVERYONE WANTED TO HELP.

WE'RE DEFINITELY SPENDING LONGER THAN JUST A DAY HERE, HUH?

LOOKS LIKE. I DON'T THINK WE'LL BE GETTING TO YU DAO ANYTIME SOON.

IN THAT CASE, I'M GONNA SEND A MESSENGER HAWK TO SUKI AND TELL HER TO JOIN US HERE.

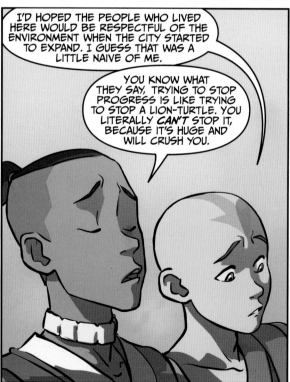

I'D HOPED THE PEOPLE WHO LIVED HERE WOULD BE RESPECTFUL OF THE ENVIRONMENT WHEN THE CITY STARTED TO EXPAND. I GUESS THAT WAS A LITTLE NAIVE OF ME.

YOU KNOW WHAT THEY SAY, TRYING TO STOP PROGRESS IS LIKE TRYING TO STOP A LION-TURTLE. YOU LITERALLY *CAN'T* STOP IT, BECAUSE IT'S HUGE AND WILL CRUSH YOU.

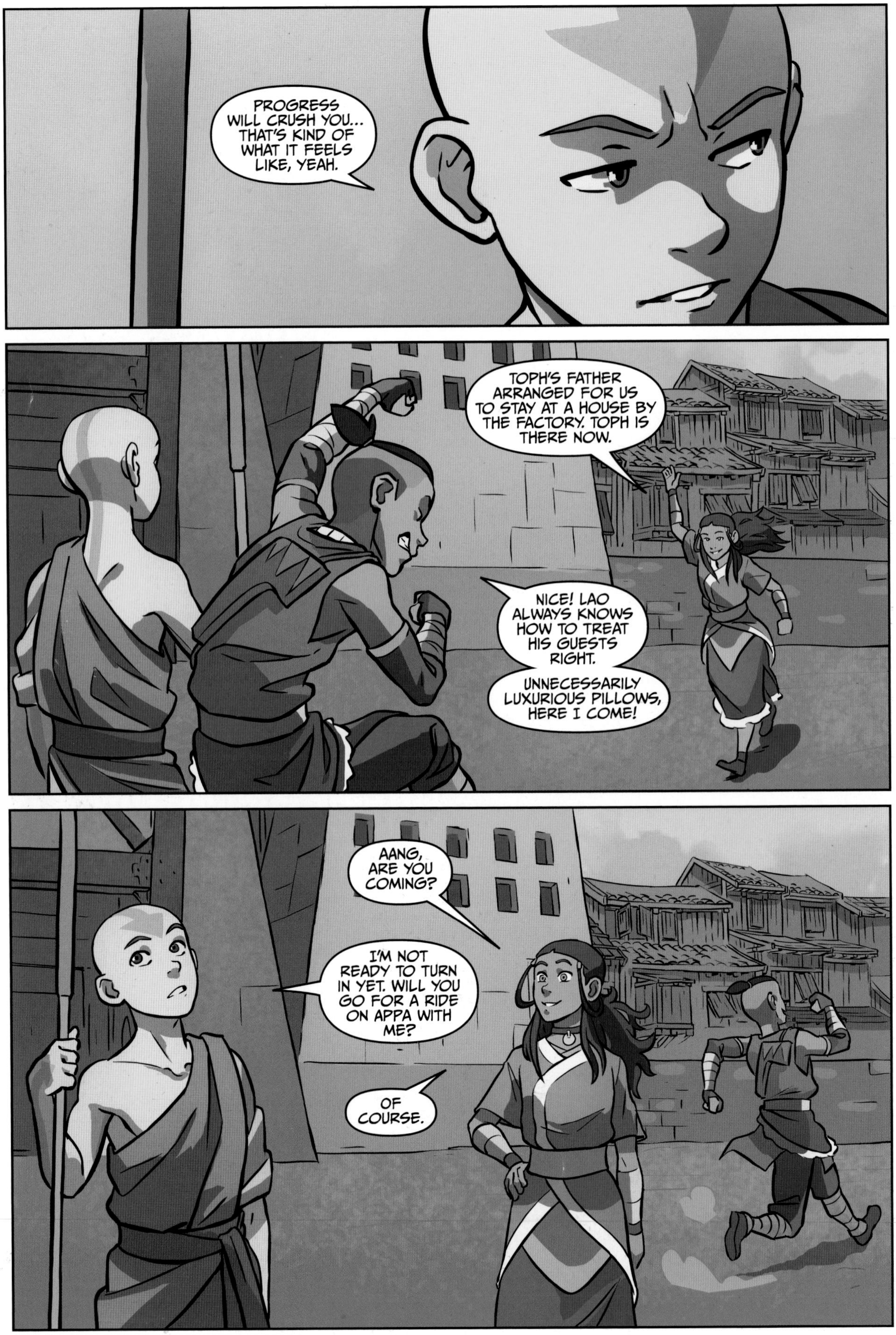
PROGRESS WILL CRUSH YOU... THAT'S KIND OF WHAT IT FEELS LIKE, YEAH.
TOPH'S FATHER ARRANGED FOR US TO STAY AT A HOUSE BY THE FACTORY. TOPH IS THERE NOW.
NICE! LAO ALWAYS KNOWS HOW TO TREAT HIS GUESTS RIGHT.
UNNECESSARILY LUXURIOUS PILLOWS, HERE I COME!
AANG, ARE YOU COMING?
I'M NOT READY TO TURN IN YET. WILL YOU GO FOR A RIDE ON APPA WITH ME?
OF COURSE.

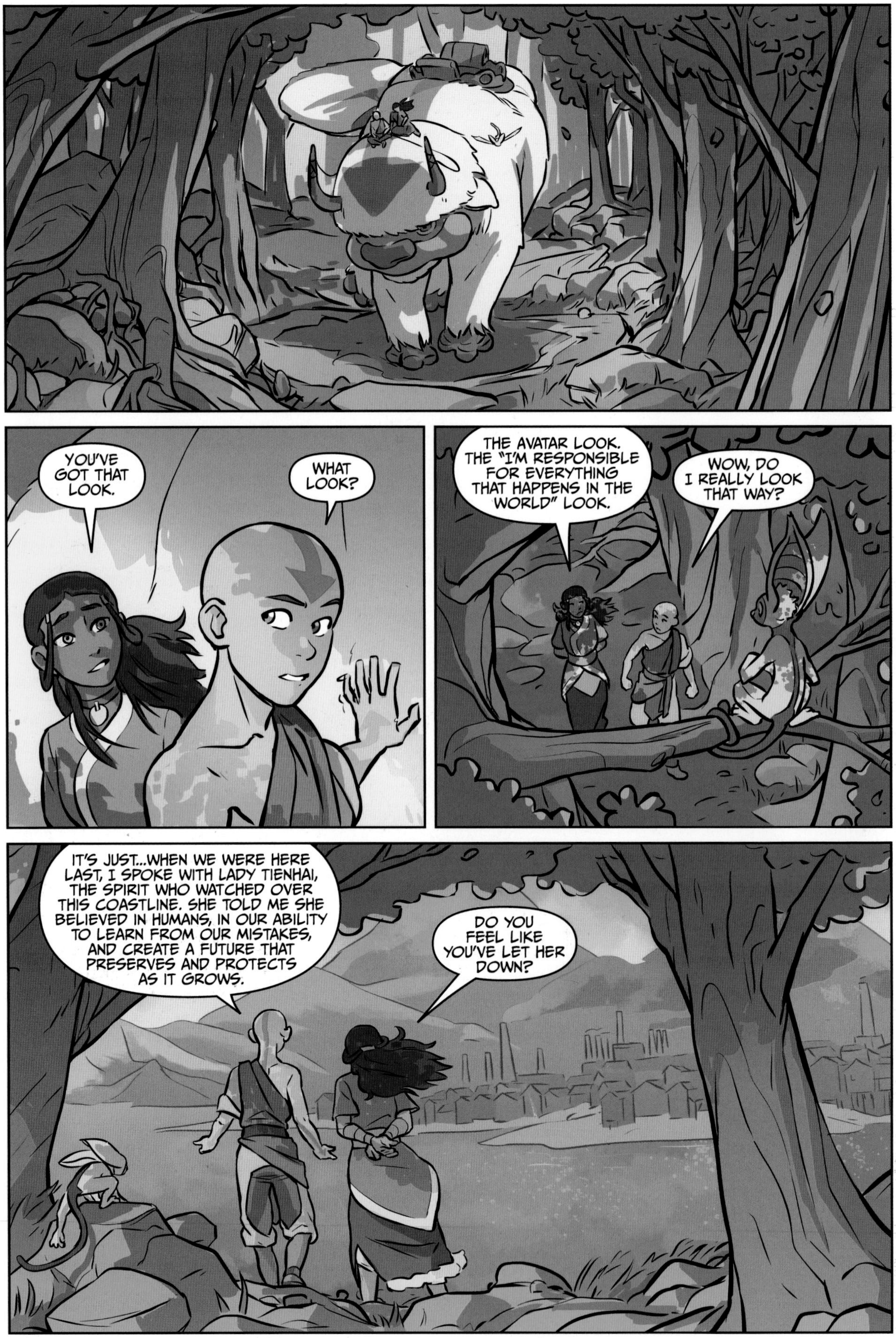
YOU'VE GOT THAT LOOK.
WHAT LOOK?
THE AVATAR LOOK. THE "I'M RESPONSIBLE FOR EVERYTHING THAT HAPPENS IN THE WORLD" LOOK.
WOW, DO I REALLY LOOK THAT WAY?
IT'S JUST...WHEN WE WERE HERE LAST, I SPOKE WITH LADY TIENHAI, THE SPIRIT WHO WATCHED OVER THIS COASTLINE. SHE TOLD ME SHE BELIEVED IN HUMANS, IN OUR ABILITY TO LEARN FROM OUR MISTAKES, AND CREATE A FUTURE THAT PRESERVES AND PROTECTS AS IT GROWS.
DO YOU FEEL LIKE YOU'VE LET HER DOWN?

PW: *This scene on the island is one of my favorites in all of the books. It's a nice, quiet moment before things fall apart.*

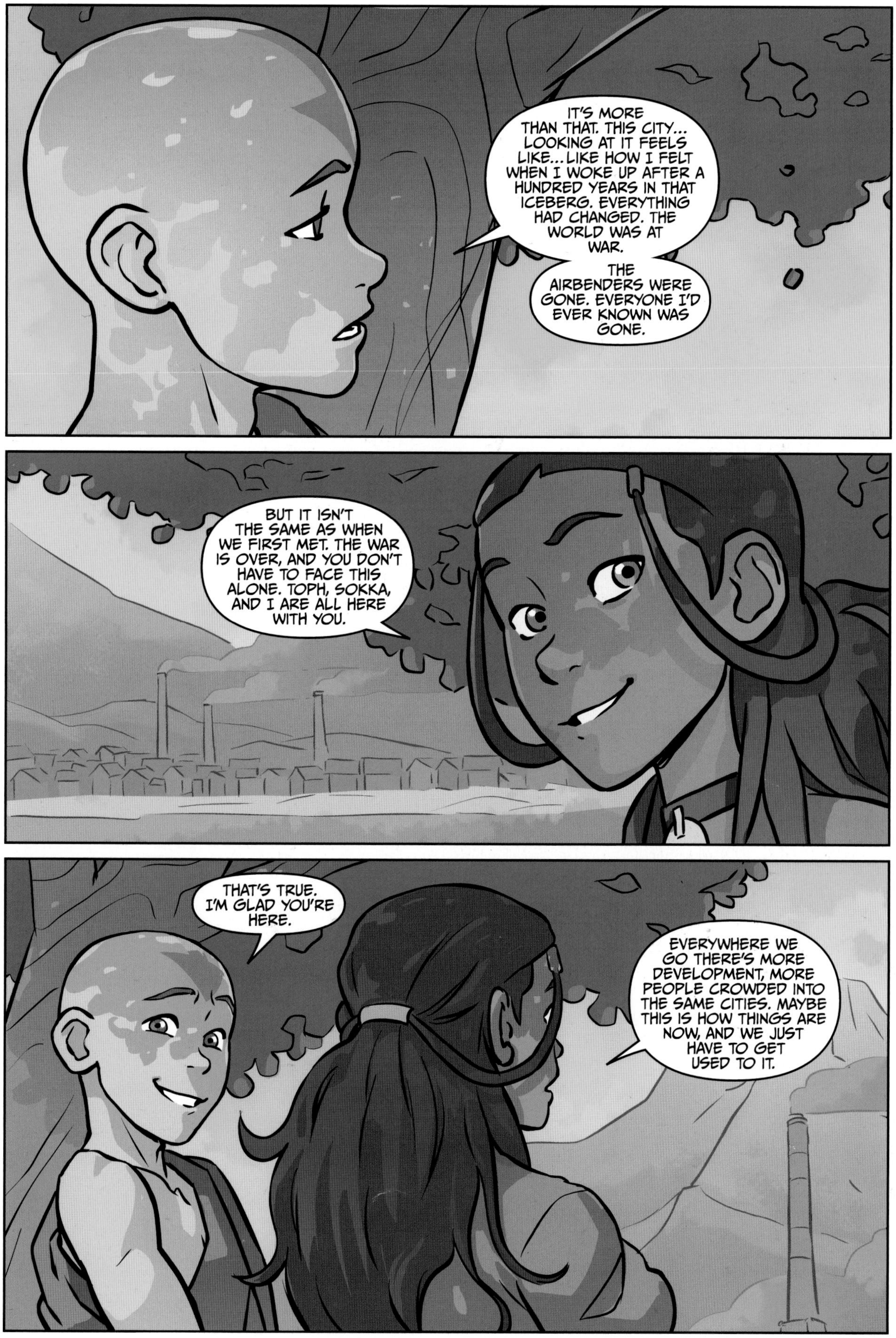
IT'S MORE THAN THAT. THIS CITY... LOOKING AT IT FEELS LIKE... LIKE HOW I FELT WHEN I WOKE UP AFTER A HUNDRED YEARS IN THAT ICEBERG. EVERYTHING HAD CHANGED. THE WORLD WAS AT WAR.
THE AIRBENDERS WERE GONE. EVERYONE I'D EVER KNOWN WAS GONE.
BUT IT ISN'T THE SAME AS WHEN WE FIRST MET. THE WAR IS OVER, AND YOU DON'T HAVE TO FACE THIS ALONE. TOPH, SOKKA, AND I ARE ALL HERE WITH YOU.
THAT'S TRUE. I'M GLAD YOU'RE HERE.
EVERYWHERE WE GO THERE'S MORE DEVELOPMENT, MORE PEOPLE CROWDED INTO THE SAME CITIES. MAYBE THIS IS HOW THINGS ARE NOW, AND WE JUST HAVE TO GET USED TO IT.

PW: *I really like how Faith transitioned from hopeful musings between Aang and Katara to a door getting kicked in.*

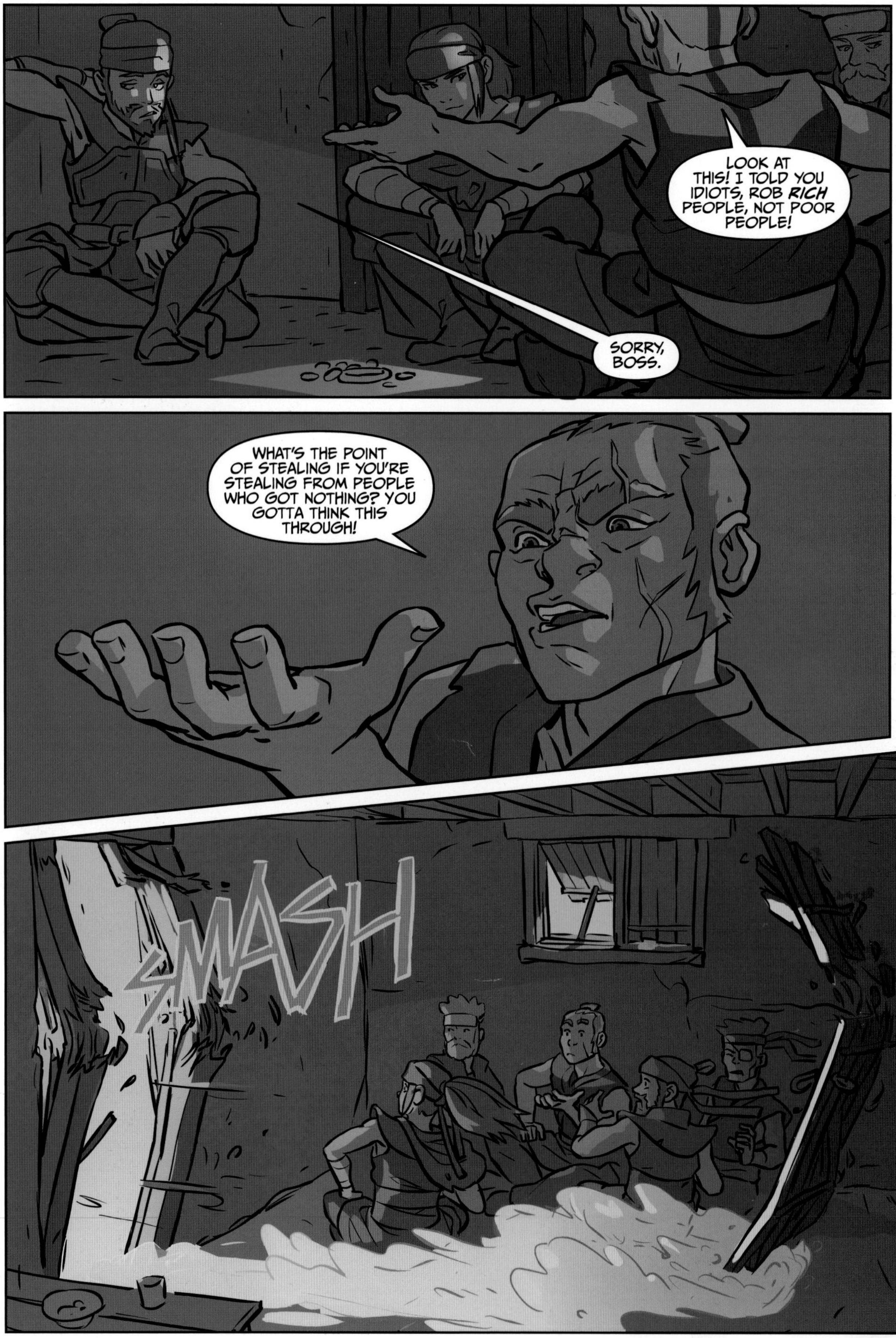
LOOK AT THIS! I TOLD YOU IDIOTS, ROB RICH PEOPLE, NOT POOR PEOPLE!
SORRY, BOSS.
WHAT'S THE POINT OF STEALING IF YOU'RE STEALING FROM PEOPLE WHO GOT NOTHING? YOU GOTTA THINK THIS THROUGH!
SMASH

HELLO! EXCUSE THE INTERRUPTION.

I'VE NOTICED YOU ARE ALL TALENTED BENDERS, *ROBBED* OF YOUR CHANCE TO USE YOUR SKILLS IN THIS CITY, *FORCED* INTO A LIFE OF CRIME.

FEH: *I adore scrappy girl villains. When I first started watching* Avatar, *I fell in love with Azula, Ty Lee, and Mai. They were everything I wanted in teen girl villains, and when I got the chance to write my own* Avatar *stories, I knew I had to include more evil young women.*

I WAS WONDERING IF YOU'D BE INTERESTED IN A JOB OPPORTUNITY. IF YOU DO GOOD WORK, YOU COULD BECOME PART OF A *WONDERFUL* MOVEMENT THAT WILL BENEFIT BENDERS AND THEIR FAMILIES ACROSS THE WORLD!

I DON'T *THINK* SO, LITTLE GIRL. I *LIKE* MY LIFE OF CRIME.

TURN YOURSELF AROUND AND MARCH OUT OF HERE BEFORE YOU GET HURT.

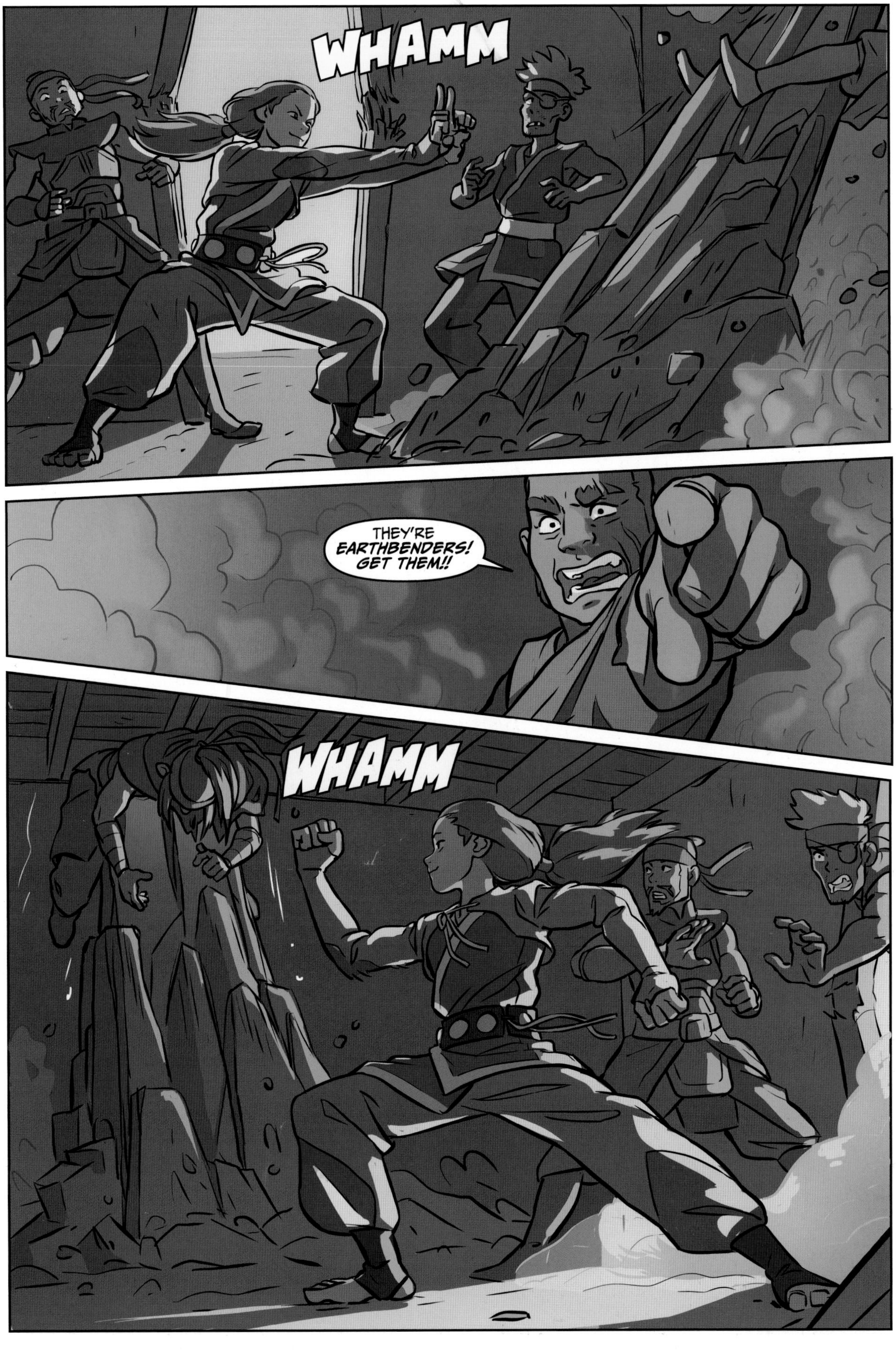
WHAMM
THEY'RE EARTHBENDERS! GET THEM!!
WHAMM

PW: *I don't know much about kung-fu, and figuring out how to draw it was one of the scariest things I had to tackle when I started this project. Having the characters move right is extremely important in* Avatar, *and so much of what made the show great was the excellent choreography and the way the various martial arts styles matched up with the characters' personalities.*

Luckily for me, I happen to have a close friend, Todd Balthazor, who has been practicing kung-fu for many years. All of the cool poses in the fight scenes were thanks to him—I would have been completely lost without his help (which goes to show how important collaboration is in projects like this!).

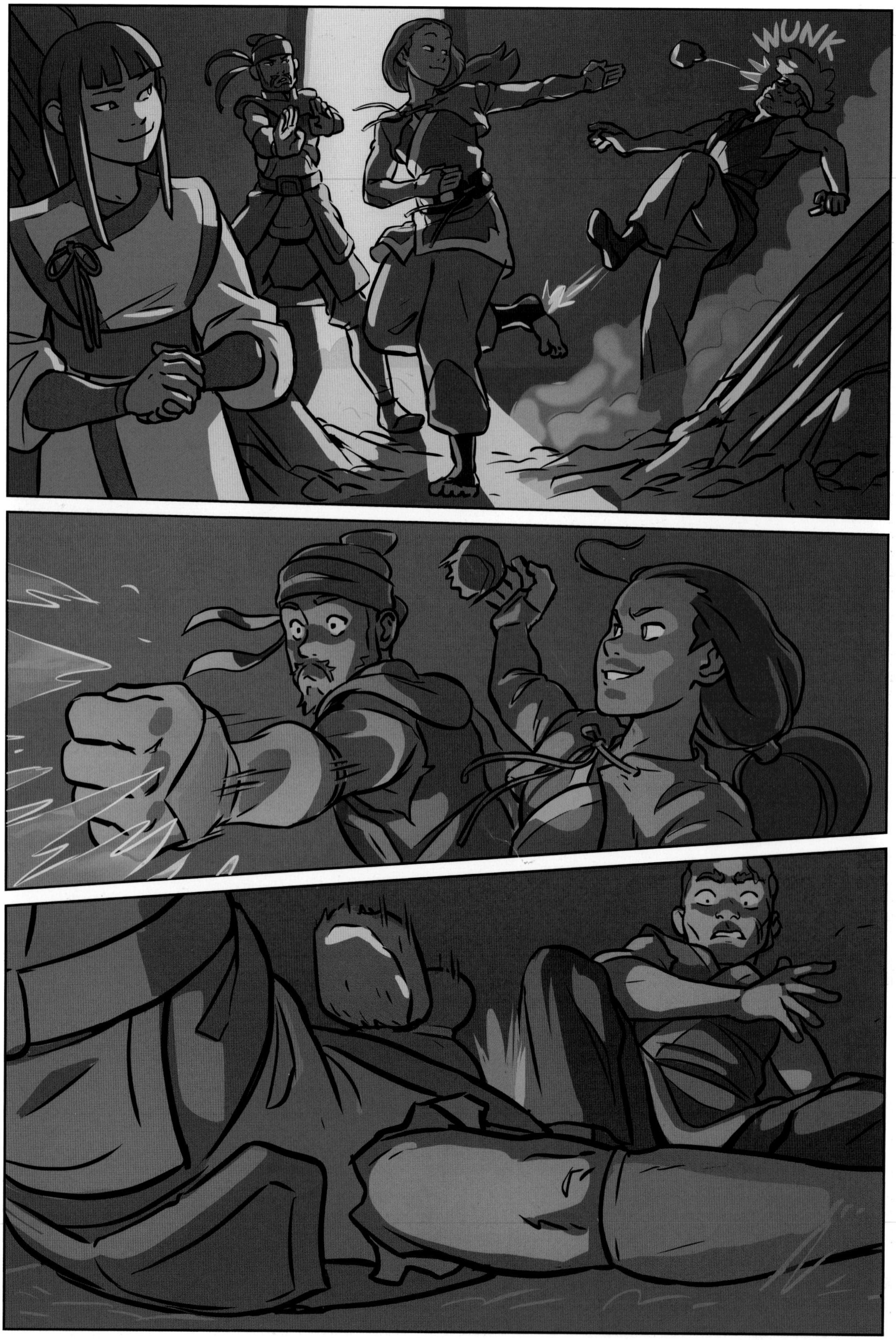
WUNK

FEH: *I love how Yaling just walks in and wipes the floor with everyone.*

PW: *Only Toph could pull off making statues of herself.*

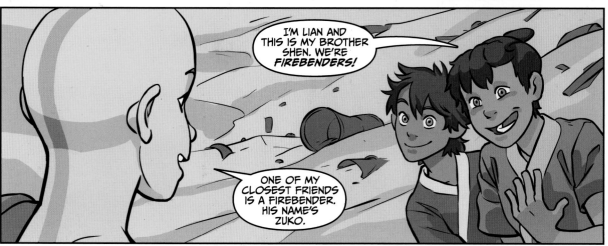

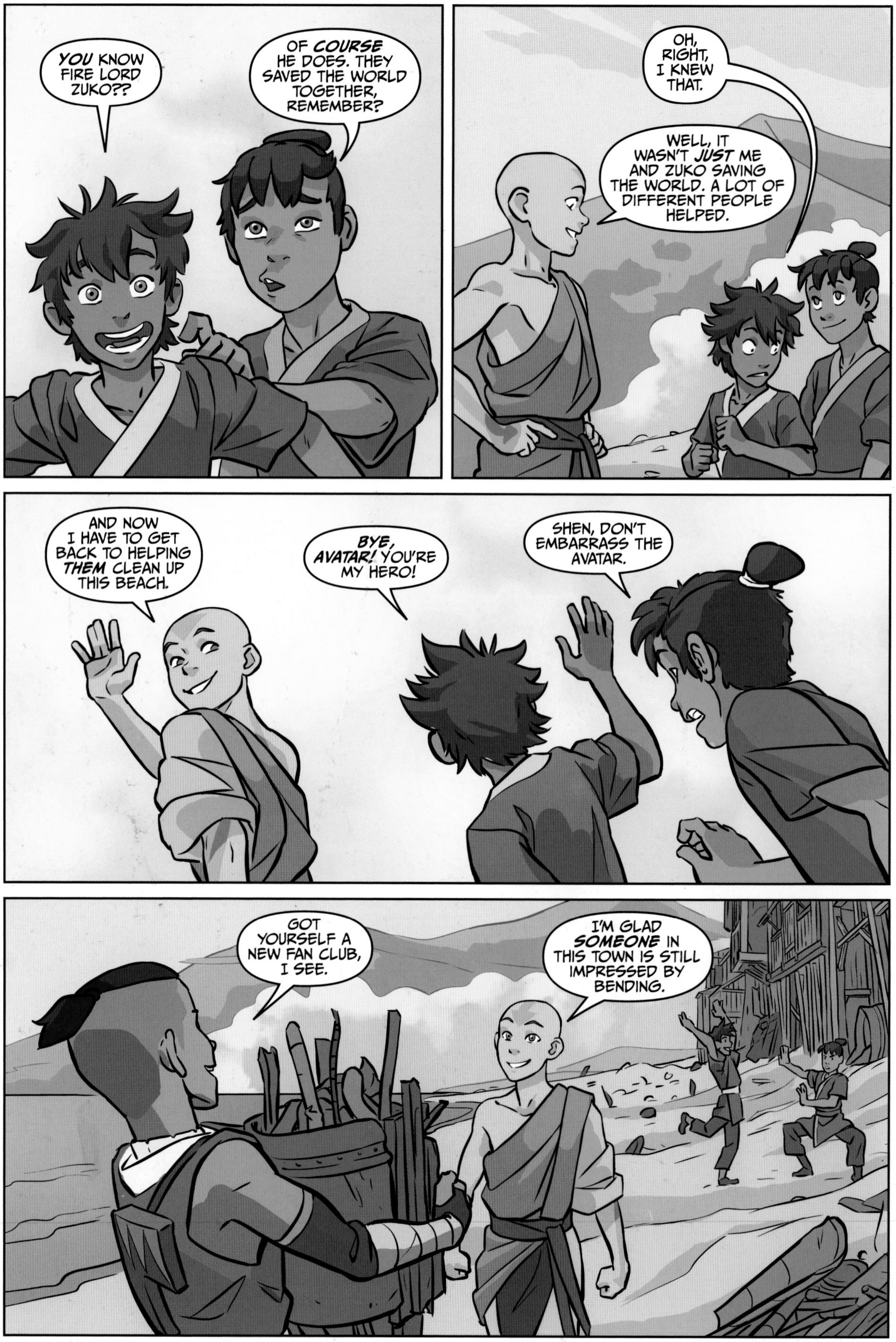
YOU KNOW FIRE LORD ZUKO??
OF COURSE HE DOES. THEY SAVED THE WORLD TOGETHER, REMEMBER?
OH, RIGHT, I KNEW THAT.
WELL, IT WASN'T JUST ME AND ZUKO SAVING THE WORLD. A LOT OF DIFFERENT PEOPLE HELPED.
AND NOW I HAVE TO GET BACK TO HELPING THEM CLEAN UP THIS BEACH.
BYE, AVATAR! YOU'RE MY HERO!
SHEN, DON'T EMBARRASS THE AVATAR.
GOT YOURSELF A NEW FAN CLUB, I SEE.
I'M GLAD SOMEONE IN THIS TOWN IS STILL IMPRESSED BY BENDING.

PW: *I considered having Toph's hair down in this scene, but it was too weird.*

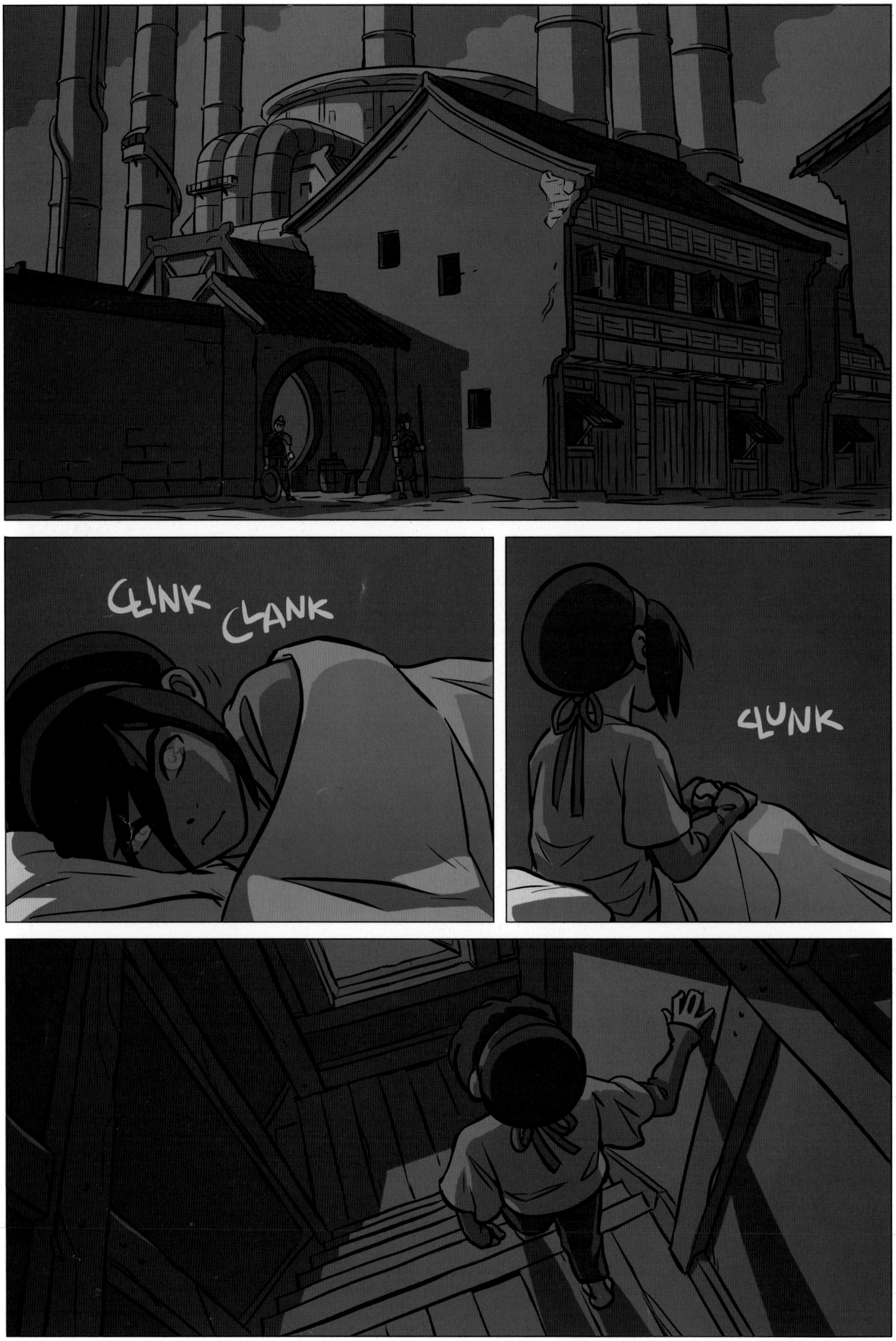
CLINK
CLANK
CLUNK

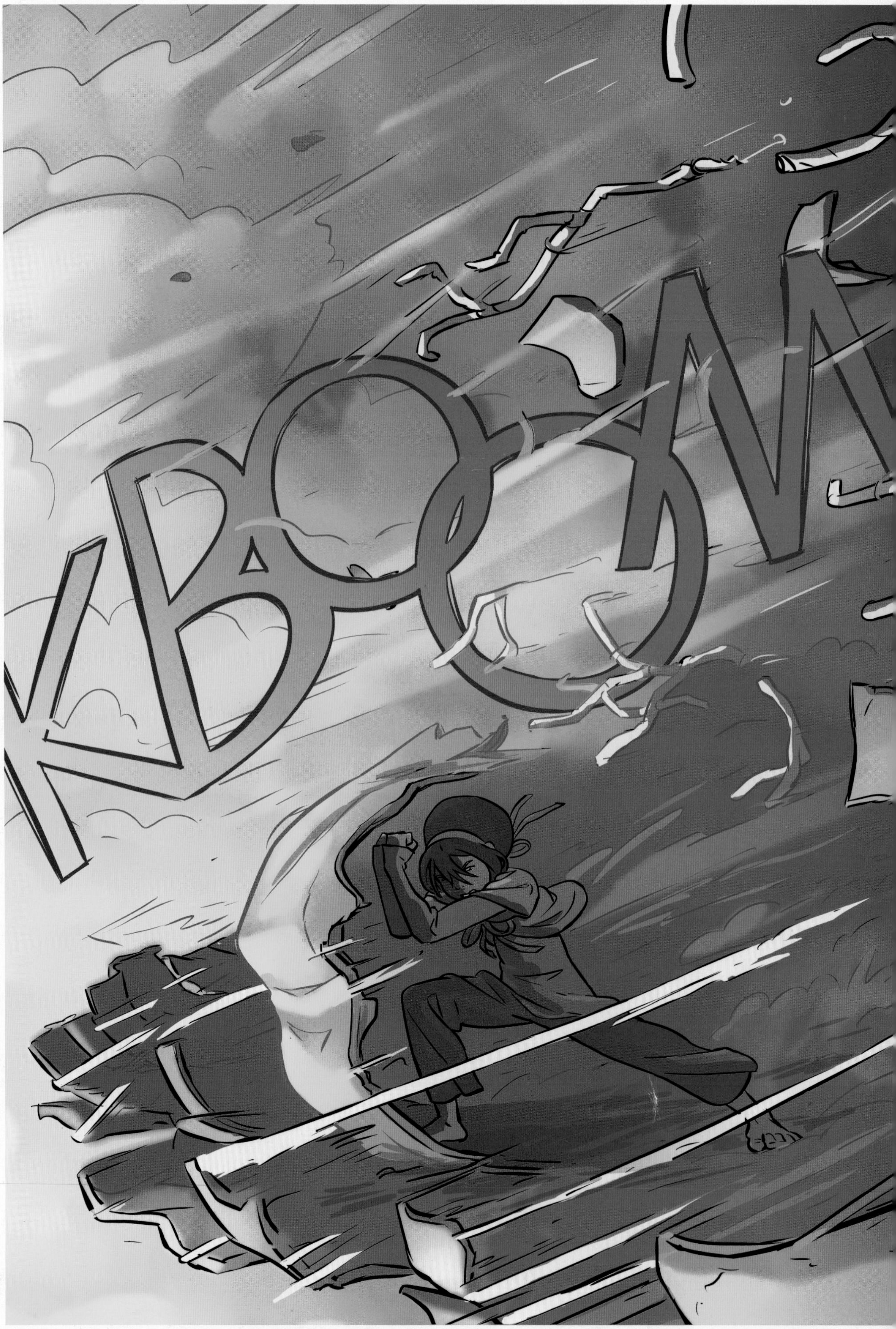
KBOOM

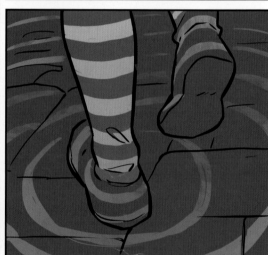

PW: *I really like how this Toph pose turned out (and Ryan's colors in this whole scene, for that matter). She's so cool.*

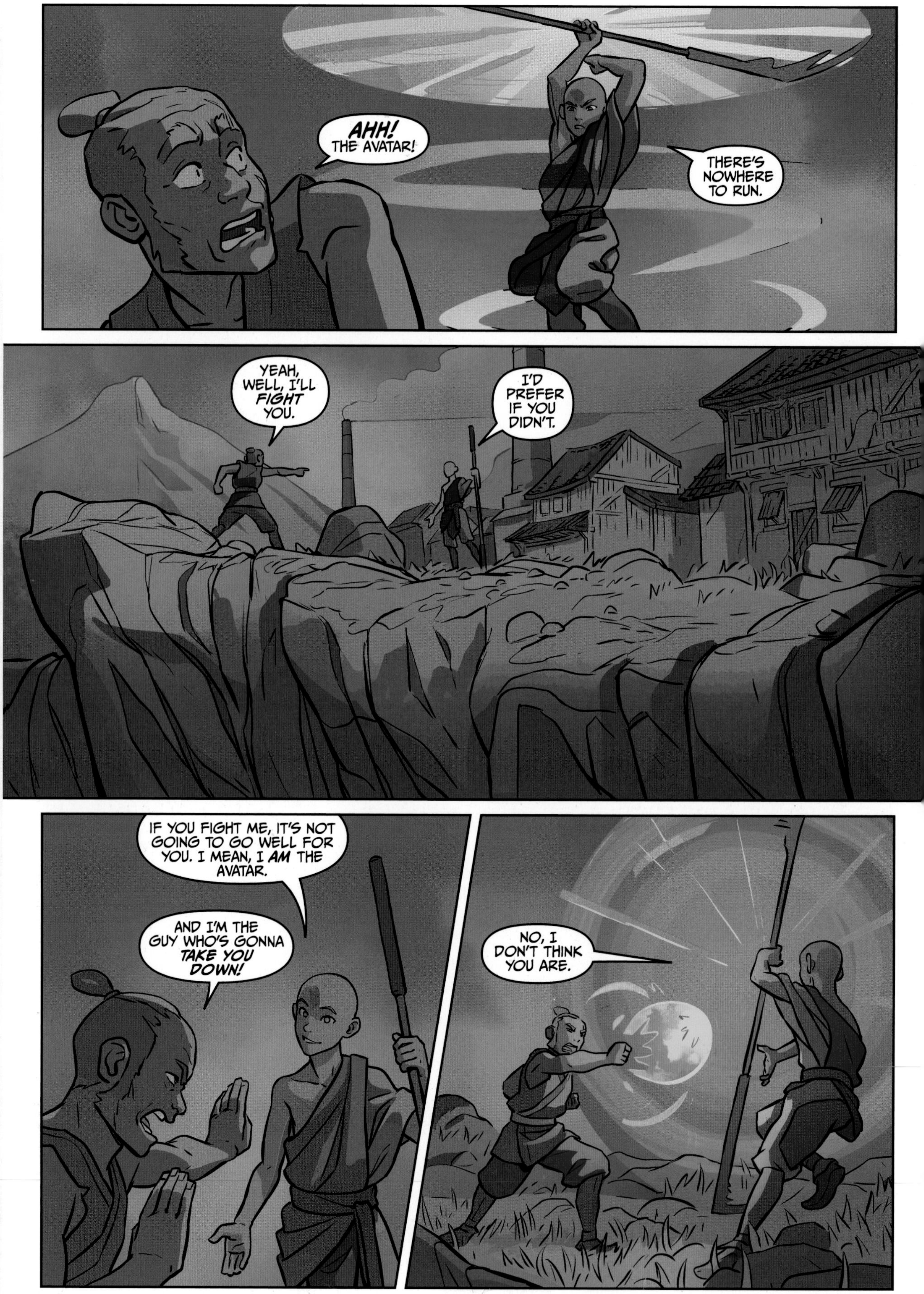
AHH! THE AVATAR!
THERE'S NOWHERE TO RUN.
YEAH, WELL, I'LL FIGHT YOU.
I'D PREFER IF YOU DIDN'T.
IF YOU FIGHT ME, IT'S NOT GOING TO GO WELL FOR YOU. I MEAN, I AM THE AVATAR.
AND I'M THE GUY WHO'S GONNA TAKE YOU DOWN!
NO, I DON'T THINK YOU ARE.

FEH: *It cracks me up that this guy is so sure he's going to win a fight with the Avatar. I think I'd just surrender.*

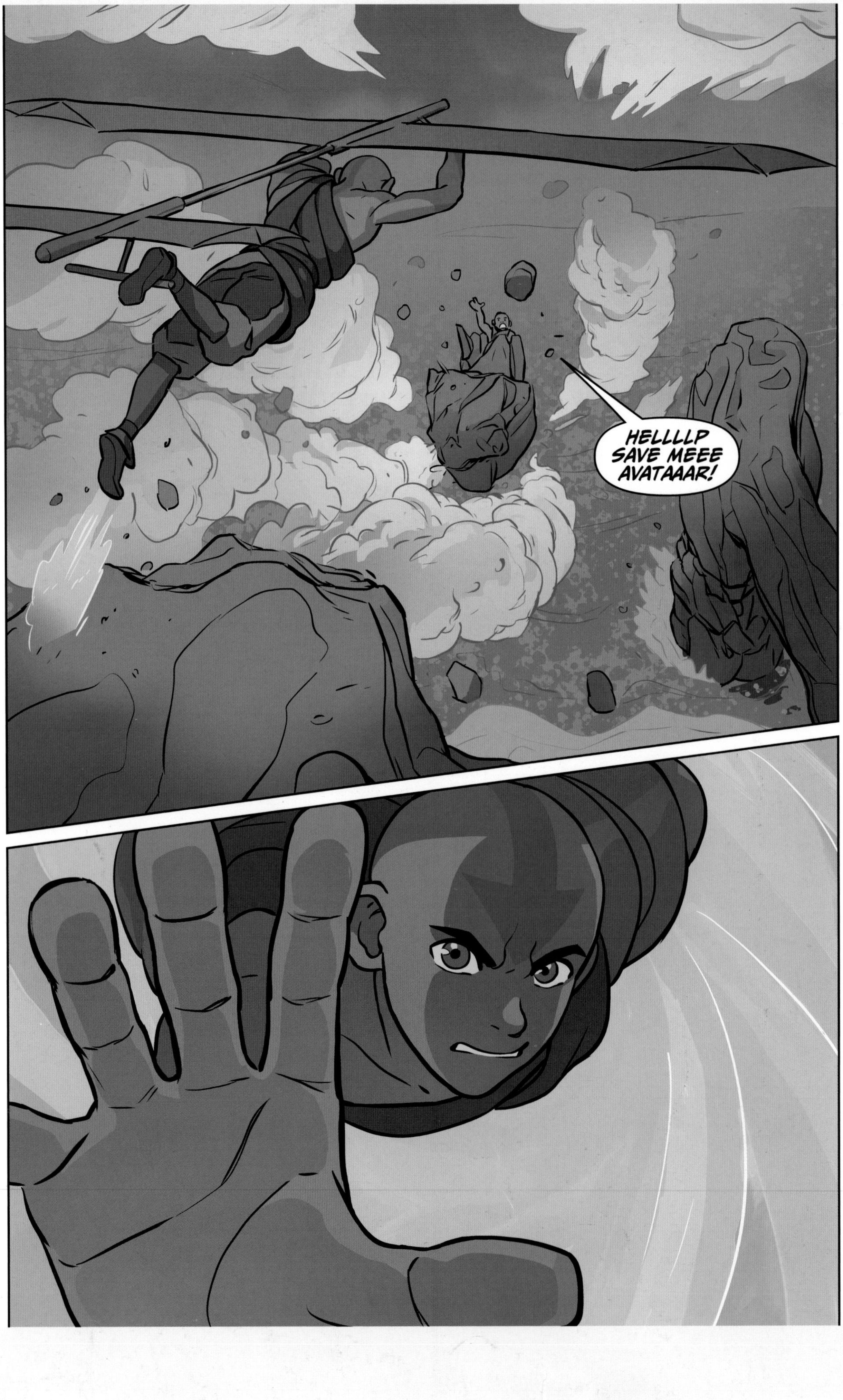
HELLLLP SAVE MEEE AVATAAAR!

UH OH.
SO THE AVATAR CAPTURED THE MAN YOU HIRED?
I *TRIED* TO MAKE SURE THE AVATAR COULDN'T GET HIM! RU DIDN'T HELP AT *ALL*--
THAT'S NOT FAIR, YALING! IT'S NOT *MY* FAULT THE AVATAR INTERFERED!
STOP.

PW: *I was trying to make the contrast between Liling's big, nice house and the surrounding city clear here.*

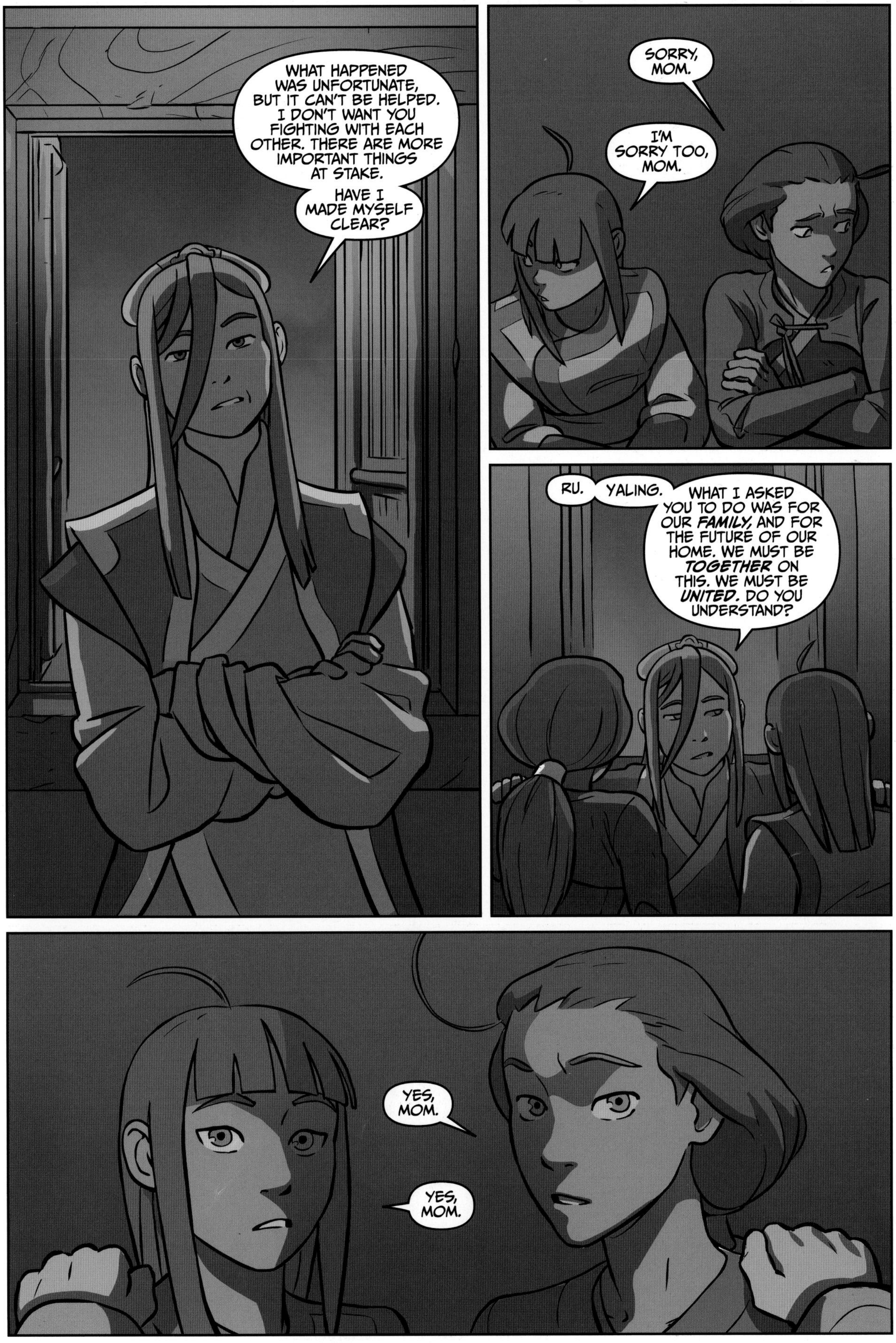
WHAT HAPPENED WAS UNFORTUNATE, BUT IT CAN'T BE HELPED. I DON'T WANT YOU FIGHTING WITH EACH OTHER. THERE ARE MORE IMPORTANT THINGS AT STAKE.
HAVE I MADE MYSELF CLEAR?
SORRY, MOM.
I'M SORRY TOO, MOM.
RU.
YALING.
WHAT I ASKED YOU TO DO WAS FOR OUR ***FAMILY,*** AND FOR THE FUTURE OF OUR HOME. WE MUST BE ***TOGETHER*** ON THIS. WE MUST BE ***UNITED.*** DO YOU UNDERSTAND?
YES, MOM.
YES, MOM.

FEH: *And twist! Councilwoman Liling is a bad person!* Avatar *has some powerful Evil Dad characters, and I thought it would be fun to make* Imbalance*'s main villain an Evil Mom, who's using her own children to further her plans. The family dynamic is my favorite thing here: the tension between Yaling and Ru wanting to make their mom proud, but also having to deal with her asking them to do terrible things. We'll see how they deal with that later in the story.*

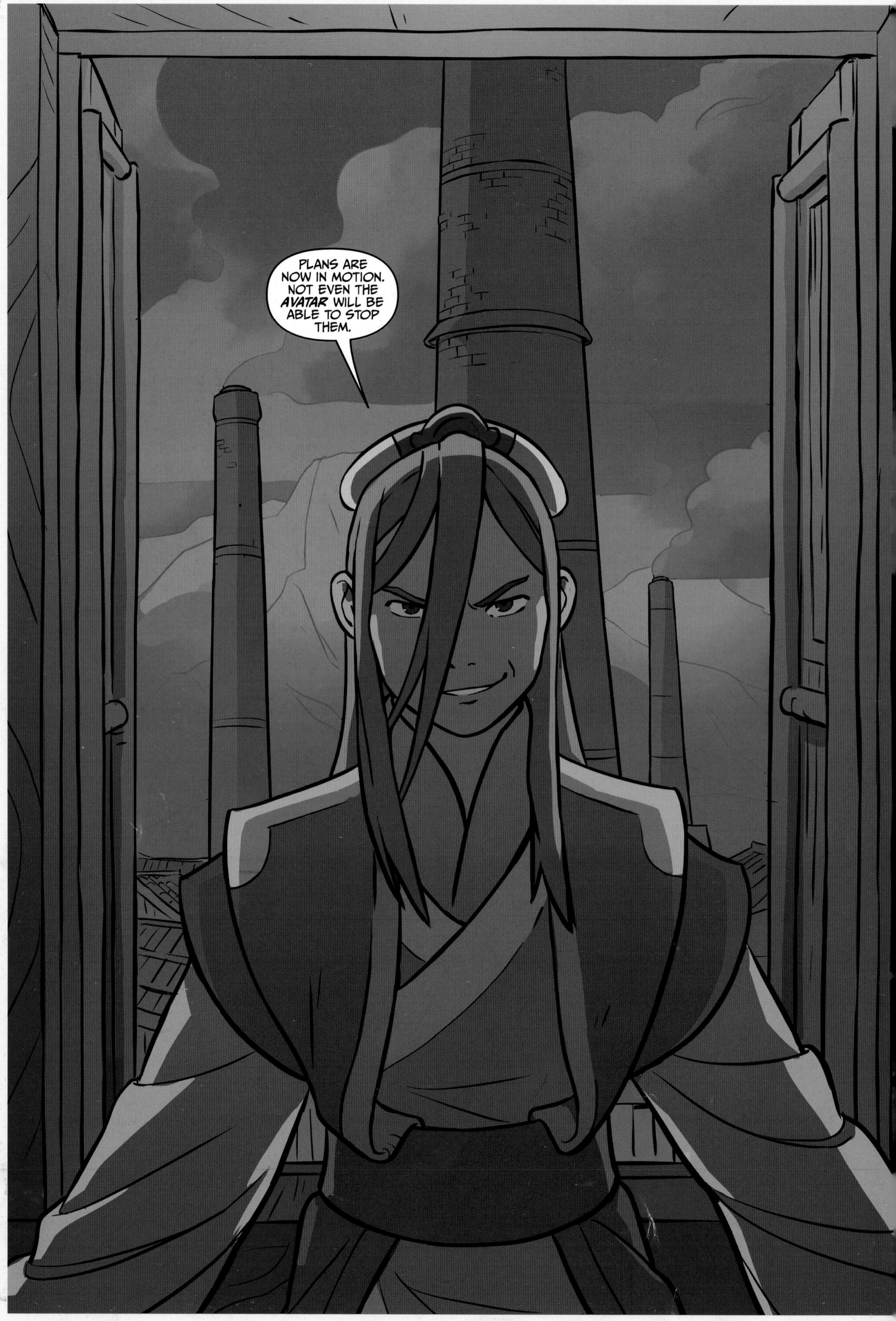
PLANS ARE NOW IN MOTION. NOT EVEN THE AVATAR WILL BE ABLE TO STOP THEM.

PETER WARTMAN: *Avatar was a huge influence on me—the show was coming out roughly around the same time I was in college and basically set the standard for what I appreciate in good storytelling. Drawing this first page was a bit surreal and intimidating, especially coming on the heels of Gene Yang and Gurihiru's long run on the comics. No easing into things either—not only was I immediately drawing every major character from the show, I had to figure out how all of them acted on the fly.*

I quickly discovered that Sokka is extremely fun to draw.

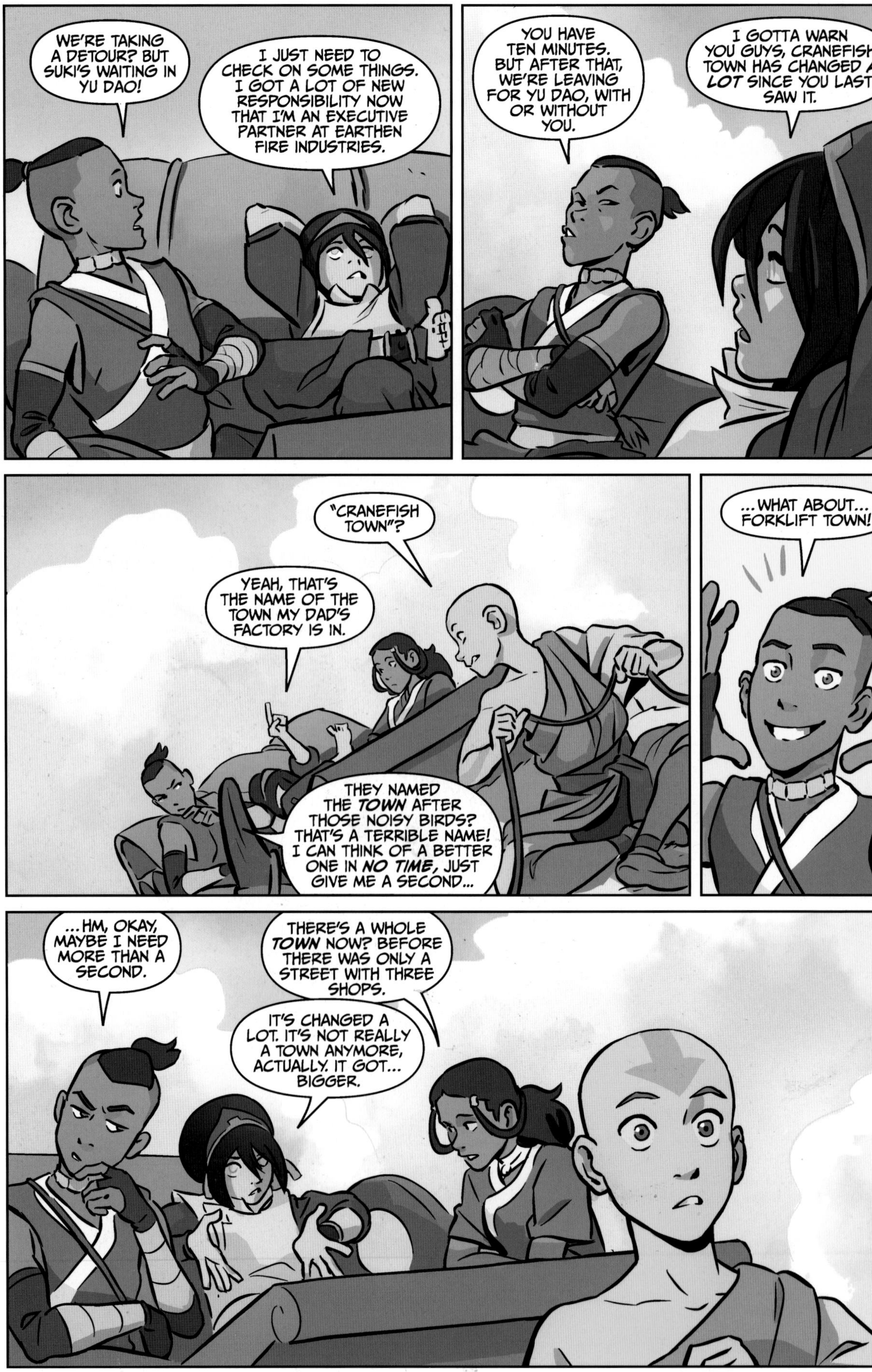
WE'RE TAKING A DETOUR? BUT SUKI'S WAITING IN YU DAO!
I JUST NEED TO CHECK ON SOME THINGS. I GOT A LOT OF NEW RESPONSIBILITY NOW THAT I'M AN EXECUTIVE PARTNER AT EARTHEN FIRE INDUSTRIES.
YOU HAVE TEN MINUTES. BUT AFTER THAT, WE'RE LEAVING FOR YU DAO, WITH OR WITHOUT YOU.
I GOTTA WARN YOU GUYS, CRANEFISH TOWN HAS CHANGED *A LOT* SINCE YOU LAST SAW IT.
"CRANEFISH TOWN"?
YEAH, THAT'S THE NAME OF THE TOWN MY DAD'S FACTORY IS IN.
THEY NAMED THE *TOWN* AFTER THOSE NOISY BIRDS? THAT'S A TERRIBLE NAME! I CAN THINK OF A BETTER ONE IN *NO TIME*, JUST GIVE ME A SECOND...
...WHAT ABOUT... FORKLIFT TOWN!
...HM, OKAY, MAYBE I NEED MORE THAN A SECOND.
THERE'S A WHOLE *TOWN* NOW? BEFORE THERE WAS ONLY A STREET WITH THREE SHOPS.
IT'S CHANGED A LOT. IT'S NOT REALLY A TOWN ANYMORE, ACTUALLY. IT GOT... BIGGER.

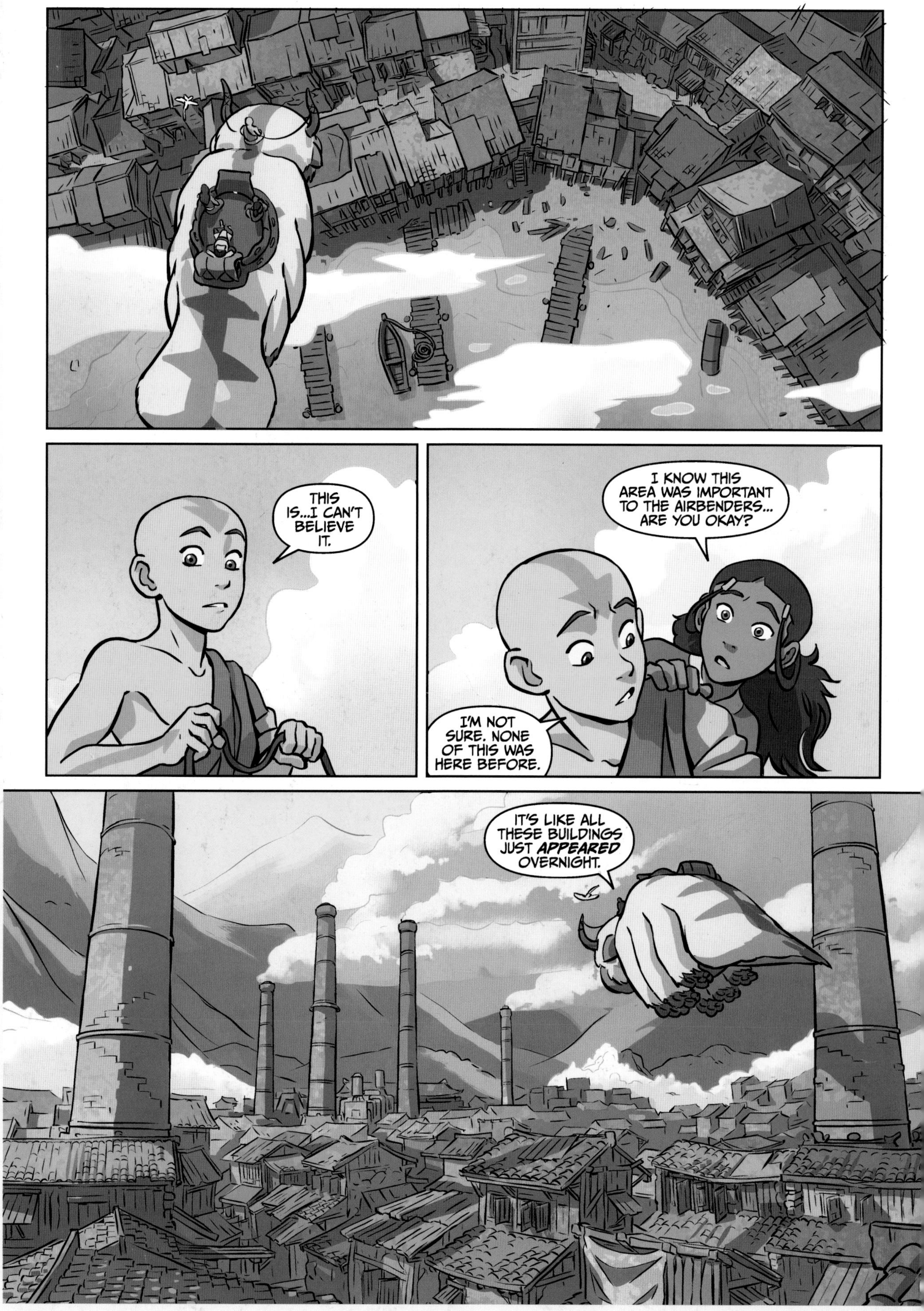
THIS IS...I CAN'T BELIEVE IT.
I KNOW THIS AREA WAS IMPORTANT TO THE AIRBENDERS... ARE YOU OKAY?
I'M NOT SURE. NONE OF THIS WAS HERE BEFORE.
IT'S LIKE ALL THESE BUILDINGS JUST ***APPEARED*** OVERNIGHT.

FEH: *Peter did an amazing job bringing this young, sprawling, messy city to life. It feels so lived-in and full of stories.*

PW: *This city took* **forever** *to draw. I'm still pretty happy with how Cranefish Town looks—I wanted it to feel very slapped together, a place that grew far too quickly and without much regard for the people living in it. I doubt anyone was paying much attention to building codes.*

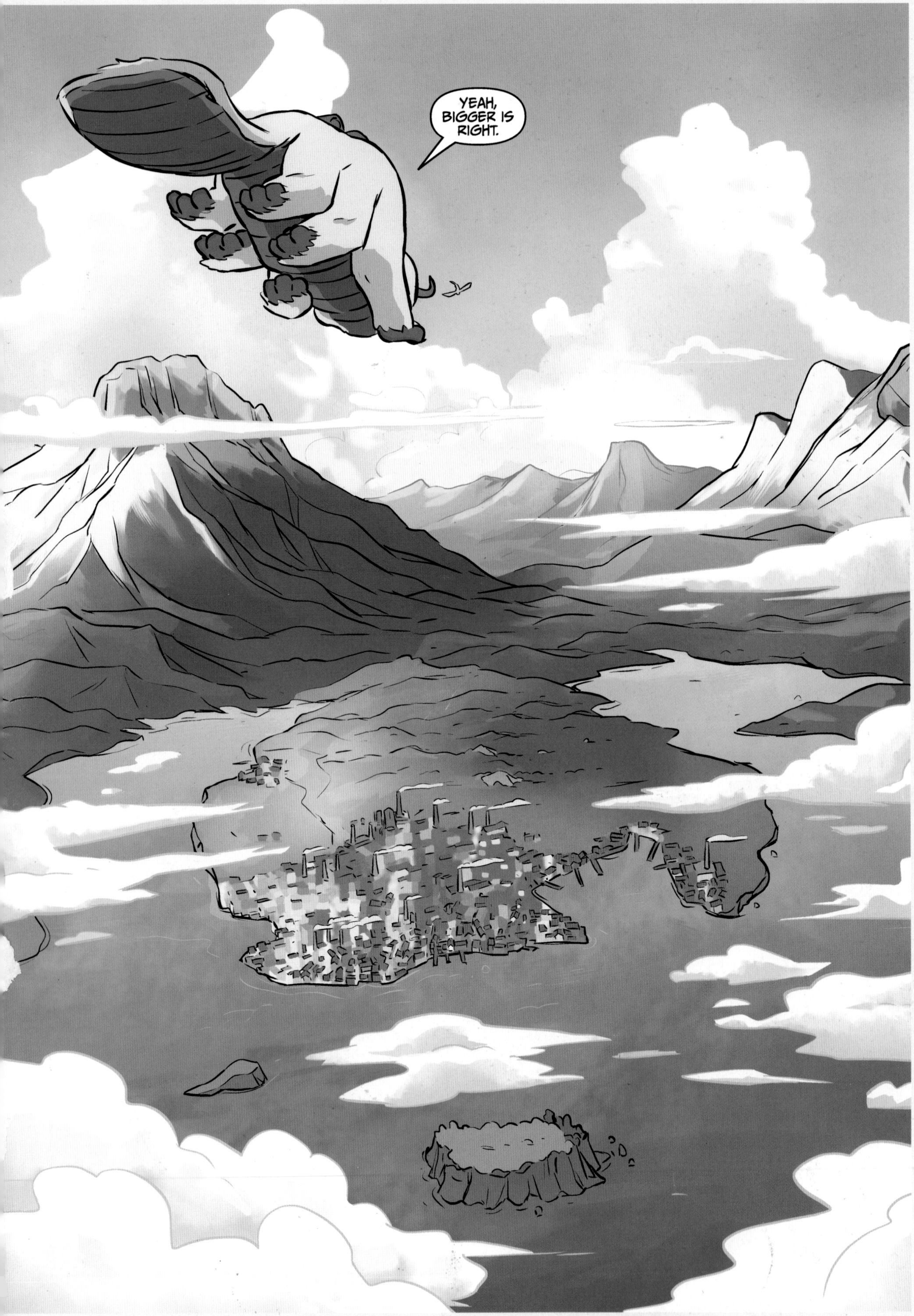
YEAH, BIGGER IS RIGHT.

FAITH ERIN HICKS: *Here's the beginnings of what would eventually become Republic City! Much of the story of* Imbalance *was inspired by season one of* The Legend of Korra. *I thought a lot about the challenges of going from a world divided between the elements to a multicultural city where different benders lived side by side.*

PW: *A lot of this comic was looking at reference images from Korra and trying to figure out how things looked a generation or so earlier.*

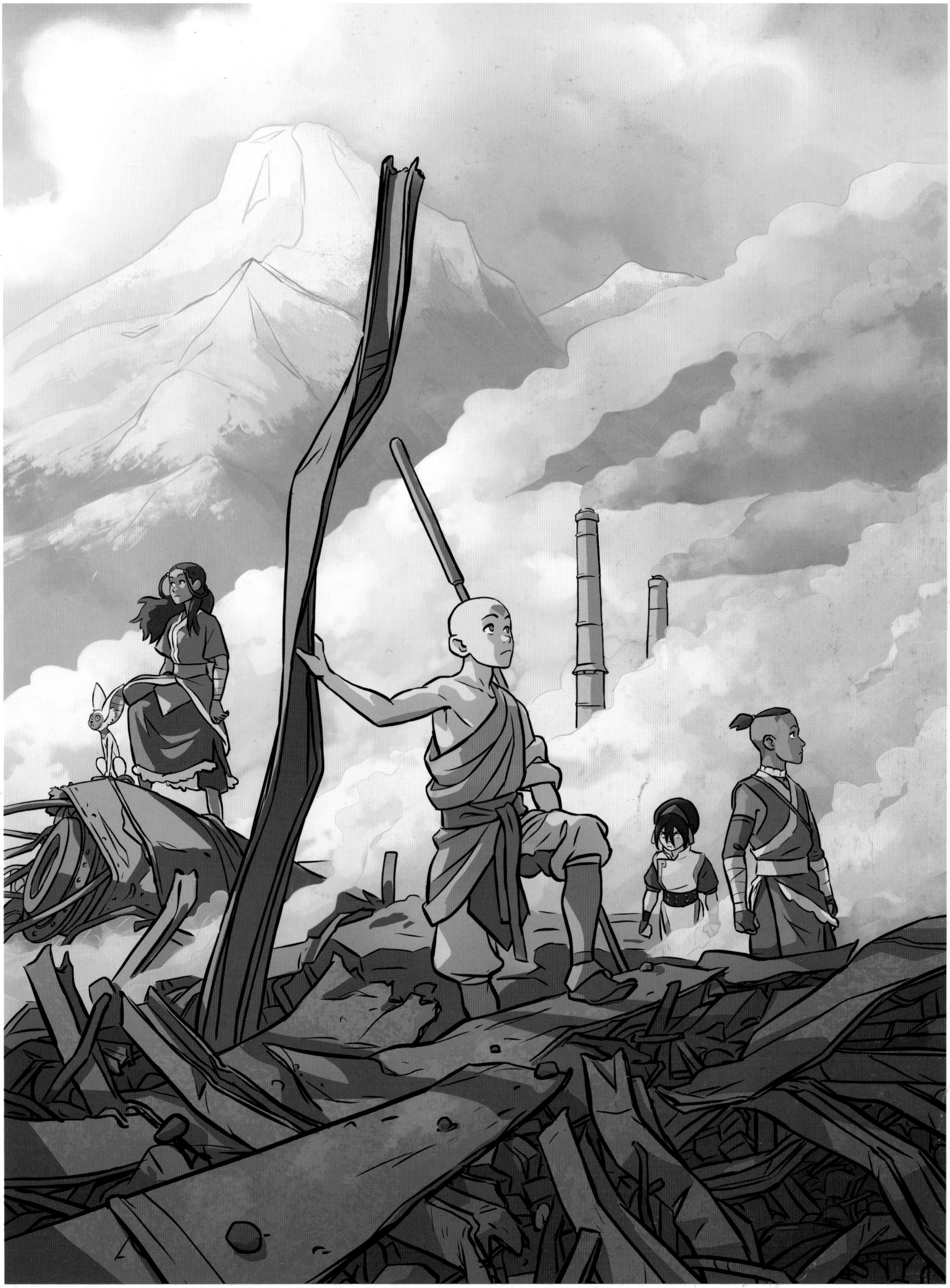

THERE'S AANG!

WELCOME BACK, TWINKLE TOES. TELL ME YOU CAUGHT THE GUY WHO EXPLODED MY DAD'S FACTORY.

I CAUGHT HIM, LITERALLY.

PW: *I enjoyed slowly destroying the factory over the course of the story— it's fun to have a visual history of everything that's happened.*

LITERALLY?

HE FELL OFF A CLIFF, SO I HAD TO RESCUE HIM. HE WAS SO GRATEFUL HE GAVE UP WHO HIRED HIM TO ATTACK EARTHEN FIRE INDUSTRIES.

WHO WAS IT? ME AND THEM ARE GOING TO HAVE *WORDS.*

FEH: *The return of Sokka's detective hat! He probably has all his disguises from the show hidden away somewhere. You never know when you're going to need them.*

PW: *Clearly Sokka has access to the same pocket dimension that cartoon and video game characters store their gear in.*

I CAN'T BELIEVE YOU STILL HAVE THAT HAT.

I CAN'T BELIEVE YOU EVER THOUGHT I'D GET RID OF THIS AMAZING HAT. DO YOU KNOW ME AT ALL?

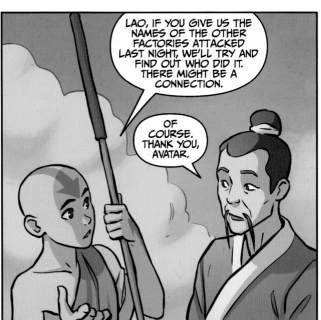

LAO, IF YOU GIVE US THE NAMES OF THE OTHER FACTORIES ATTACKED LAST NIGHT, WE'LL TRY AND FIND OUT WHO DID IT. THERE MIGHT BE A CONNECTION.

OF COURSE. THANK YOU, AVATAR.

DON'T LOOK SO DOWN, SIS. IT'S JUST A HAT.

IT'S NOT THE HAT. IT'S WHAT YOU JUST SAID. THERE'S SOMETHING GOING ON BENEATH THE SURFACE OF CRANEFISH TOWN, BUT WE HAVEN'T SEEN IT YET.

HAD ENOUGH OF HANGING OUT WITH APPA, MOMO? LET'S GO FOR A WALK IN THE CITY.

WHATEVER'S HAPPENING HERE, WE'LL BE ABLE TO HANDLE IT. WE'RE TEAM AVATAR INVESTIGATIONS.

I HOPE SO.

PW: *In addition to rooftops, one of the main visual themes in* Imbalance *was a lot of debris. I got good at debris.*

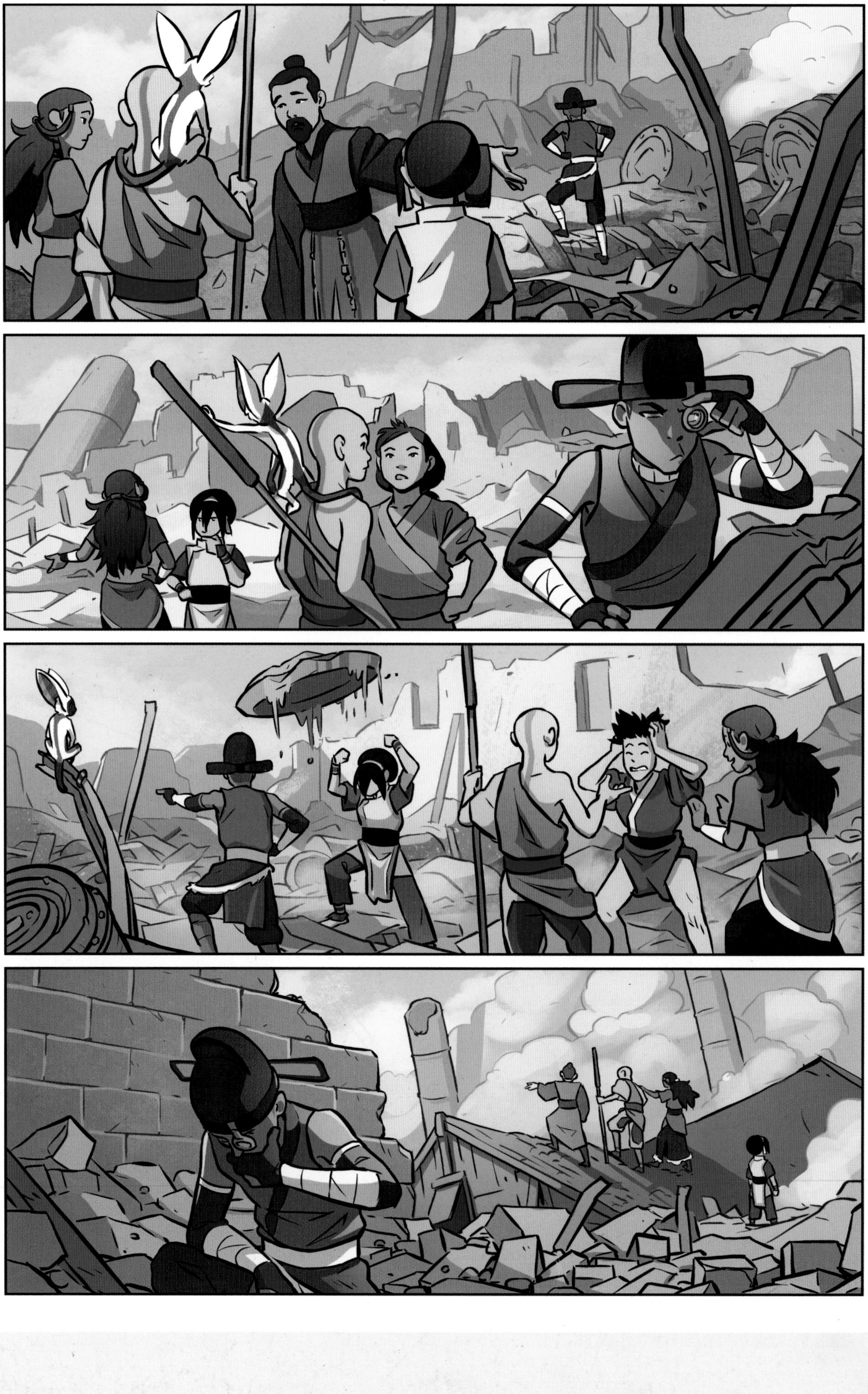

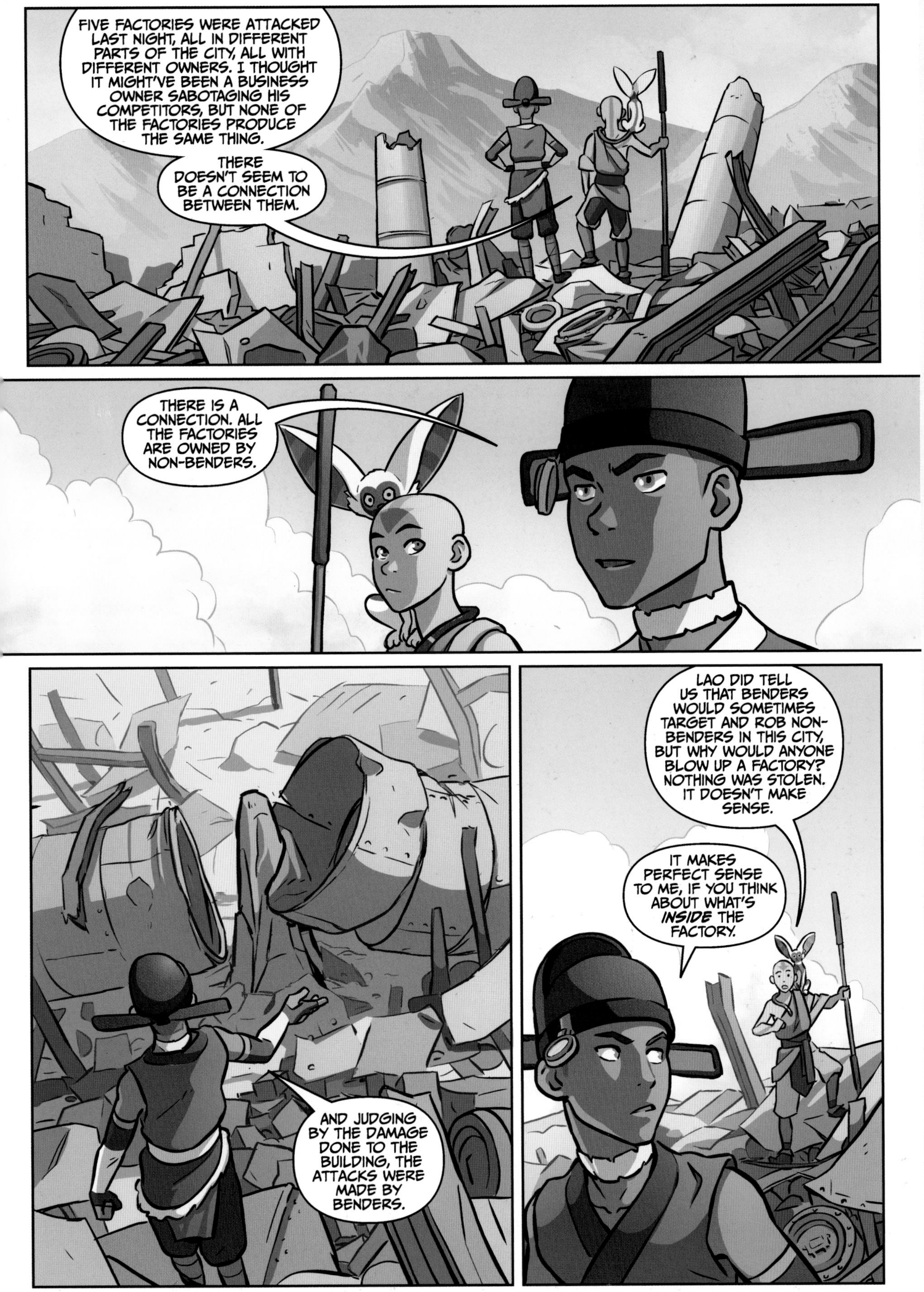
FIVE FACTORIES WERE ATTACKED LAST NIGHT, ALL IN DIFFERENT PARTS OF THE CITY, ALL WITH DIFFERENT OWNERS. I THOUGHT IT MIGHT'VE BEEN A BUSINESS OWNER SABOTAGING HIS COMPETITORS, BUT NONE OF THE FACTORIES PRODUCE THE SAME THING.
THERE DOESN'T SEEM TO BE A CONNECTION BETWEEN THEM.
THERE IS A CONNECTION. ALL THE FACTORIES ARE OWNED BY NON-BENDERS.
AND JUDGING BY THE DAMAGE DONE TO THE BUILDING, THE ATTACKS WERE MADE BY BENDERS.
LAO DID TELL US THAT BENDERS WOULD SOMETIMES TARGET AND ROB NON-BENDERS IN THIS CITY, BUT WHY WOULD ANYONE BLOW UP A FACTORY? NOTHING WAS STOLEN. IT DOESN'T MAKE SENSE.
IT MAKES PERFECT SENSE TO ME, IF YOU THINK ABOUT WHAT'S *INSIDE* THE FACTORY.

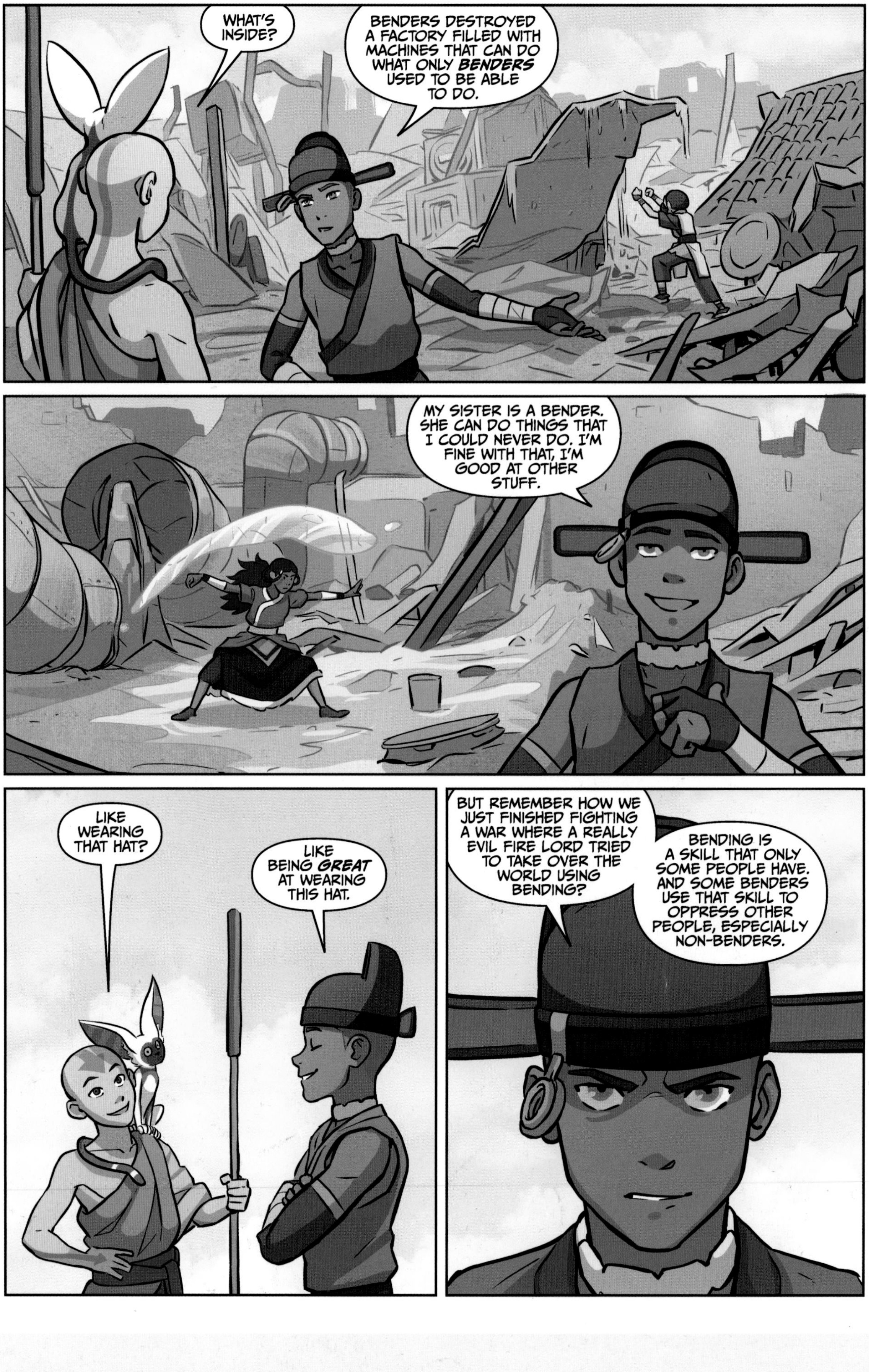
WHAT'S INSIDE?
BENDERS DESTROYED A FACTORY FILLED WITH MACHINES THAT CAN DO WHAT ONLY BENDERS USED TO BE ABLE TO DO.
MY SISTER IS A BENDER. SHE CAN DO THINGS THAT I COULD NEVER DO. I'M FINE WITH THAT, I'M GOOD AT OTHER STUFF.
LIKE WEARING THAT HAT?
LIKE BEING GREAT AT WEARING THIS HAT.
BUT REMEMBER HOW WE JUST FINISHED FIGHTING A WAR WHERE A REALLY EVIL FIRE LORD TRIED TO TAKE OVER THE WORLD USING BENDING?
BENDING IS A SKILL THAT ONLY SOME PEOPLE HAVE. AND SOME BENDERS USE THAT SKILL TO OPPRESS OTHER PEOPLE, ESPECIALLY NON-BENDERS.

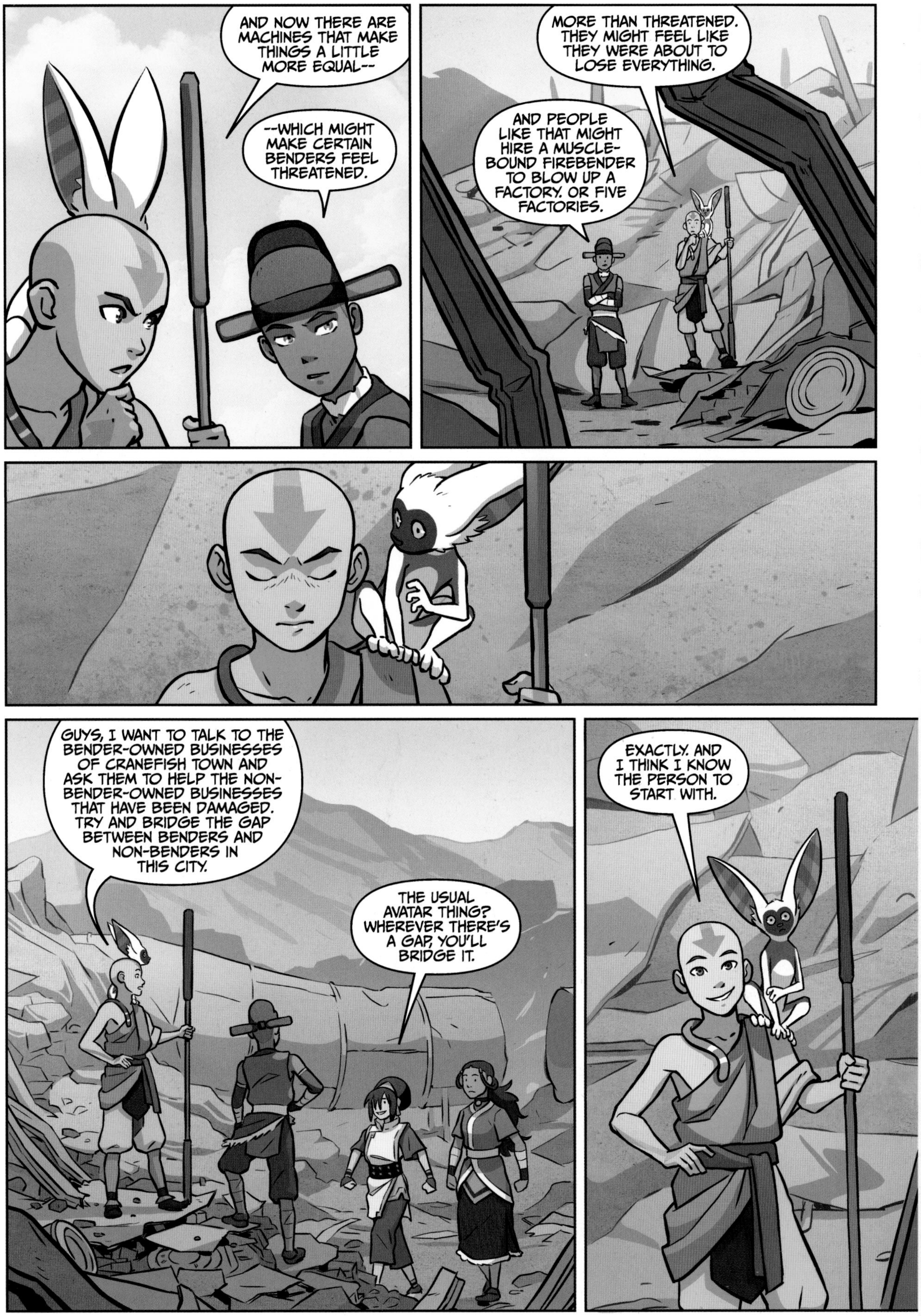
AND NOW THERE ARE MACHINES THAT MAKE THINGS A LITTLE MORE EQUAL--
--WHICH MIGHT MAKE CERTAIN BENDERS FEEL THREATENED.
MORE THAN THREATENED. THEY MIGHT FEEL LIKE THEY WERE ABOUT TO LOSE EVERYTHING.
AND PEOPLE LIKE THAT MIGHT HIRE A MUSCLE-BOUND FIREBENDER TO BLOW UP A FACTORY. OR FIVE FACTORIES.
GUYS, I WANT TO TALK TO THE BENDER-OWNED BUSINESSES OF CRANEFISH TOWN AND ASK THEM TO HELP THE NON-BENDER-OWNED BUSINESSES THAT HAVE BEEN DAMAGED. TRY AND BRIDGE THE GAP BETWEEN BENDERS AND NON-BENDERS IN THIS CITY.
THE USUAL AVATAR THING? WHEREVER THERE'S A GAP, YOU'LL BRIDGE IT.
EXACTLY. AND I THINK I KNOW THE PERSON TO START WITH.

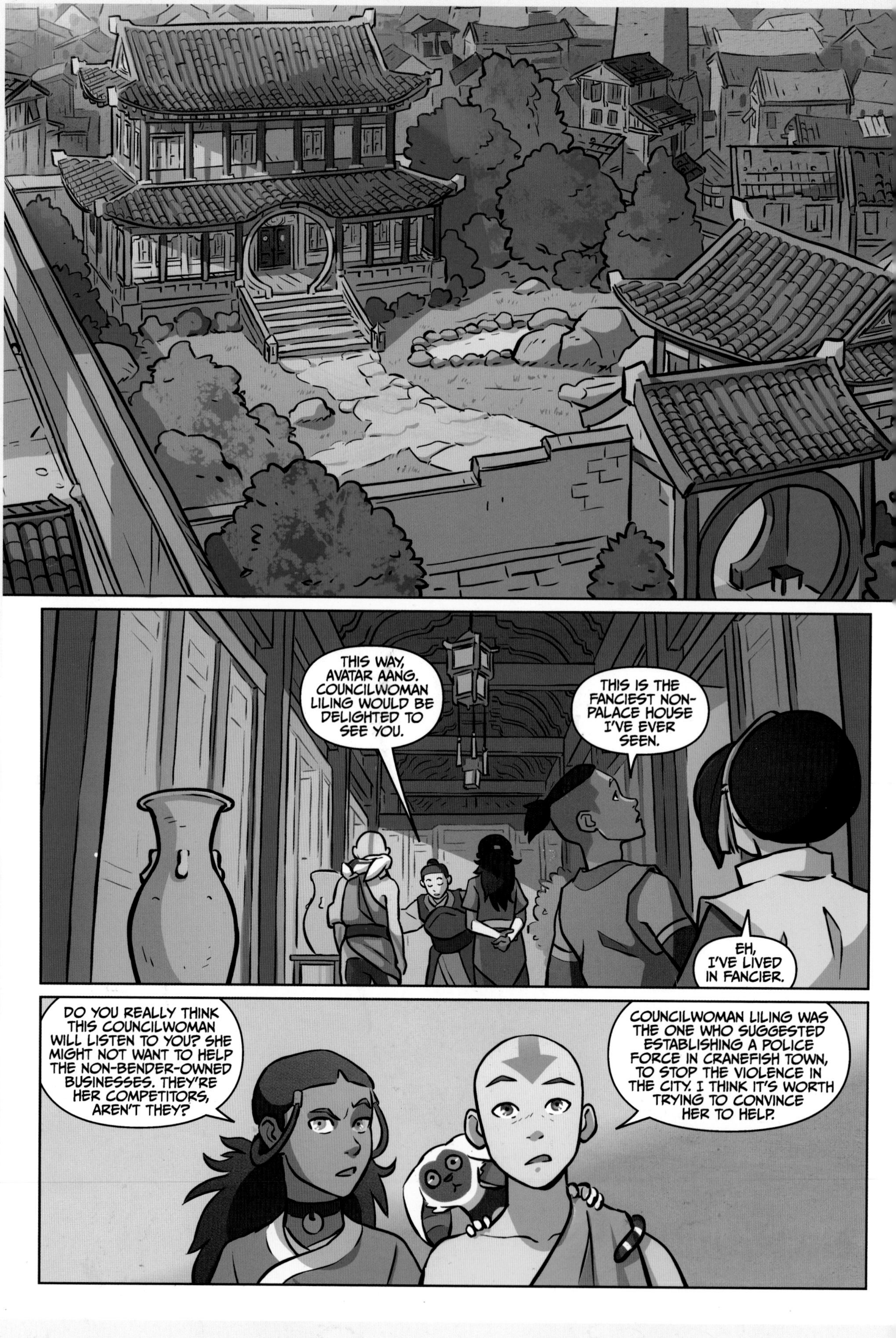
THIS WAY, AVATAR AANG. COUNCILWOMAN LILING WOULD BE DELIGHTED TO SEE YOU.
THIS IS THE FANCIEST NON-PALACE HOUSE I'VE EVER SEEN.
EH, I'VE LIVED IN FANCIER.
DO YOU REALLY THINK THIS COUNCILWOMAN WILL LISTEN TO YOU? SHE MIGHT NOT WANT TO HELP THE NON-BENDER-OWNED BUSINESSES. THEY'RE HER COMPETITORS, AREN'T THEY?
COUNCILWOMAN LILING WAS THE ONE WHO SUGGESTED ESTABLISHING A POLICE FORCE IN CRANEFISH TOWN, TO STOP THE VIOLENCE IN THE CITY. I THINK IT'S WORTH TRYING TO CONVINCE HER TO HELP.

PW: *I really like the atmospheric perspective Adele added in the colors here!*

PW: *This interior was one of the hardest things to figure out, and had to go through quite a few revisions.*

YOU KNOW, I HEARD THE AREA CRANEFISH TOWN IS BUILT ON WAS SACRED TO THE AIRBENDERS. IS THAT TRUE?

YES! THERE WAS A FESTIVAL HERE, A LONG TIME AGO. IT HONORED ONE OF THE PREVIOUS AVATARS, YANGCHEN.

IS IT DIFFICULT FOR YOU TO SEE HOW MUCH THIS AREA HAS CHANGED? IT MUST BE VERY DIFFERENT FROM WHEN THE AIRBENDERS WERE HERE.

WELL, IT CAN BE.

FEH: I asked Mike [DiMartino] if there were any animals in the Avatar universe that a rich person might have as pet. He pointed out that there was a Persian cat in the "Blue Spirit" episode of the show. Liling's cat is more of a jerk than Miyuki was, though.

I KNOW PROGRESS IS IMPORTANT, BUT I'D HOPED THIS CITY HAD PROGRESSED A LITTLE MORE...SLOWLY. OR AT LEAST WITH MORE RESPECT FOR THE ENVIRONMENT.

I UNDERSTAND, AVATAR. I GREW UP IN A SMALL VILLAGE NOT FAR FROM HERE. WHEN I WAS A CHILD, THIS REGION WAS MOSTLY PRISTINE WILDERNESS.

IT'S STRANGE HOW WE ALWAYS SEEM TO WANT TO RETURN TO THE SAFETY OF OUR CHILD-HOOD HOMES, ISN'T IT? I SPENT MOST OF MY ADULT LIFE IN BA SING SE, BUT THE MOMENT THE WAR WAS OVER, I CAME BACK HERE AND STARTED MY BUSINESS.

RRRRRR

I ONLY WISH I COULD HAVE DONE MORE TO, WELL, *GUIDE* THIS CITY'S DEVELOPMENT. I REGRET THAT, AVATAR, I REALLY DO.

THAT WAS WHAT I WANTED TO TALK TO YOU ABOUT, THE FUTURE OF CRANEFISH TOWN.

ARE YOU PLANNING TO...*STAY* IN OUR HUMBLE TOWN, AVATAR? THAT IS A SURPRISE.

I'M NOT SURE YET, BUT THERE'S A PROBLEM I WANT TO HELP SOLVE, AND THAT MIGHT TAKE SOME TIME.

WHY DOES SHE KEEP CALLING THINGS HUMBLE WHEN THEY'RE REALLY NOT HUMBLE?

SHH!

LAST NIGHT, SEVERAL FACTORIES WERE SABOTAGED.

I KNOW, I HEARD. HOW HORRIBLE.

I SAW A LOT OF TENSION BETWEEN BENDERS AND NON-BENDERS WHEN I ARRIVED IN THE CITY YESTERDAY. LAST NIGHT'S ATTACKS MAY HAVE BEEN BENDERS TARGETING NON-BENDER-OWNED BUSINESSES.

FEH: *Ru is a non-bender born into a family of benders. I'm fascinated by that idea: her entire family has these incredible abilities, and a common bond, but Ru doesn't have any of that. How would that make her feel?*

YOU--YOU CAN METALBEND?

UM, ARE YOU AN EARTHBENDER TOO, RU?

I'M NOT ANY KIND OF BENDER.

RU HAS OTHER TALENTS.

LIKE ME! THERE'S NO WAY KATARA CAN WATERBEND A BOOMERANG. THAT REQUIRES PURE NON-BENDER SKILL.

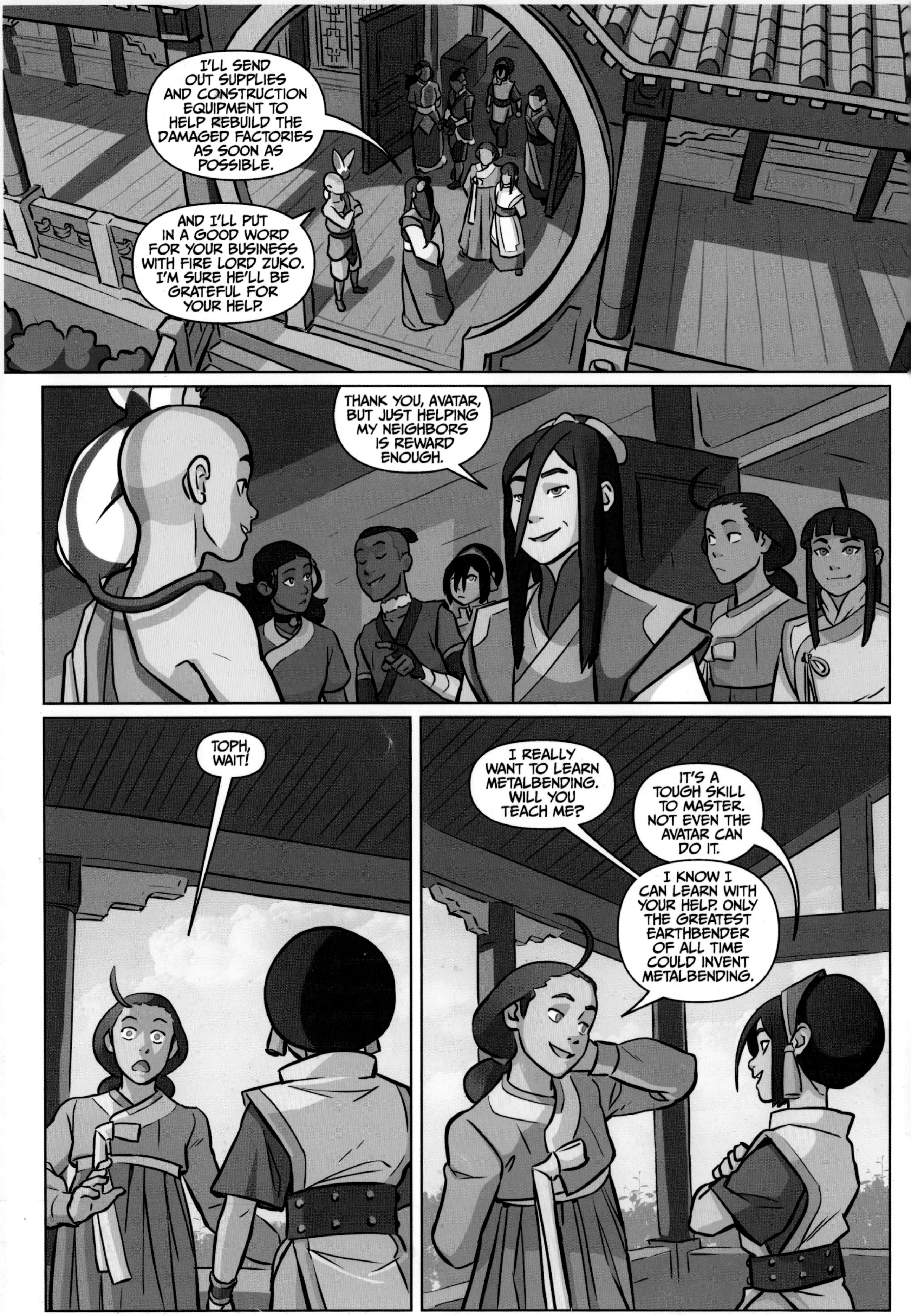
I'LL SEND OUT SUPPLIES AND CONSTRUCTION EQUIPMENT TO HELP REBUILD THE DAMAGED FACTORIES AS SOON AS POSSIBLE.
AND I'LL PUT IN A GOOD WORD FOR YOUR BUSINESS WITH FIRE LORD ZUKO. I'M SURE HE'LL BE GRATEFUL FOR YOUR HELP.
THANK YOU, AVATAR, BUT JUST HELPING MY NEIGHBORS IS REWARD ENOUGH.
TOPH, WAIT!
I REALLY WANT TO LEARN METALBENDING. WILL YOU TEACH ME?
IT'S A TOUGH SKILL TO MASTER. NOT EVEN THE AVATAR CAN DO IT.
I KNOW I CAN LEARN WITH YOUR HELP. ONLY THE GREATEST EARTHBENDER OF ALL TIME COULD INVENT METALBENDING.

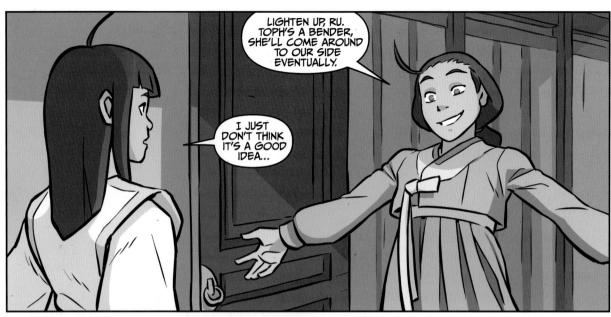

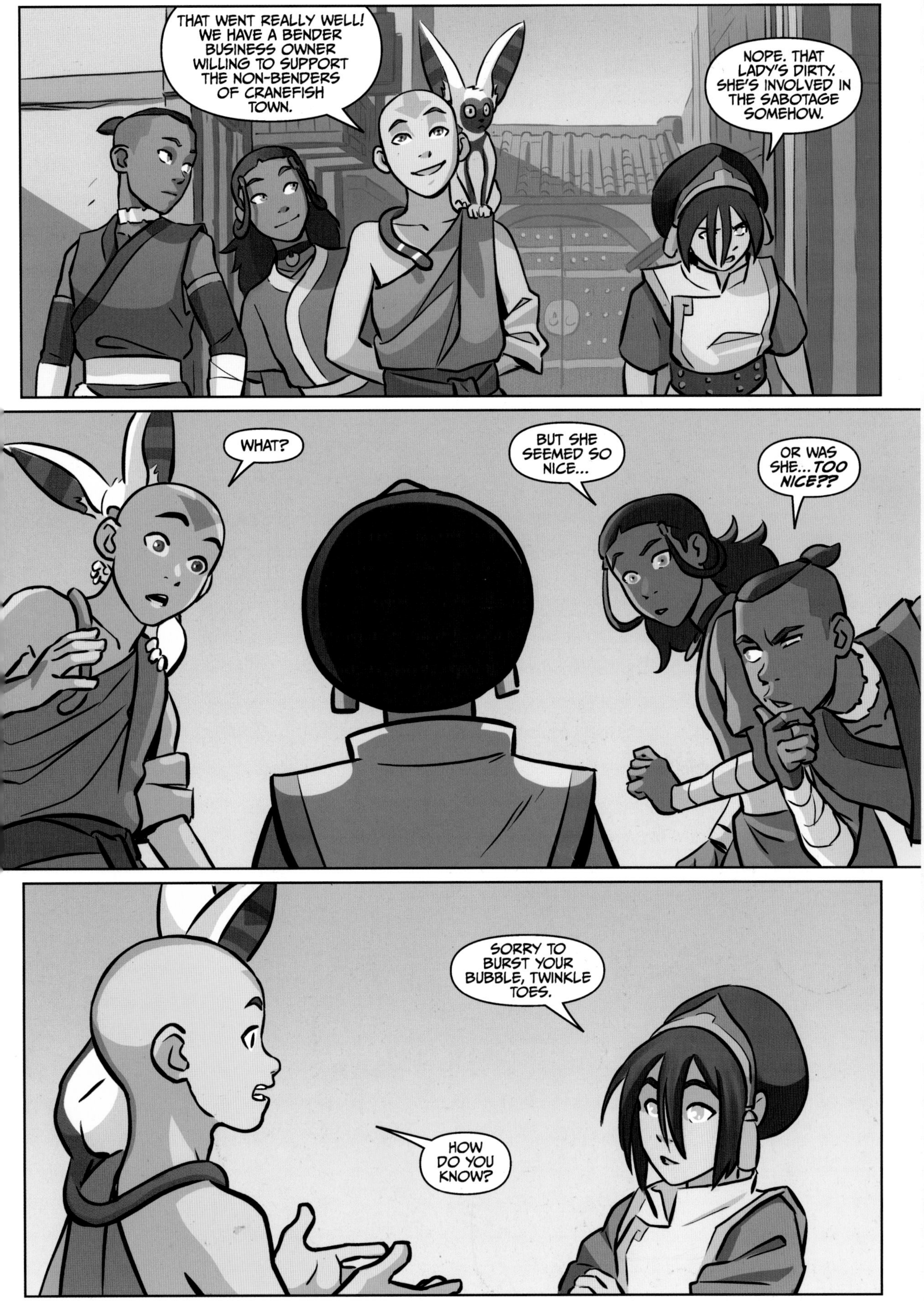
THAT WENT REALLY WELL! WE HAVE A BENDER BUSINESS OWNER WILLING TO SUPPORT THE NON-BENDERS OF CRANEFISH TOWN.
NOPE. THAT LADY'S DIRTY. SHE'S INVOLVED IN THE SABOTAGE SOMEHOW.
WHAT?
BUT SHE SEEMED SO NICE...
OR WAS SHE... *TOO NICE??*
SORRY TO BURST YOUR BUBBLE, TWINKLE TOES.
HOW DO YOU KNOW?

FEH: *Nothing gets past Sokka!*

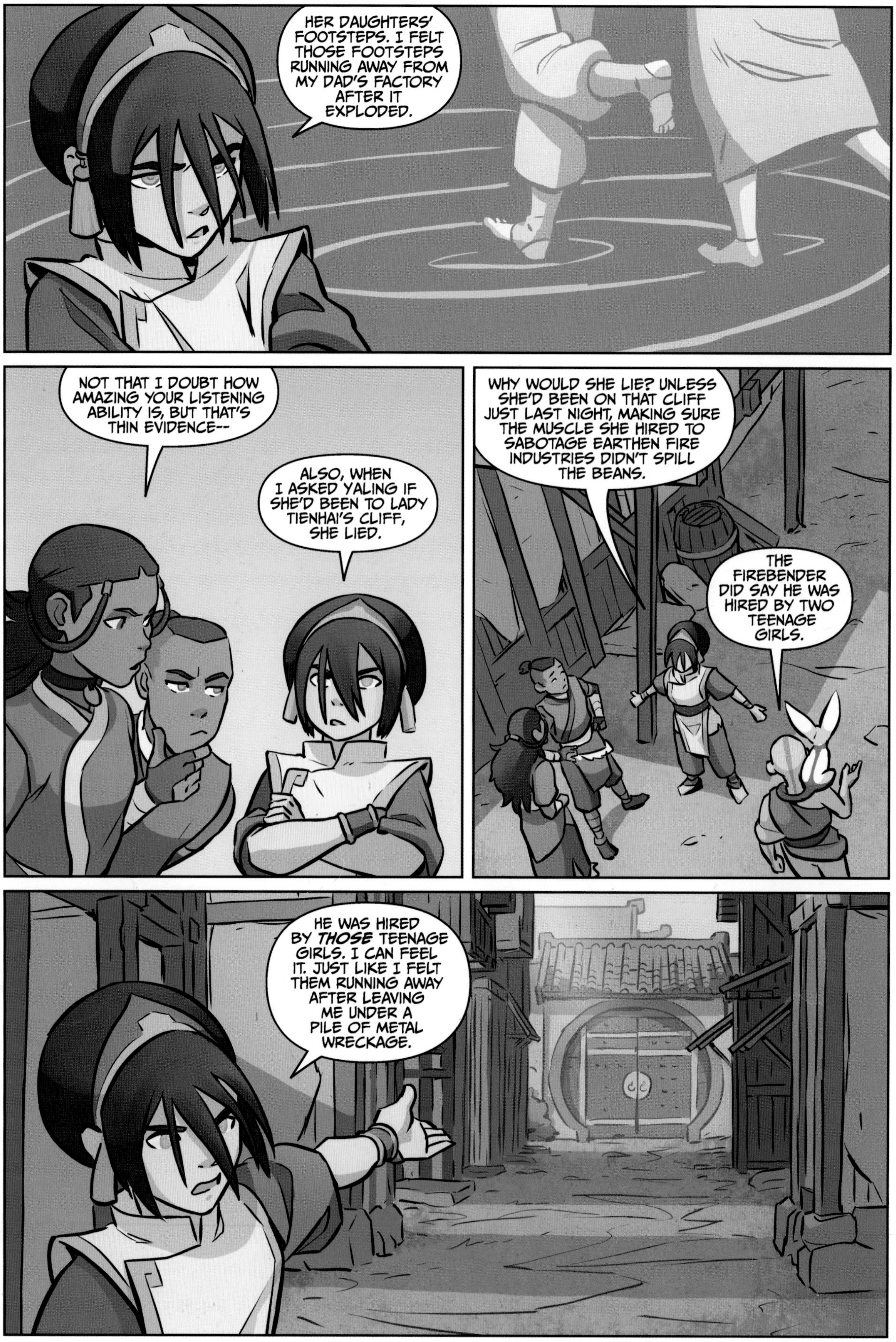
HER DAUGHTERS' FOOTSTEPS. I FELT THOSE FOOTSTEPS RUNNING AWAY FROM MY DAD'S FACTORY AFTER IT EXPLODED.
NOT THAT I DOUBT HOW AMAZING YOUR LISTENING ABILITY IS, BUT THAT'S THIN EVIDENCE--
ALSO, WHEN I ASKED YALING IF SHE'D BEEN TO LADY TIENHAI'S CLIFF, SHE LIED.
WHY WOULD SHE LIE? UNLESS SHE'D BEEN ON THAT CLIFF JUST LAST NIGHT, MAKING SURE THE MUSCLE SHE HIRED TO SABOTAGE EARTHEN FIRE INDUSTRIES DIDN'T SPILL THE BEANS.
THE FIREBENDER DID SAY HE WAS HIRED BY TWO TEENAGE GIRLS.
HE WAS HIRED BY *THOSE* TEENAGE GIRLS. I CAN FEEL IT. JUST LIKE I FELT THEM RUNNING AWAY AFTER LEAVING ME UNDER A PILE OF METAL WRECKAGE.

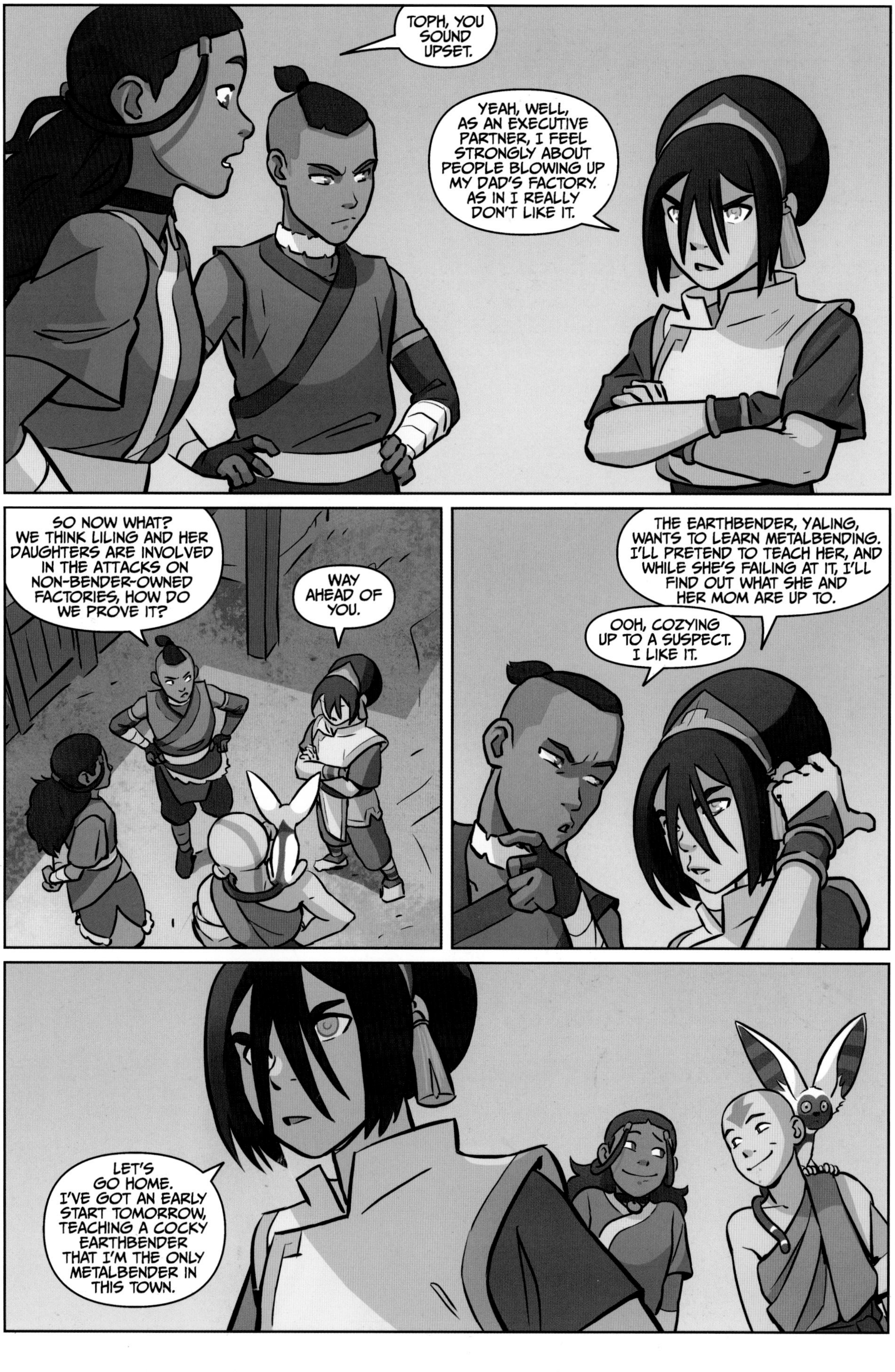
TOPH, YOU SOUND UPSET.
YEAH, WELL, AS AN EXECUTIVE PARTNER, I FEEL STRONGLY ABOUT PEOPLE BLOWING UP MY DAD'S FACTORY. AS IN I REALLY DON'T LIKE IT.
SO NOW WHAT? WE THINK LILING AND HER DAUGHTERS ARE INVOLVED IN THE ATTACKS ON NON-BENDER-OWNED FACTORIES, HOW DO WE PROVE IT?
WAY AHEAD OF YOU.
THE EARTHBENDER, YALING, WANTS TO LEARN METALBENDING. I'LL PRETEND TO TEACH HER, AND WHILE SHE'S FAILING AT IT, I'LL FIND OUT WHAT SHE AND HER MOM ARE UP TO.
OOH, COZYING UP TO A SUSPECT. I LIKE IT.
LET'S GO HOME. I'VE GOT AN EARLY START TOMORROW, TEACHING A COCKY EARTHBENDER THAT I'M THE ONLY METALBENDER IN THIS TOWN.

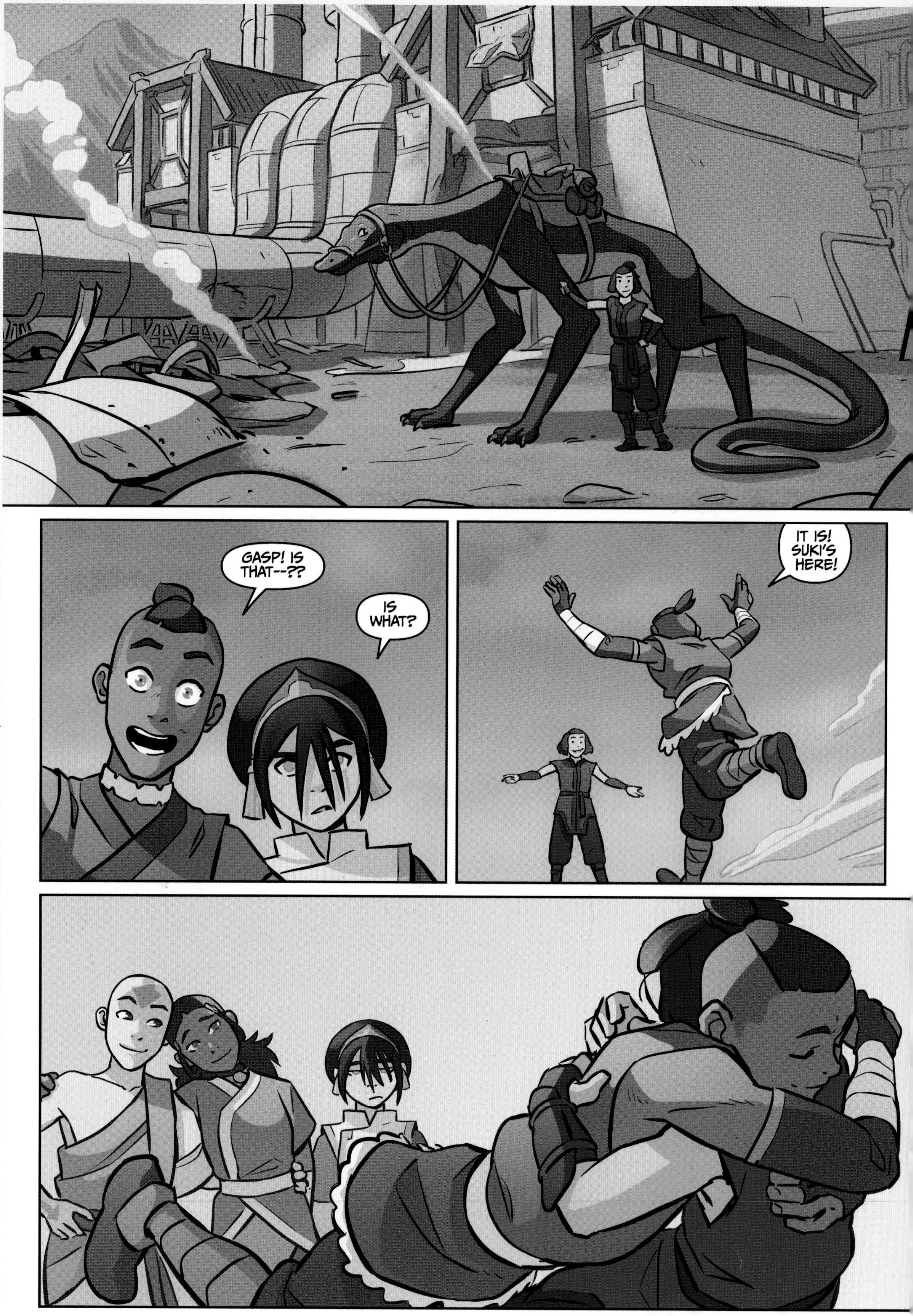
GASP! IS THAT--??
IS WHAT?
IT IS! SUKI'S HERE!

FEH: *Sokka and Suki have spent a lot of time apart in the other* Avatar *comics! I thought it was time to get them back together.*

PW: *Sometimes hugs are more fun to draw than fights.*

PW: *On the other hand, Toph's reaction here is usually mine as well.*

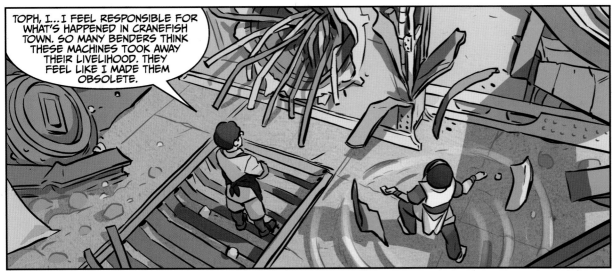

TOPH, I...I FEEL RESPONSIBLE FOR WHAT'S HAPPENED IN CRANEFISH TOWN. SO MANY BENDERS THINK THESE MACHINES TOOK AWAY THEIR LIVELIHOOD. THEY FEEL LIKE I MADE THEM OBSOLETE.

COME ON, YOU KNOW THAT'S NOT TRUE.

I DON'T KNOW. THEY MAY HAVE A POINT.

SATORU, EVEN IF YOU HADN'T MADE THESE MACHINES, THERE STILL WOULDN'T BE ENOUGH JOBS IN CRANEFISH TOWN FOR EVERY SKILLED BENDER. PEOPLE ARE JUST LOOKING FOR SOMEONE TO BLAME.

AND I SHOULD STOP FEELING GUILTY, RIGHT?

TOOK THE WORDS RIGHT OUT OF MY MOUTH.

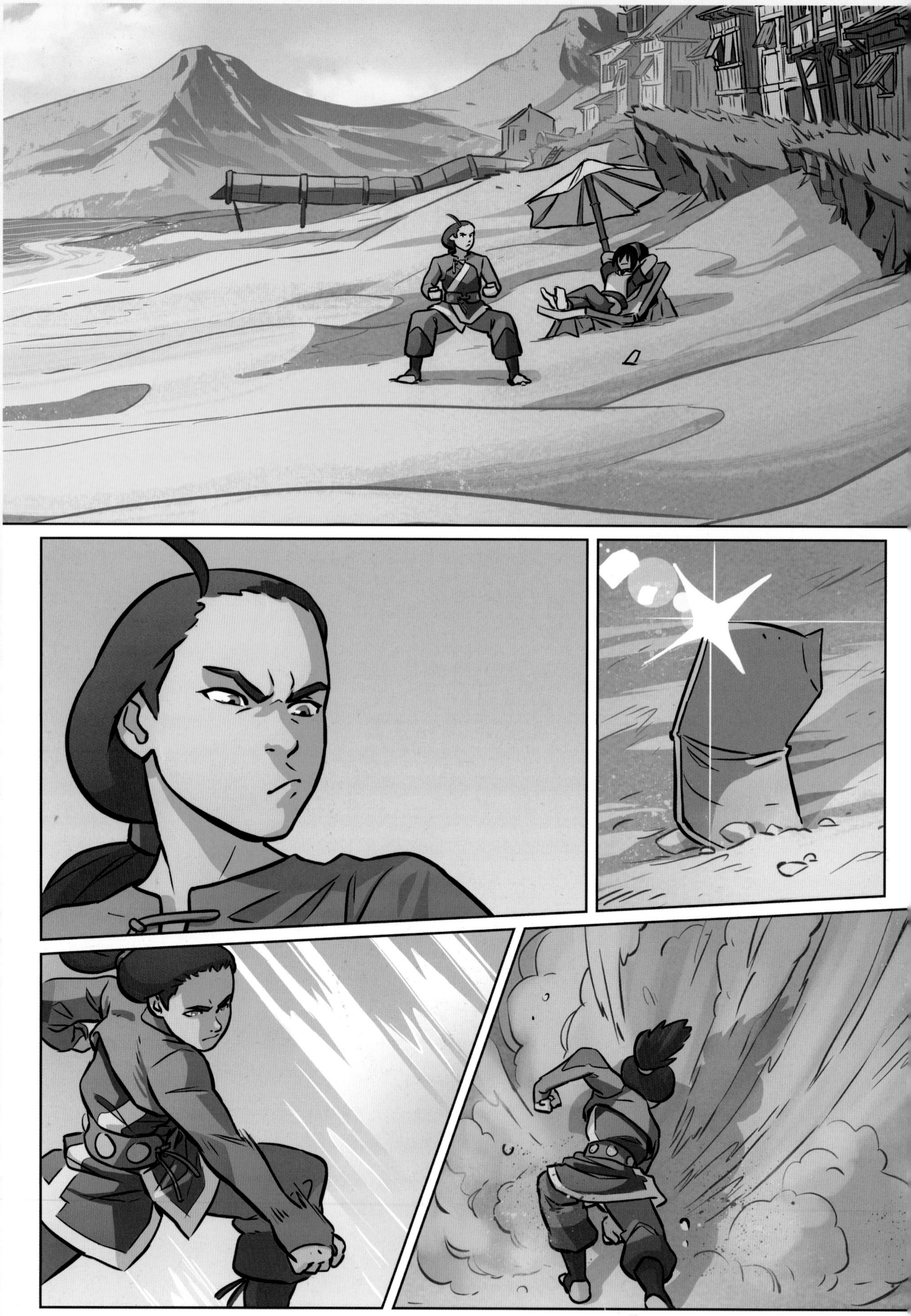

PW: *Toph isn't* **all** *brute force. She can use guile when she needs it. I like how Faith is setting up Toph's eventual role as a police captain.*

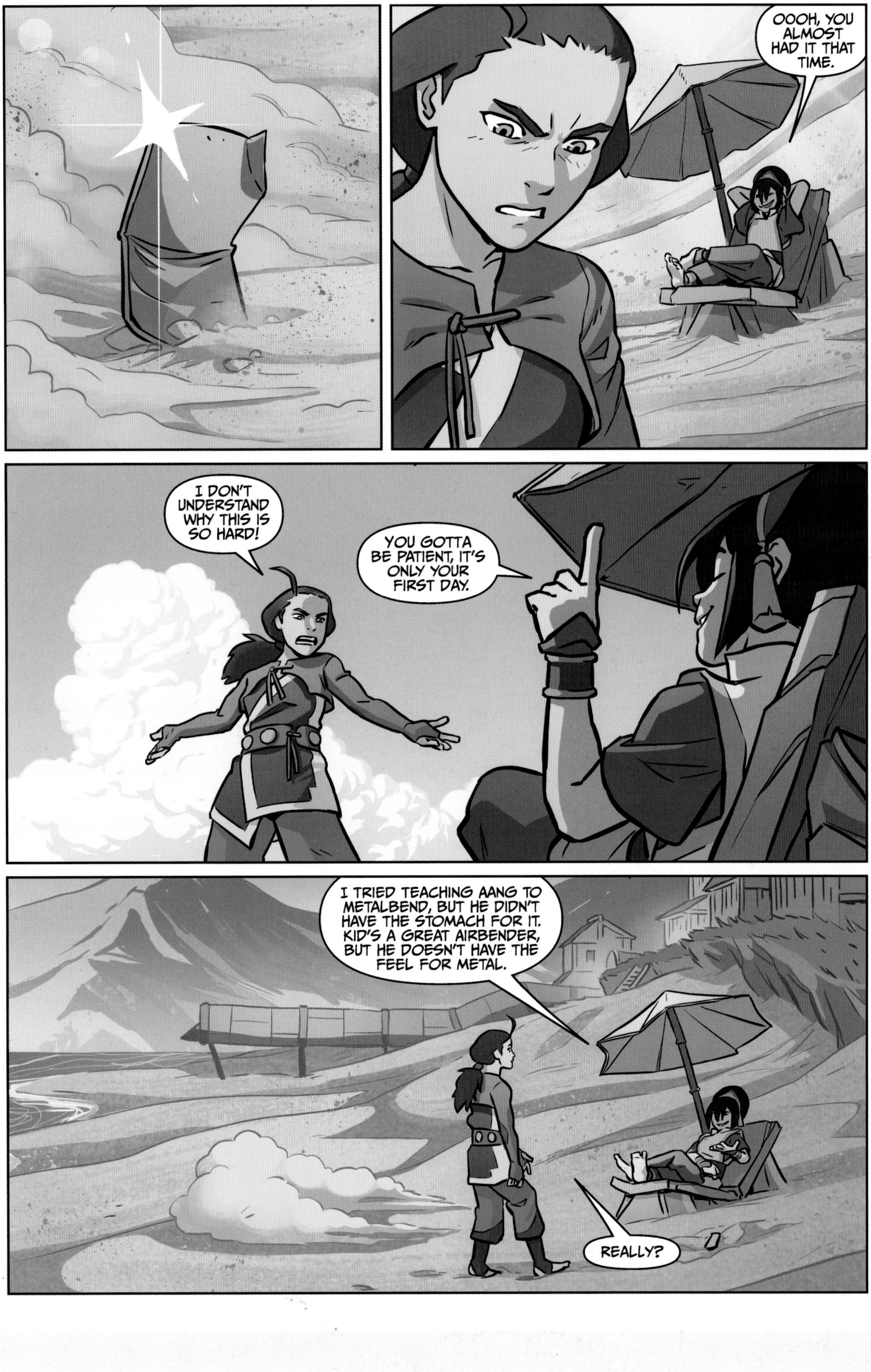
OOOH, YOU ALMOST HAD IT THAT TIME.
I DON'T UNDERSTAND WHY THIS IS SO HARD!
YOU GOTTA BE PATIENT, IT'S ONLY YOUR FIRST DAY.
I TRIED TEACHING AANG TO METALBEND, BUT HE DIDN'T HAVE THE STOMACH FOR IT. KID'S A GREAT AIRBENDER, BUT HE DOESN'T HAVE THE FEEL FOR METAL.
REALLY?

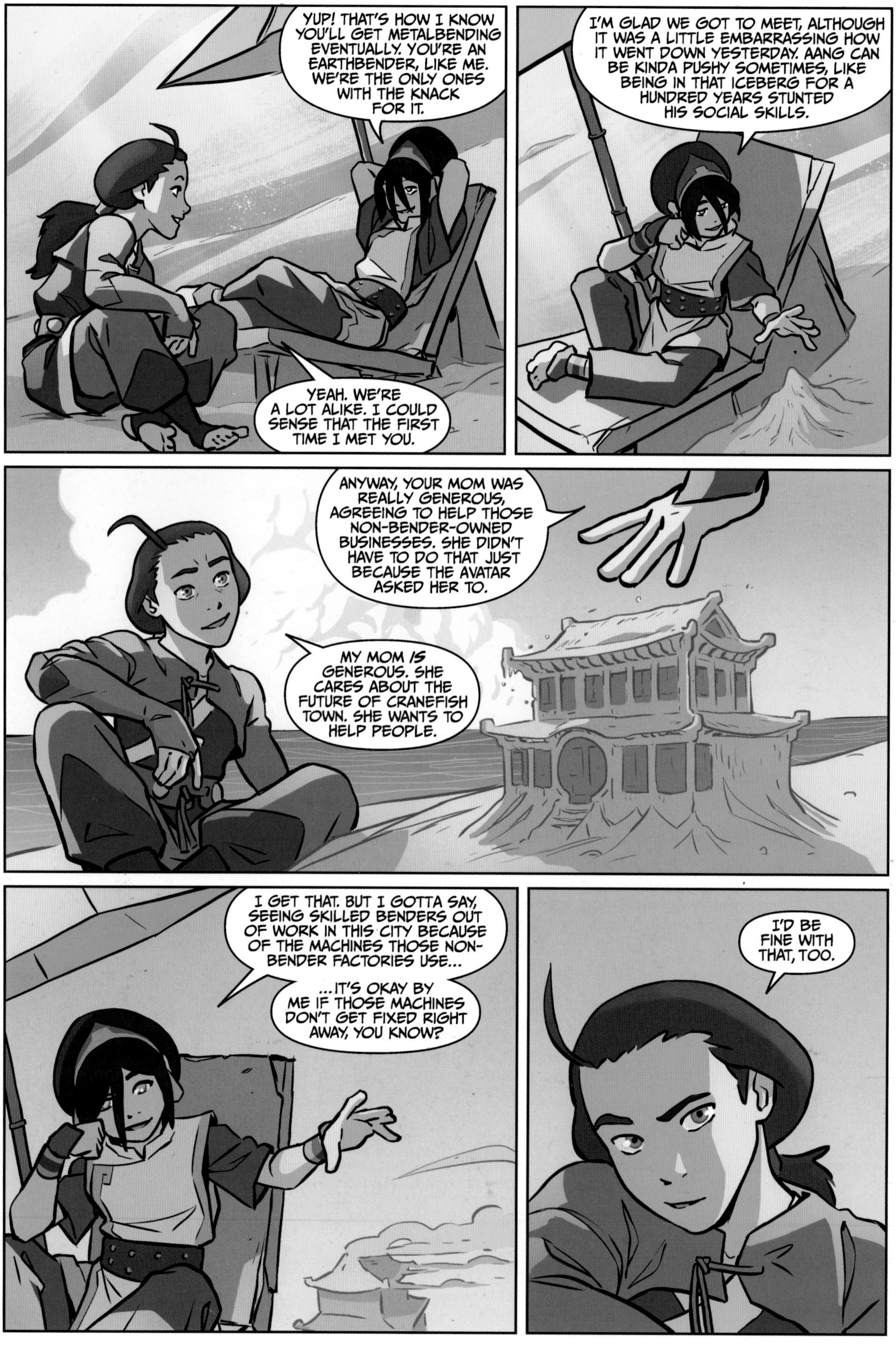
YUP! THAT'S HOW I KNOW YOU'LL GET METALBENDING EVENTUALLY. YOU'RE AN EARTHBENDER, LIKE ME. WE'RE THE ONLY ONES WITH THE KNACK FOR IT.
YEAH. WE'RE A LOT ALIKE. I COULD SENSE THAT THE FIRST TIME I MET YOU.
I'M GLAD WE GOT TO MEET, ALTHOUGH IT WAS A LITTLE EMBARRASSING HOW IT WENT DOWN YESTERDAY. AANG CAN BE KINDA PUSHY SOMETIMES, LIKE BEING IN THAT ICEBERG FOR A HUNDRED YEARS STUNTED HIS SOCIAL SKILLS.
ANYWAY, YOUR MOM WAS REALLY GENEROUS, AGREEING TO HELP THOSE NON-BENDER-OWNED BUSINESSES. SHE DIDN'T HAVE TO DO THAT JUST BECAUSE THE AVATAR ASKED HER TO.
MY MOM *IS* GENEROUS. SHE CARES ABOUT THE FUTURE OF CRANEFISH TOWN. SHE WANTS TO HELP PEOPLE.
I GET THAT. BUT I GOTTA SAY, SEEING SKILLED BENDERS OUT OF WORK IN THIS CITY BECAUSE OF THE MACHINES THOSE NON-BENDER FACTORIES USE...
...IT'S OKAY BY ME IF THOSE MACHINES DON'T GET FIXED RIGHT AWAY, YOU KNOW?
I'D BE FINE WITH THAT, TOO.

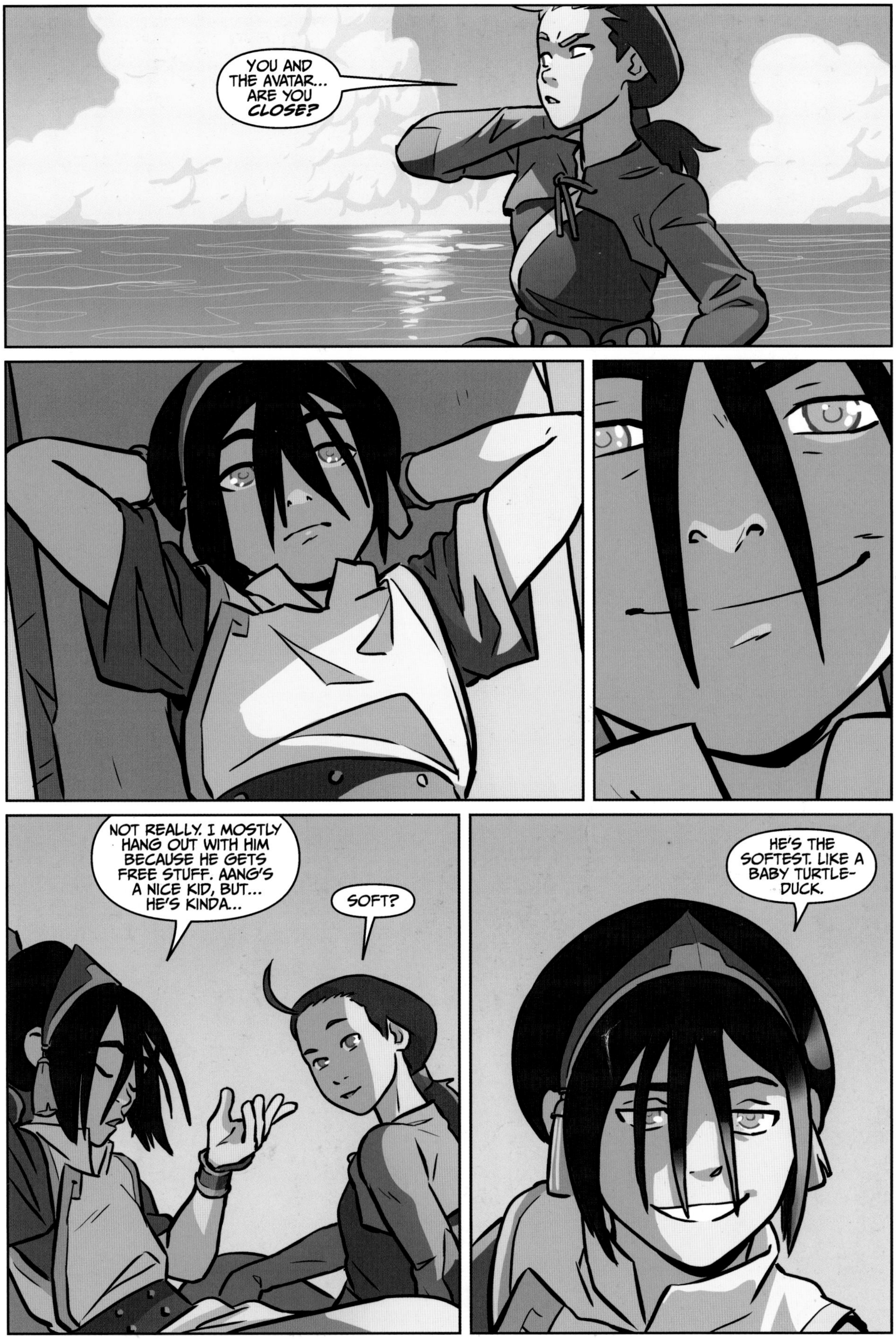
YOU AND THE AVATAR... ARE YOU CLOSE?
NOT REALLY. I MOSTLY HANG OUT WITH HIM BECAUSE HE GETS FREE STUFF. AANG'S A NICE KID, BUT... HE'S KINDA...
SOFT?
HE'S THE SOFTEST. LIKE A BABY TURTLE-DUCK.

FEH: *Toph's little smirk here is so delightful! She knows she's got Yaling right where she wants her.*

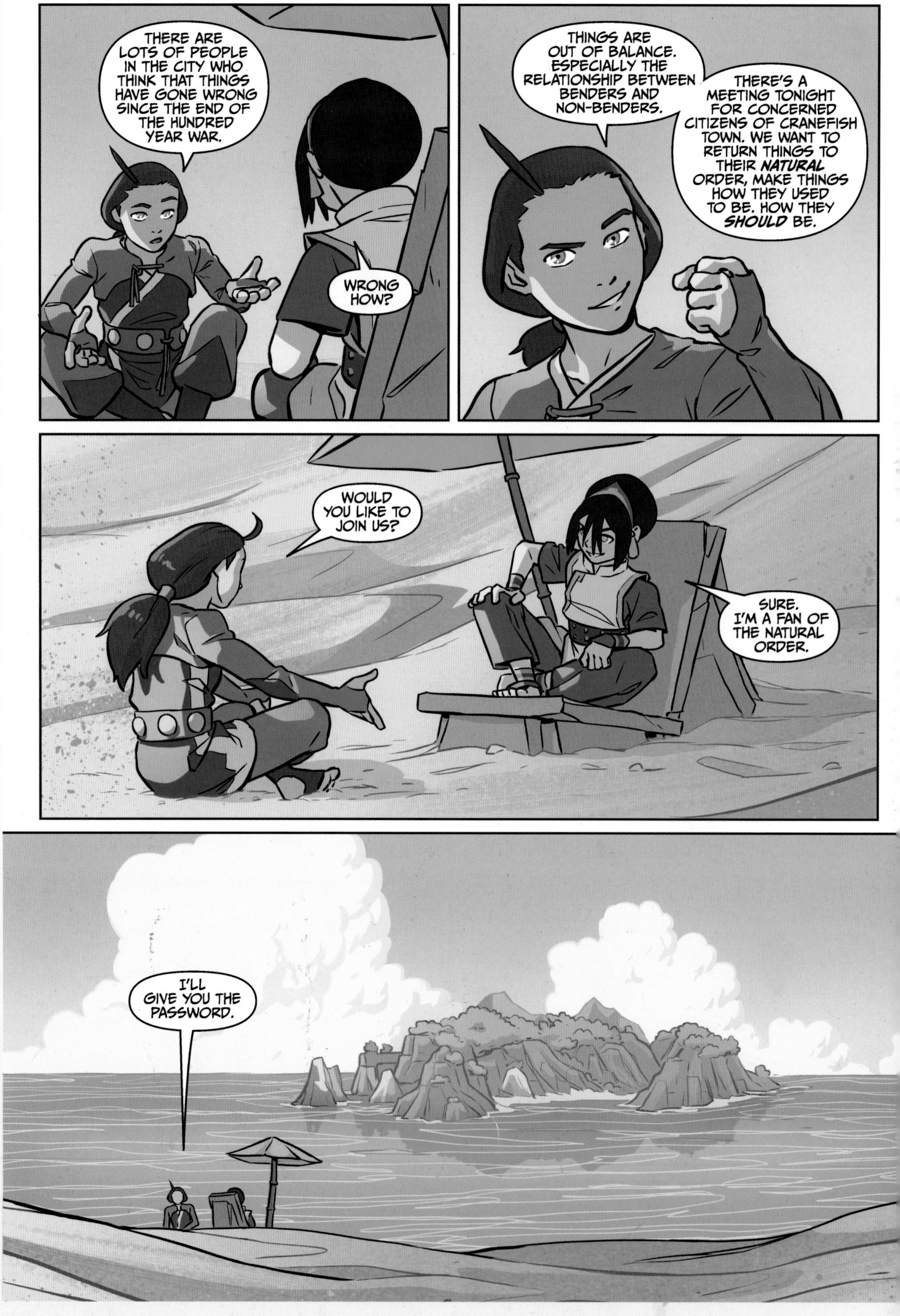
THERE ARE LOTS OF PEOPLE IN THE CITY WHO THINK THAT THINGS HAVE GONE WRONG SINCE THE END OF THE HUNDRED YEAR WAR.
WRONG HOW?
THINGS ARE OUT OF BALANCE. ESPECIALLY THE RELATIONSHIP BETWEEN BENDERS AND NON-BENDERS.
THERE'S A MEETING TONIGHT FOR CONCERNED CITIZENS OF CRANEFISH TOWN. WE WANT TO RETURN THINGS TO THEIR NATURAL ORDER, MAKE THINGS HOW THEY USED TO BE. HOW THEY SHOULD BE.
WOULD YOU LIKE TO JOIN US?
SURE. I'M A FAN OF THE NATURAL ORDER.
I'LL GIVE YOU THE PASSWORD.

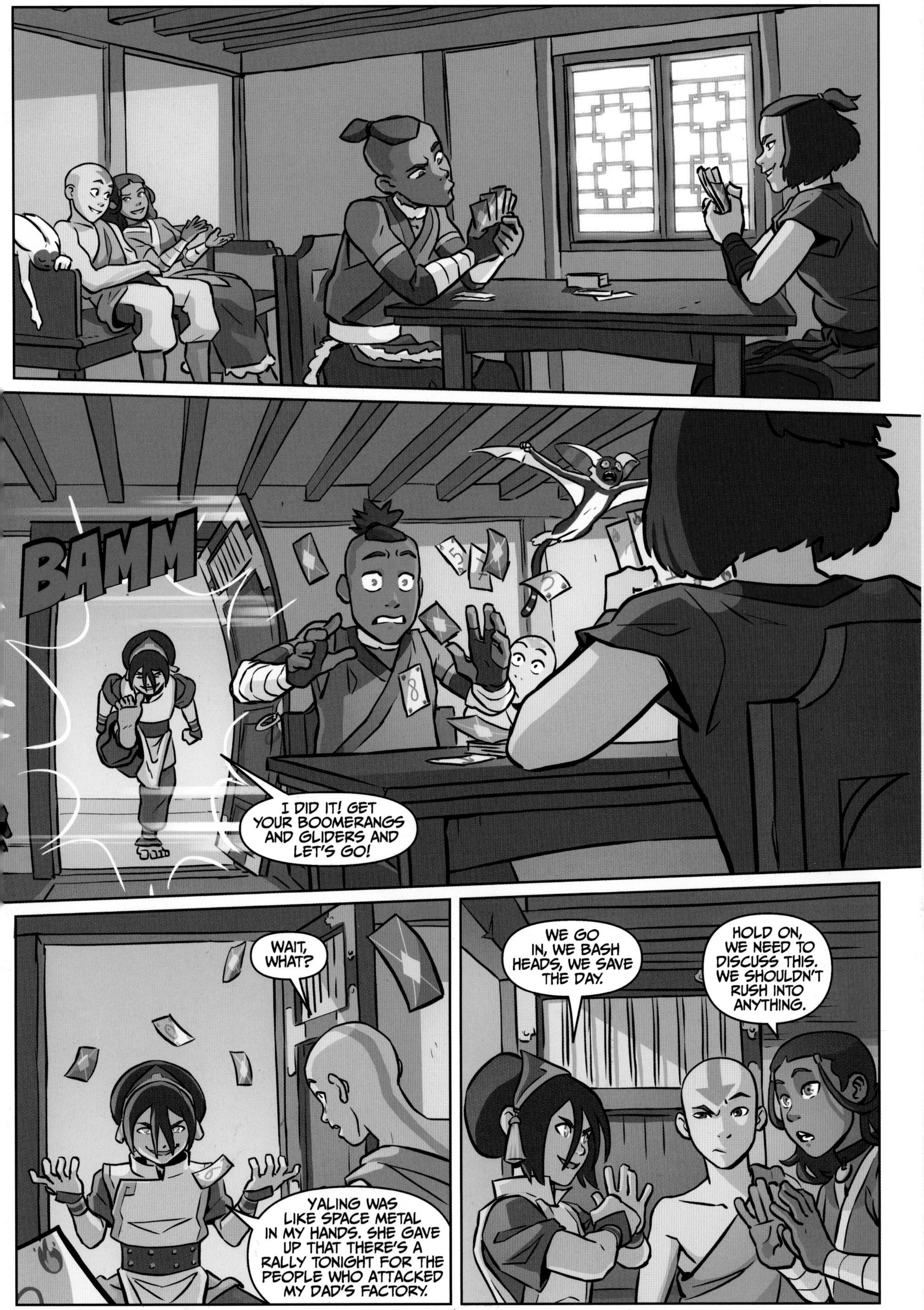
BAMM
I DID IT! GET YOUR BOOMERANGS AND GLIDERS AND LET'S GO!
WAIT, WHAT?
YALING WAS LIKE SPACE METAL IN MY HANDS. SHE GAVE UP THAT THERE'S A RALLY TONIGHT FOR THE PEOPLE WHO ATTACKED MY DAD'S FACTORY.
WE GO IN, WE BASH HEADS, WE SAVE THE DAY.
HOLD ON, WE NEED TO DISCUSS THIS. WE SHOULDN'T RUSH INTO ANYTHING.

WHAT'S TO DISCUSS?

WE DON'T KNOW WHY THE FACTORIES WERE ATTACKED, OR WHAT LILING'S INVOLVEMENT IS. SHE'S ON CRANEFISH TOWN'S BUSINESS COUNCIL. WE CAN'T ARREST HER WITHOUT PROOF SHE DID SOMETHING WRONG.

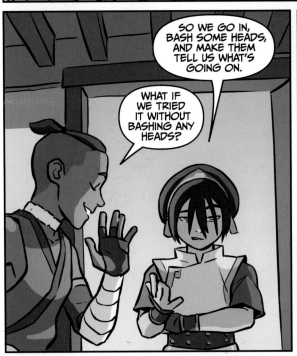

SO WE GO IN, BASH SOME HEADS, AND MAKE THEM TELL US WHAT'S GOING ON.

WHAT IF WE TRIED IT WITHOUT BASHING ANY HEADS?

WE COULD DO THAT, BUT... WHY?

WHAT ABOUT THIS. TOPH GOES TO THE MEETING WITH YALING, AND THE REST OF US DISGUISE OURSELVES AND SNEAK IN AFTER HER. THEN WE CAN GATHER INFORMATION.

SEEMS LIKE LESS FUN, BUT IF THAT'S THE WAY YOU WANT TO PLAY IT.

I THINK IT'S A GOOD PLAN.

IT'S A GREAT PLAN. ALSO, IT MEANS--

FEH: *WANG FIRE RETURNS! I was so excited that the story's need for disguises meant Sokka could whip out his Wang Fire beard. "The Headband" is one of my favorite episodes.*

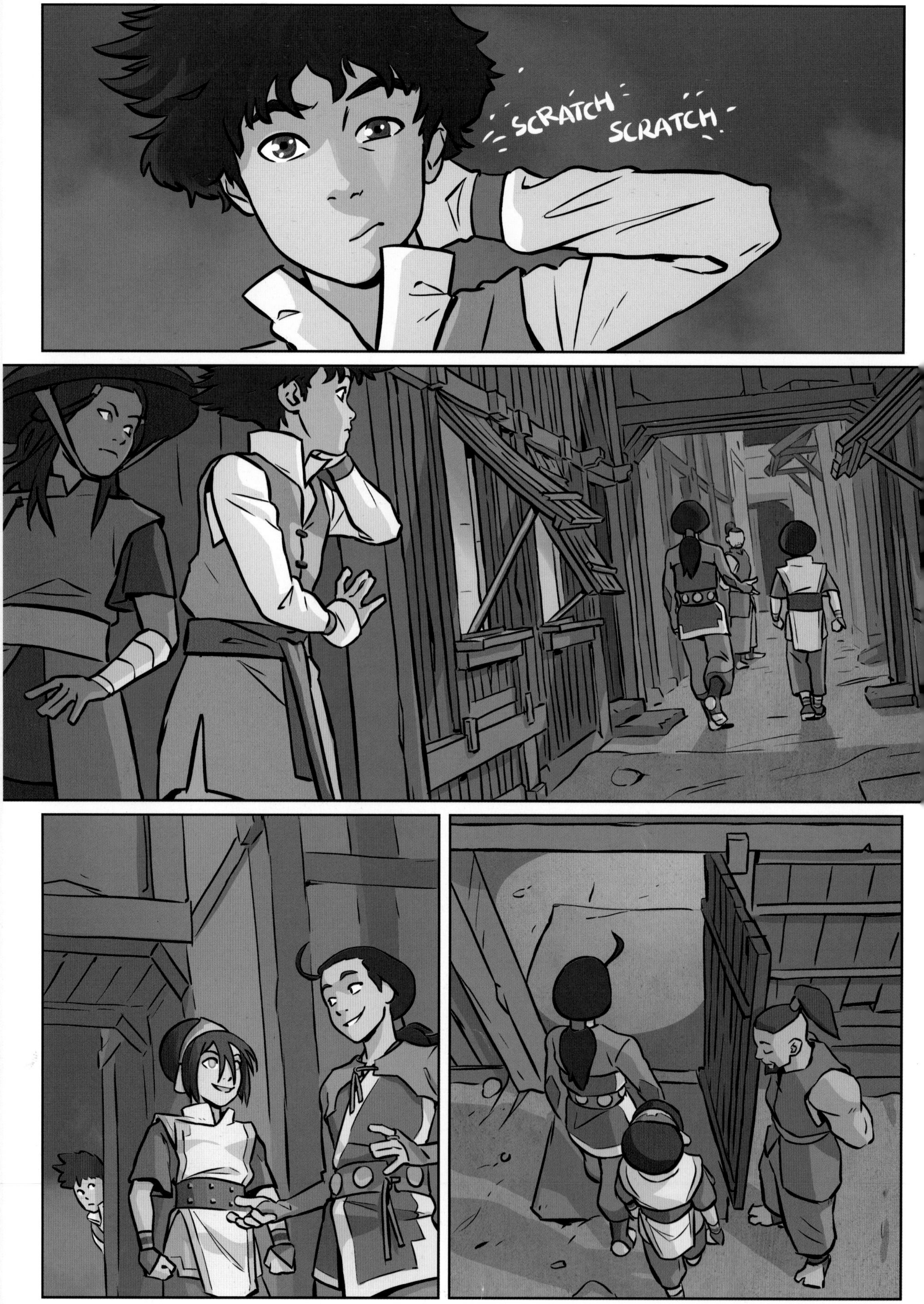
SCRATCH
SCRATCH

PW: *Giving Aang massive anime hair was the highlight of this book for me.*

SUKI, I JUST WANT TO SAY YOU LOOK ABSOLUTELY BEAUTIFUL IN YOUR DISGUISE.
THANK YOU, SOKKA! YOU LOOK SO HANDSOME IN YOURS.
DO YOU THINK WE'RE LIKE THAT?
HAHA! PROBABLY A LITTLE.
OKAY, LET'S GO.

PW: *Sokka and Suki are basically just wearing their Fire Nation clothes, although Suki added a headband (they're good for sneaky missions).*

I gave Aang and Katara Earth Kingdom disguises (I figure there was some stuff they found in the house they were staying in).

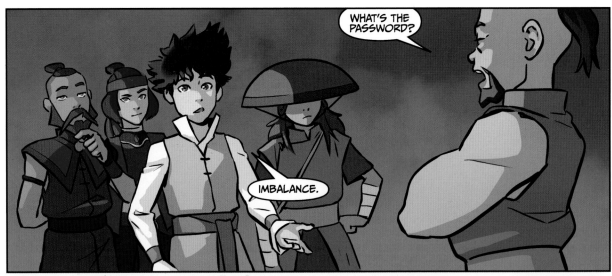

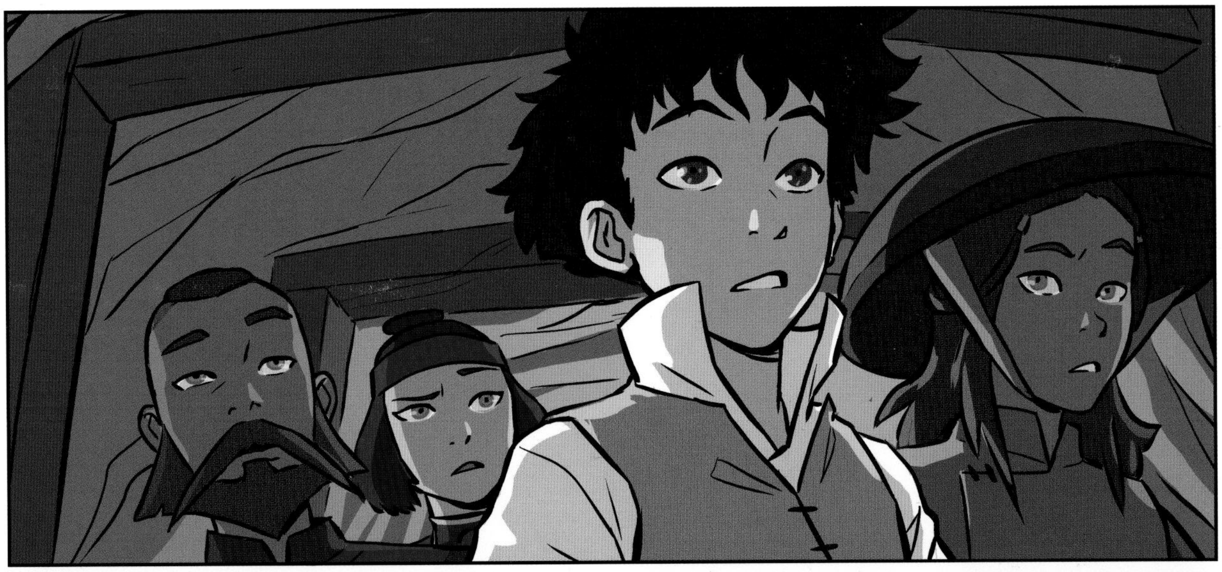

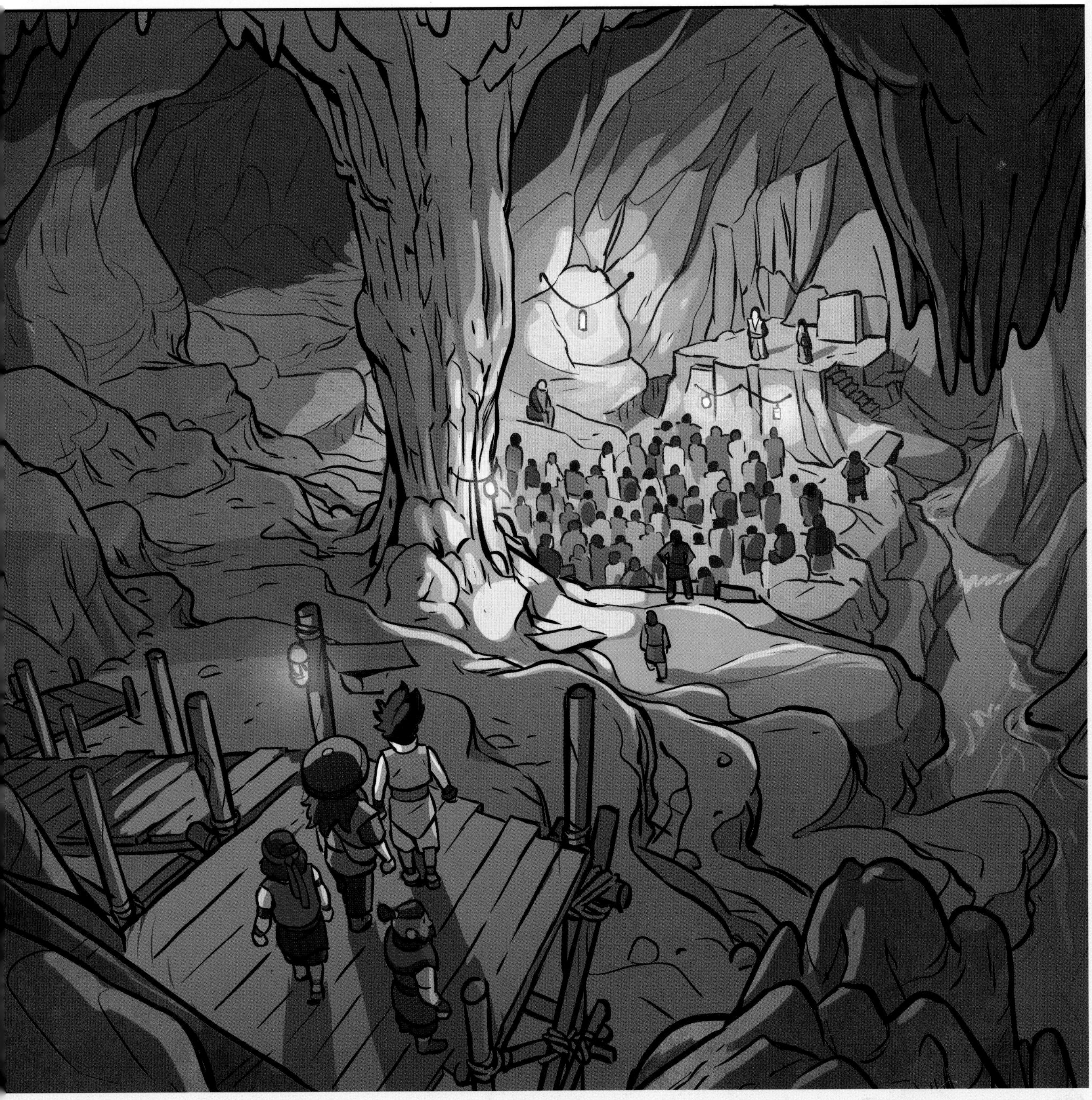

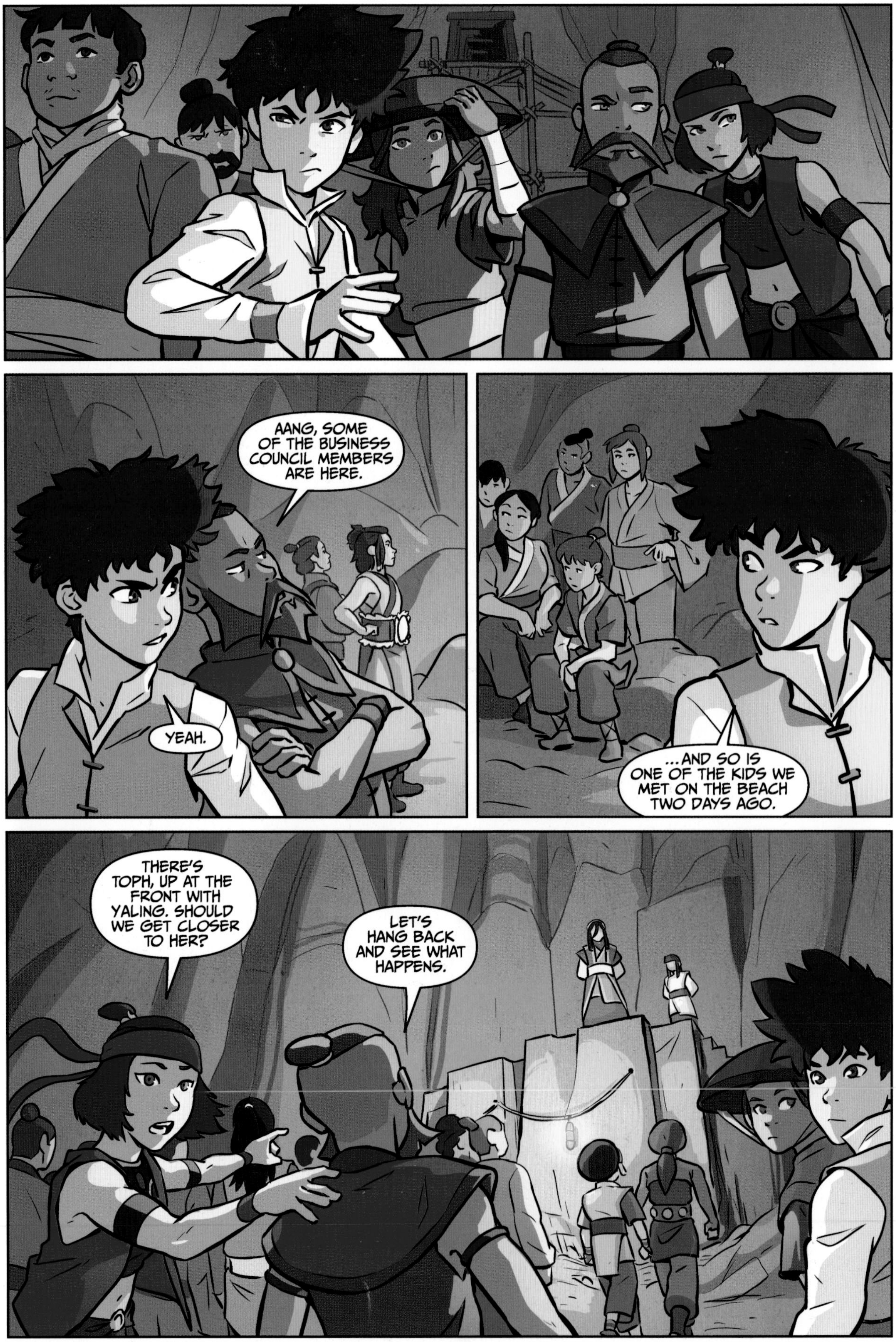
AANG, SOME OF THE BUSINESS COUNCIL MEMBERS ARE HERE.
YEAH.
...AND SO IS ONE OF THE KIDS WE MET ON THE BEACH TWO DAYS AGO.
THERE'S TOPH, UP AT THE FRONT WITH YALING. SHOULD WE GET CLOSER TO HER?
LET'S HANG BACK AND SEE WHAT HAPPENS.

FEH: *Fear fuels benders' bigotry and fear of what might happen if non-benders had the same privileges they did. The rise of bender supremacy has begun.*

123

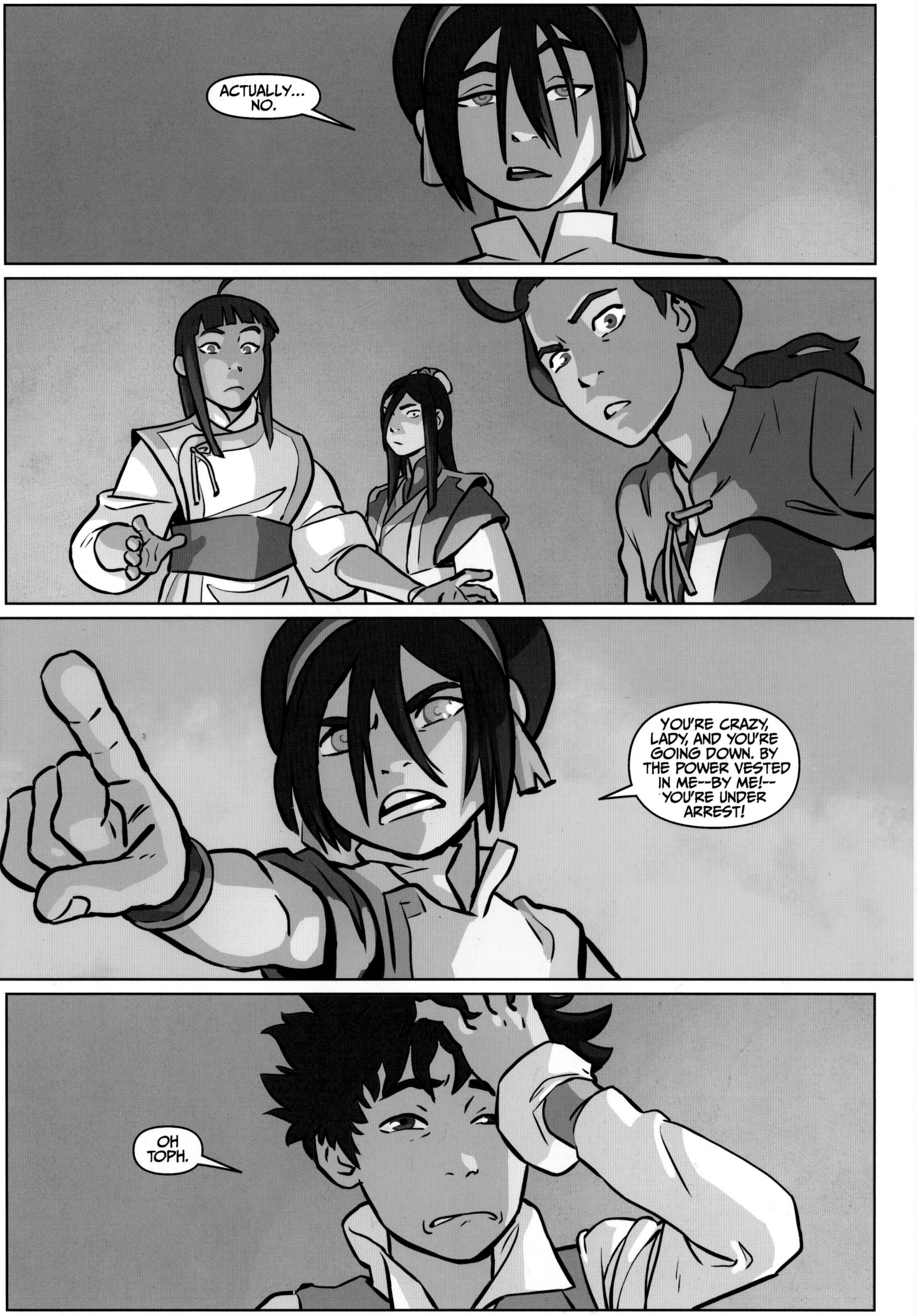
ACTUALLY... NO.
YOU'RE CRAZY, LADY, AND YOU'RE GOING DOWN. BY THE POWER VESTED IN ME--BY ME!--YOU'RE UNDER ARREST!
OH TOPH.

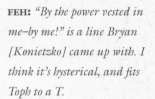

FEH: *"By the power vested in me–by me!" is a line Bryan [Konietzko] came up with. I think it's hysterical, and fits Toph to a T.*

PW: *I guess Toph only has so much patience for subtlety.*

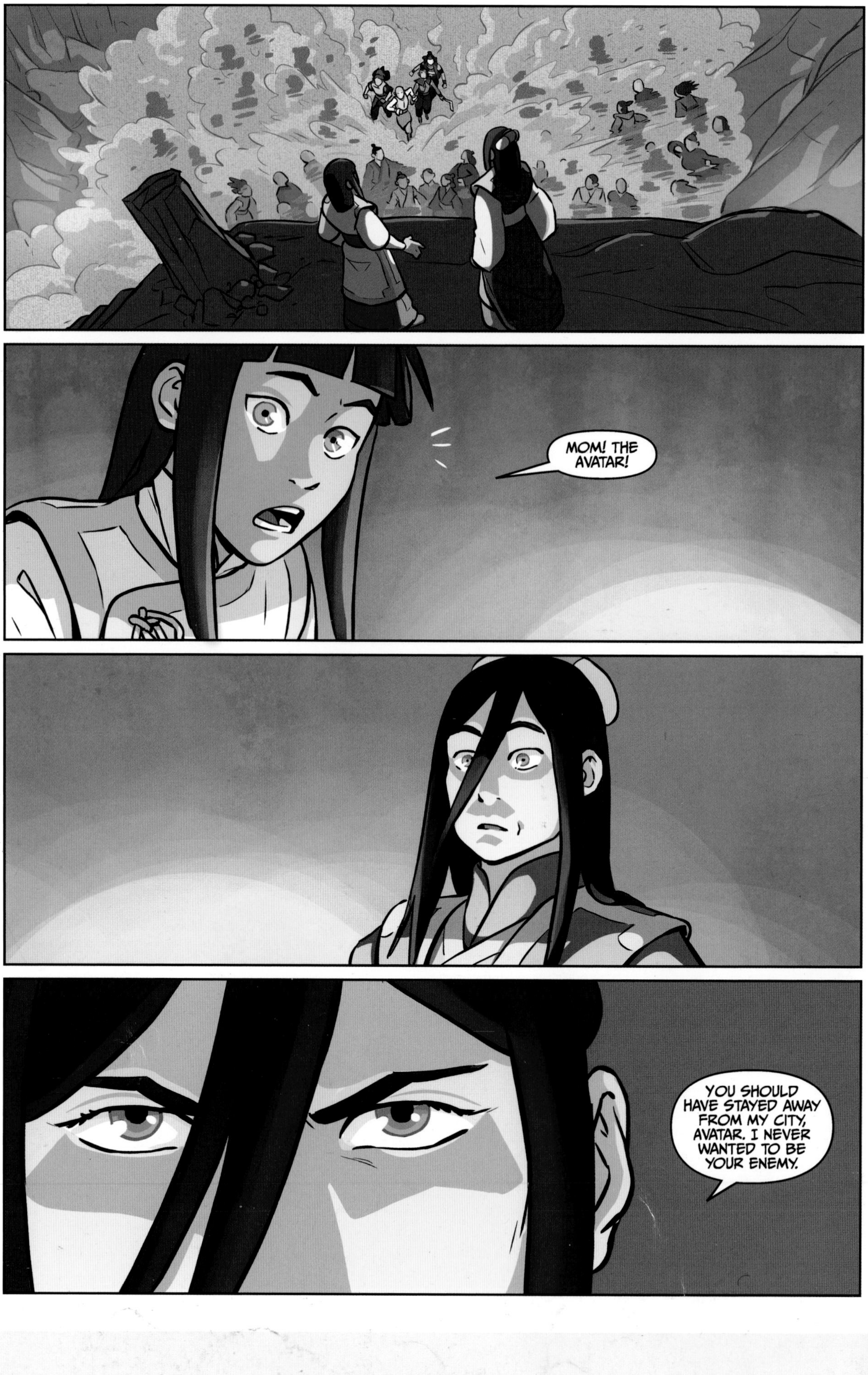
MOM! THE AVATAR!
YOU SHOULD HAVE STAYED AWAY FROM MY CITY, AVATAR. I NEVER WANTED TO BE YOUR ENEMY.

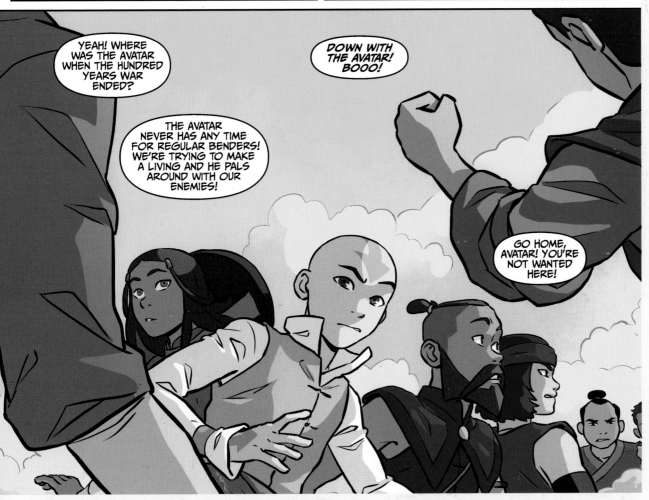

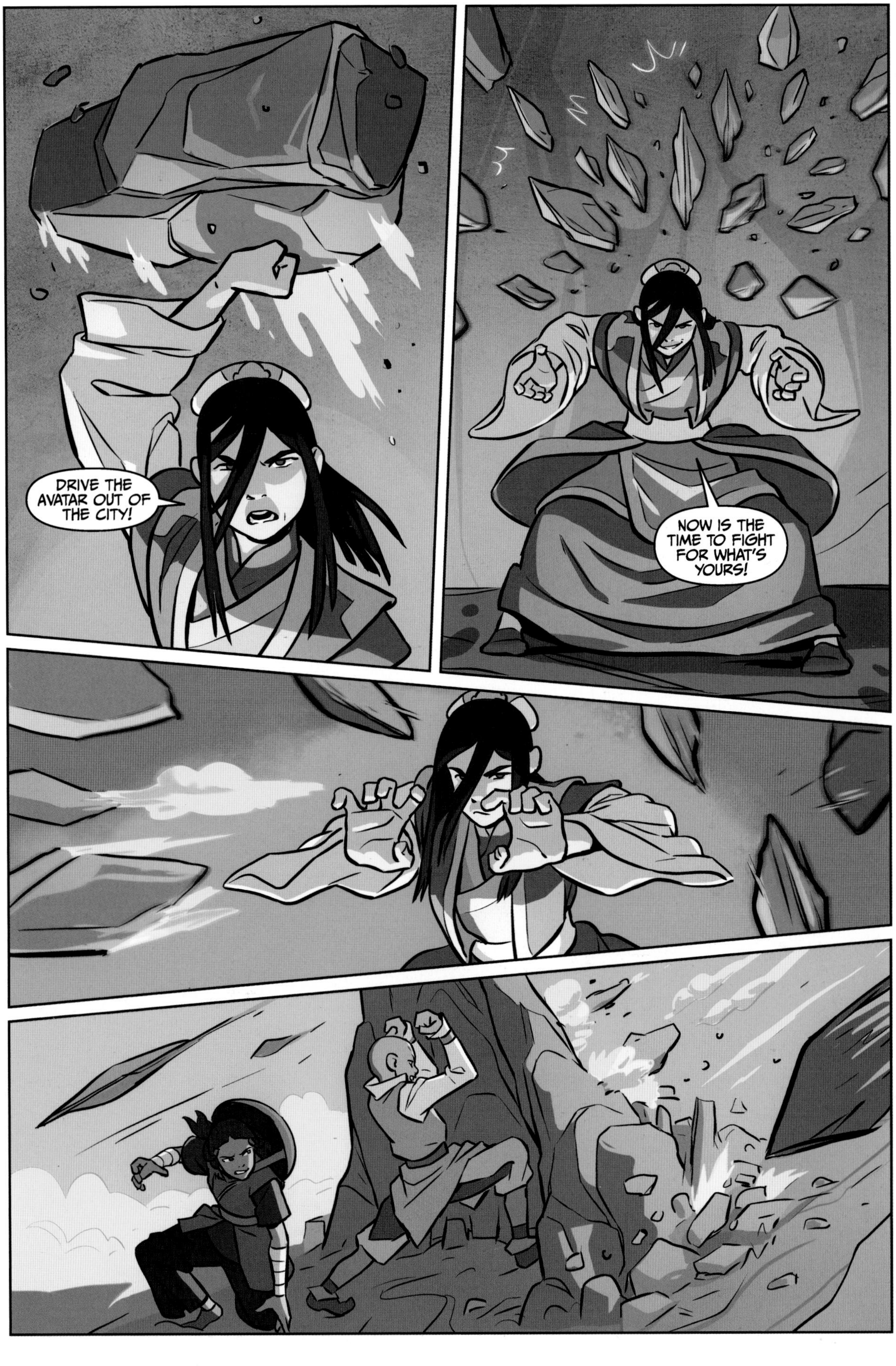
DRIVE THE AVATAR OUT OF THE CITY!
NOW IS THE TIME TO FIGHT FOR WHAT'S YOURS!

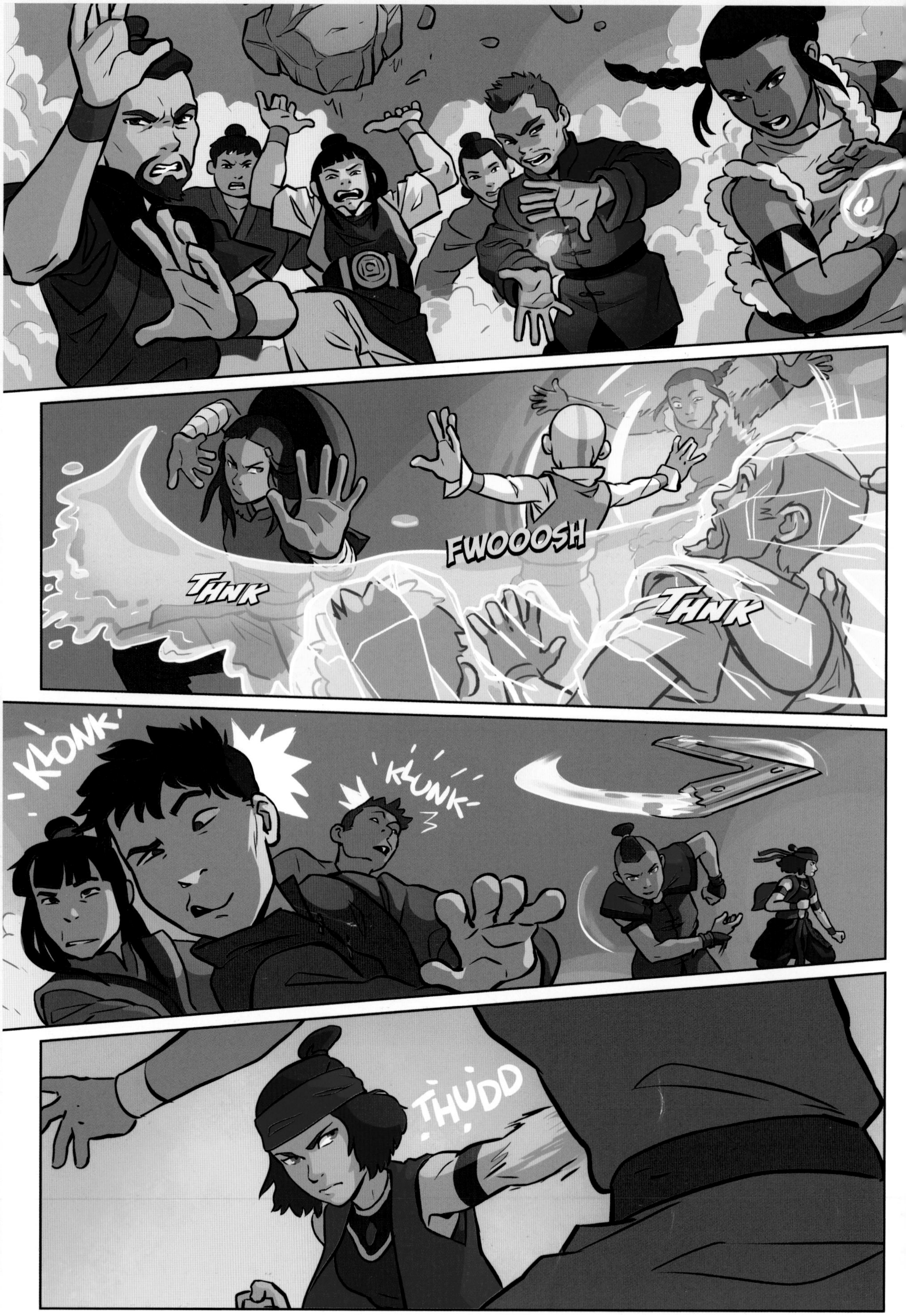
FWOOOSH
THNK
THNK
KLONK
KLUNK
THUDD

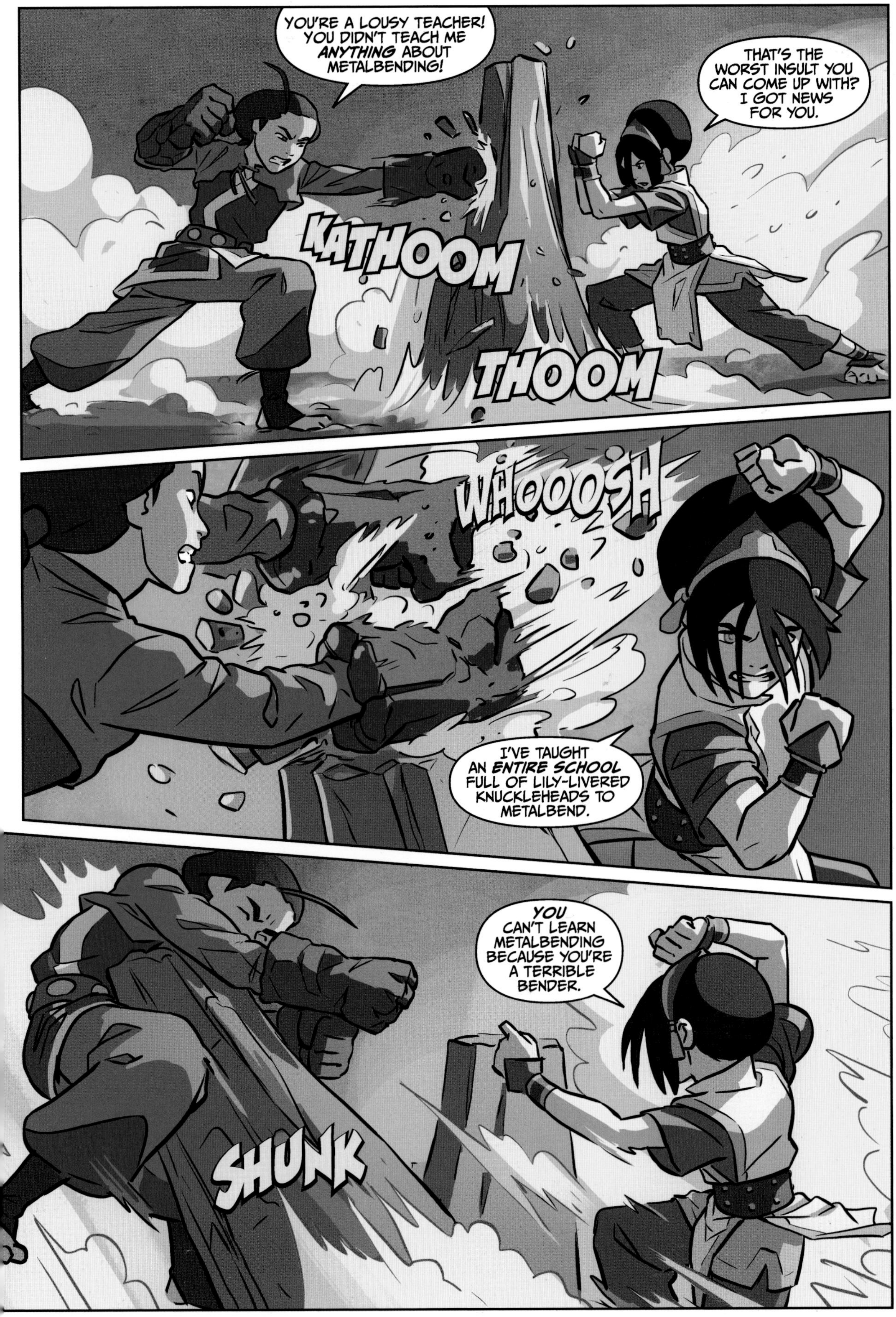
YOU'RE A LOUSY TEACHER! YOU DIDN'T TEACH ME ANYTHING ABOUT METALBENDING!
THAT'S THE WORST INSULT YOU CAN COME UP WITH? I GOT NEWS FOR YOU.
KATHOOM
THOOM
WHOOOSH
I'VE TAUGHT AN ENTIRE SCHOOL FULL OF LILY-LIVERED KNUCKLEHEADS TO METALBEND.
YOU CAN'T LEARN METALBENDING BECAUSE YOU'RE A TERRIBLE BENDER.
SHUNK

FEH: Avatar *is known for its detailed and amazing fight scenes. It's hard to do complicated fight scenes in a comic with a limited page count, but I think Peter did an amazing job!*

PW: *Todd (my friend who helped with choreography) had to handle both sides of all the fights, which made for some rather amusing photographs. His help was crucial for this scene, making sure all the punches and dodges flowed and made sense.*

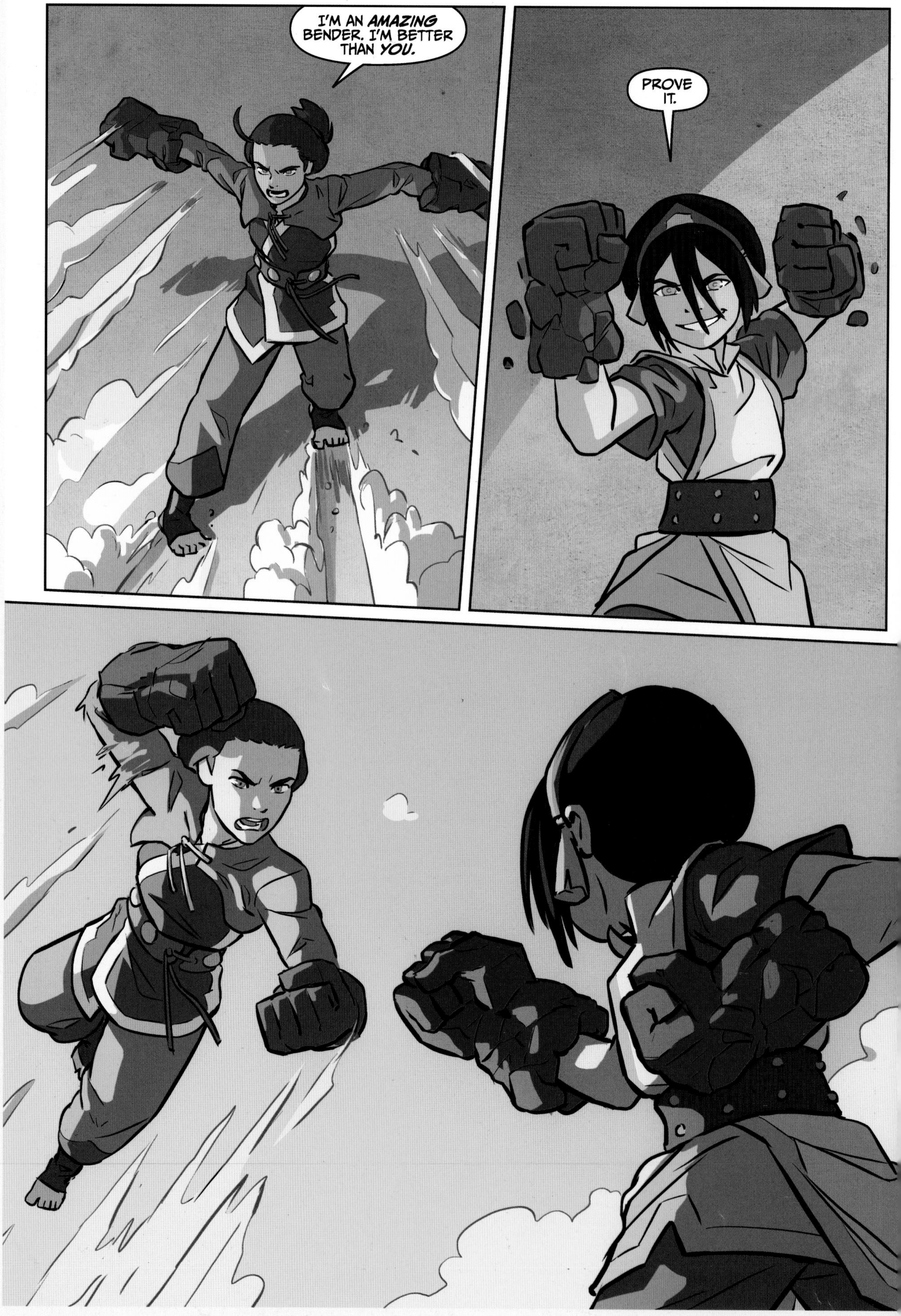
I'M AN AMAZING BENDER. I'M BETTER THAN YOU.
PROVE IT.

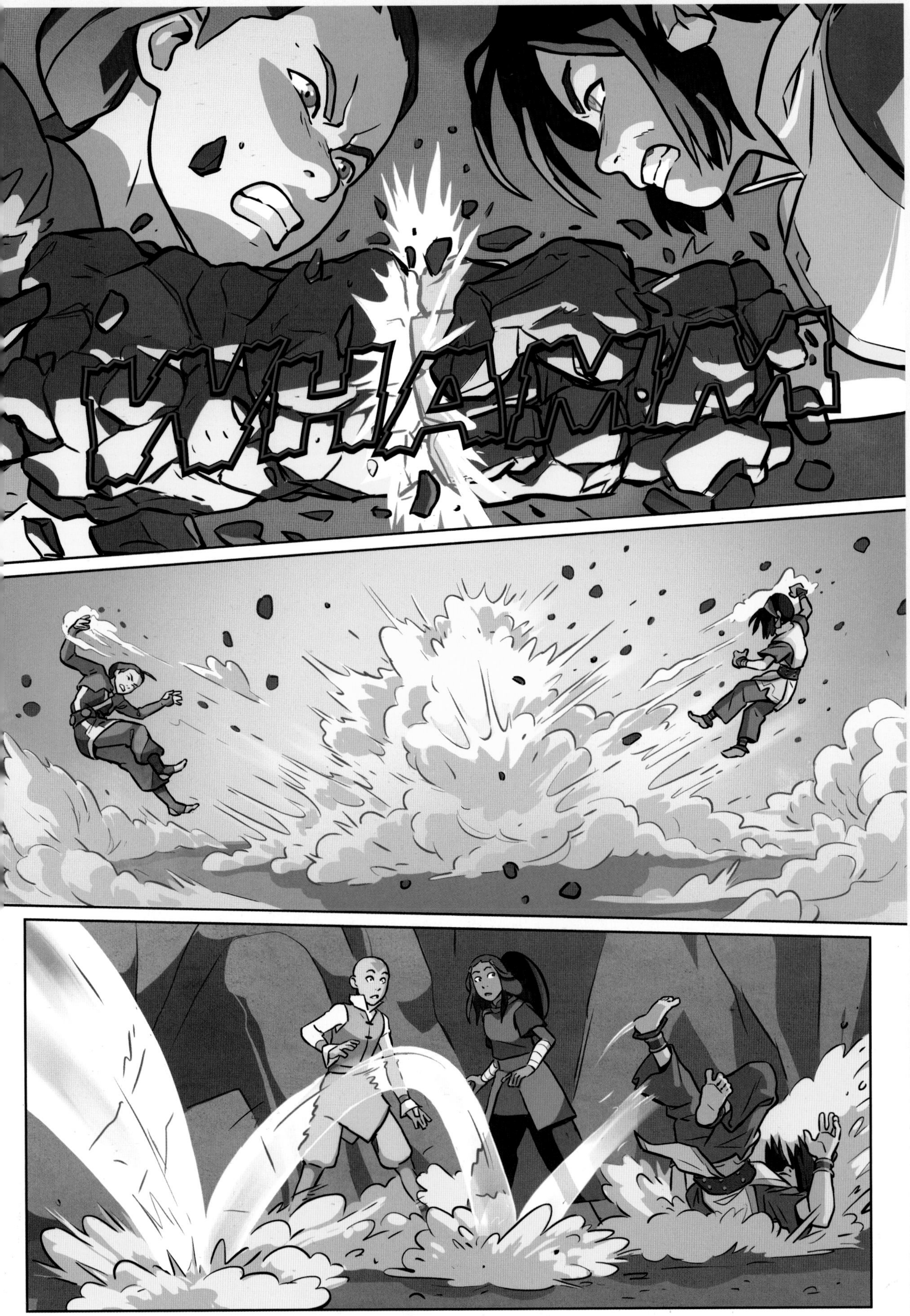

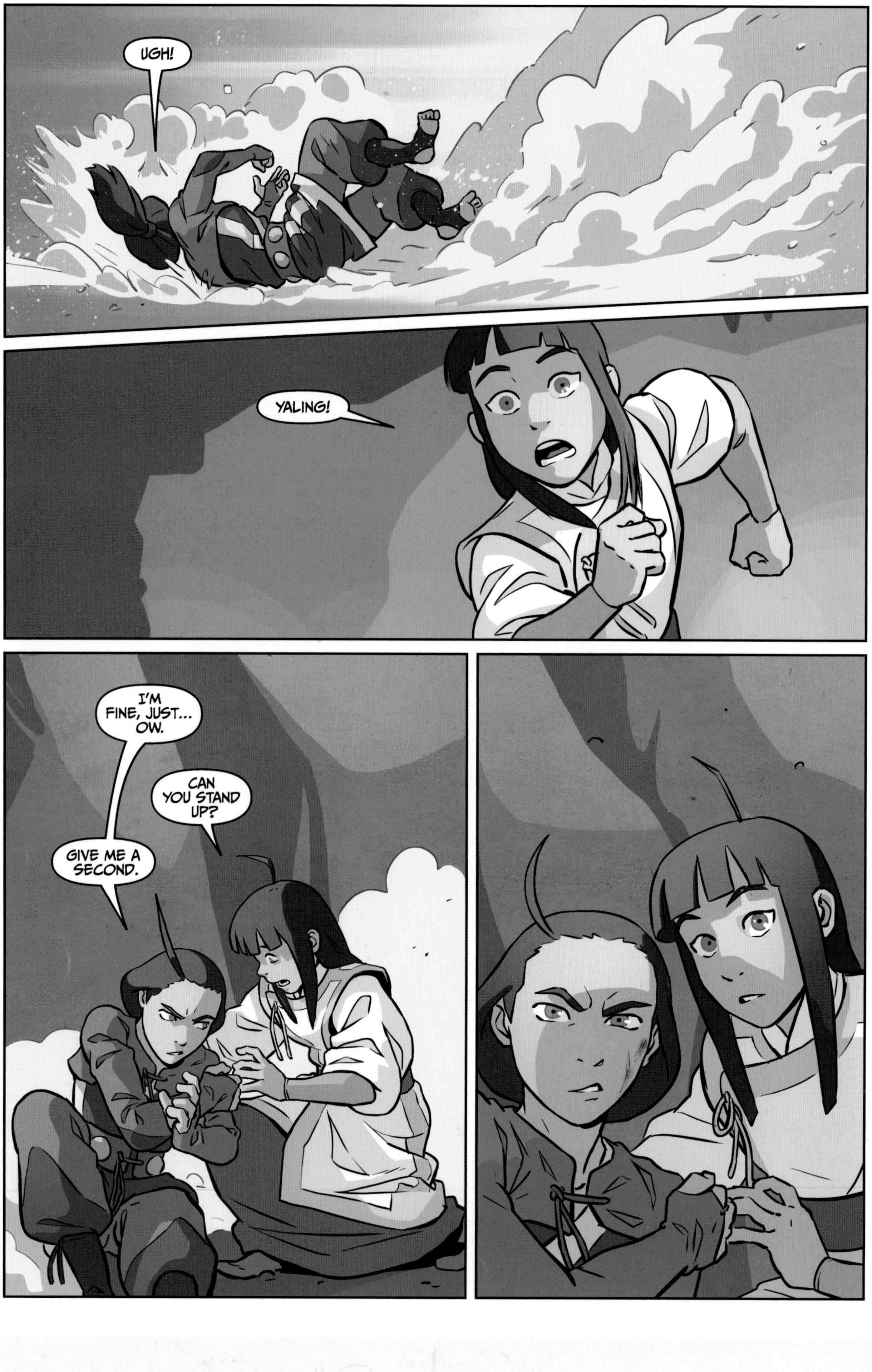
UGH!
YALING!
I'M FINE, JUST... OW.
CAN YOU STAND UP?
GIVE ME A SECOND.

SORRY GUYS, YOU'RE NOT GOING ANYWHERE.

YEAH, LIKE YOU CAN STOP US WITH YOUR TOY BOOMERANG. TRY AGAIN WHEN YOU HAVE A REAL WEAPON.

RU, YOU'RE A NON-BENDER. HOW CAN YOU BE OKAY WITH WHAT YOUR MOM IS DOING? SHE'S TARGETING PEOPLE LIKE YOU.

PW: *I'm really glad Faith gave Sokka a chance to shine in this story. He's not just a goofy character, and I think he has the clearest understanding of what's going on out of anyone in Imbalance.*

PEOPLE LIKE *US.*

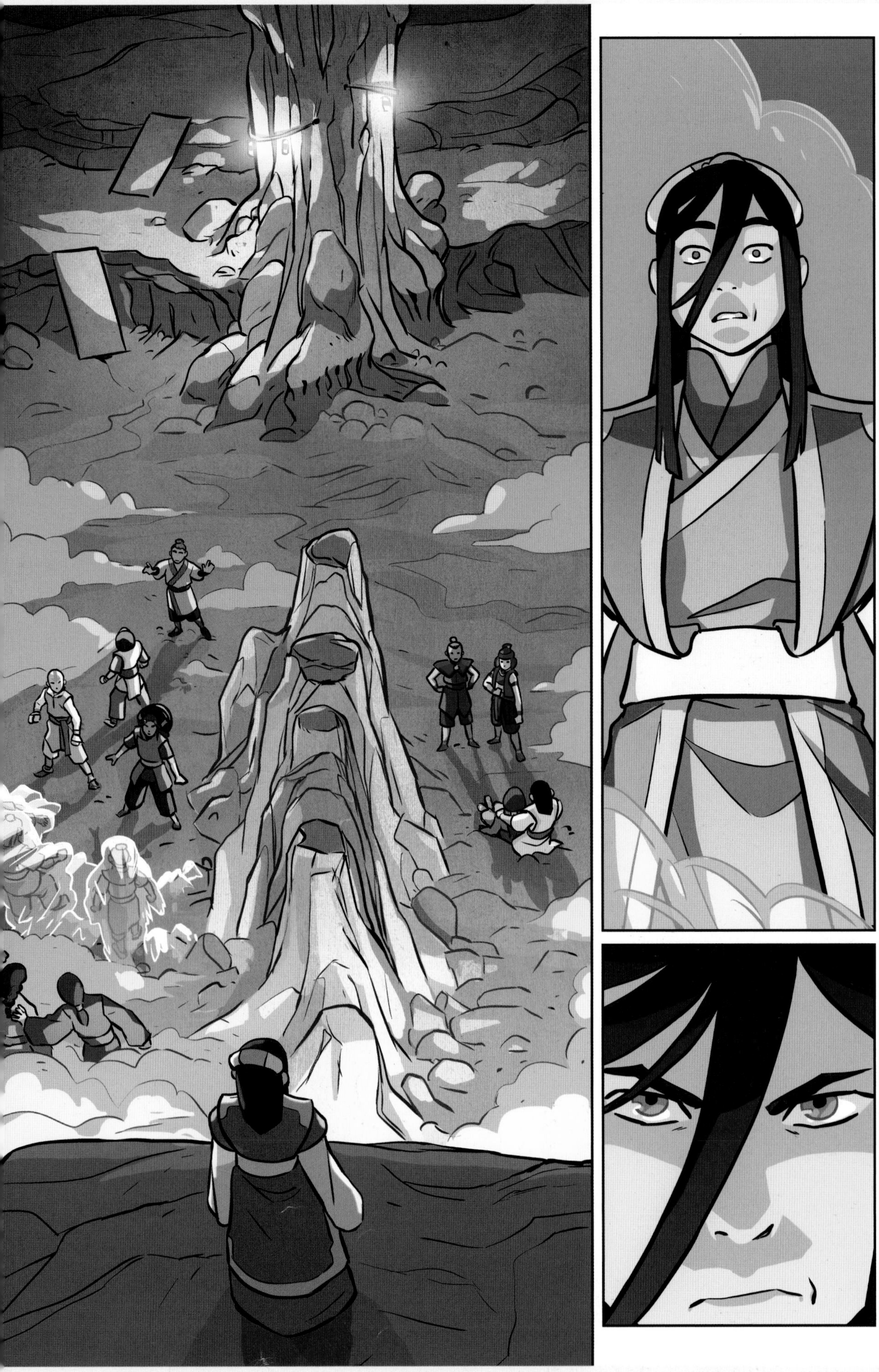

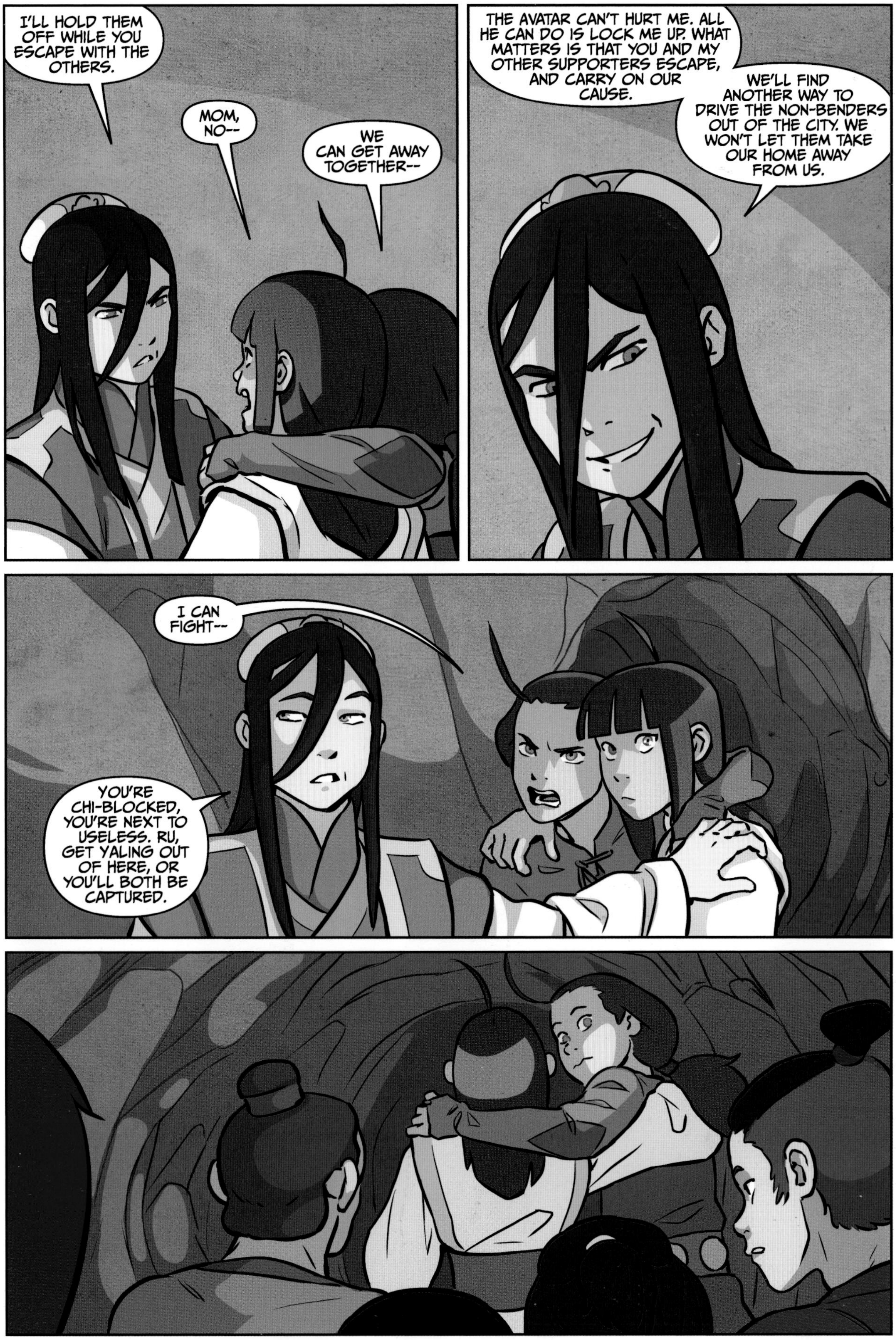
I'LL HOLD THEM OFF WHILE YOU ESCAPE WITH THE OTHERS.
MOM, NO--
WE CAN GET AWAY TOGETHER--
THE AVATAR CAN'T HURT ME. ALL HE CAN DO IS LOCK ME UP. WHAT MATTERS IS THAT YOU AND MY OTHER SUPPORTERS ESCAPE, AND CARRY ON OUR CAUSE.
WE'LL FIND ANOTHER WAY TO DRIVE THE NON-BENDERS OUT OF THE CITY. WE WON'T LET THEM TAKE OUR HOME AWAY FROM US.
I CAN FIGHT--
YOU'RE CHI-BLOCKED, YOU'RE NEXT TO USELESS. RU, GET YALING OUT OF HERE, OR YOU'LL BOTH BE CAPTURED.

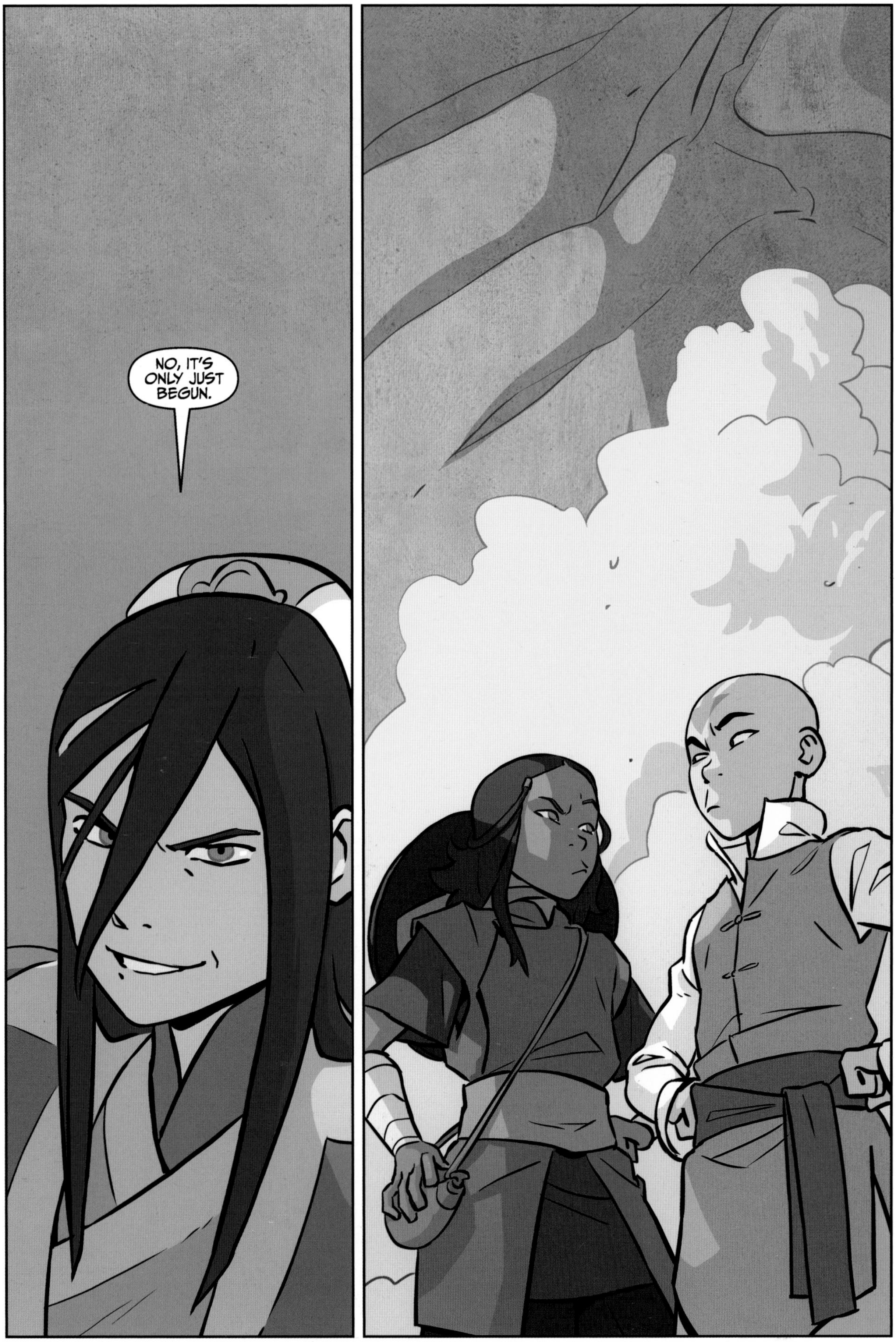
NO, IT'S ONLY JUST BEGUN.

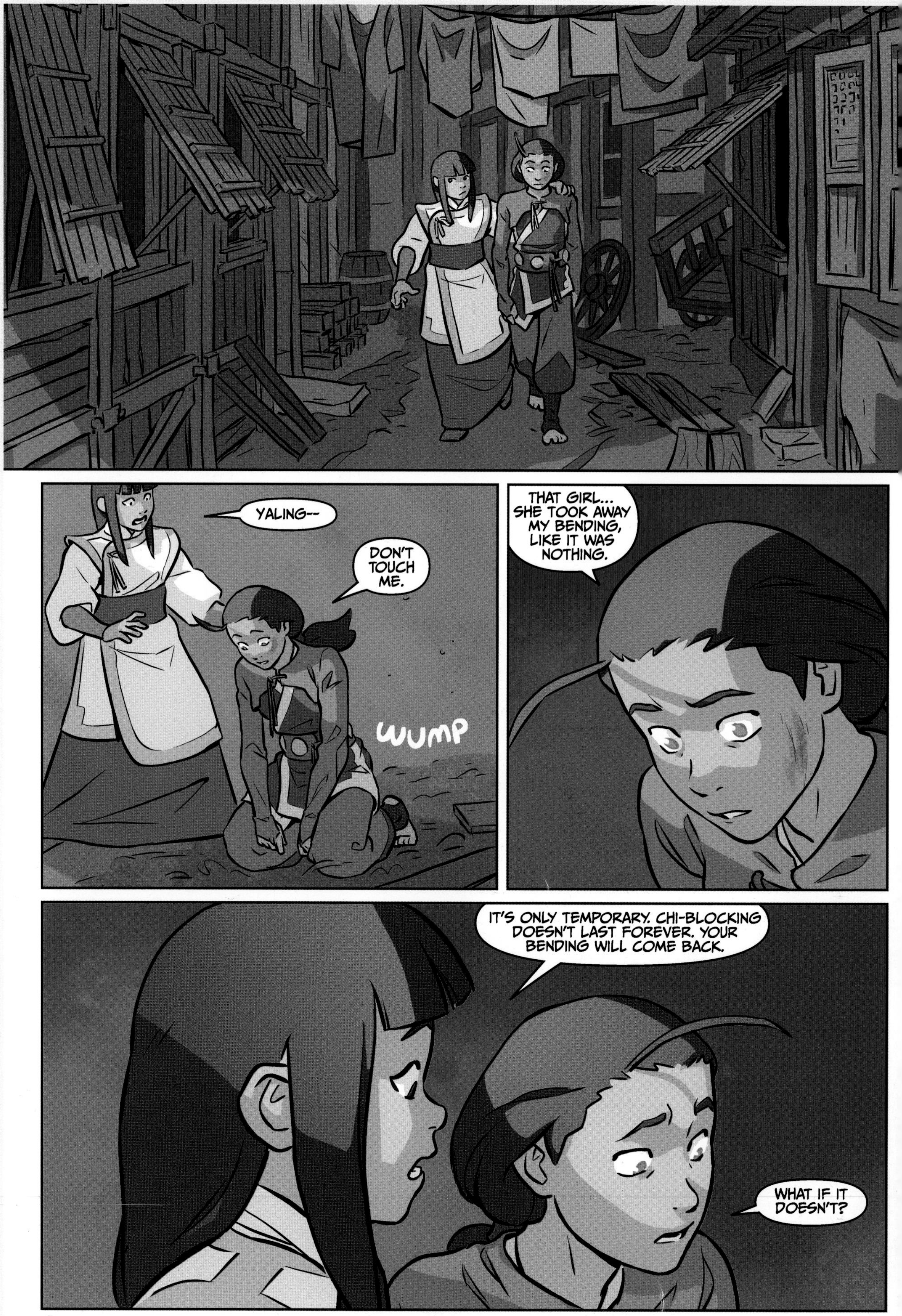
YALING--
DON'T TOUCH ME.
WUMP
THAT GIRL... SHE TOOK AWAY MY BENDING, LIKE IT WAS NOTHING.
IT'S ONLY TEMPORARY. CHI-BLOCKING DOESN'T LAST FOREVER. YOUR BENDING WILL COME BACK.
WHAT IF IT DOESN'T?

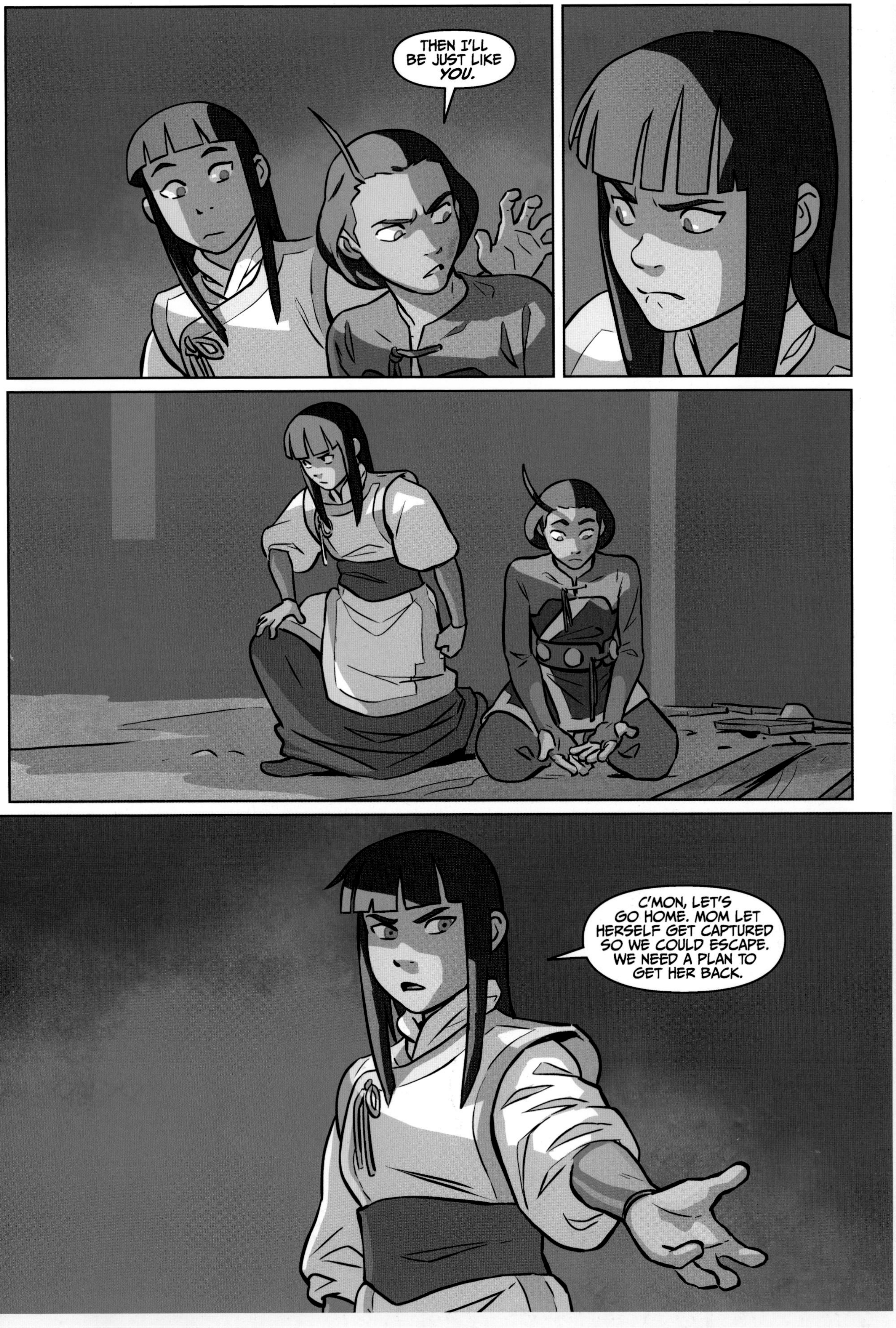
THEN I'LL BE JUST LIKE YOU.
C'MON, LET'S GO HOME. MOM LET HERSELF GET CAPTURED SO WE COULD ESCAPE. WE NEED A PLAN TO GET HER BACK.

FEH: *Yaling's worst nightmare is to lose her bending, which would make her the same as her sister, a non-bender. It's probably something Ru has always suspected, but Yaling coming right out and saying it has to be brutal for her.*

AVATAR: THE LAST AIRBENDER—IMBALANCE PART TWO

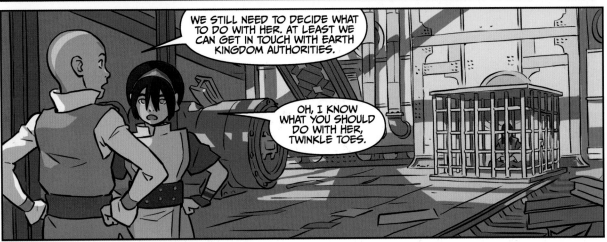

151

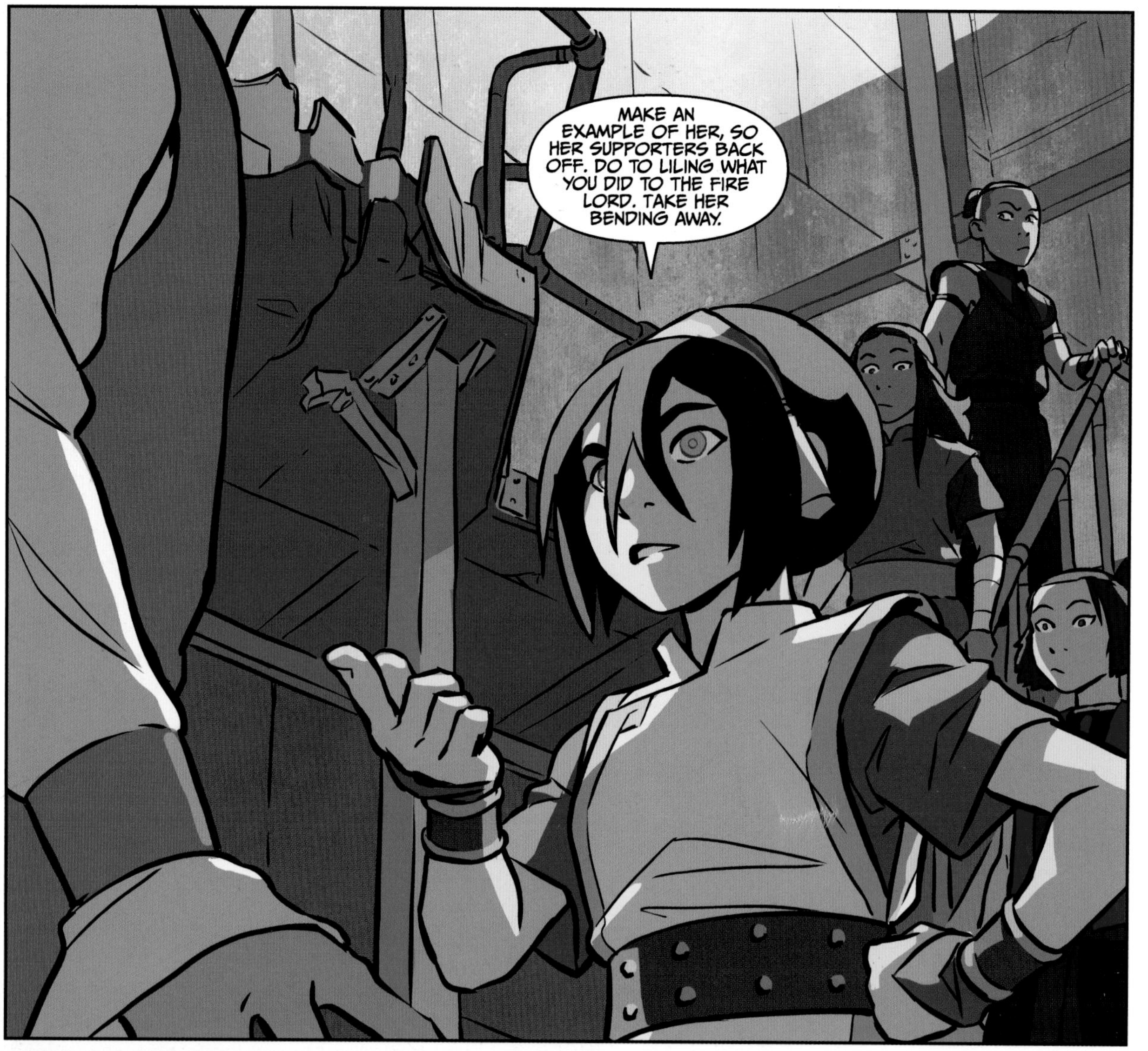
MAKE AN EXAMPLE OF HER, SO HER SUPPORTERS BACK OFF. DO TO LILING WHAT YOU DID TO THE FIRE LORD. TAKE HER BENDING AWAY.

FEH: *At this point in time, Aang has taken away someone's bending only once: when he fought Fire Lord Ozai. It's a power only he seems to possess, and he's used it only as an alternative to killing Ozai. But what if he chooses to use this power on a captured bender supremacist? Is this a power he should use to resolve conflict, or only in a life or death situation? At this point, I suspect Aang himself doesn't even know.*

PW: *I'm still partial to these drawings of Toph and Aang!*

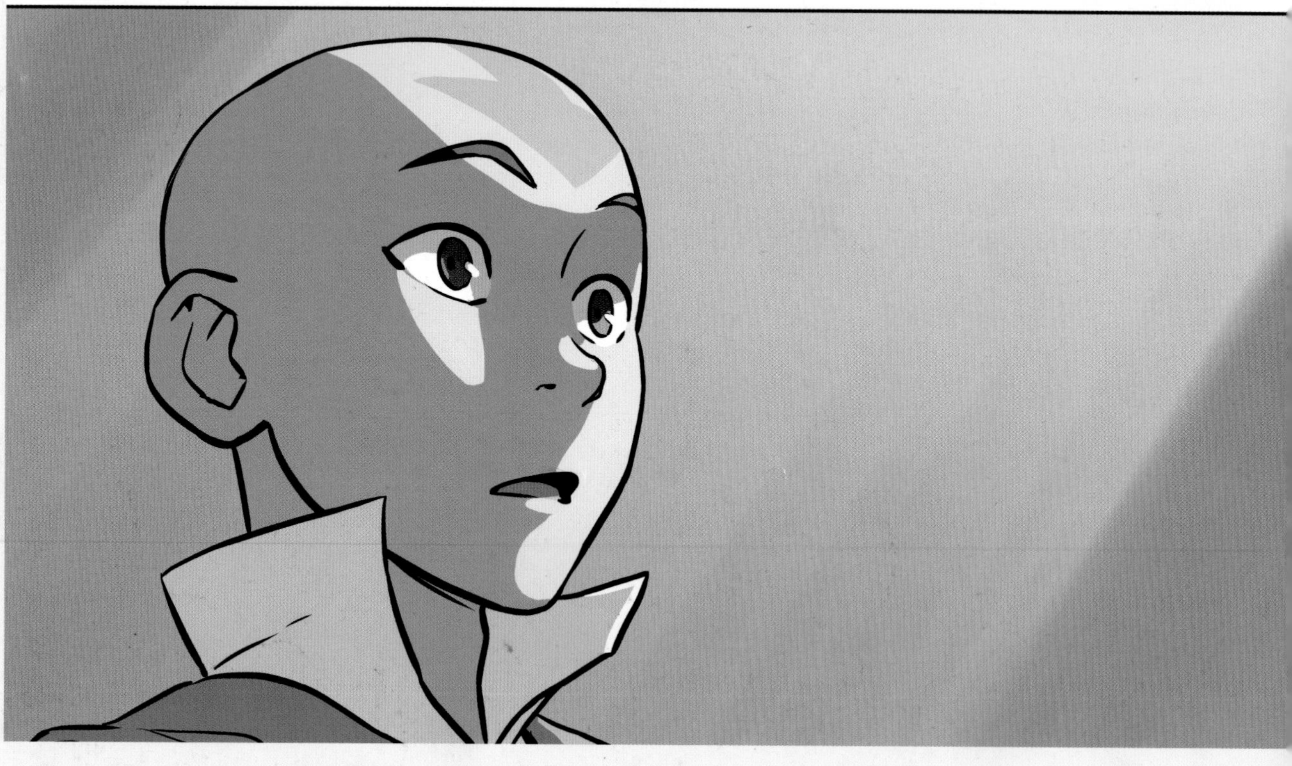

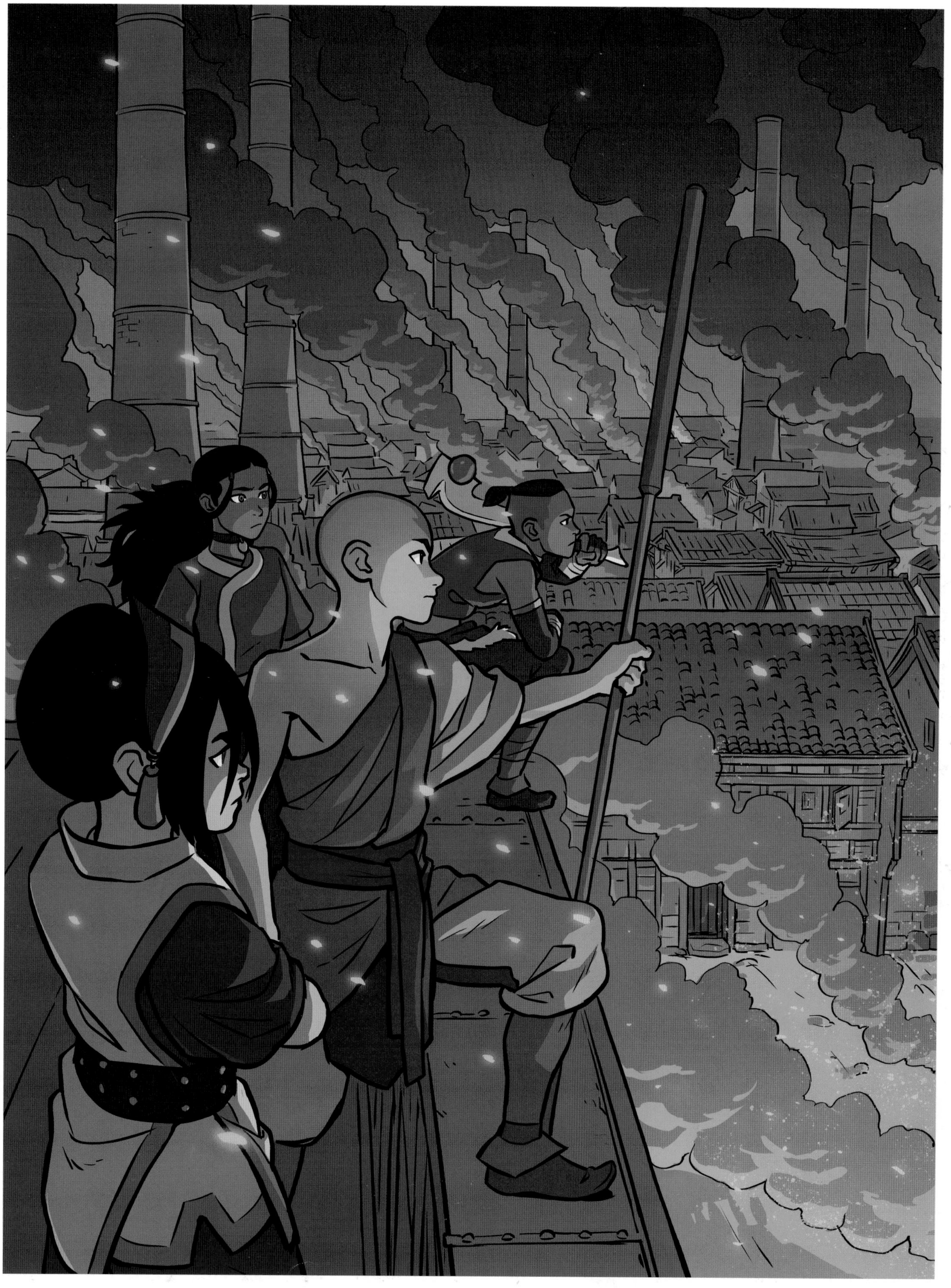

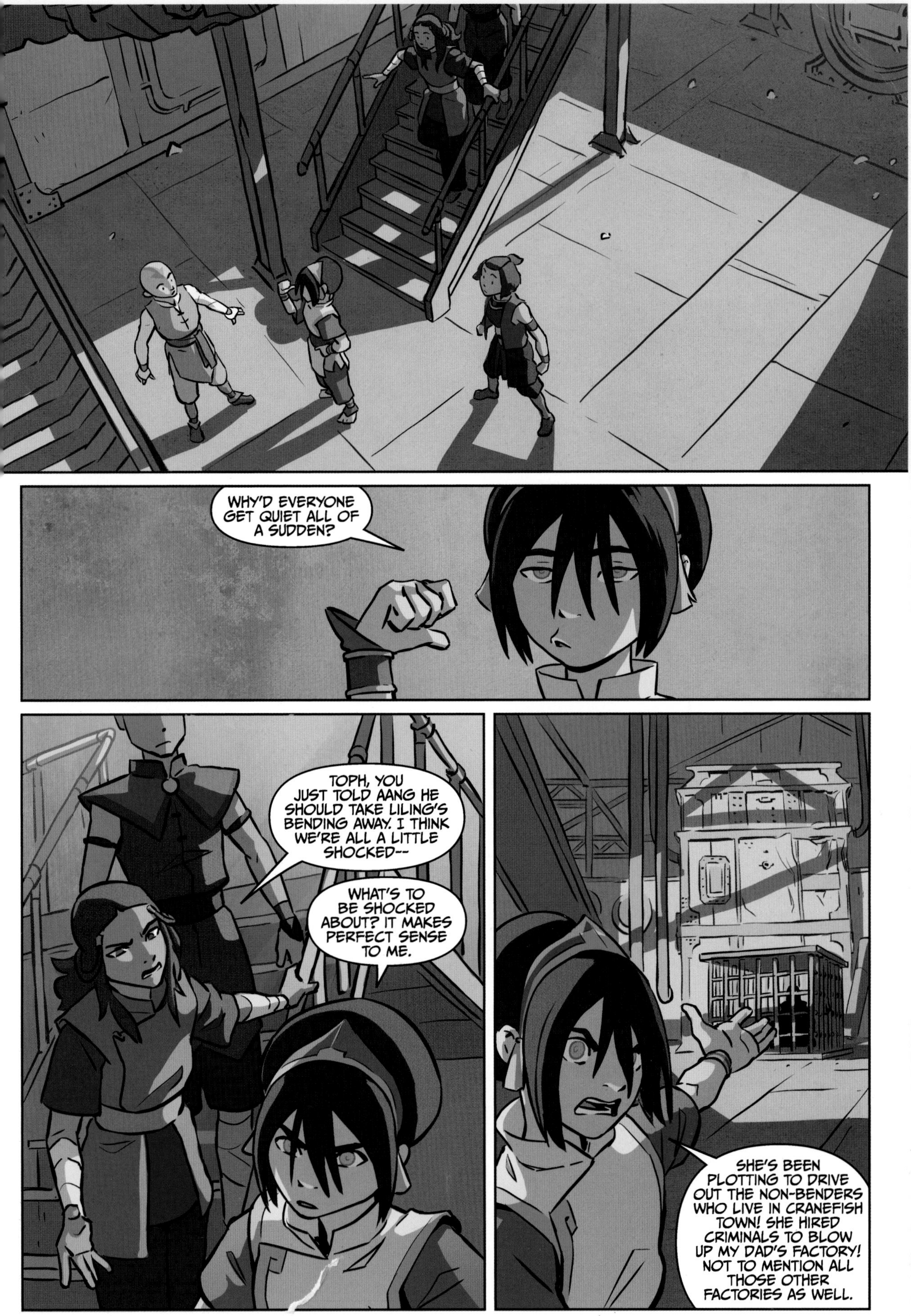
WHY'D EVERYONE GET QUIET ALL OF A SUDDEN?
TOPH, YOU JUST TOLD AANG HE SHOULD TAKE LILING'S BENDING AWAY. I THINK WE'RE ALL A LITTLE SHOCKED--
WHAT'S TO BE SHOCKED ABOUT? IT MAKES PERFECT SENSE TO ME.
SHE'S BEEN PLOTTING TO DRIVE OUT THE NON-BENDERS WHO LIVE IN CRANEFISH TOWN! SHE HIRED CRIMINALS TO BLOW UP MY DAD'S FACTORY! NOT TO MENTION ALL THOSE OTHER FACTORIES AS WELL.

SHE CAN'T LEAD A BUNCH OF BENDER SUPREMACISTS IF SHE'S NOT A BENDER ANYMORE.

AANG HAS ONLY TAKEN AWAY SOMEONE'S BENDING ONCE BEFORE, AND THAT WAS THE FIRE LORD! LILING ISN'T HIM! SHE'S NOT THREATENING THE WORLD WITH DESTRUCTION.

NO, SHE'S JUST THREATENING THIS CITY. DID YOU MISS THE PART WHERE I GOT BURIED IN RUBBLE BECAUSE SHE BLEW UP MY DAD'S FACTORY?

PW: I think Adele knocked it out of the park with her colors in general in this book, but the god rays and lighting in this panel are really special.

WHY ARE YOU SO UPSET ABOUT WHAT I SAID?

TOPH, IT'S TAKING AWAY SOMEONE'S BENDING. IT'S REMOVING A PART OF WHO THEY ARE. IT'S NOT A DECISION TO BE MADE LIGHTLY.

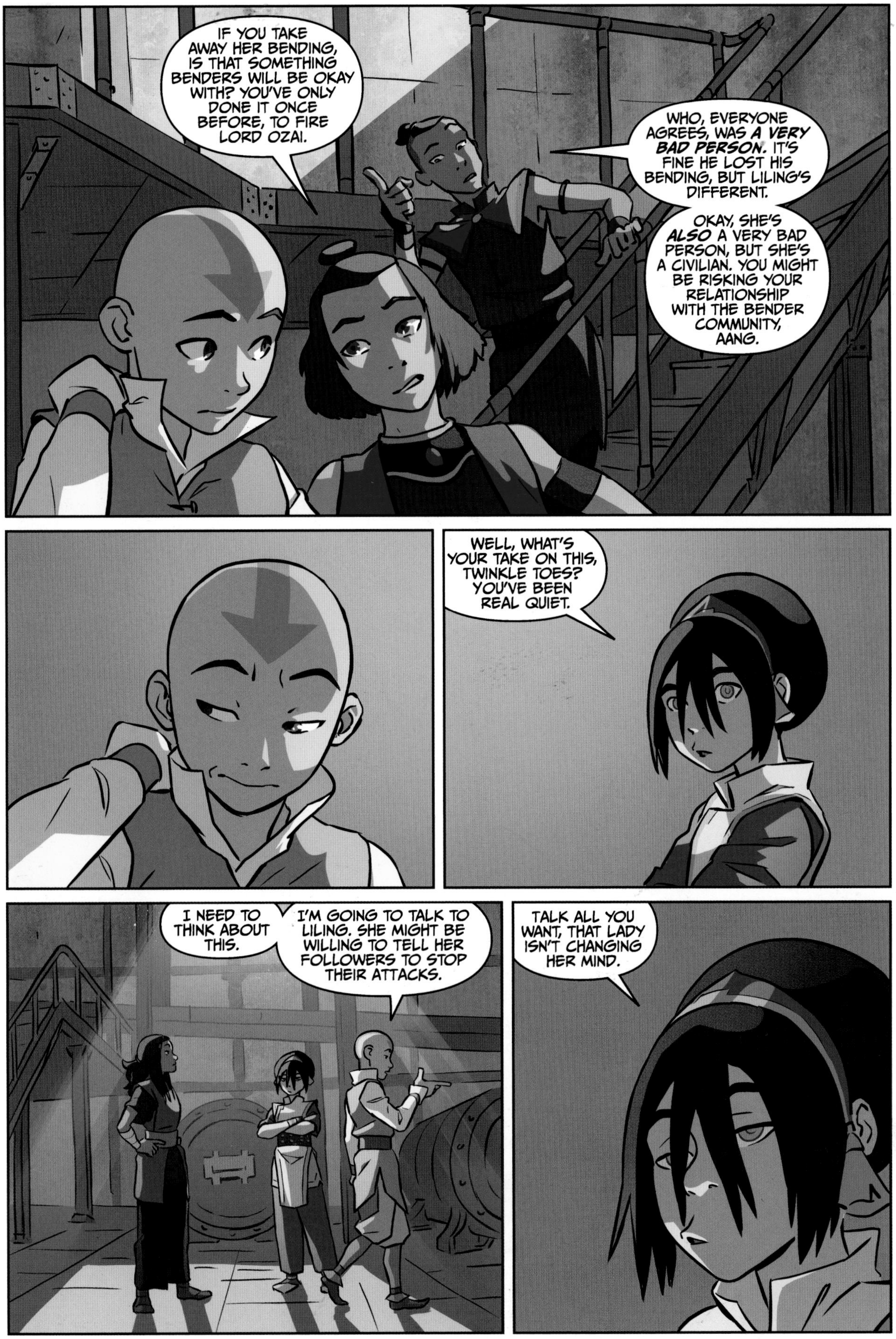
IF YOU TAKE AWAY HER BENDING, IS THAT SOMETHING BENDERS WILL BE OKAY WITH? YOU'VE ONLY DONE IT ONCE BEFORE, TO FIRE LORD OZAI.
WHO, EVERYONE AGREES, WAS A VERY BAD PERSON. IT'S FINE HE LOST HIS BENDING, BUT LILING'S DIFFERENT.
OKAY, SHE'S ALSO A VERY BAD PERSON, BUT SHE'S A CIVILIAN. YOU MIGHT BE RISKING YOUR RELATIONSHIP WITH THE BENDER COMMUNITY, AANG.
WELL, WHAT'S YOUR TAKE ON THIS, TWINKLE TOES? YOU'VE BEEN REAL QUIET.
I NEED TO THINK ABOUT THIS.
I'M GOING TO TALK TO LILING. SHE MIGHT BE WILLING TO TELL HER FOLLOWERS TO STOP THEIR ATTACKS.
TALK ALL YOU WANT, THAT LADY ISN'T CHANGING HER MIND.

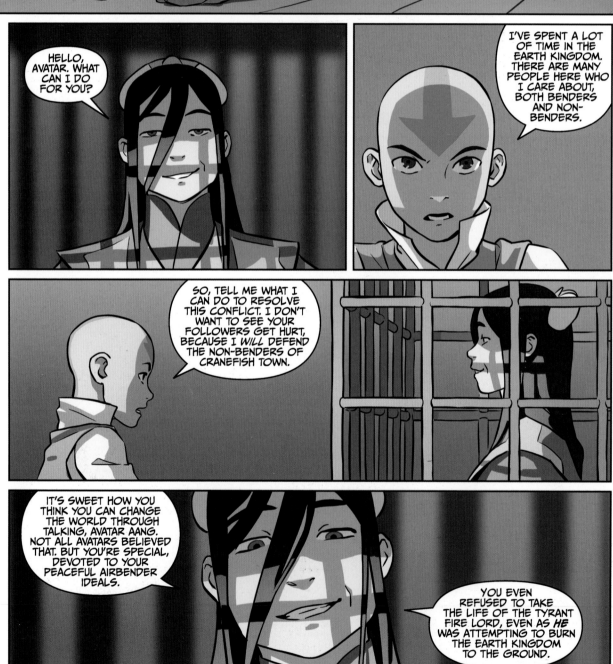

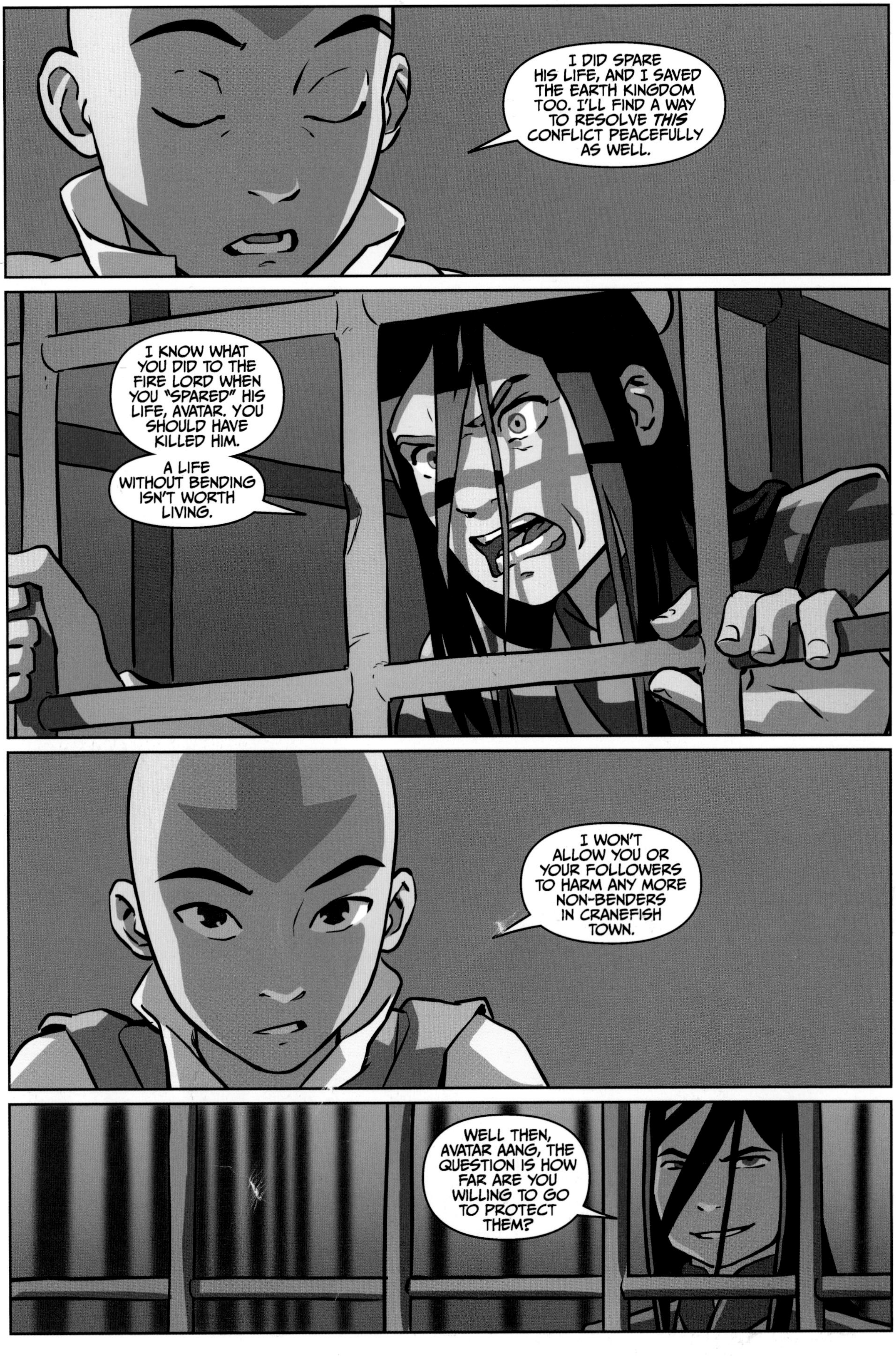
I DID SPARE HIS LIFE, AND I SAVED THE EARTH KINGDOM TOO. I'LL FIND A WAY TO RESOLVE *THIS* CONFLICT PEACEFULLY AS WELL.
I KNOW WHAT YOU DID TO THE FIRE LORD WHEN YOU "SPARED" HIS LIFE, AVATAR. YOU SHOULD HAVE KILLED HIM.
A LIFE WITHOUT BENDING ISN'T WORTH LIVING.
I WON'T ALLOW YOU OR YOUR FOLLOWERS TO HARM ANY MORE NON-BENDERS IN CRANEFISH TOWN.
WELL THEN, AVATAR AANG, THE QUESTION IS HOW FAR ARE YOU WILLING TO GO TO PROTECT THEM?

PW: *Yaling has one solution to all problems. She's a good foil for Toph in that way—I really like how Faith handles their arc (more on that later in this book).*

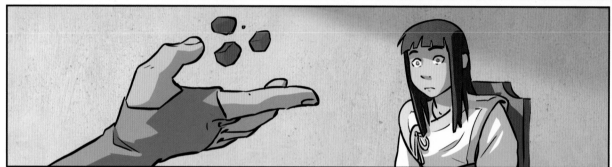

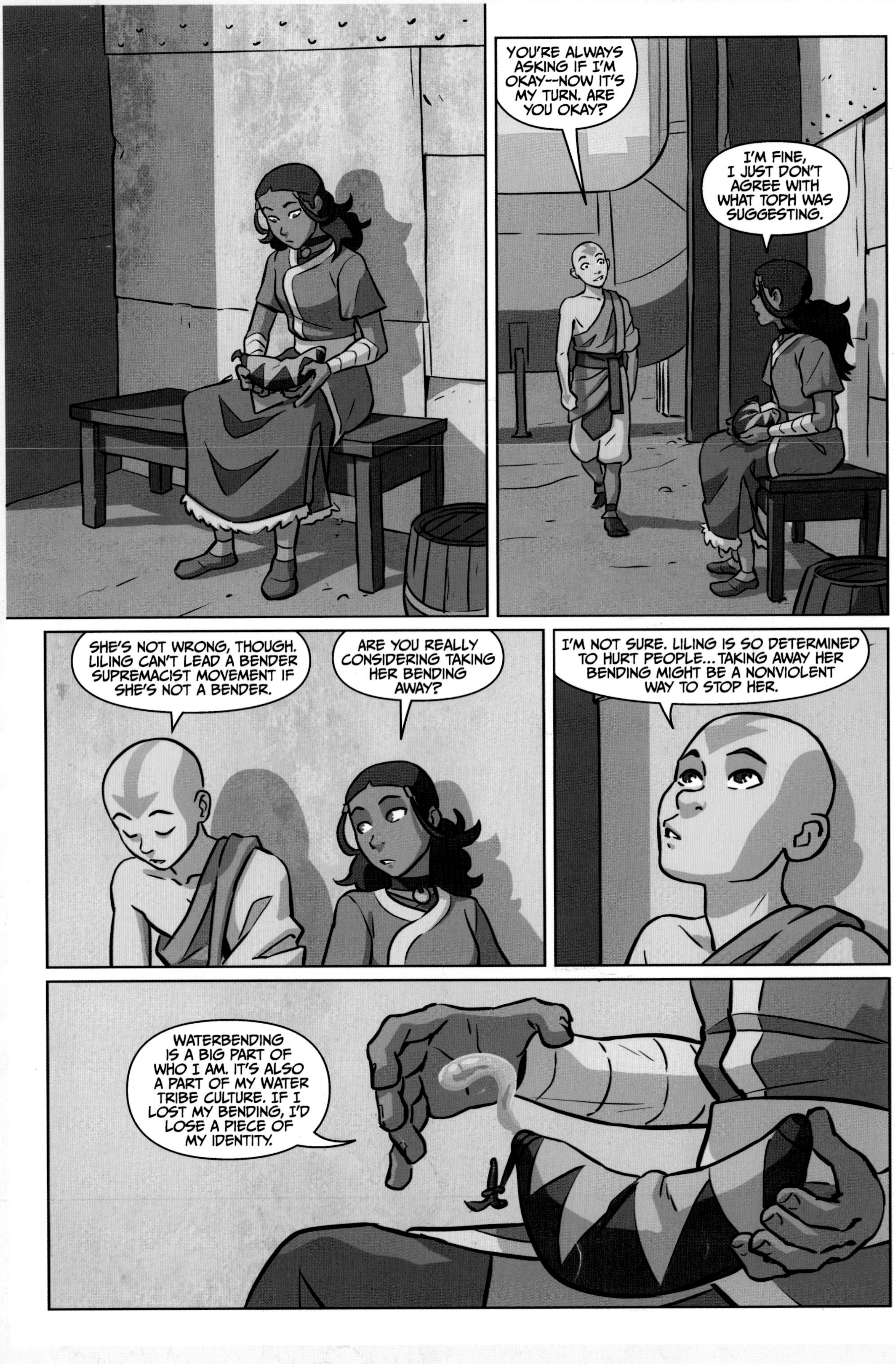
YOU'RE ALWAYS ASKING IF I'M OKAY--NOW IT'S MY TURN. ARE YOU OKAY?
I'M FINE, I JUST DON'T AGREE WITH WHAT TOPH WAS SUGGESTING.
SHE'S NOT WRONG, THOUGH. LILING CAN'T LEAD A BENDER SUPREMACIST MOVEMENT IF SHE'S NOT A BENDER.
ARE YOU REALLY CONSIDERING TAKING HER BENDING AWAY?
I'M NOT SURE. LILING IS SO DETERMINED TO HURT PEOPLE... TAKING AWAY HER BENDING MIGHT BE A NONVIOLENT WAY TO STOP HER.
WATERBENDING IS A BIG PART OF WHO I AM. IT'S ALSO A PART OF MY WATER TRIBE CULTURE. IF I LOST MY BENDING, I'D LOSE A PIECE OF MY IDENTITY.

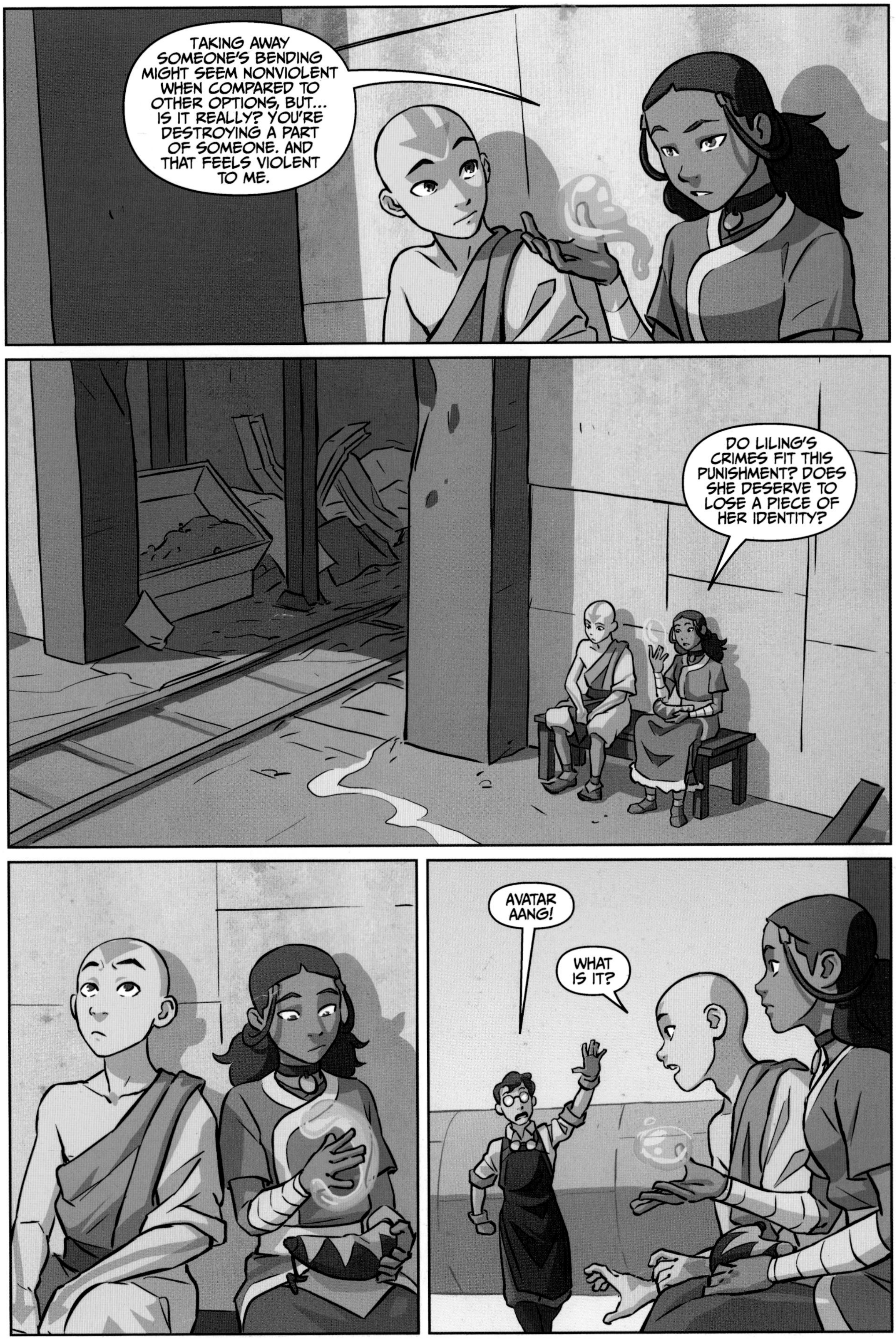
TAKING AWAY SOMEONE'S BENDING MIGHT SEEM NONVIOLENT WHEN COMPARED TO OTHER OPTIONS, BUT... IS IT REALLY? YOU'RE DESTROYING A PART OF SOMEONE. AND THAT FEELS VIOLENT TO ME.
DO LILING'S CRIMES FIT THIS PUNISHMENT? DOES SHE DESERVE TO LOSE A PIECE OF HER IDENTITY?
AVATAR AANG!
WHAT IS IT?

FEH: *A lot of Katara's thoughts on taking away someone's bending came from my reaction to Amon taking away Korra's bending in season one of* The Legend of Korra. *That moment felt incredibly violent to me. Even though Korra wasn't harmed physically, the loss of her bending must have felt like the loss of a limb.*

PW: *Everyone knows Toph is best.*

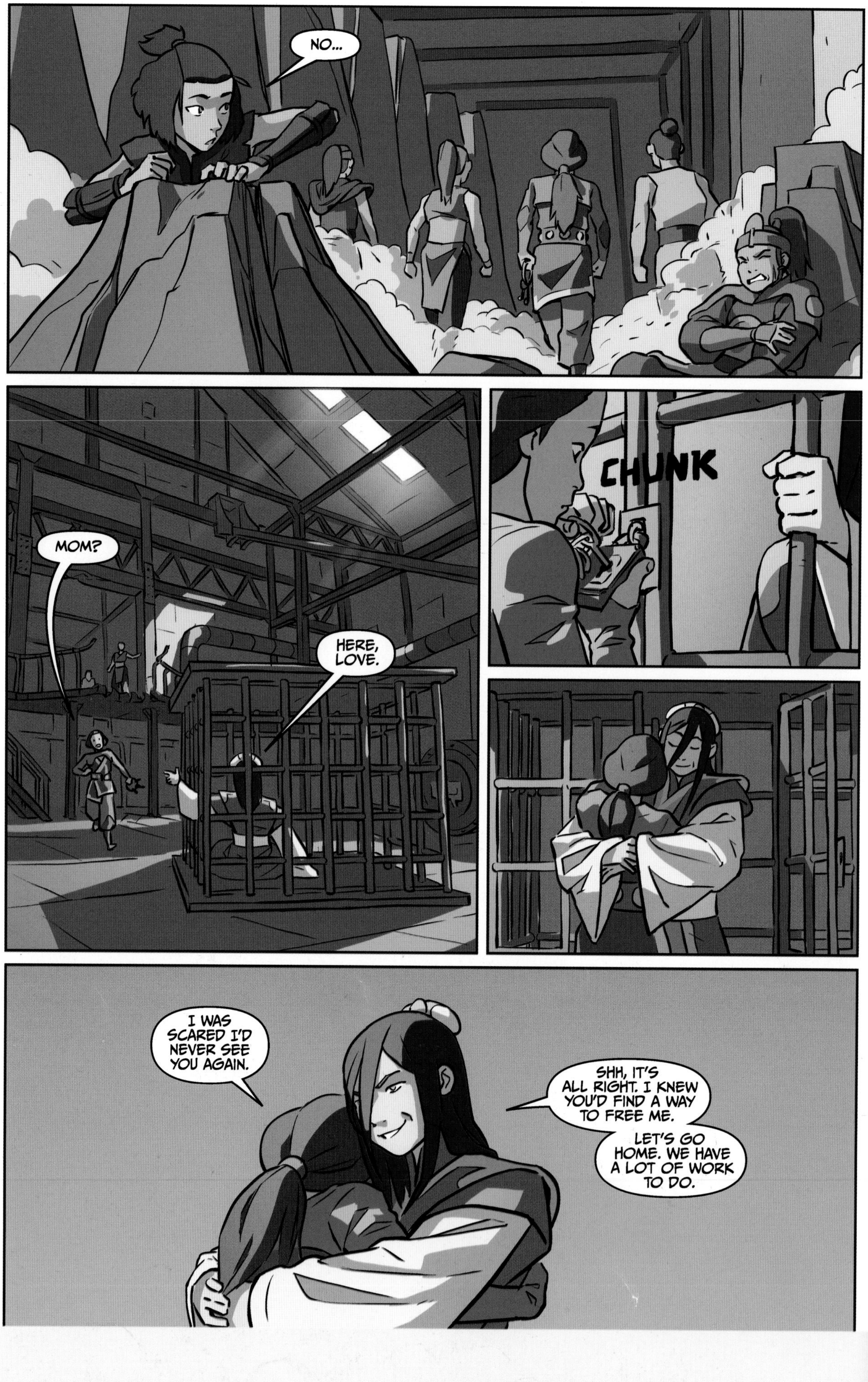
NO...
MOM?
HERE, LOVE.
CHUNK
I WAS SCARED I'D NEVER SEE YOU AGAIN.
SHH, IT'S ALL RIGHT. I KNEW YOU'D FIND A WAY TO FREE ME.
LET'S GO HOME. WE HAVE A LOT OF WORK TO DO.

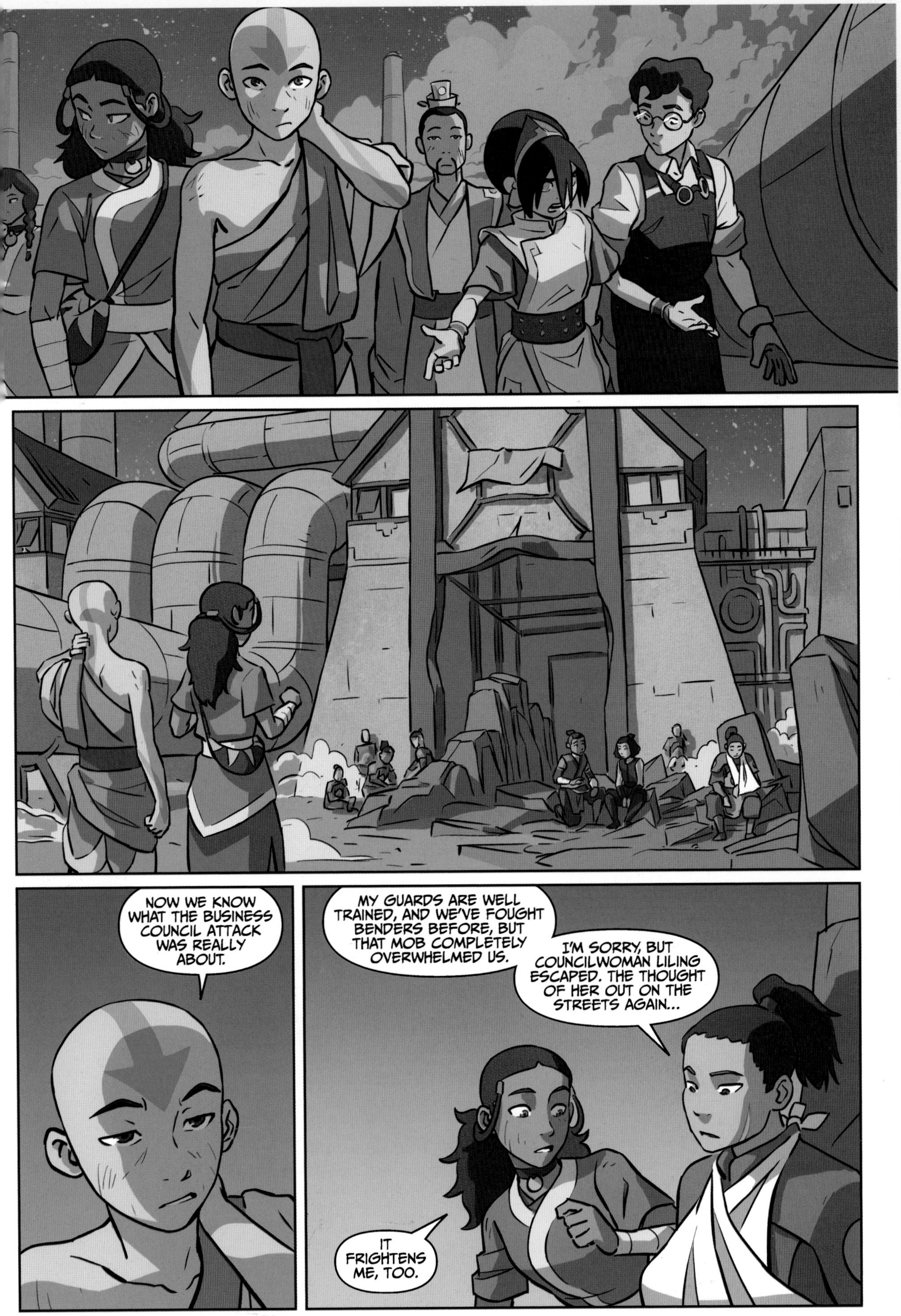
NOW WE KNOW WHAT THE BUSINESS COUNCIL ATTACK WAS REALLY ABOUT.
MY GUARDS ARE WELL TRAINED, AND WE'VE FOUGHT BENDERS BEFORE, BUT THAT MOB COMPLETELY OVERWHELMED US.
I'M SORRY, BUT COUNCILWOMAN LILING ESCAPED. THE THOUGHT OF HER OUT ON THE STREETS AGAIN...
IT FRIGHTENS ME, TOO.

PW: *This factory really goes through a lot.*

AANG ASKED THE COUNCIL MEMBERS TO STAY AT THE FACTORY, WHERE WE CAN PROTECT THEM. BUT AS LONG AS LILING AND HER FOLLOWERS ARE FREE, EVERY NON-BENDER IN THE CITY IS IN DANGER.

FEH: *Another nod to* The Legend of Korra. *In Aang's time, the ability to chi-block was quite rare. But in Korra's time it was a weapon wielded by many Equalists. Teaching that particular skill must have spread more widely as Team Avatar got older. I assume Suki learned chi-blocking from Ty Lee, who joined the Kyoshi Warriors after the events of the TV show.*

SHE ALWAYS SEEMS TO BE ONE STEP AHEAD OF US. IT'S FRUSTRATING, I FEEL LIKE WE NEED TO BE DOING MORE.

AT LEAST I CAN HEAL YOUR ARM.

THANK YOU.

THERE'S SOMETHING I WANTED TO ASK...

WHAT IS IT?

YOUR FRIEND, THE KYOSHI WARRIOR, DO YOU THINK SHE'D TEACH MY OFFICERS HOW TO CHI-BLOCK?

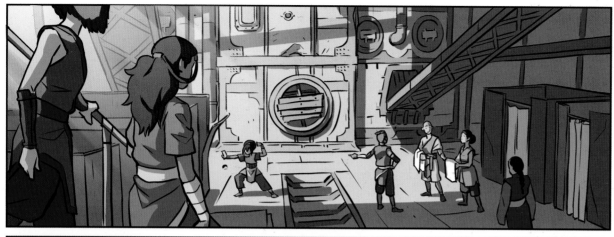

AANG, SUKI AND I HAVE BEEN TALKING.

WE WANT TO BE READY THE NEXT TIME LILING'S FOLLOWERS ATTACK.

I'M GOING TO TEACH LAO'S SECURITY GUARDS HOW TO CHI-BLOCK.

THAT'S A GREAT IDEA! YOU'RE SO SMART, SUKI. AND TALENTED! EVERYTHING YOU DO IS AMAZING.

HOW FAST COULD THEY LEARN? WE DON'T KNOW WHEN LILING WILL ATTACK AGAIN. IT COULD BE SOON.

IT'LL TAKE A WHILE, MAYBE MORE TIME THAN WE HAVE. BUT THE SECURITY GUARDS ARE ALREADY WELL-TRAINED FIGHTERS. I CAN AT LEAST START TO TEACH THEM THE BASICS.

OKAY. WE'LL NEED ALL THE HELP WE CAN GET.

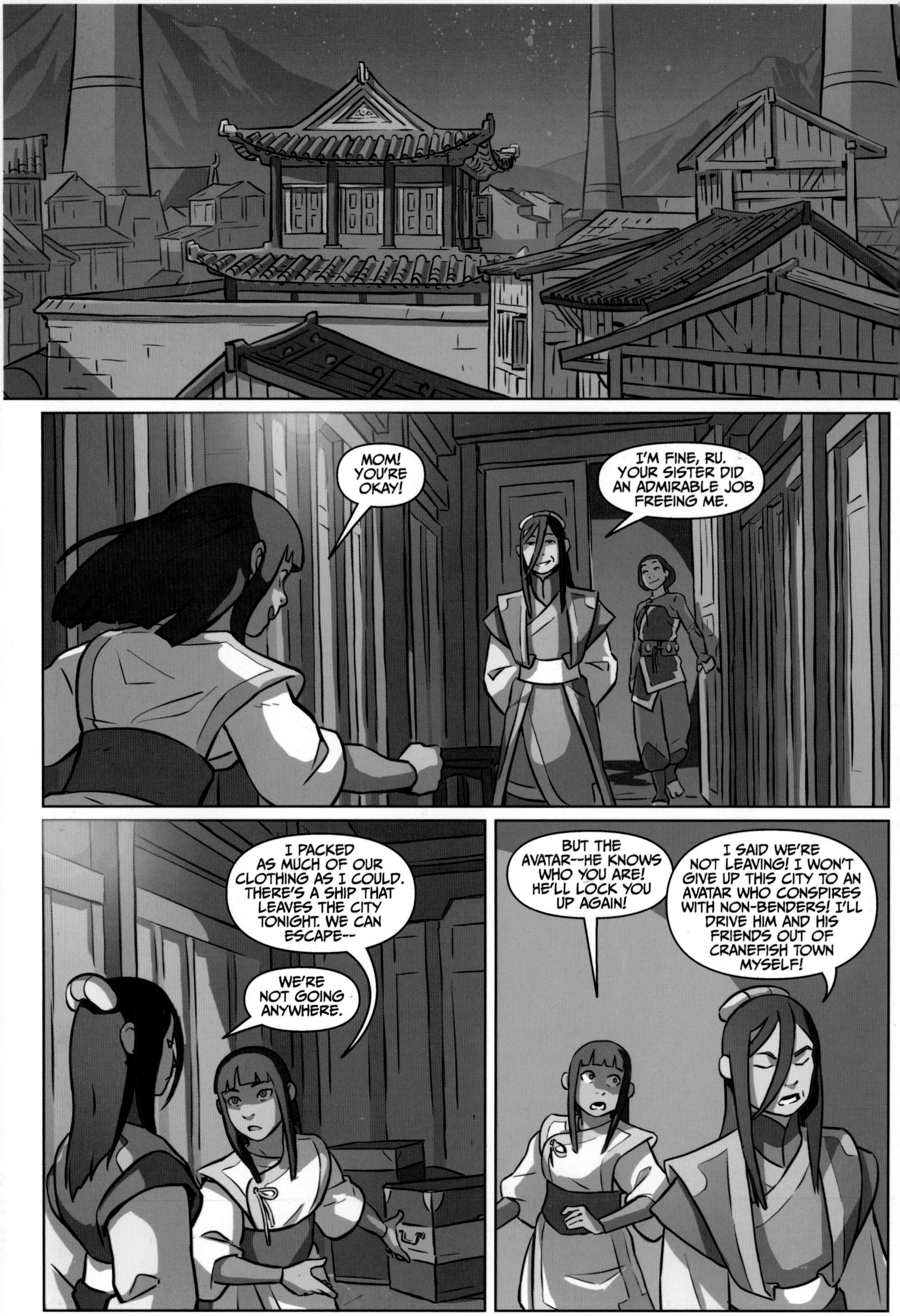
MOM! YOU'RE OKAY!
I'M FINE, RU. YOUR SISTER DID AN ADMIRABLE JOB FREEING ME.
I PACKED AS MUCH OF OUR CLOTHING AS I COULD. THERE'S A SHIP THAT LEAVES THE CITY TONIGHT. WE CAN ESCAPE--
WE'RE NOT GOING ANYWHERE.
BUT THE AVATAR--HE KNOWS WHO YOU ARE! HE'LL LOCK YOU UP AGAIN!
I SAID WE'RE NOT LEAVING! I WON'T GIVE UP THIS CITY TO AN AVATAR WHO CONSPIRES WITH NON-BENDERS! I'LL DRIVE HIM AND HIS FRIENDS OUT OF CRANEFISH TOWN MYSELF!

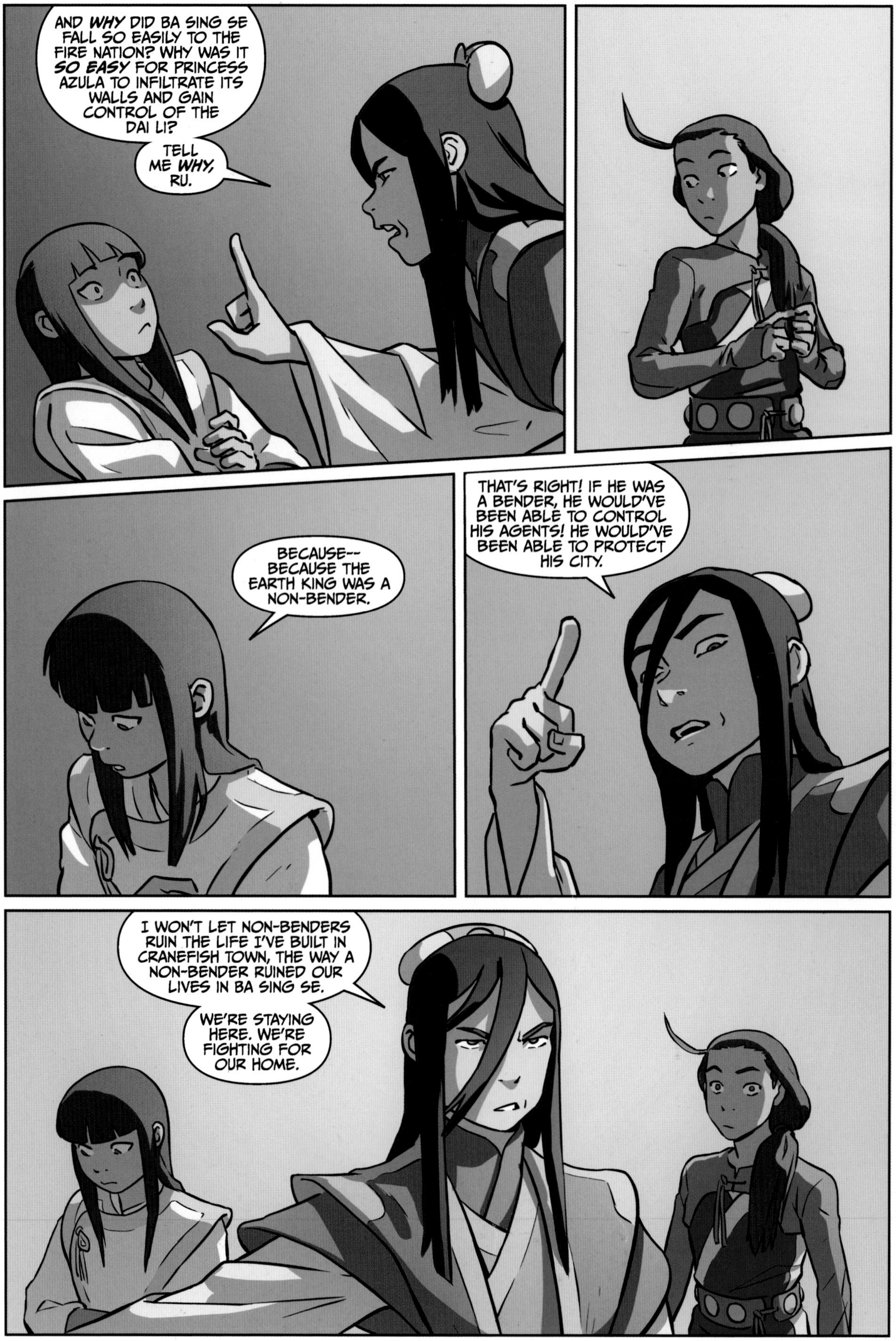
AND WHY DID BA SING SE FALL SO EASILY TO THE FIRE NATION? WHY WAS IT SO EASY FOR PRINCESS AZULA TO INFILTRATE ITS WALLS AND GAIN CONTROL OF THE DAI LI?
TELL ME WHY, RU.
BECAUSE-- BECAUSE THE EARTH KING WAS A NON-BENDER.
THAT'S RIGHT! IF HE WAS A BENDER, HE WOULD'VE BEEN ABLE TO CONTROL HIS AGENTS! HE WOULD'VE BEEN ABLE TO PROTECT HIS CITY.
I WON'T LET NON-BENDERS RUIN THE LIFE I'VE BUILT IN CRANEFISH TOWN, THE WAY A NON-BENDER RUINED OUR LIVES IN BA SING SE.
WE'RE STAYING HERE. WE'RE FIGHTING FOR OUR HOME.

FEH: *Ru finally stands up for herself. I love the emotion on her face here.*

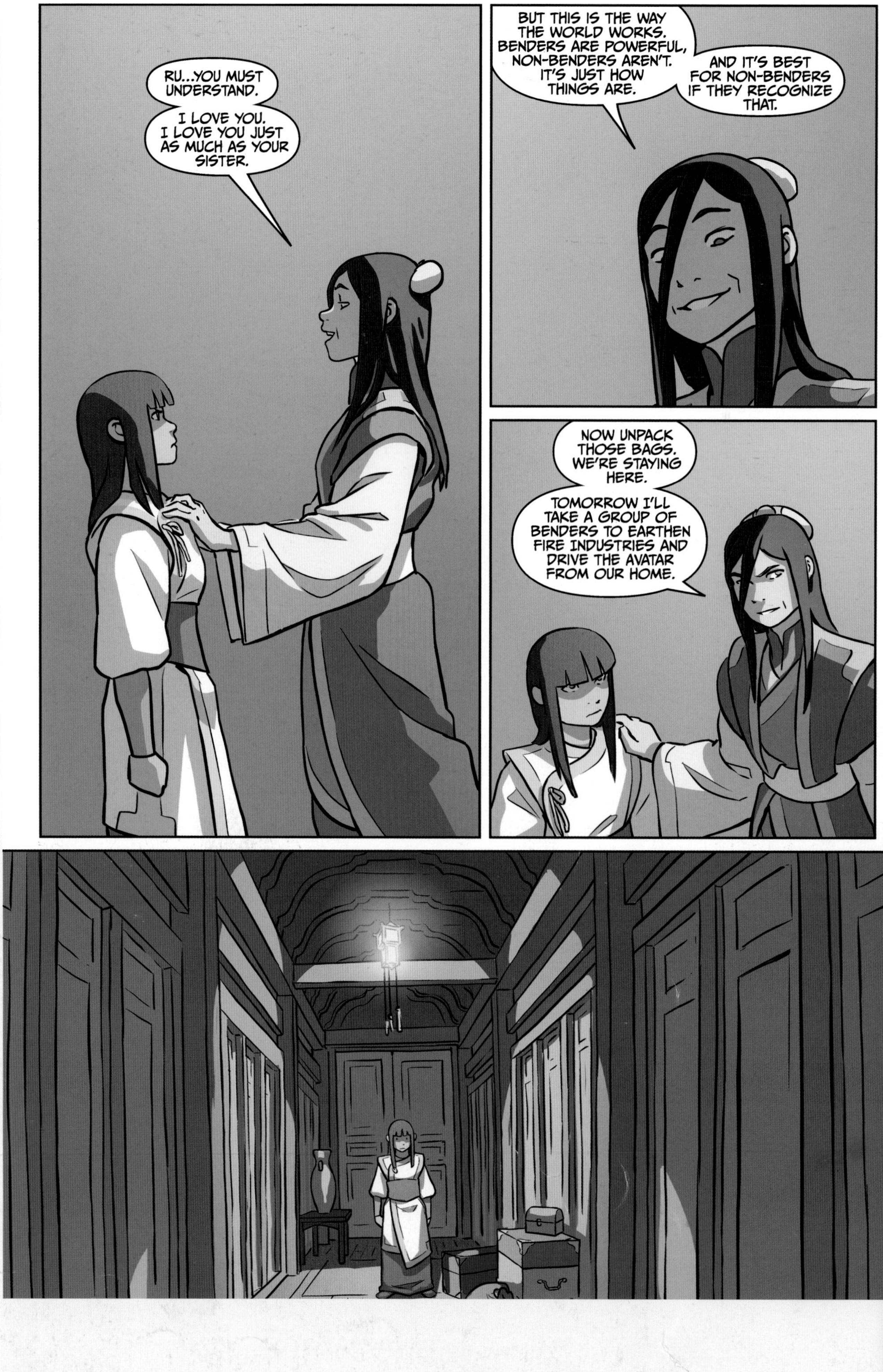
RU...YOU MUST UNDERSTAND.
I LOVE YOU. I LOVE YOU JUST AS MUCH AS YOUR SISTER.
BUT THIS IS THE WAY THE WORLD WORKS. BENDERS ARE POWERFUL, NON-BENDERS AREN'T. IT'S JUST HOW THINGS ARE.
AND IT'S BEST FOR NON-BENDERS IF THEY RECOGNIZE THAT.
NOW UNPACK THOSE BAGS. WE'RE STAYING HERE.
TOMORROW I'LL TAKE A GROUP OF BENDERS TO EARTHEN FIRE INDUSTRIES AND DRIVE THE AVATAR FROM OUR HOME.

PW: *Poor Ru. I really tried to make her look lost and alone in this panel, and I'm really happy with how Adele brought the colors together here.*

IF I'D DONE WHAT TOPH SAID AND TAKEN AWAY LILING'S BENDING WHEN WE'D CAPTURED HER, EVERYTHING MIGHT BE OVER BY NOW.

THIS BENDER SUPREMACIST MOVEMENT IS MORE THAN ONE PERSON. REMEMBER ALL THE BENDERS WE SAW AT THAT UNDERGROUND RALLY? SOME OF THEM WERE EVEN ON THE BUSINESS COUNCIL.

PW: It was fun having Aang and Sokka emote in this scene—especially because Sokka is serious for most of it, a side of him we don't always get to see. I'm really happy Faith gave boomerang guy so much time in this comic.

ARE YOU WILLING TO TAKE AWAY THE BENDING OF ALL LILING'S FOLLOWERS, TOO?

ARGH! NO, OF COURSE NOT.

ALL OF THIS... THE POLLUTION, THE TENSION BETWEEN BENDERS AND NON-BENDERS, IT STARTED WITH THE FACTORY MACHINES.

IT'S THE SAME AS WHEN THE FIRE NATION ATTACKED THE OTHER NATIONS USING TANKS AND STEAM SHIPS. THEY NEVER WOULD'VE GONE TO WAR IF THEY DIDN'T HAVE THAT TECHNOLOGY.

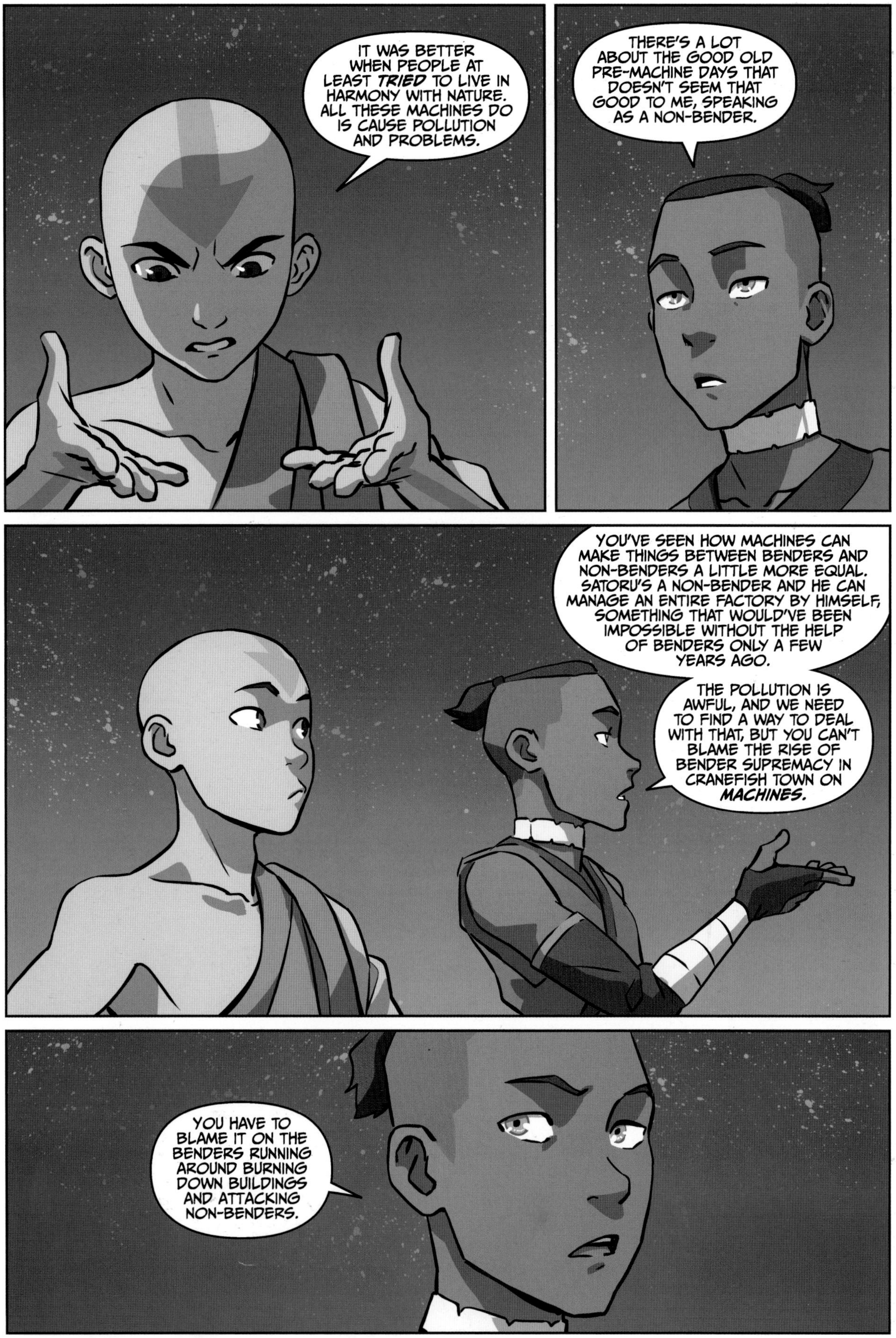
IT WAS BETTER WHEN PEOPLE AT LEAST *TRIED* TO LIVE IN HARMONY WITH NATURE. ALL THESE MACHINES DO IS CAUSE POLLUTION AND PROBLEMS.
THERE'S A LOT ABOUT THE GOOD OLD PRE-MACHINE DAYS THAT DOESN'T SEEM THAT GOOD TO ME, SPEAKING AS A NON-BENDER.
YOU'VE SEEN HOW MACHINES CAN MAKE THINGS BETWEEN BENDERS AND NON-BENDERS A LITTLE MORE EQUAL. SATORU'S A NON-BENDER AND HE CAN MANAGE AN ENTIRE FACTORY BY HIMSELF, SOMETHING THAT WOULD'VE BEEN IMPOSSIBLE WITHOUT THE HELP OF BENDERS ONLY A FEW YEARS AGO.
THE POLLUTION IS AWFUL, AND WE NEED TO FIND A WAY TO DEAL WITH THAT, BUT YOU CAN'T BLAME THE RISE OF BENDER SUPREMACY IN CRANEFISH TOWN ON *MACHINES.*
YOU HAVE TO BLAME IT ON THE BENDERS RUNNING AROUND BURNING DOWN BUILDINGS AND ATTACKING NON-BENDERS.

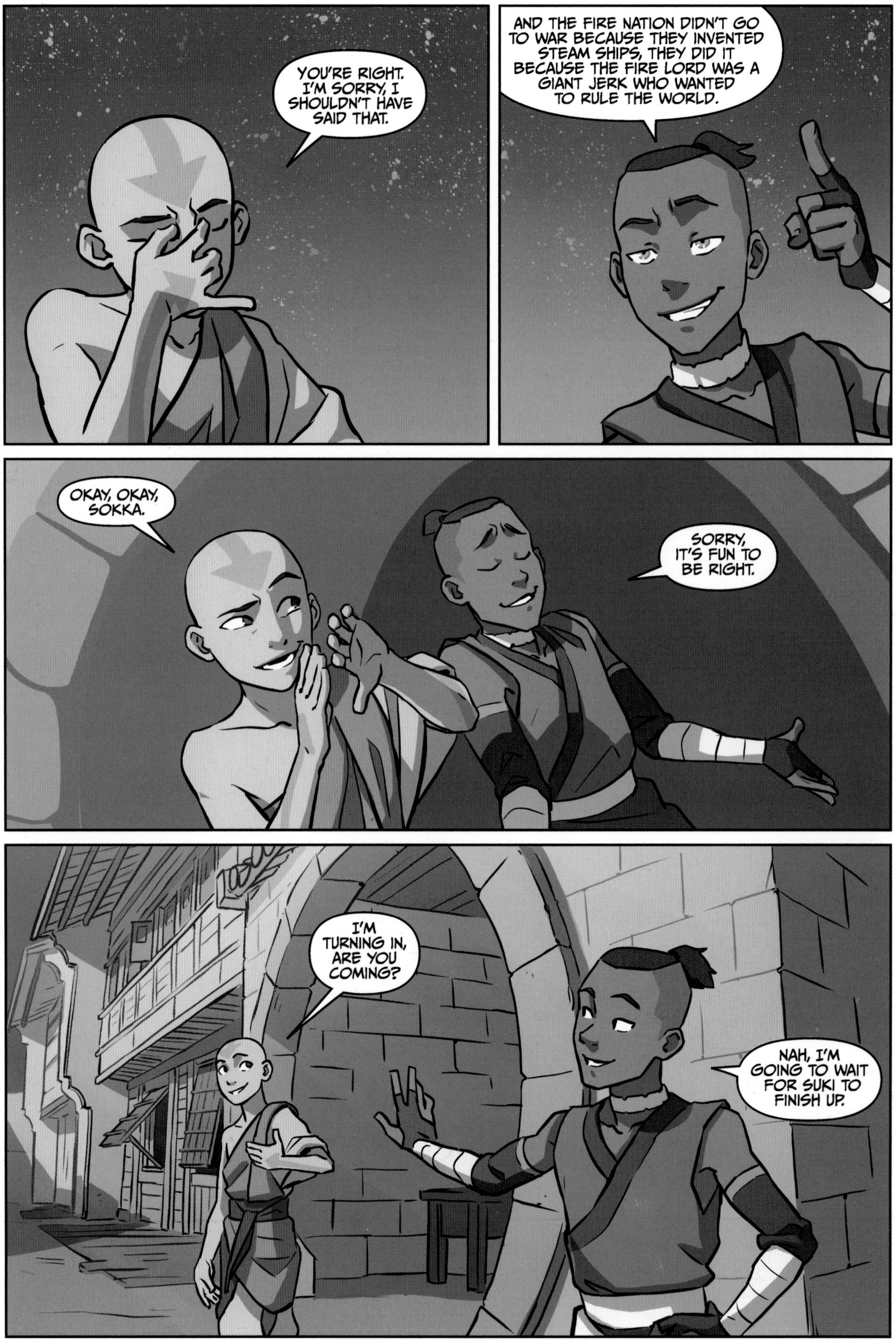
YOU'RE RIGHT. I'M SORRY, I SHOULDN'T HAVE SAID THAT.
AND THE FIRE NATION DIDN'T GO TO WAR BECAUSE THEY INVENTED STEAM SHIPS, THEY DID IT BECAUSE THE FIRE LORD WAS A GIANT JERK WHO WANTED TO RULE THE WORLD.
OKAY, OKAY, SOKKA.
SORRY, IT'S FUN TO BE RIGHT.
I'M TURNING IN, ARE YOU COMING?
NAH, I'M GOING TO WAIT FOR SUKI TO FINISH UP.

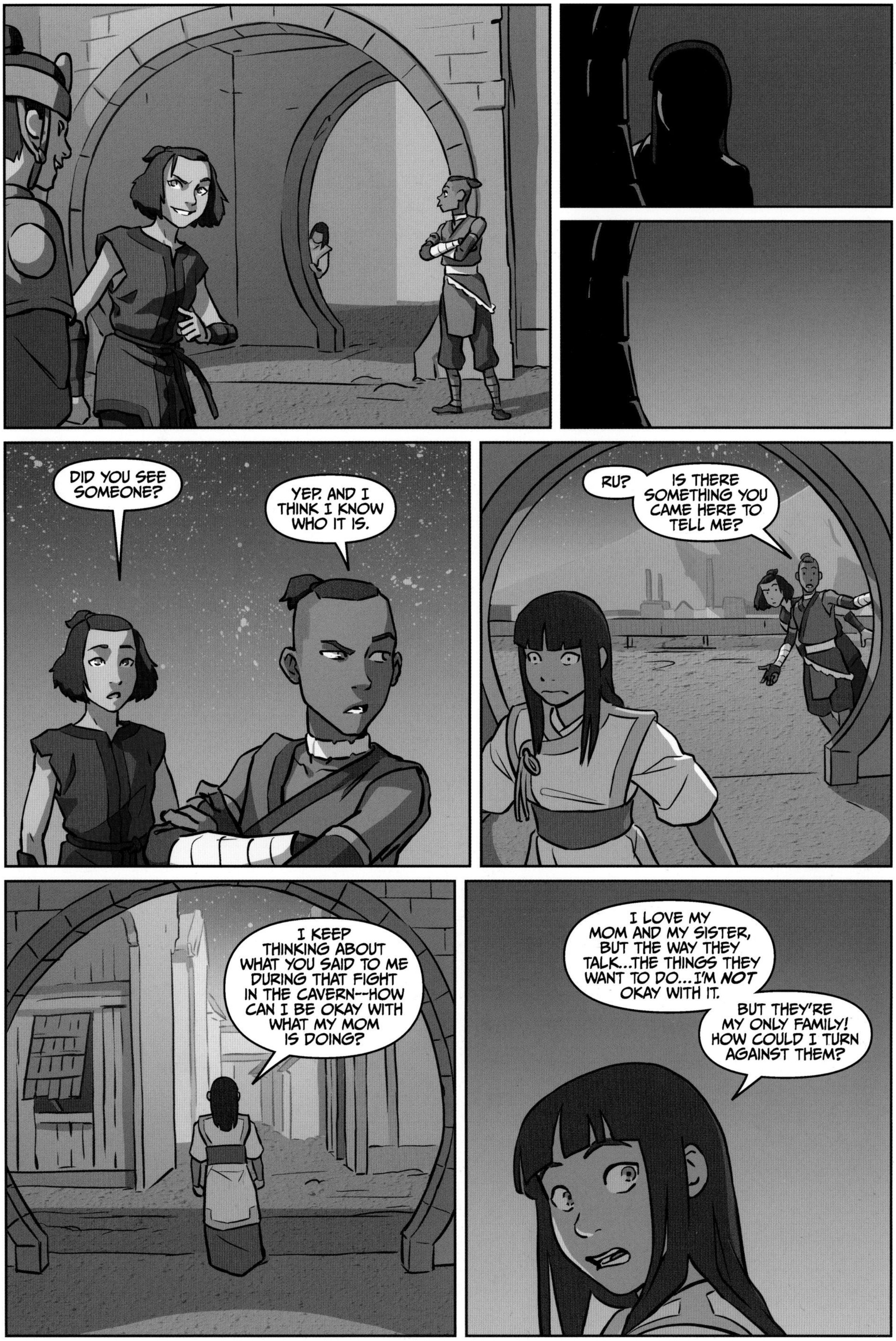
DID YOU SEE SOMEONE?
YEP. AND I THINK I KNOW WHO IT IS.
RU?
IS THERE SOMETHING YOU CAME HERE TO TELL ME?
I KEEP THINKING ABOUT WHAT YOU SAID TO ME DURING THAT FIGHT IN THE CAVERN--HOW CAN I BE OKAY WITH WHAT MY MOM IS DOING?
I LOVE MY MOM AND MY SISTER, BUT THE WAY THEY TALK...THE THINGS THEY WANT TO DO...I'M ***NOT*** OKAY WITH IT.
BUT THEY'RE MY ONLY FAMILY! HOW COULD I TURN AGAINST THEM?

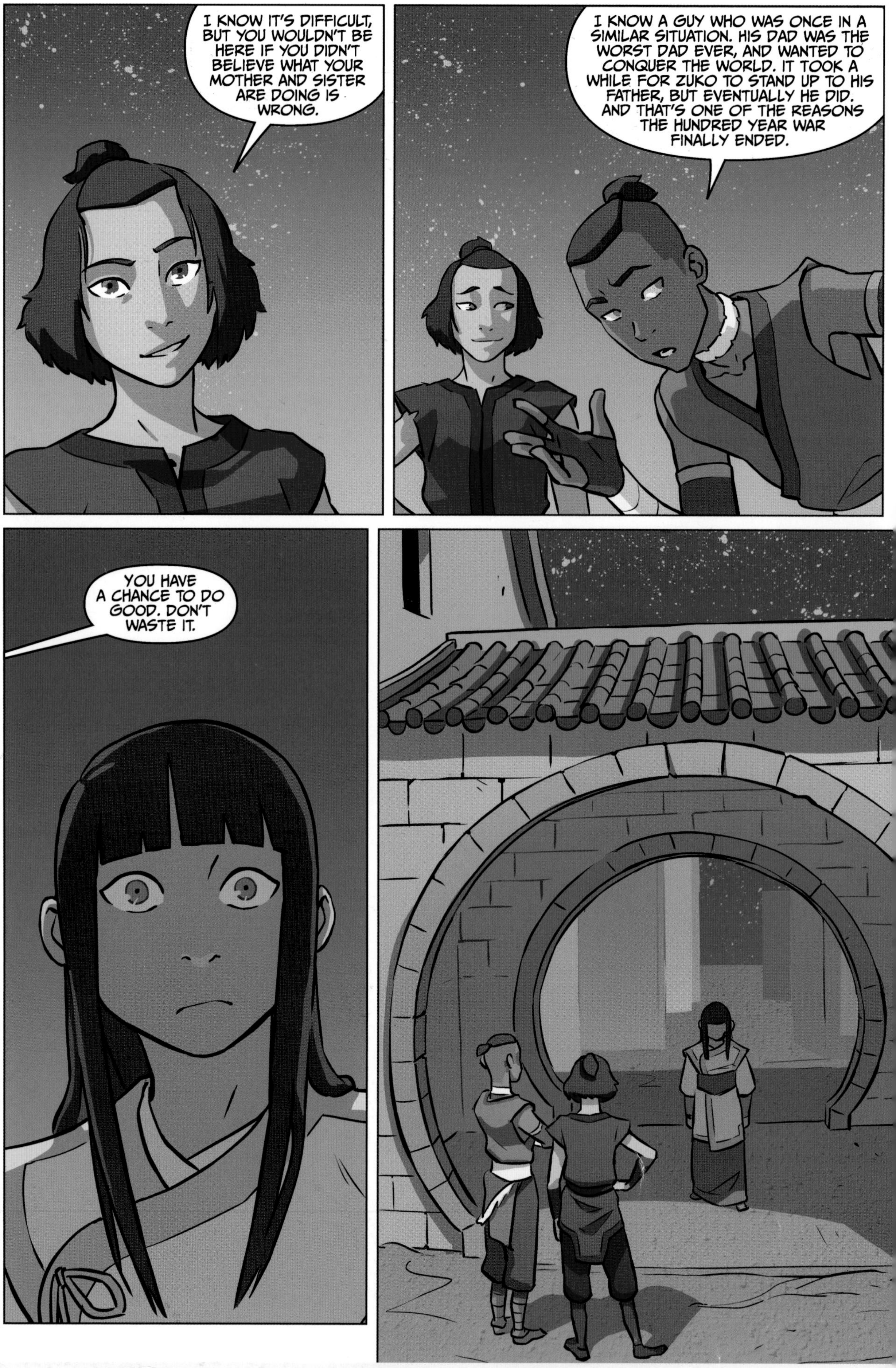
I KNOW IT'S DIFFICULT, BUT YOU WOULDN'T BE HERE IF YOU DIDN'T BELIEVE WHAT YOUR MOTHER AND SISTER ARE DOING IS WRONG.
I KNOW A GUY WHO WAS ONCE IN A SIMILAR SITUATION. HIS DAD WAS THE WORST DAD EVER, AND WANTED TO CONQUER THE WORLD. IT TOOK A WHILE FOR ZUKO TO STAND UP TO HIS FATHER, BUT EVENTUALLY HE DID. AND THAT'S ONE OF THE REASONS THE HUNDRED YEAR WAR FINALLY ENDED.
YOU HAVE A CHANCE TO DO GOOD. DON'T WASTE IT.

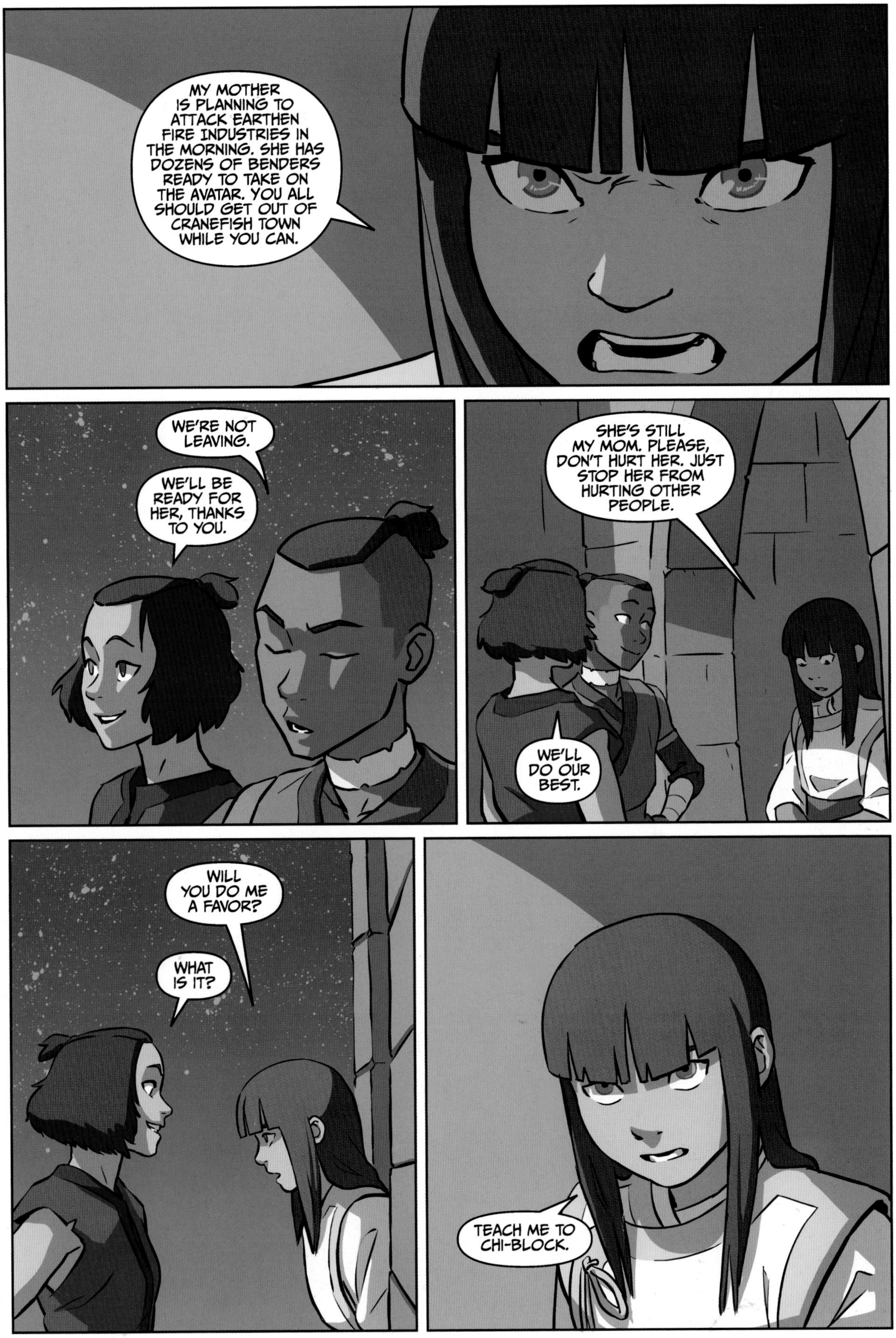
MY MOTHER IS PLANNING TO ATTACK EARTHEN FIRE INDUSTRIES IN THE MORNING. SHE HAS DOZENS OF BENDERS READY TO TAKE ON THE AVATAR. YOU ALL SHOULD GET OUT OF CRANEFISH TOWN WHILE YOU CAN.
WE'RE NOT LEAVING.
WE'LL BE READY FOR HER, THANKS TO YOU.
SHE'S STILL MY MOM. PLEASE, DON'T HURT HER. JUST STOP HER FROM HURTING OTHER PEOPLE.
WE'LL DO OUR BEST.
WILL YOU DO ME A FAVOR?
WHAT IS IT?
TEACH ME TO CHI-BLOCK.

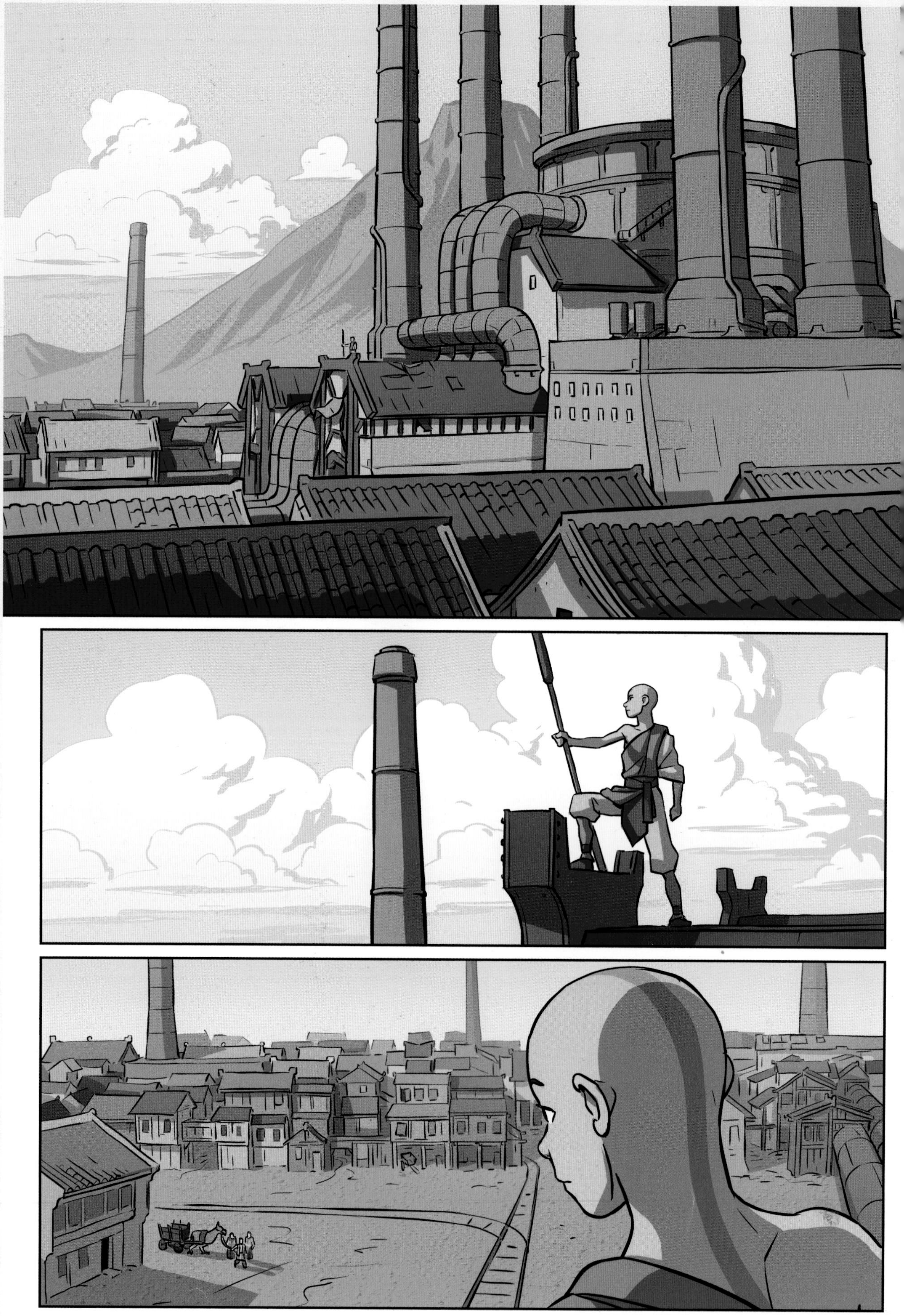

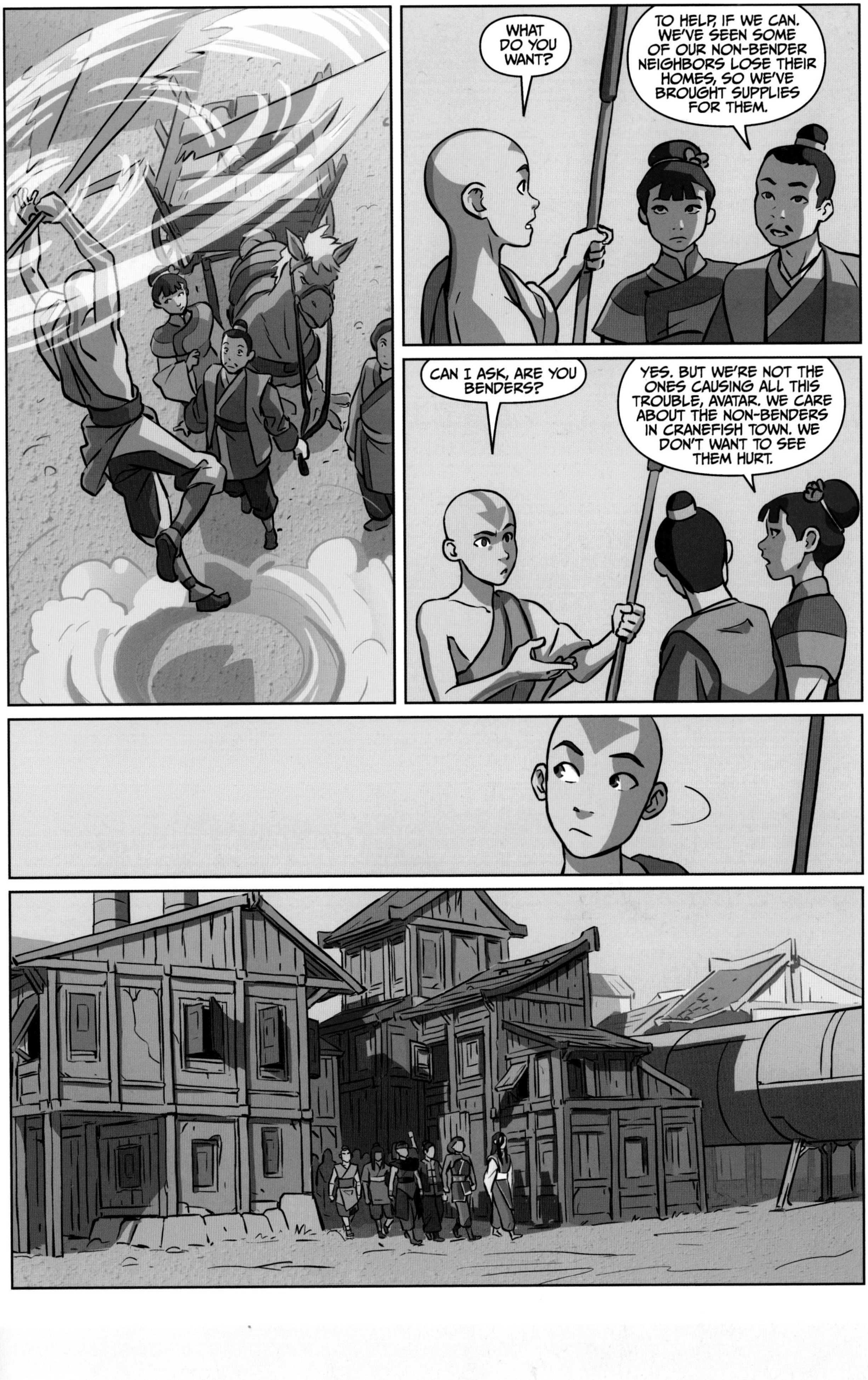
WHAT DO YOU WANT?
TO HELP, IF WE CAN. WE'VE SEEN SOME OF OUR NON-BENDER NEIGHBORS LOSE THEIR HOMES, SO WE'VE BROUGHT SUPPLIES FOR THEM.
CAN I ASK, ARE YOU BENDERS?
YES. BUT WE'RE NOT THE ONES CAUSING ALL THIS TROUBLE, AVATAR. WE CARE ABOUT THE NON-BENDERS IN CRANEFISH TOWN. WE DON'T WANT TO SEE THEM HURT.

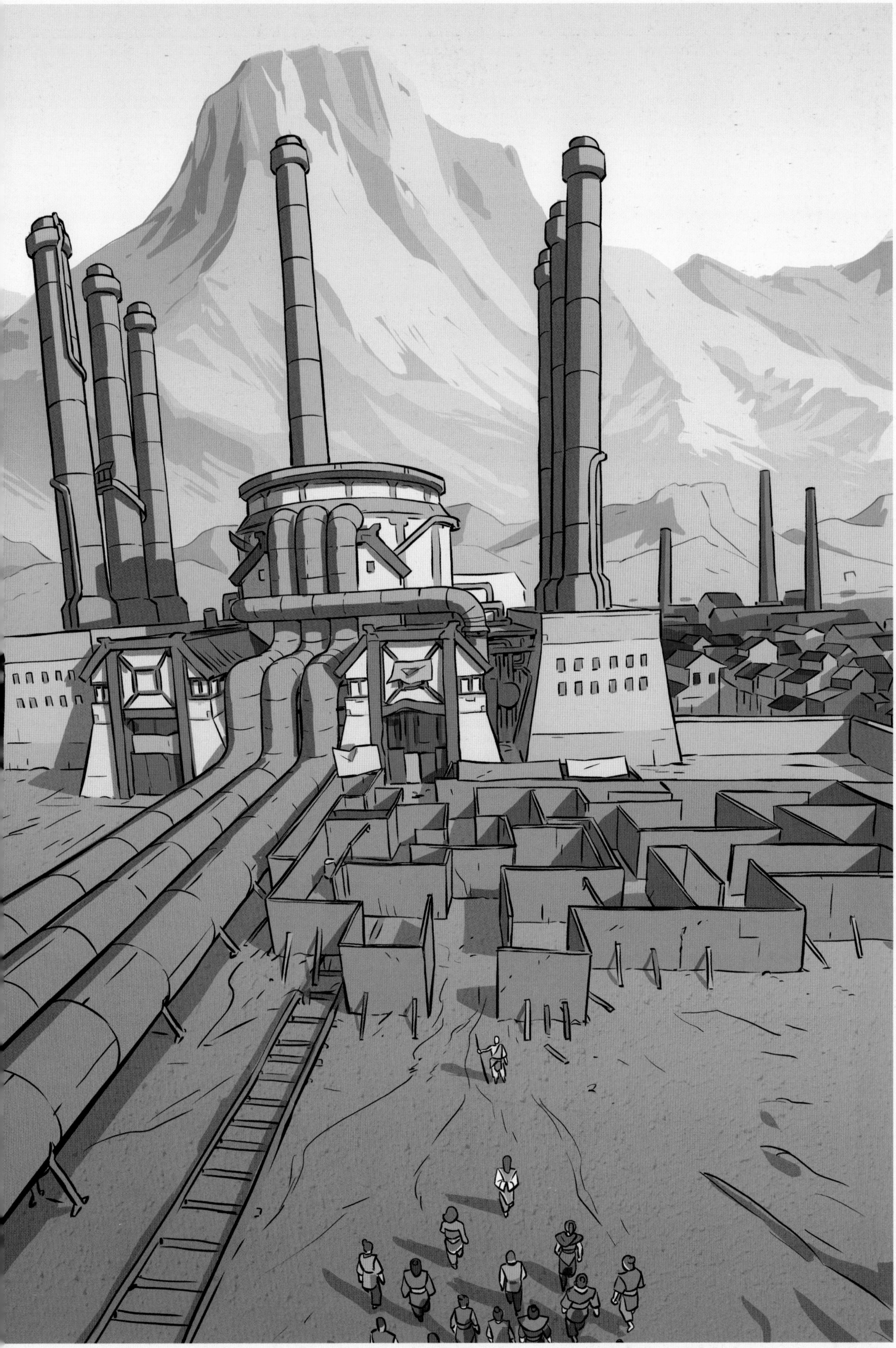

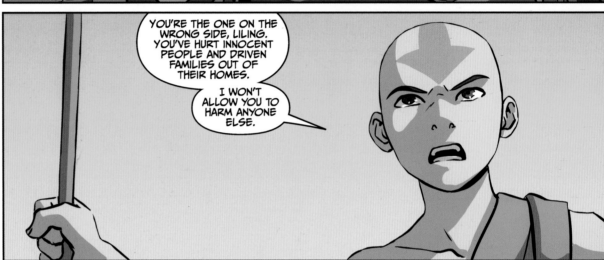

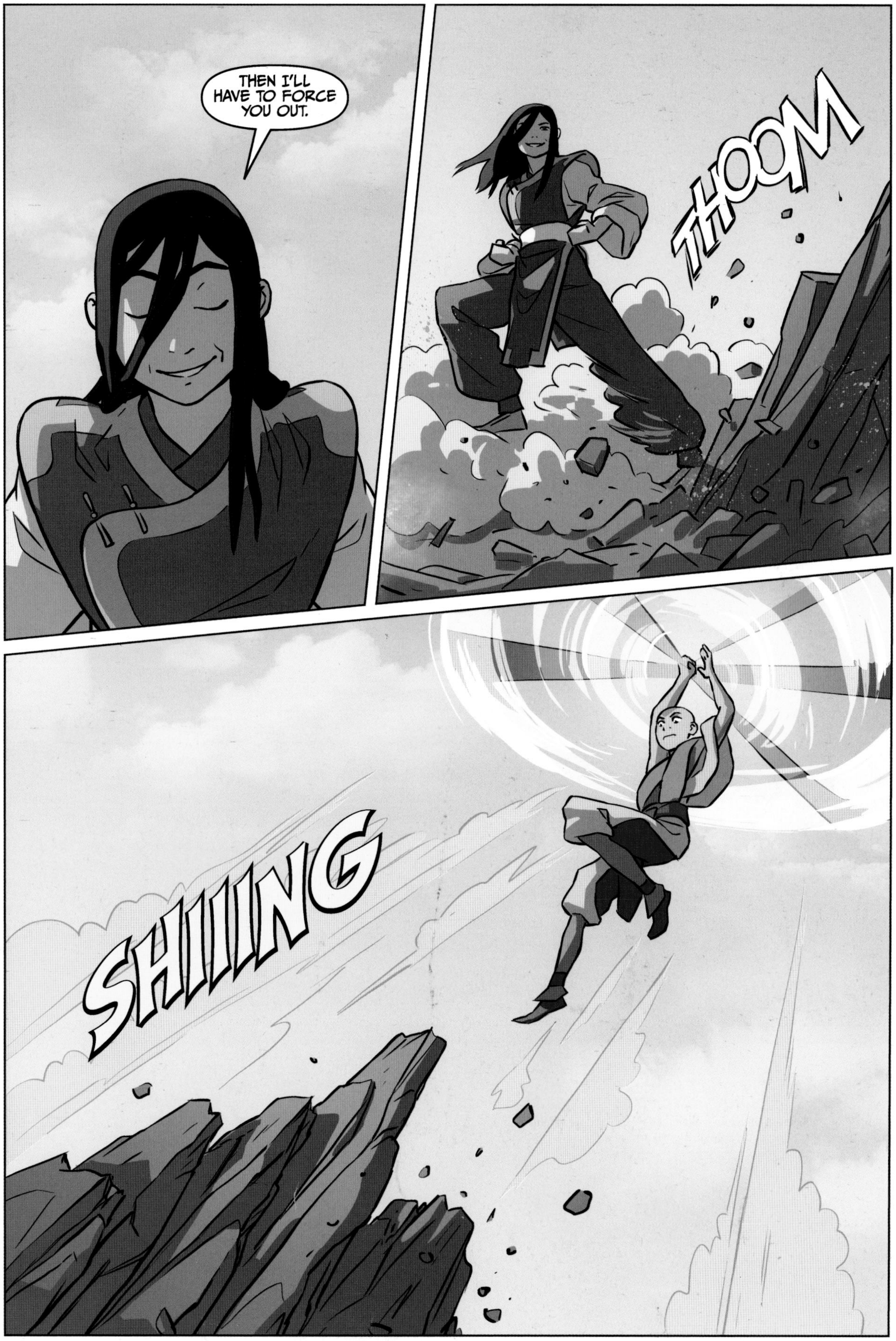
THEN I'LL HAVE TO FORCE YOU OUT.
THOOM
SHIIING

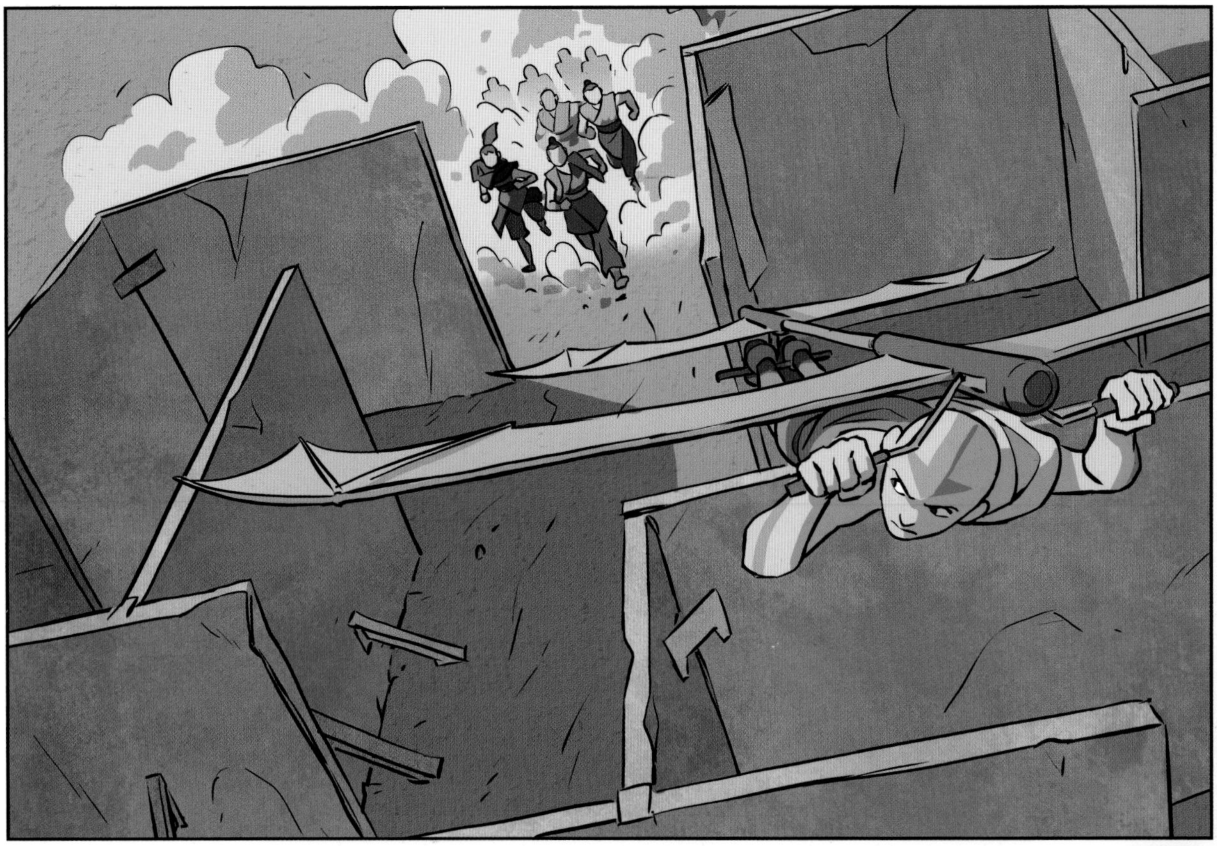

PW: *Drawing Aang on his glider is so hard.*

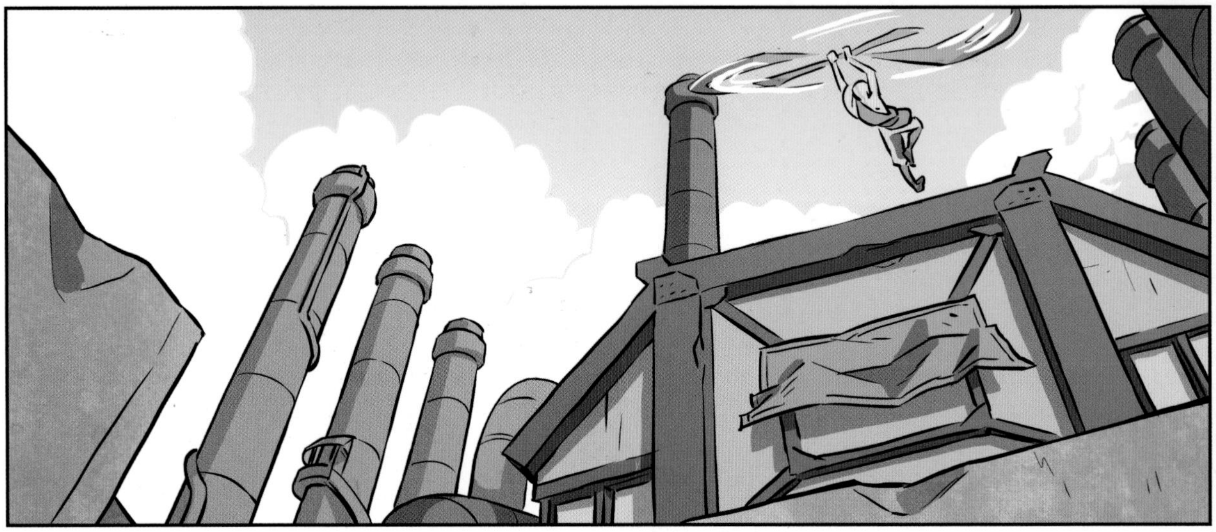

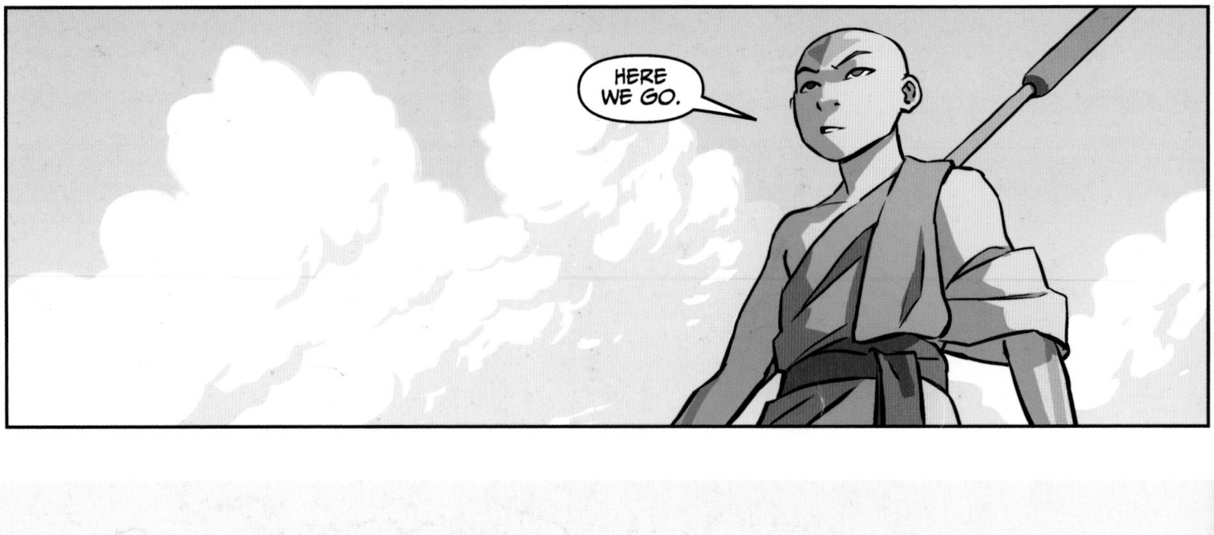
HERE WE GO.

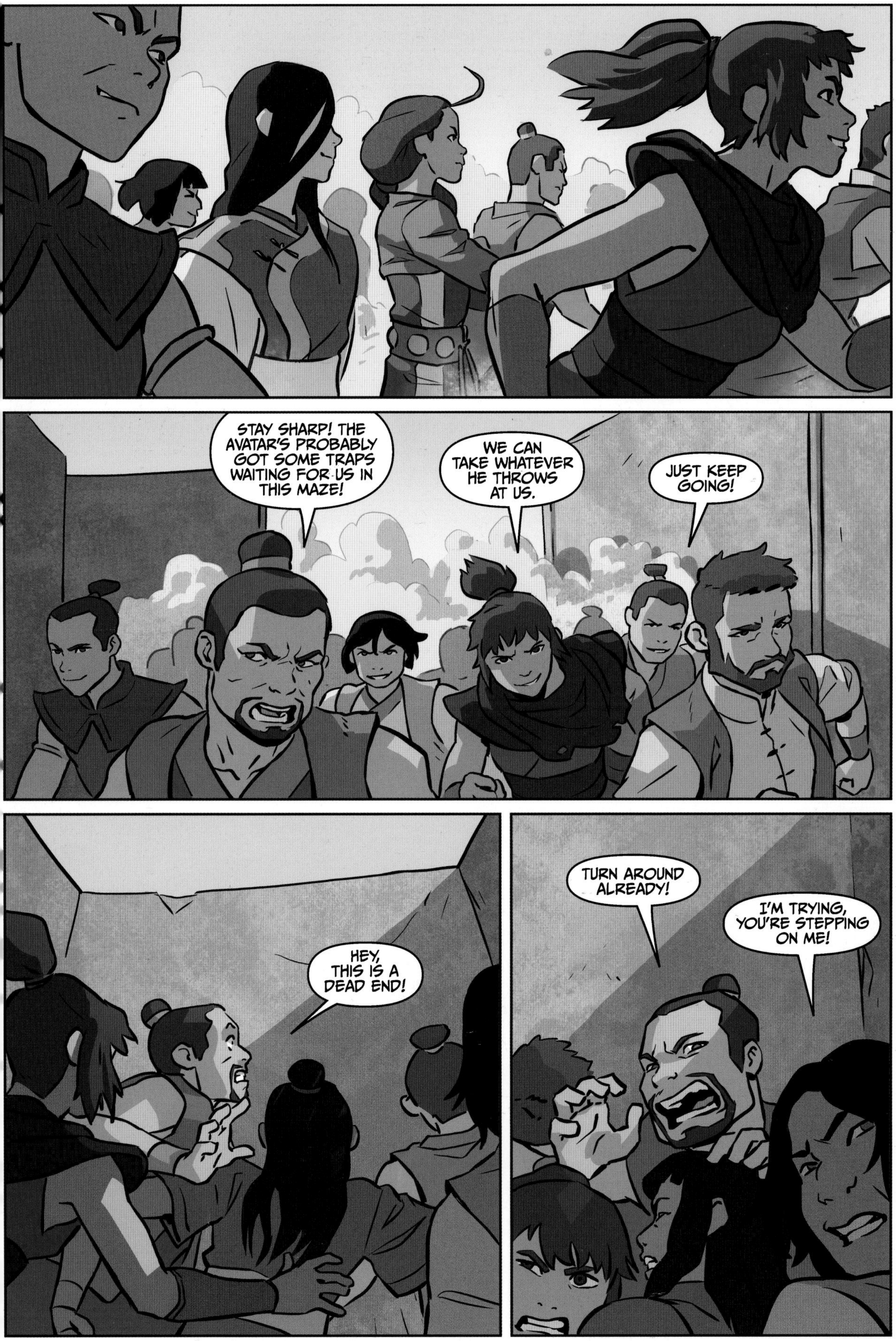
STAY SHARP! THE AVATAR'S PROBABLY GOT SOME TRAPS WAITING FOR US IN THIS MAZE!
WE CAN TAKE WHATEVER HE THROWS AT US.
JUST KEEP GOING!
HEY, THIS IS A DEAD END!
TURN AROUND ALREADY!
I'M TRYING, YOU'RE STEPPING ON ME!

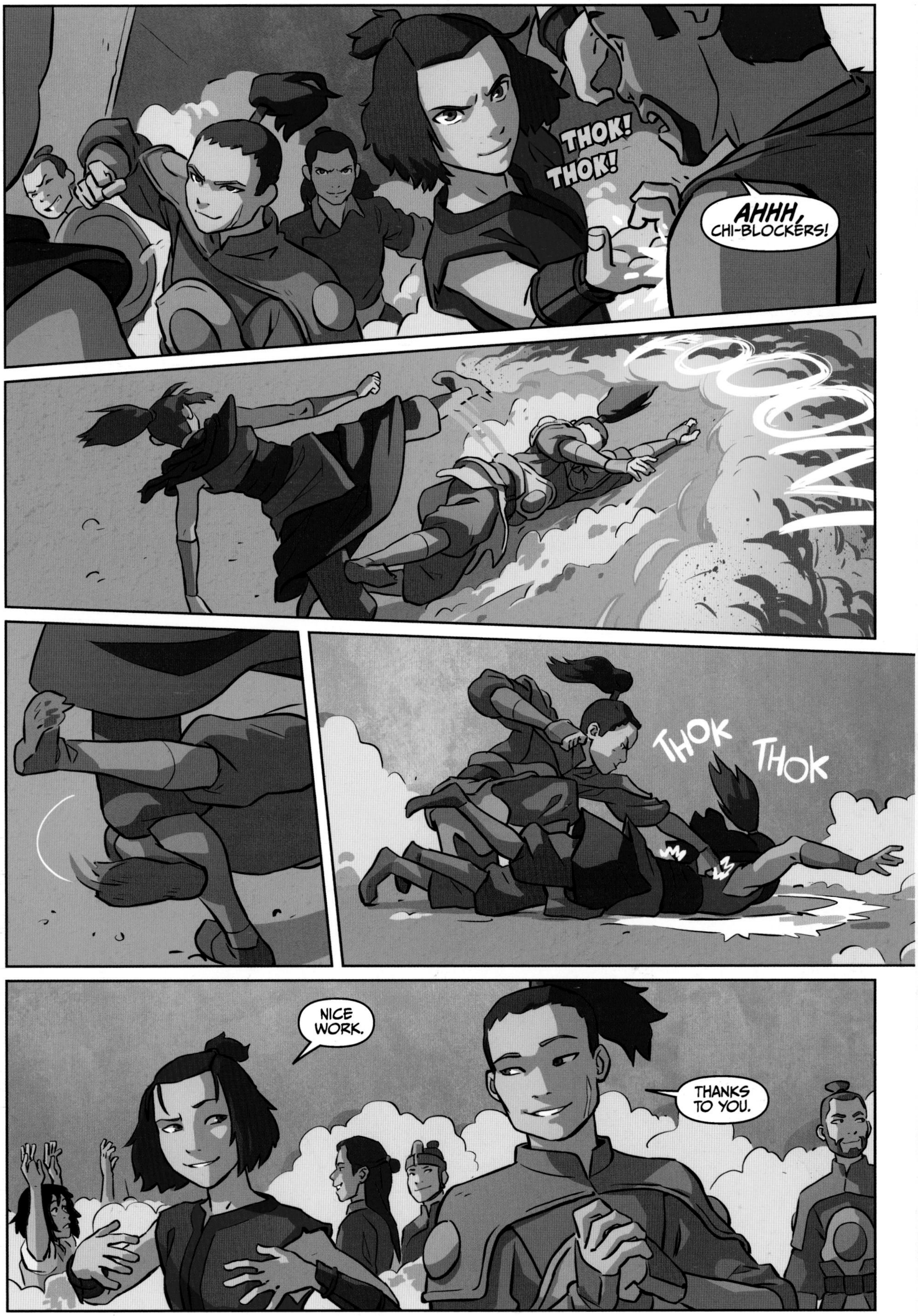
THOK!
THOK!
AHHH, CHI-BLOCKERS!
FOOOOMM
THOK
THOK
NICE WORK.
THANKS TO YOU.

PW: *I'm sure having all these chi-blockers running around won't lead to anything down the line.*

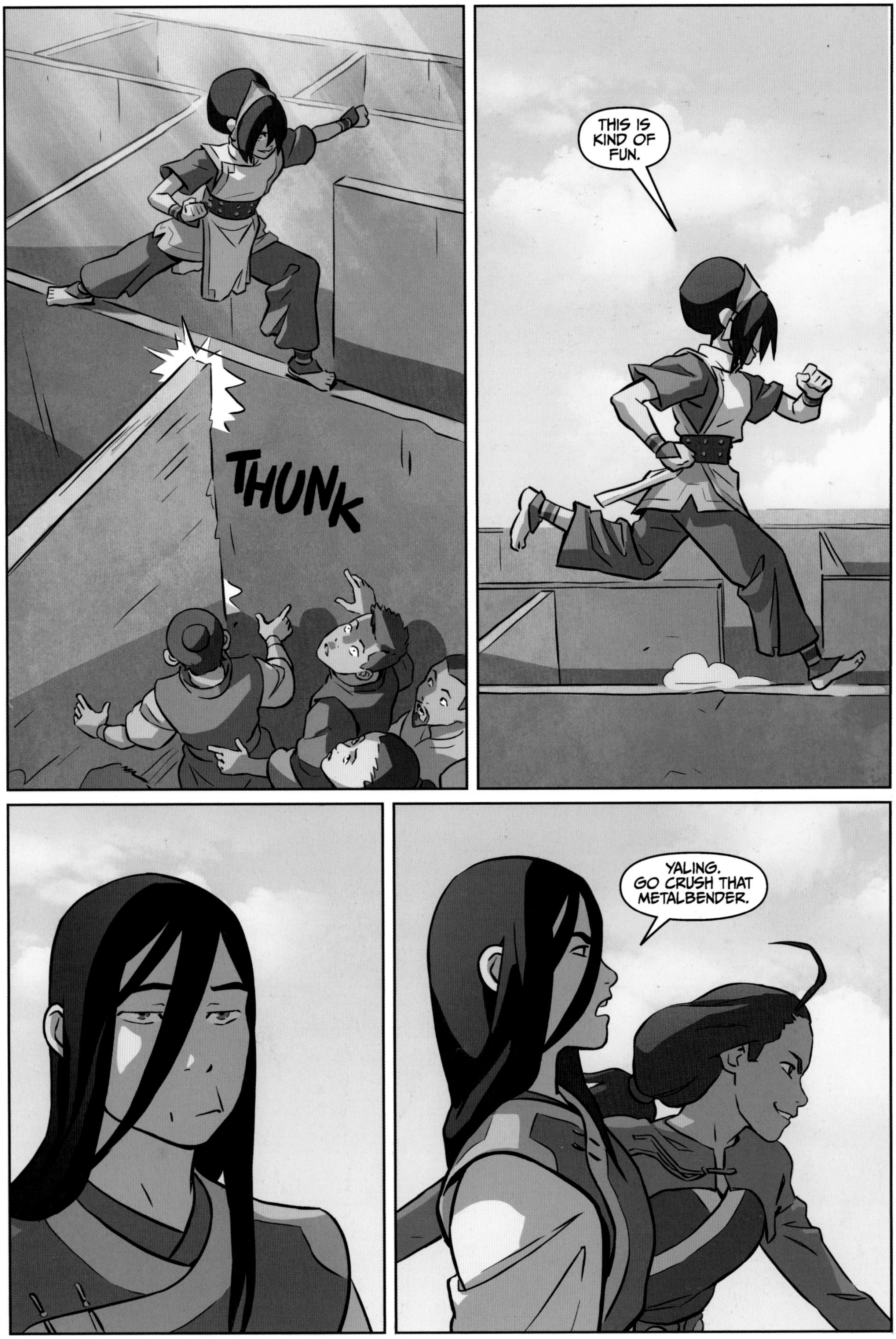
THUNK
THIS IS KIND OF FUN.
YALING. GO CRUSH THAT METALBENDER.

FEH: *I absolutely love this panel. Yaling's little smirk as she runs past her mom.*

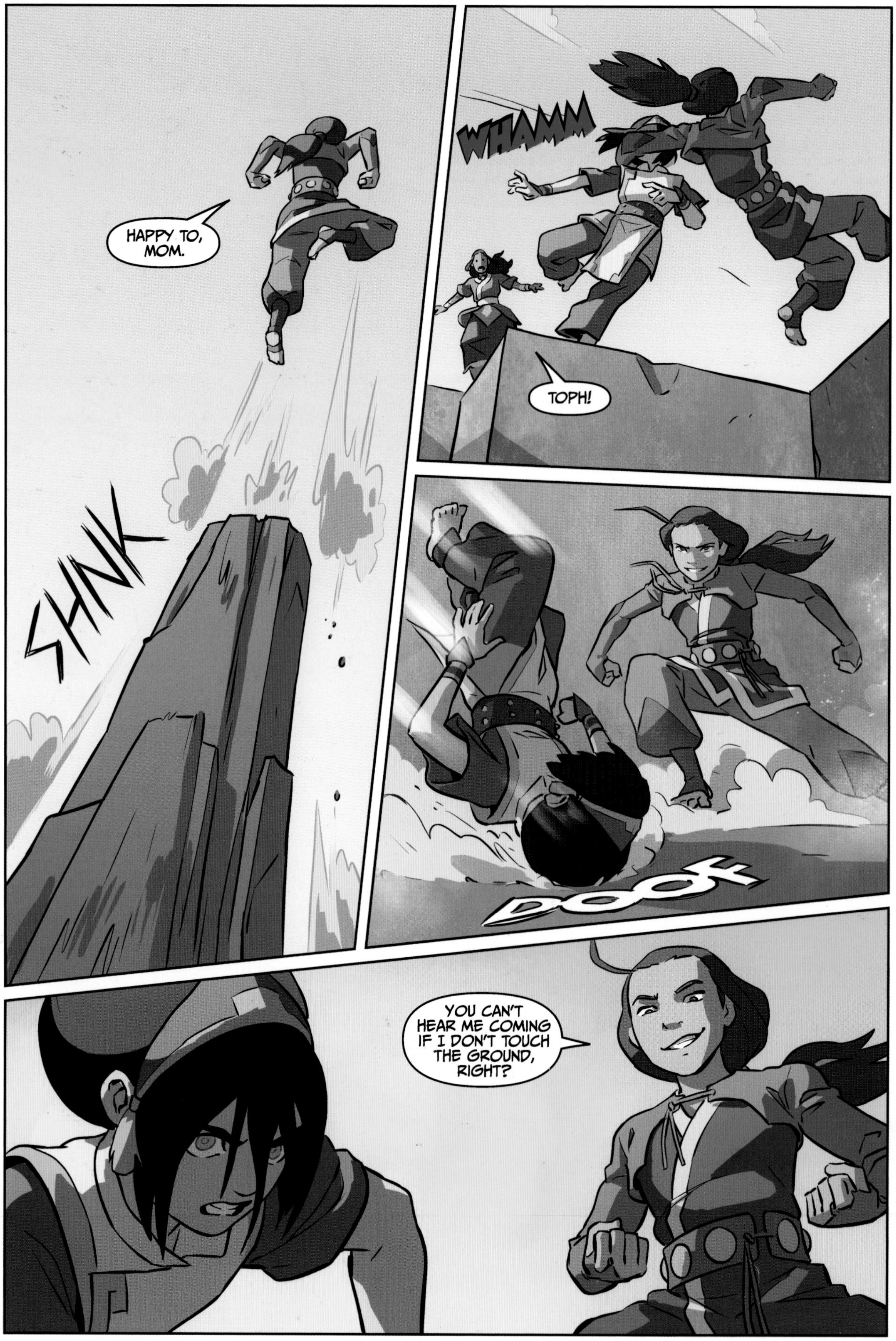
HAPPY TO, MOM.
WHAMM
TOPH!
SHNK
DOOF
YOU CAN'T HEAR ME COMING IF I DON'T TOUCH THE GROUND, RIGHT?

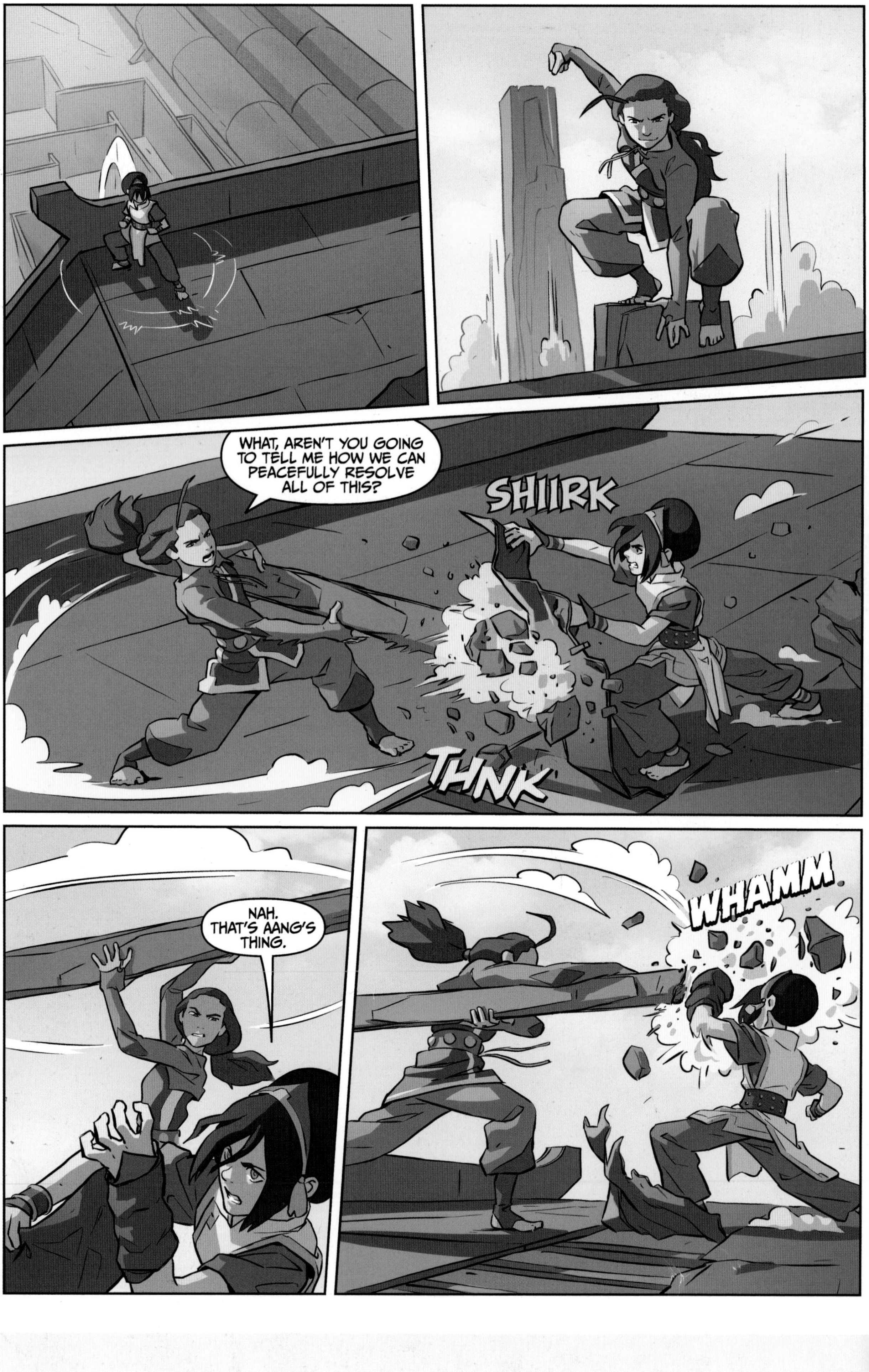
WHAT, AREN'T YOU GOING TO TELL ME HOW WE CAN PEACEFULLY RESOLVE ALL OF THIS?
SHIRK
THNK
NAH. THAT'S AANG'S THING.
WHAMM

FEH: *I wanted to find a way for Toph and Yaling to fight where Toph, the Greatest Bender in the World, wouldn't roll right over her. Sending them up to the roof of a factory seemed to work pretty well!*

PW: *Yaling swinging this rock column around as a weapon was all Todd's invention—something I think really adds to this scene and keeps things flowing.*

YOU DON'T WANT TO DO THIS.

HEY, UM, YOU AREN'T ONE OF THOSE CHI-BLOCKERS, ARE YOU?

YES! YES, I AM! I'M THE BEST CHI-BLOCKER YOU'LL EVER MEET! ALL I'VE EVER WANTED TO DO IN LIFE IS BLOCK CHI! I'M A REGULAR CHI-BLOCKING MACHINE!

WSHH

WSHH

WSHH

THERE'S ONE OF HIM AND FIVE OF US! WE CAN TAKE HIM.

YOU GO FIRST, THEN. I DIDN'T SIGN UP TO GET MY CHI BLOCKED. IT REALLY HURTS!

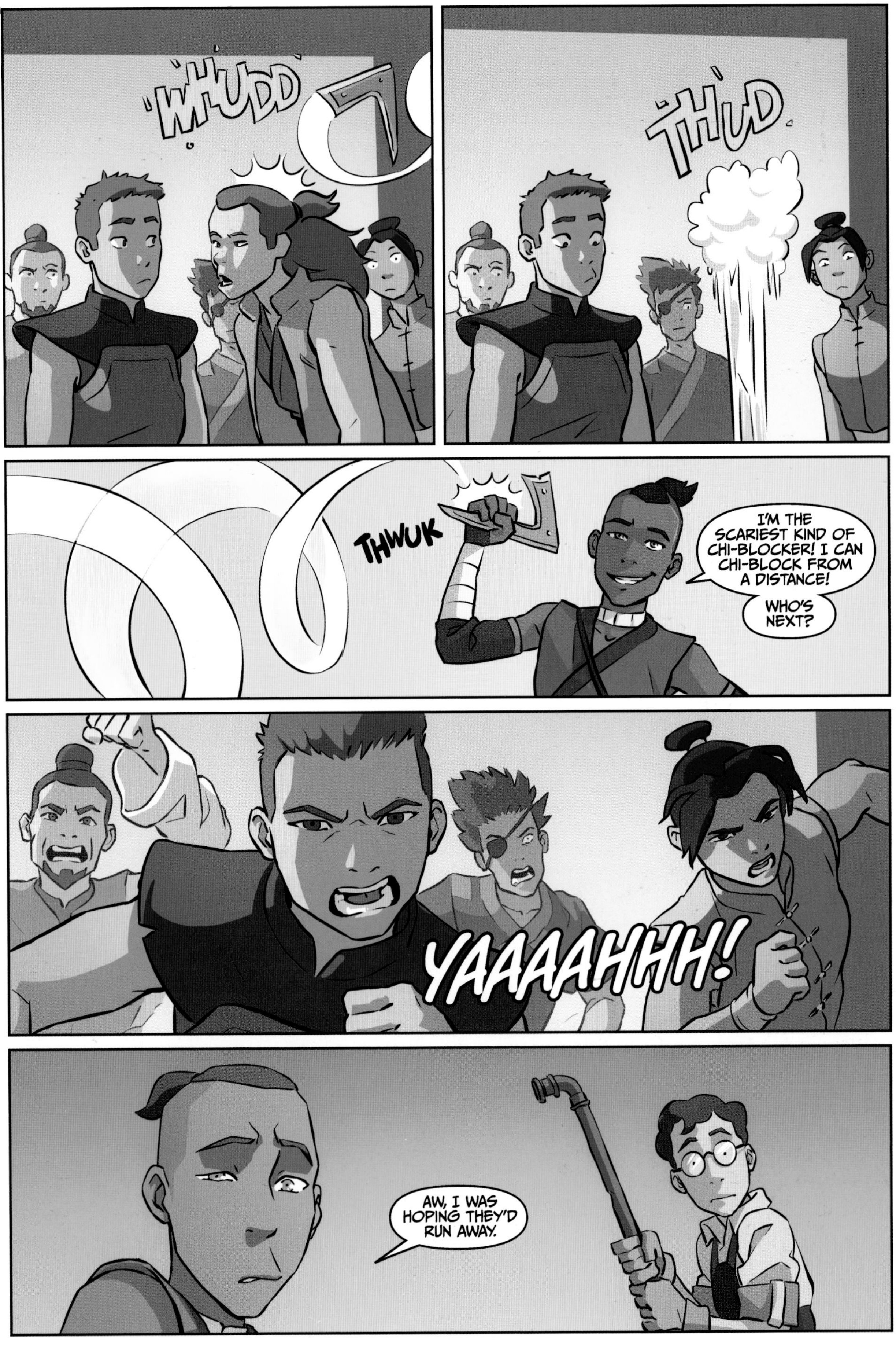
WHUDD
THUD
THWUK
I'M THE SCARIEST KIND OF CHI-BLOCKER! I CAN CHI-BLOCK FROM A DISTANCE!
WHO'S NEXT?
YAAAAHHH!
AW, I WAS HOPING THEY'D RUN AWAY.

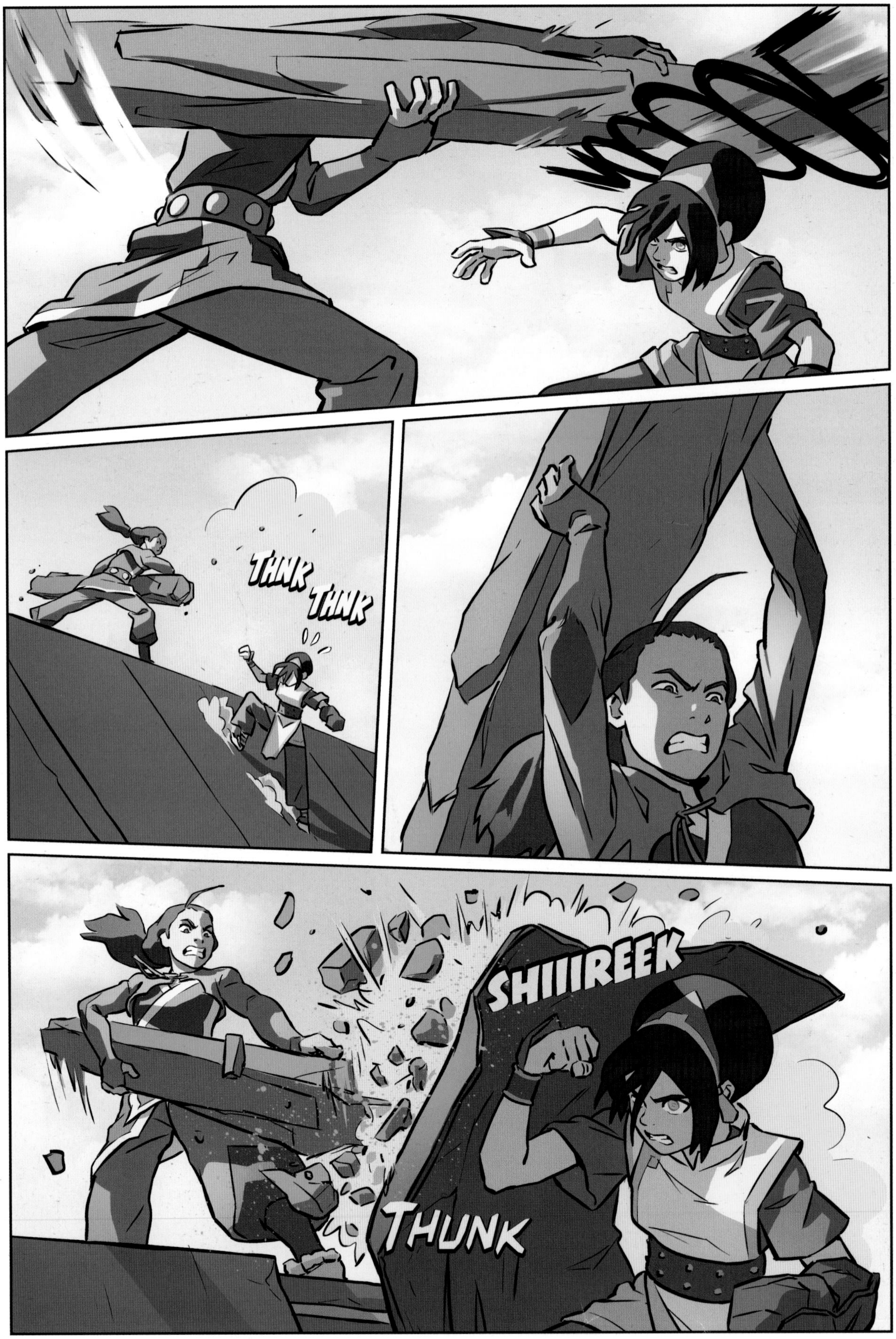
THNK
THNK
SHIIIREEK
THUNK

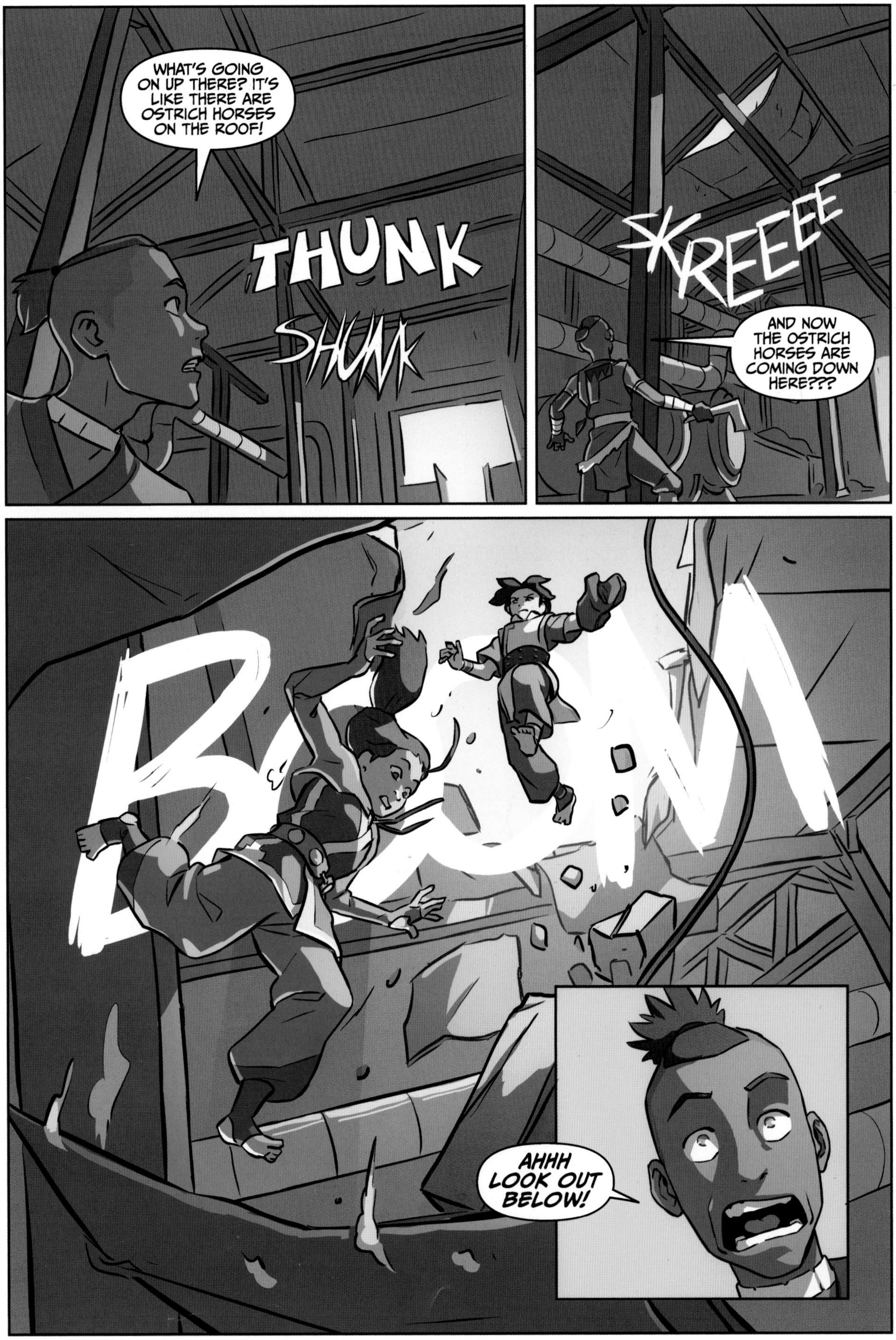
WHAT'S GOING ON UP THERE? IT'S LIKE THERE ARE OSTRICH HORSES ON THE ROOF!
THUNK
SHUNK
SKREEEE
AND NOW THE OSTRICH HORSES ARE COMING DOWN HERE???
BOOM
AHHH LOOK OUT BELOW!

FEH: *I know you should never laugh at your own jokes, but Sokka saying "And now the ostrich horses are coming down here???" kills me every time I read it.*

PW: *I love Adele's colors on this page. That hazy dust effect is so nice!*

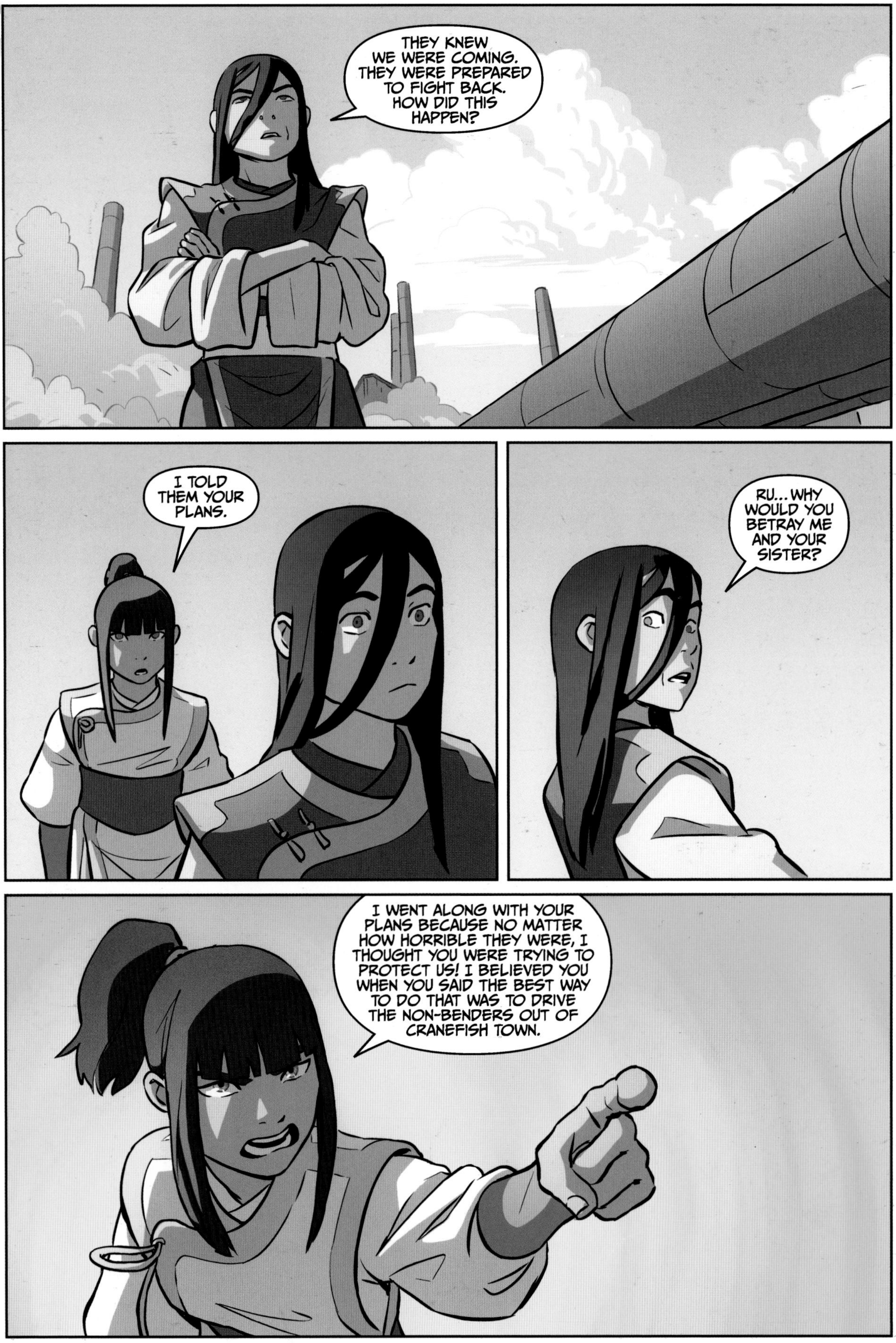
THEY KNEW WE WERE COMING. THEY WERE PREPARED TO FIGHT BACK. HOW DID THIS HAPPEN?
I TOLD THEM YOUR PLANS.
RU... WHY WOULD YOU BETRAY ME AND YOUR SISTER?
I WENT ALONG WITH YOUR PLANS BECAUSE NO MATTER HOW HORRIBLE THEY WERE, I THOUGHT YOU WERE TRYING TO PROTECT US! I BELIEVED YOU WHEN YOU SAID THE BEST WAY TO DO THAT WAS TO DRIVE THE NON-BENDERS OUT OF CRANEFISH TOWN.

THUMP.

DID YOU JUST TRY TO CHI-BLOCK YOUR OWN MOTHER?!

I'LL *BURY* YOU, YOU UNGRATEFUL CHILD!!

RUMMBI

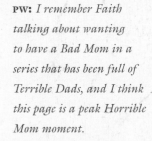

PW: *I remember Faith talking about wanting to have a Bad Mom in a series that has been full of Terrible Dads, and I think this page is a peak Horrible Mom moment.*

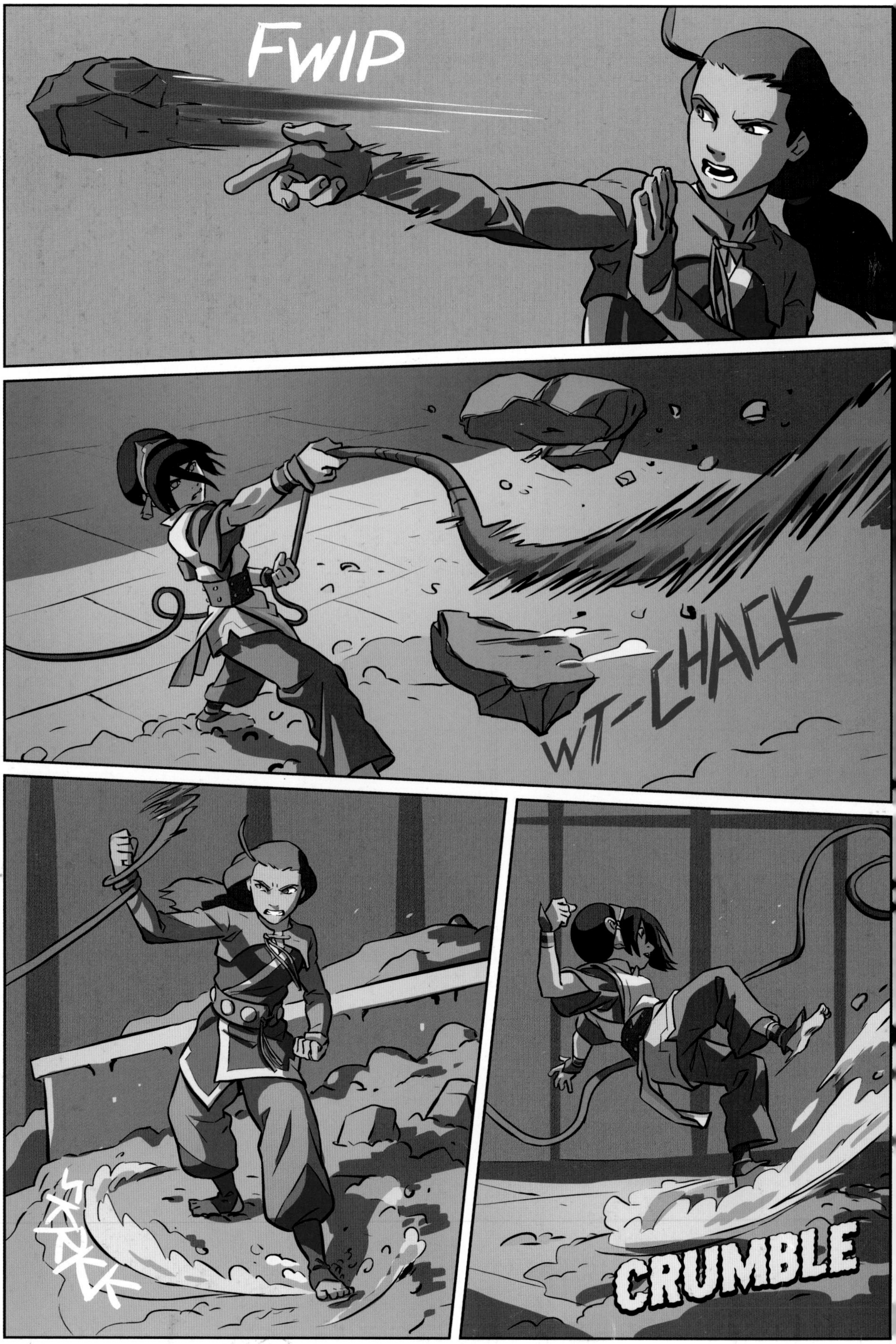
FWIP
WT-CHACK
SKKKK
CRUMBLE

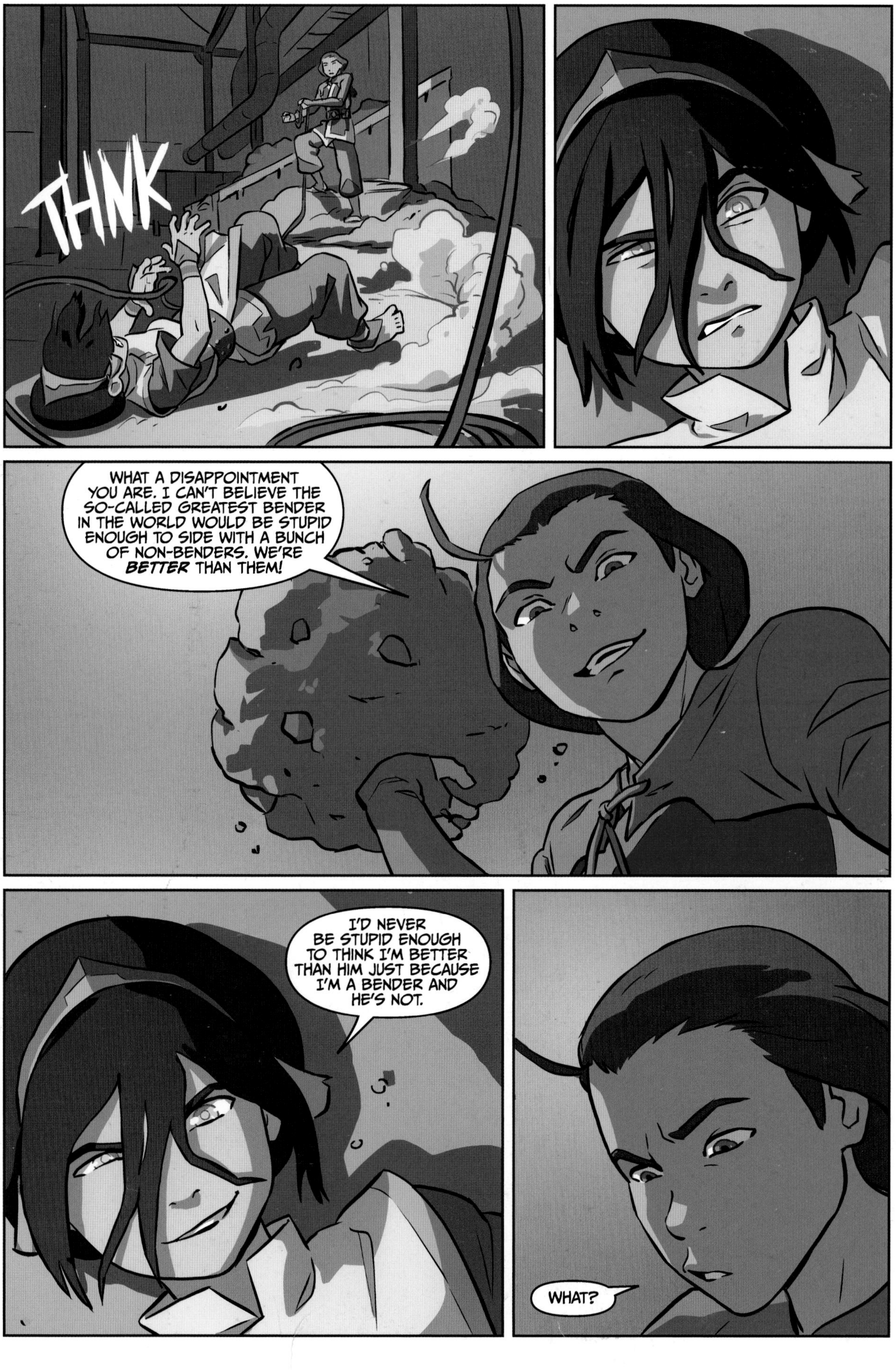
THNK
WHAT A DISAPPOINTMENT YOU ARE. I CAN'T BELIEVE THE SO-CALLED GREATEST BENDER IN THE WORLD WOULD BE STUPID ENOUGH TO SIDE WITH A BUNCH OF NON-BENDERS. WE'RE **BETTER** THAN THEM!
I'D NEVER BE STUPID ENOUGH TO THINK I'M BETTER THAN HIM JUST BECAUSE I'M A BENDER AND HE'S NOT.
WHAT?

FEH: *Punching! Feelings!*

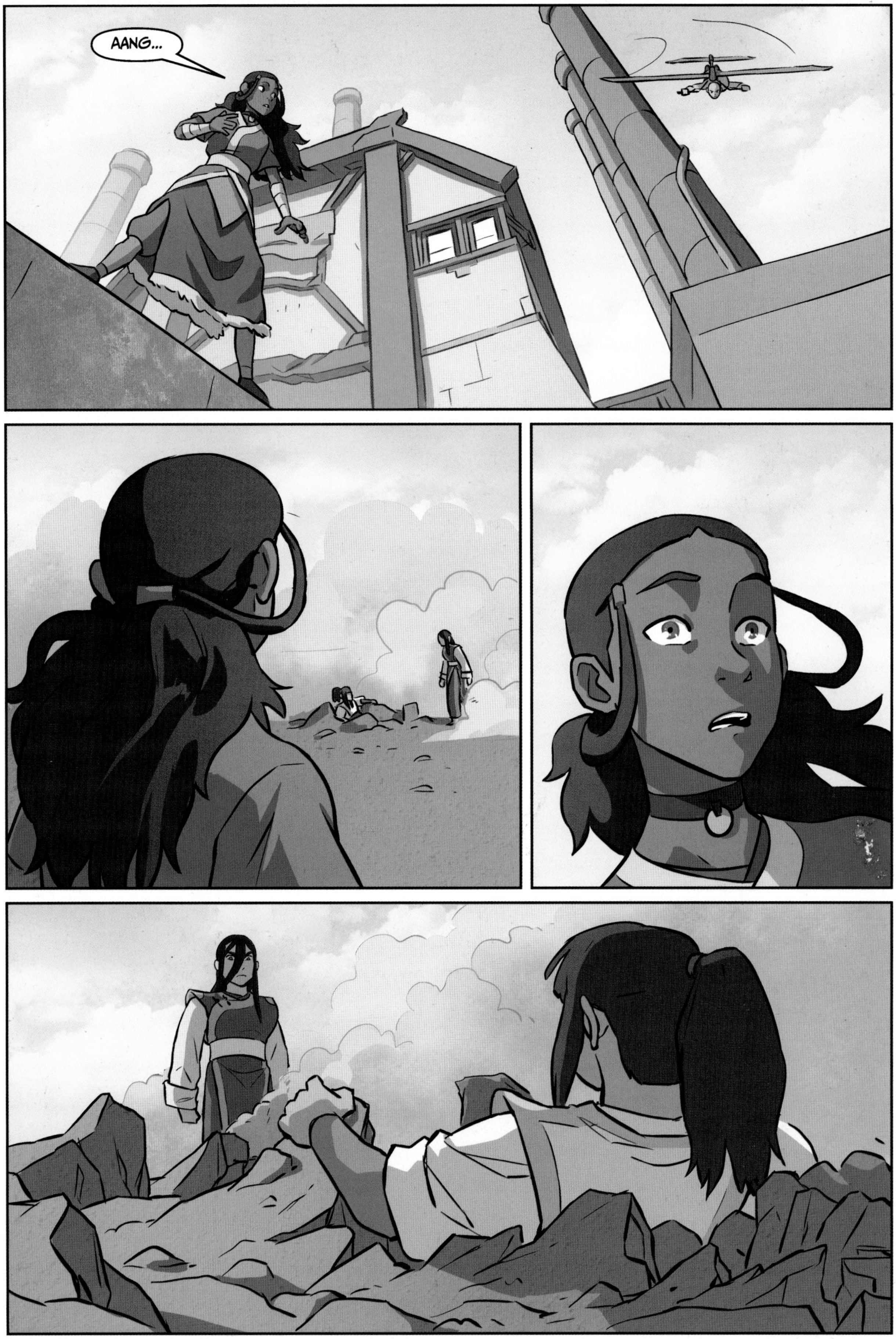
AANG...

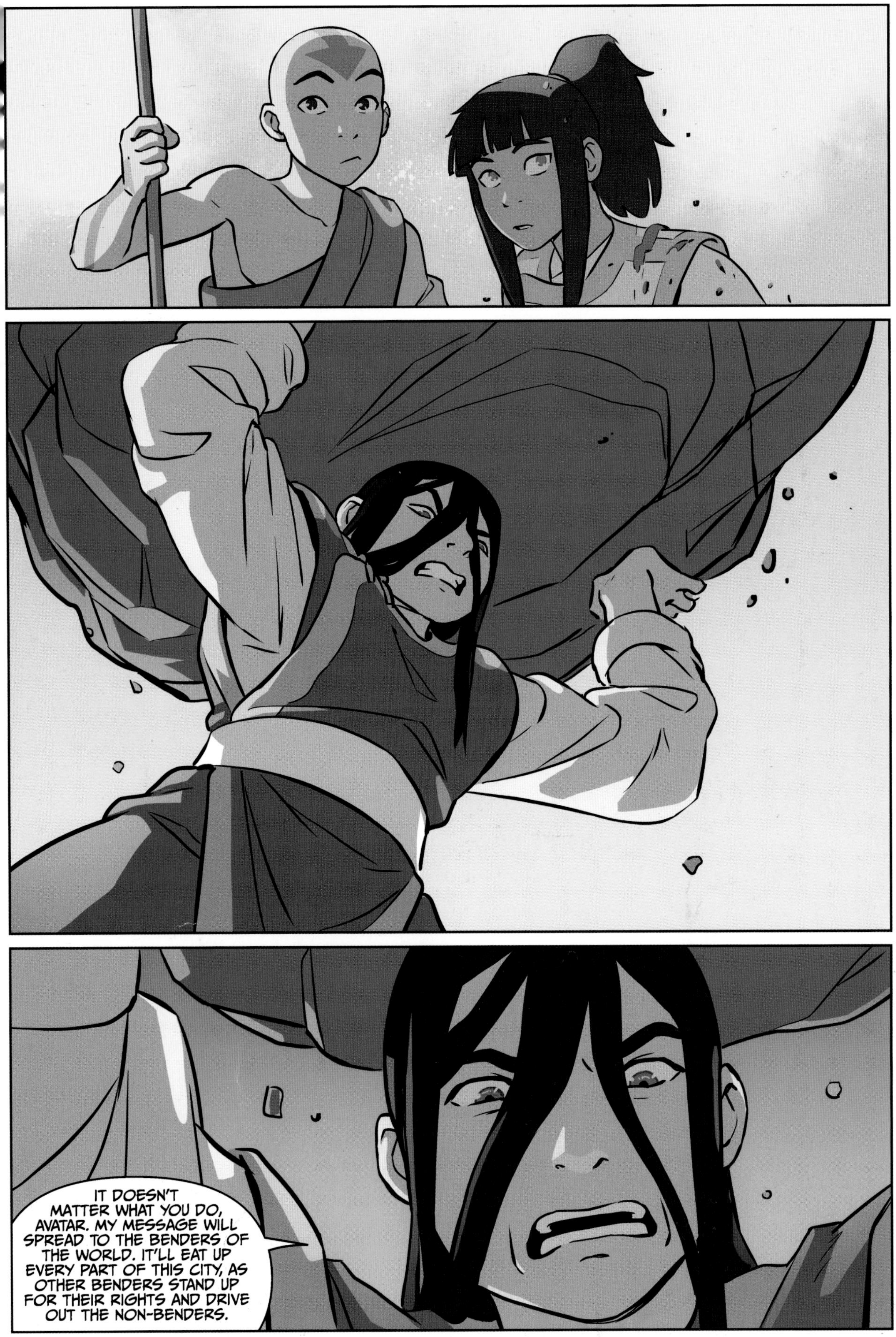
IT DOESN'T MATTER WHAT YOU DO, AVATAR. MY MESSAGE WILL SPREAD TO THE BENDERS OF THE WORLD. IT'LL EAT UP EVERY PART OF THIS CITY, AS OTHER BENDERS STAND UP FOR THEIR RIGHTS AND DRIVE OUT THE NON-BENDERS.

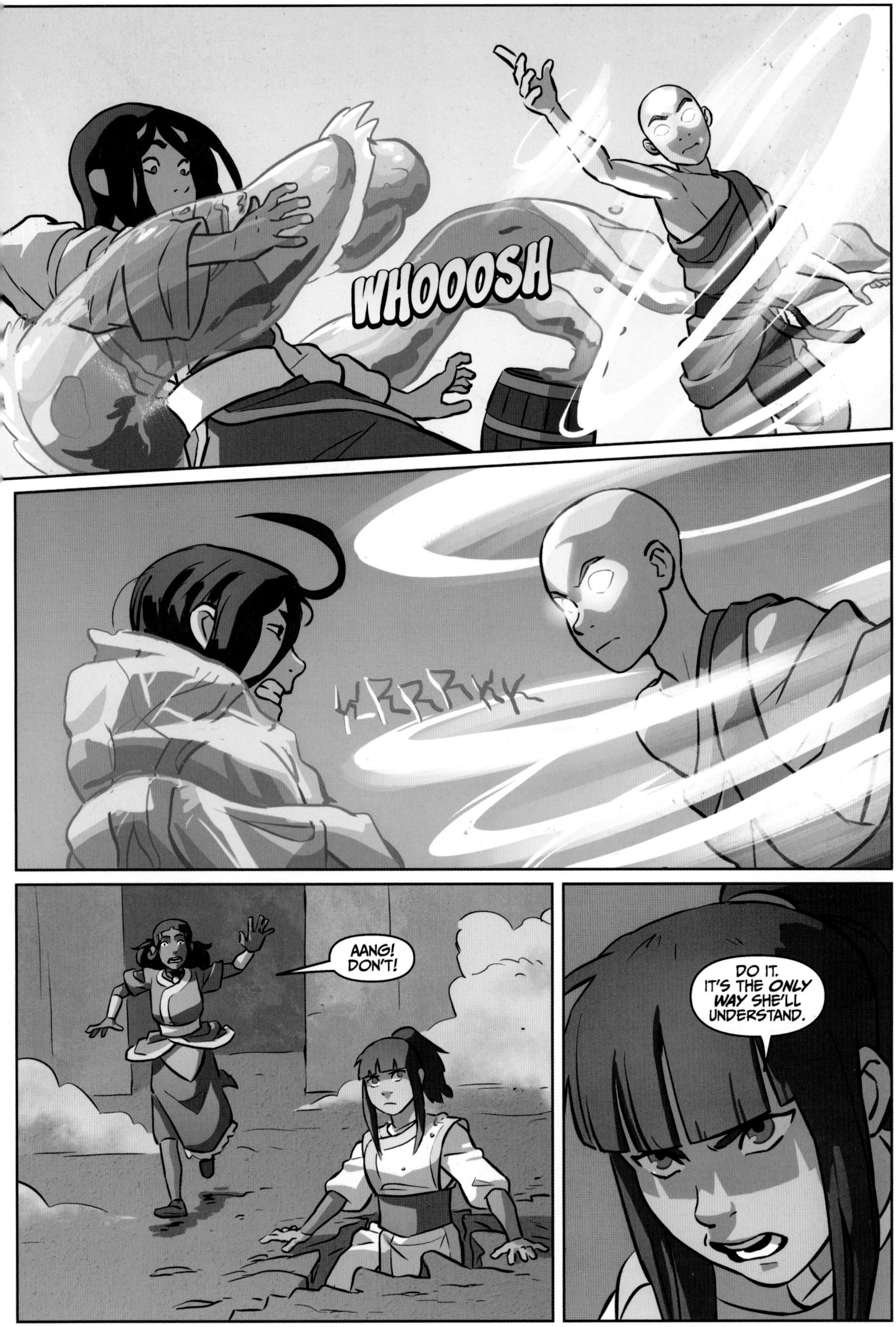
WHOOOSH
KRRRKK
AANG! DON'T!
DO IT. IT'S THE ONLY WAY SHE'LL UNDERSTAND.

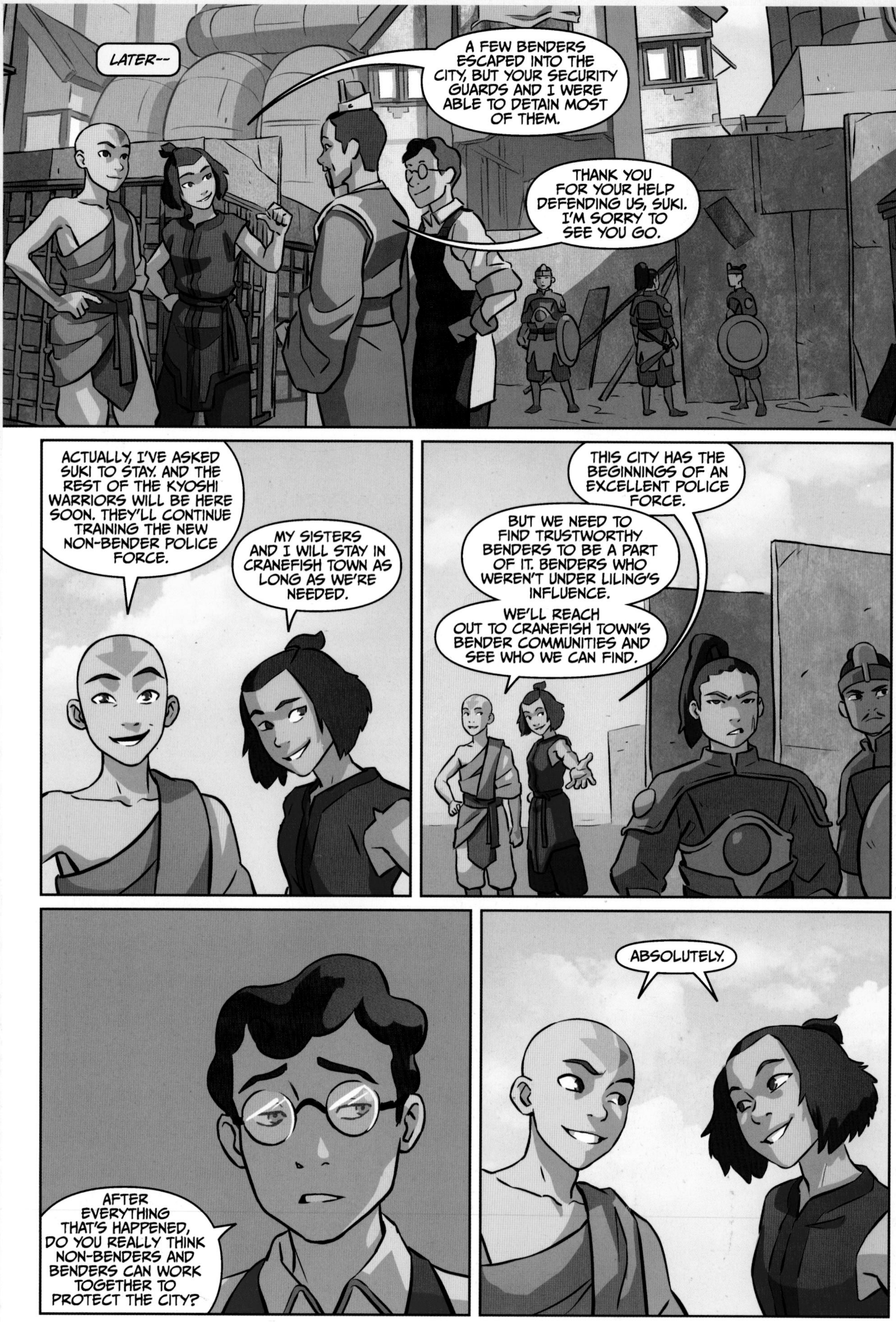
LATER--
A FEW BENDERS ESCAPED INTO THE CITY, BUT YOUR SECURITY GUARDS AND I WERE ABLE TO DETAIN MOST OF THEM.
THANK YOU FOR YOUR HELP DEFENDING US, SUKI. I'M SORRY TO SEE YOU GO.
ACTUALLY, I'VE ASKED SUKI TO STAY. AND THE REST OF THE KYOSHI WARRIORS WILL BE HERE SOON. THEY'LL CONTINUE TRAINING THE NEW NON-BENDER POLICE FORCE.
MY SISTERS AND I WILL STAY IN CRANEFISH TOWN AS LONG AS WE'RE NEEDED.
THIS CITY HAS THE BEGINNINGS OF AN EXCELLENT POLICE FORCE.
BUT WE NEED TO FIND TRUSTWORTHY BENDERS TO BE A PART OF IT. BENDERS WHO WEREN'T UNDER LILING'S INFLUENCE.
WE'LL REACH OUT TO CRANEFISH TOWN'S BENDER COMMUNITIES AND SEE WHO WE CAN FIND.
AFTER EVERYTHING THAT'S HAPPENED, DO YOU REALLY THINK NON-BENDERS AND BENDERS CAN WORK TOGETHER TO PROTECT THE CITY?
ABSOLUTELY.

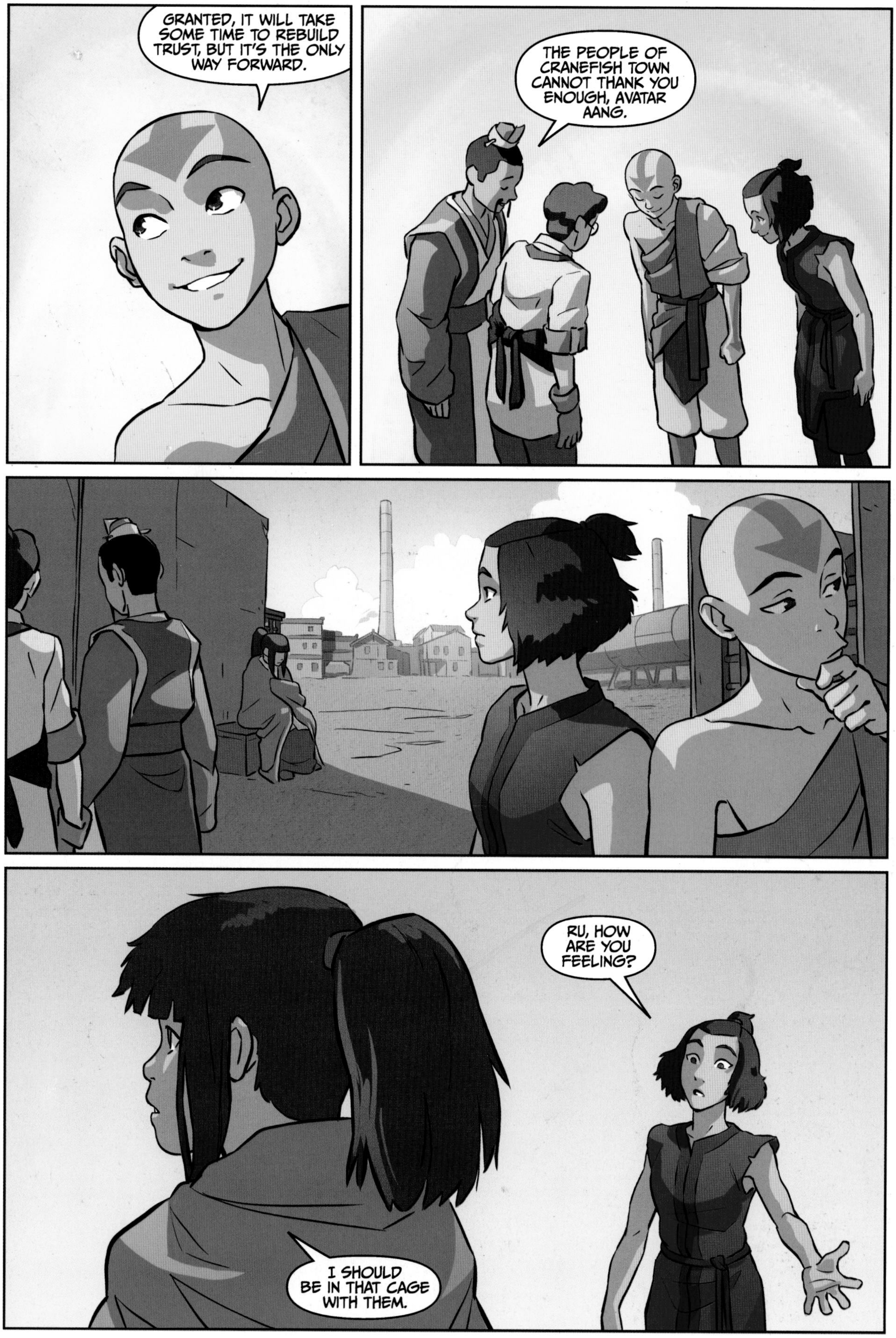
GRANTED, IT WILL TAKE SOME TIME TO REBUILD TRUST, BUT IT'S THE ONLY WAY FORWARD.
THE PEOPLE OF CRANEFISH TOWN CANNOT THANK YOU ENOUGH, AVATAR AANG.
RU, HOW ARE YOU FEELING?
I SHOULD BE IN THAT CAGE WITH THEM.

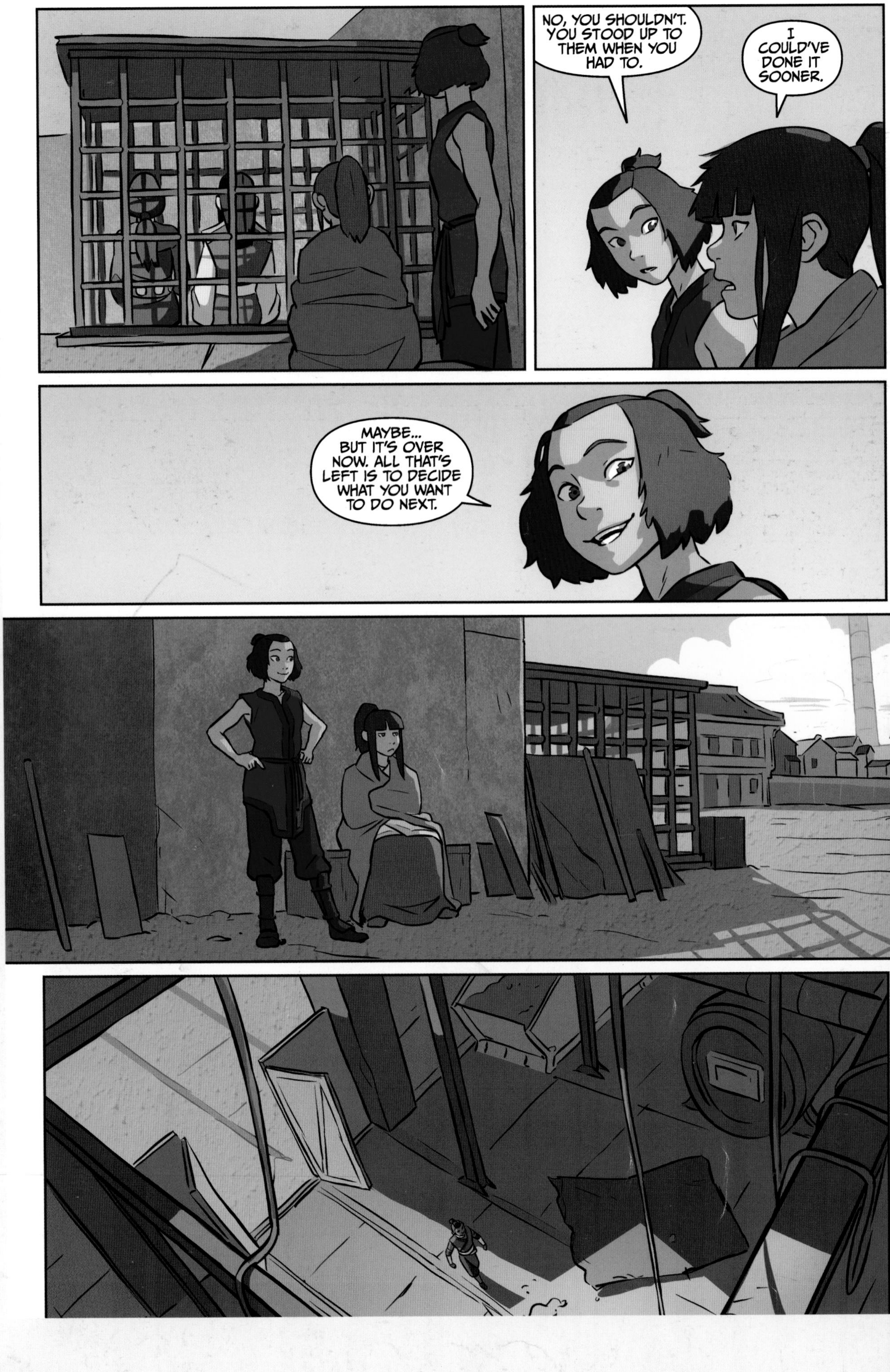
NO, YOU SHOULDN'T. YOU STOOD UP TO THEM WHEN YOU HAD TO.
I COULD'VE DONE IT SOONER.
MAYBE... BUT IT'S OVER NOW. ALL THAT'S LEFT IS TO DECIDE WHAT YOU WANT TO DO NEXT.

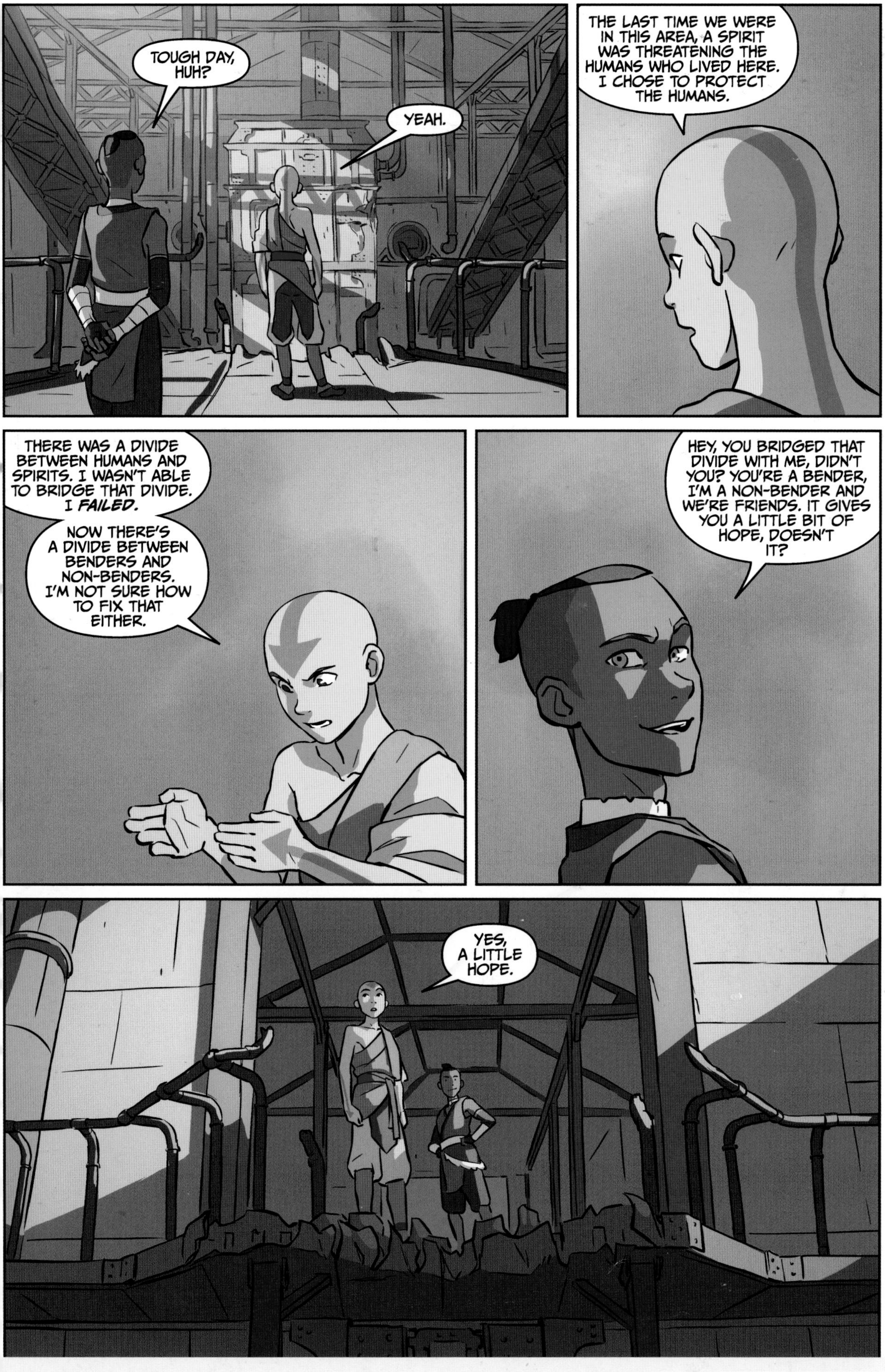
TOUGH DAY, HUH?
YEAH.
THE LAST TIME WE WERE IN THIS AREA, A SPIRIT WAS THREATENING THE HUMANS WHO LIVED HERE. I CHOSE TO PROTECT THE HUMANS.
THERE WAS A DIVIDE BETWEEN HUMANS AND SPIRITS. I WASN'T ABLE TO BRIDGE THAT DIVIDE. I *FAILED.*
NOW THERE'S A DIVIDE BETWEEN BENDERS AND NON-BENDERS. I'M NOT SURE HOW TO FIX THAT EITHER.
HEY, YOU BRIDGED THAT DIVIDE WITH ME, DIDN'T YOU? YOU'RE A BENDER, I'M A NON-BENDER AND WE'RE FRIENDS. IT GIVES YOU A LITTLE BIT OF HOPE, DOESN'T IT?
YES, A LITTLE HOPE.

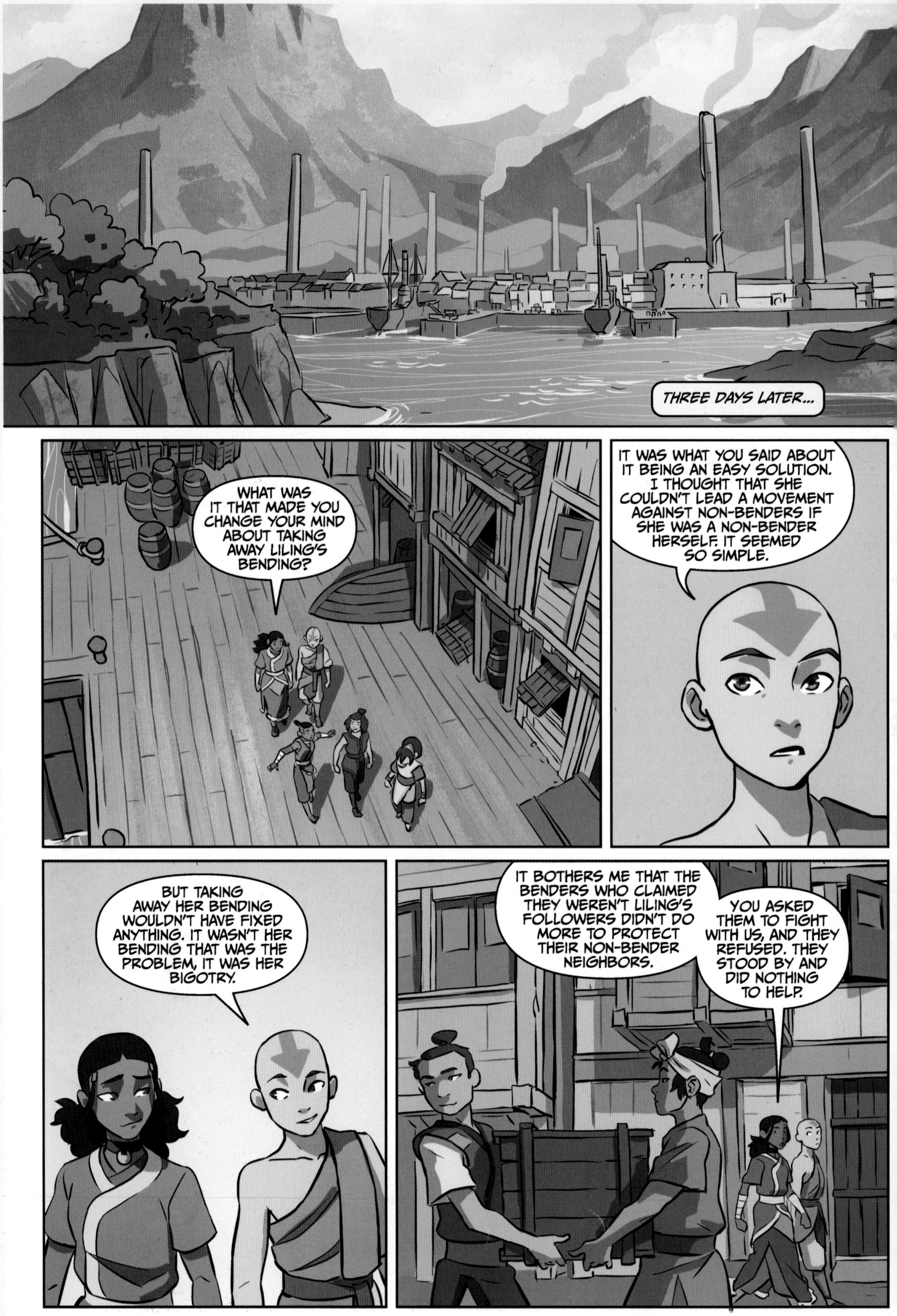
THREE DAYS LATER...
WHAT WAS IT THAT MADE YOU CHANGE YOUR MIND ABOUT TAKING AWAY LILING'S BENDING?
IT WAS WHAT YOU SAID ABOUT IT BEING AN EASY SOLUTION. I THOUGHT THAT SHE COULDN'T LEAD A MOVEMENT AGAINST NON-BENDERS IF SHE WAS A NON-BENDER HERSELF. IT SEEMED SO SIMPLE.
BUT TAKING AWAY HER BENDING WOULDN'T HAVE FIXED ANYTHING. IT WASN'T HER BENDING THAT WAS THE PROBLEM, IT WAS HER BIGOTRY.
IT BOTHERS ME THAT THE BENDERS WHO CLAIMED THEY WEREN'T LILING'S FOLLOWERS DIDN'T DO MORE TO PROTECT THEIR NON-BENDER NEIGHBORS.
YOU ASKED THEM TO FIGHT WITH US, AND THEY REFUSED. THEY STOOD BY AND DID NOTHING TO HELP.

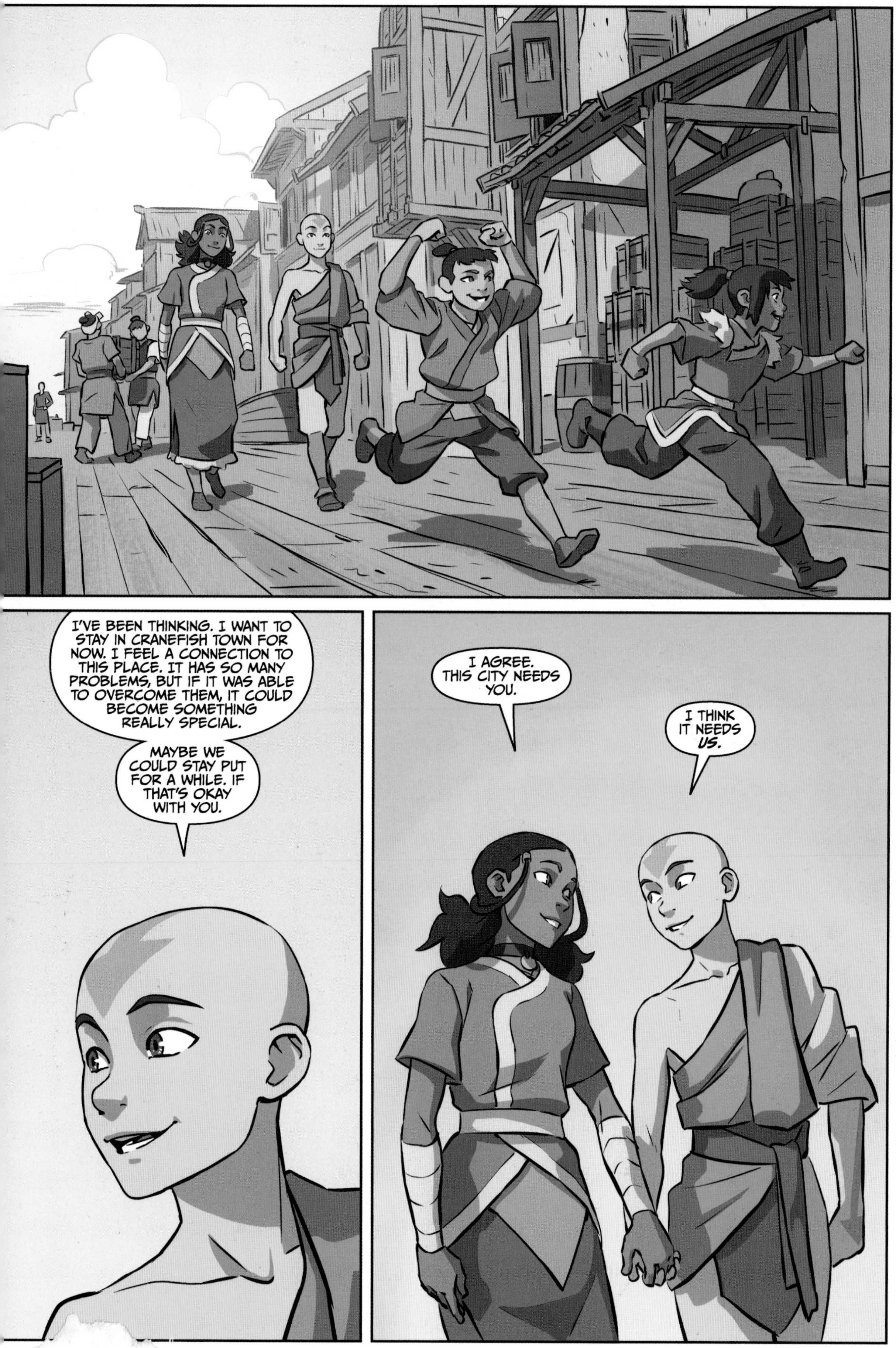
I'VE BEEN THINKING. I WANT TO STAY IN CRANEFISH TOWN FOR NOW. I FEEL A CONNECTION TO THIS PLACE. IT HAS SO MANY PROBLEMS, BUT IF IT WAS ABLE TO OVERCOME THEM, IT COULD BECOME SOMETHING REALLY SPECIAL.
MAYBE WE COULD STAY PUT FOR A WHILE. IF THAT'S OKAY WITH YOU.
I AGREE. THIS CITY NEEDS YOU.
I THINK IT NEEDS *US*.

FEH: *And someday that messy port city called Cranefish Town would become Republic City! As for who eventually got the credit for naming it, maybe we'll find out someday.*

PW: *And we end, fittingly enough, with a whole lot of rooftops!*

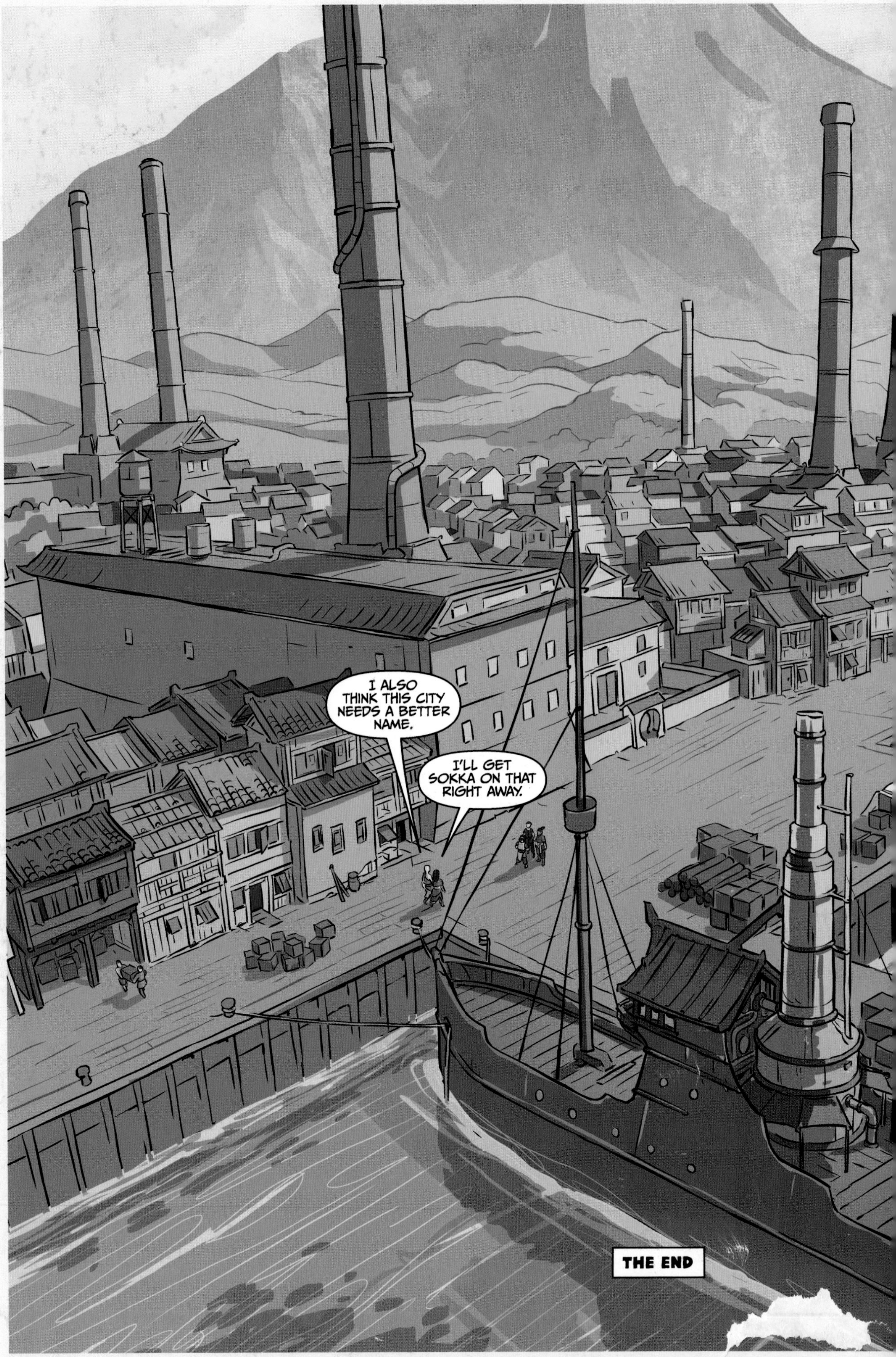
I ALSO THINK THIS CITY NEEDS A BETTER NAME.
I'LL GET SOKKA ON THAT RIGHT AWAY.
THE END

These two drawings were early concepts for Katara's look in the comic. I ended up
going with something close to this, although I changed her undershirt a little.

LILING

The final concept of Liling, the Bad Mom of the comic. I based her costume mostly on Earth Kingdom styles (especially from the Ba Sing Se arc), but gave her some broad, somewhat spiky shoulders to hint at her villainous role.

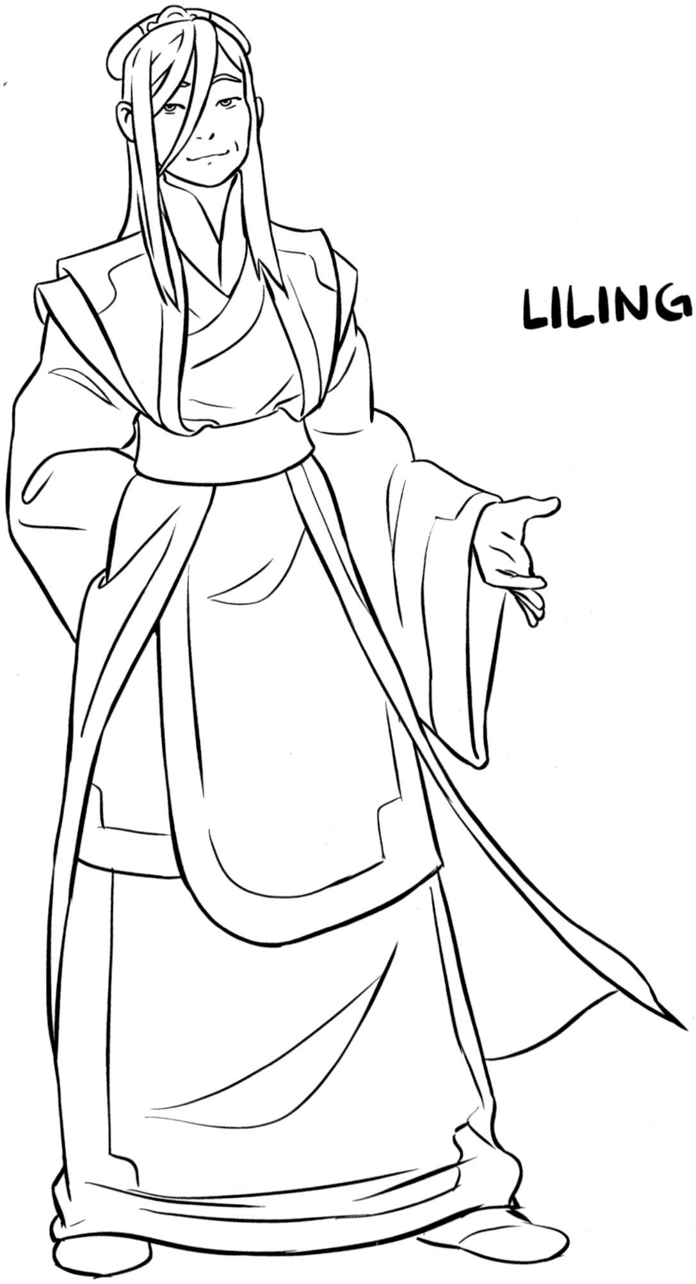
LILING

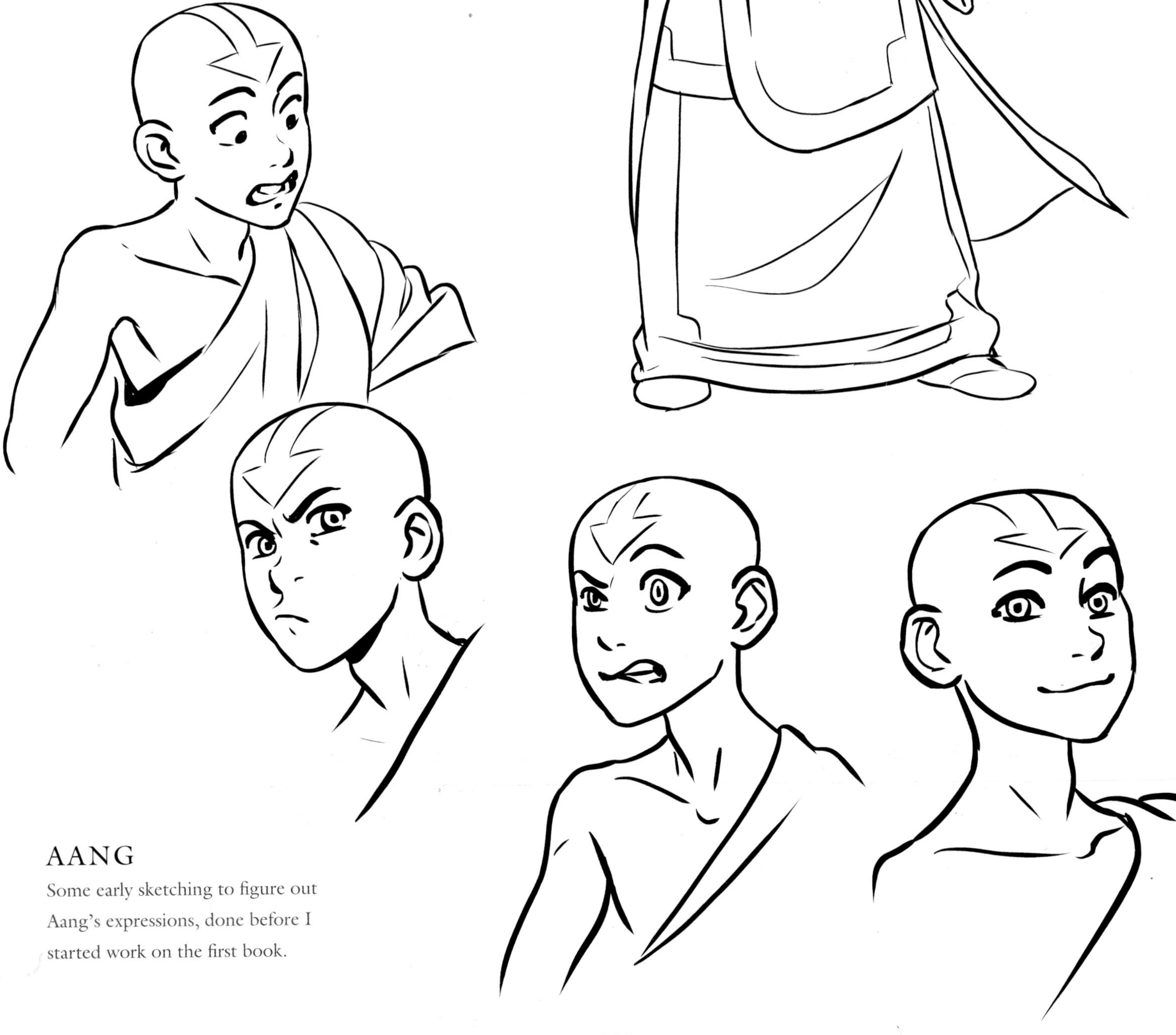

AANG

Some early sketching to figure out Aang's expressions, done before I started work on the first book.

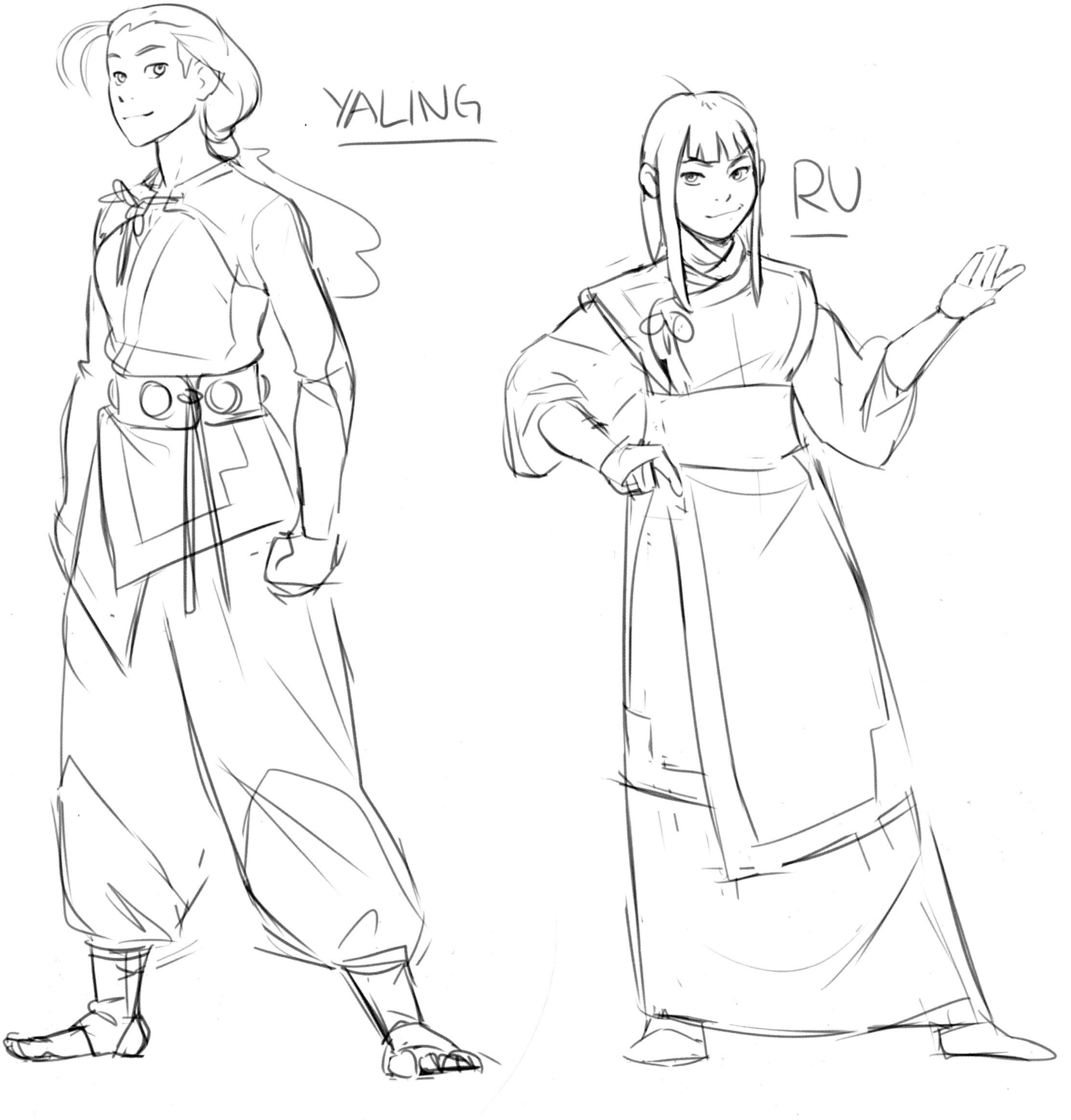
YALING
RU

Yaling and Ru went through a few revisions, but the designs here were what we landed on. I wanted to make sure their costumes reflected their personalities and roles in the stories: Yaling is a fighter who punches first and maybe doesn't even ask questions later, whereas Ru relies more on her wits to get out of problems.

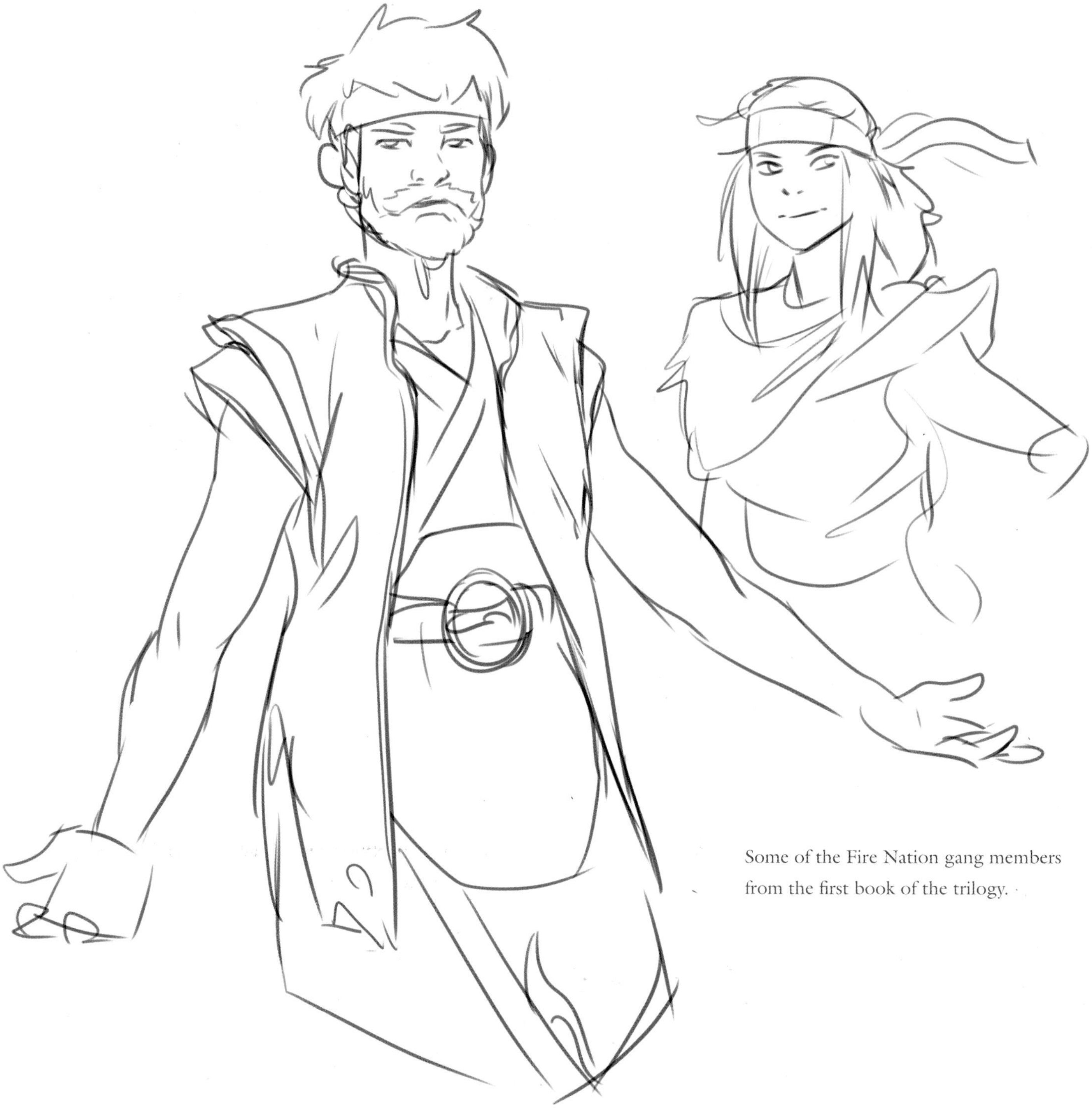

Some of the Fire Nation gang members from the first book of the trilogy.

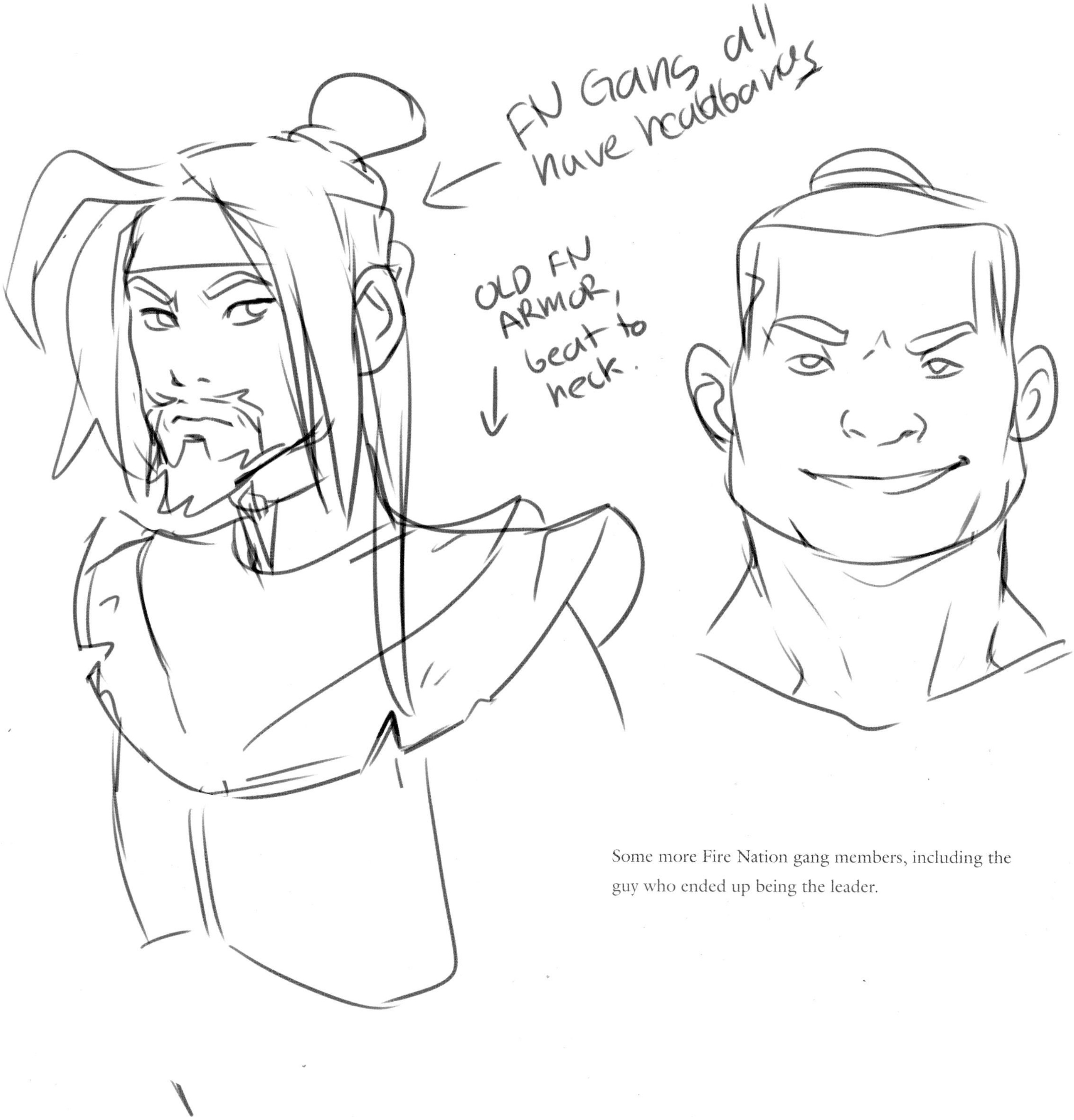
FN Gangs all have headbands
OLD FN ARMOR, beat to heck.

Some more Fire Nation gang members, including the guy who ended up being the leader.

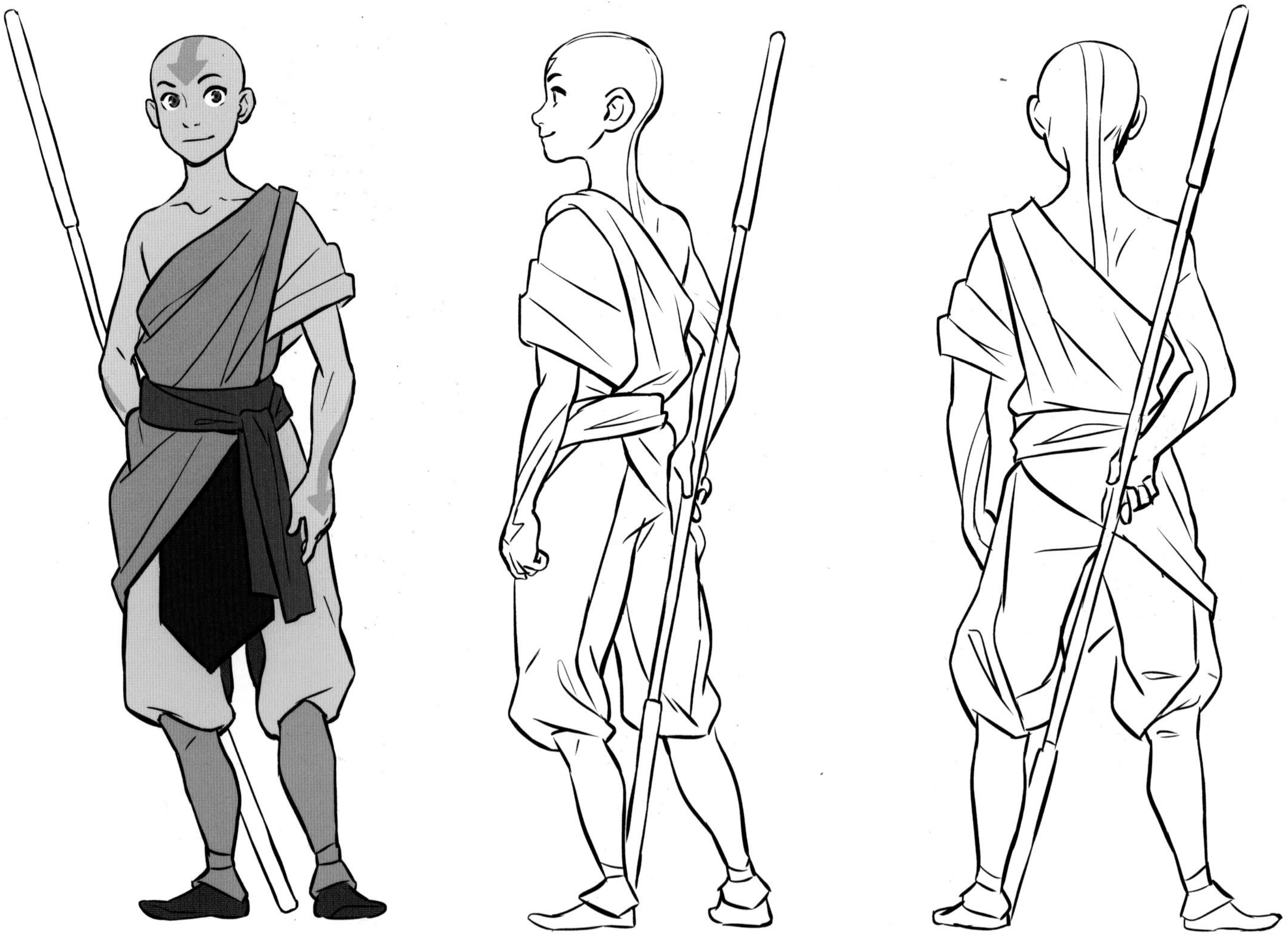

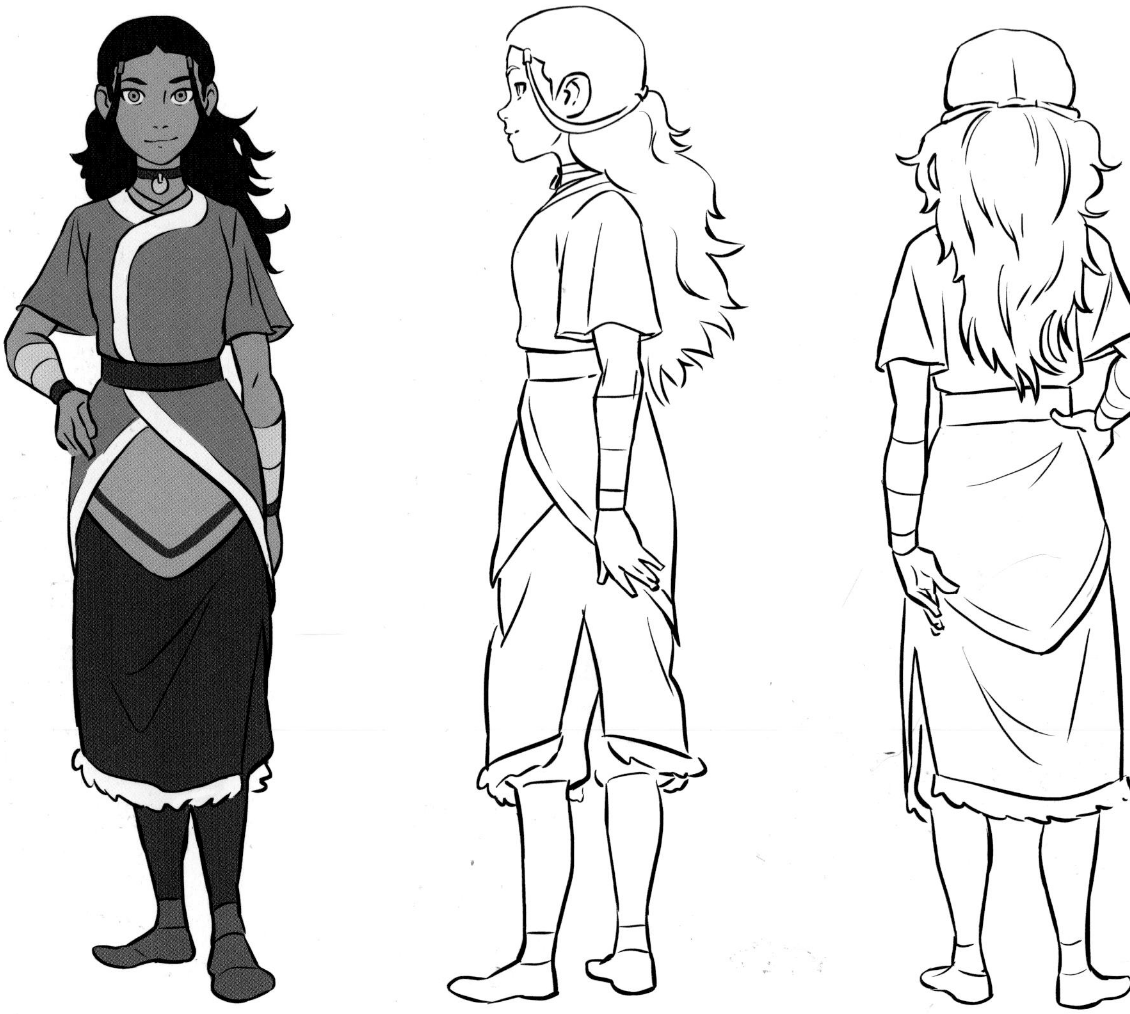

Turnarounds for most of the main characters as they appear in *Imbalance*, which were also the first thing I really did for the project. Mostly I stuck close to what the show (and later Guruhiru) depicted, but some characters (like Katara) took me a little longer.

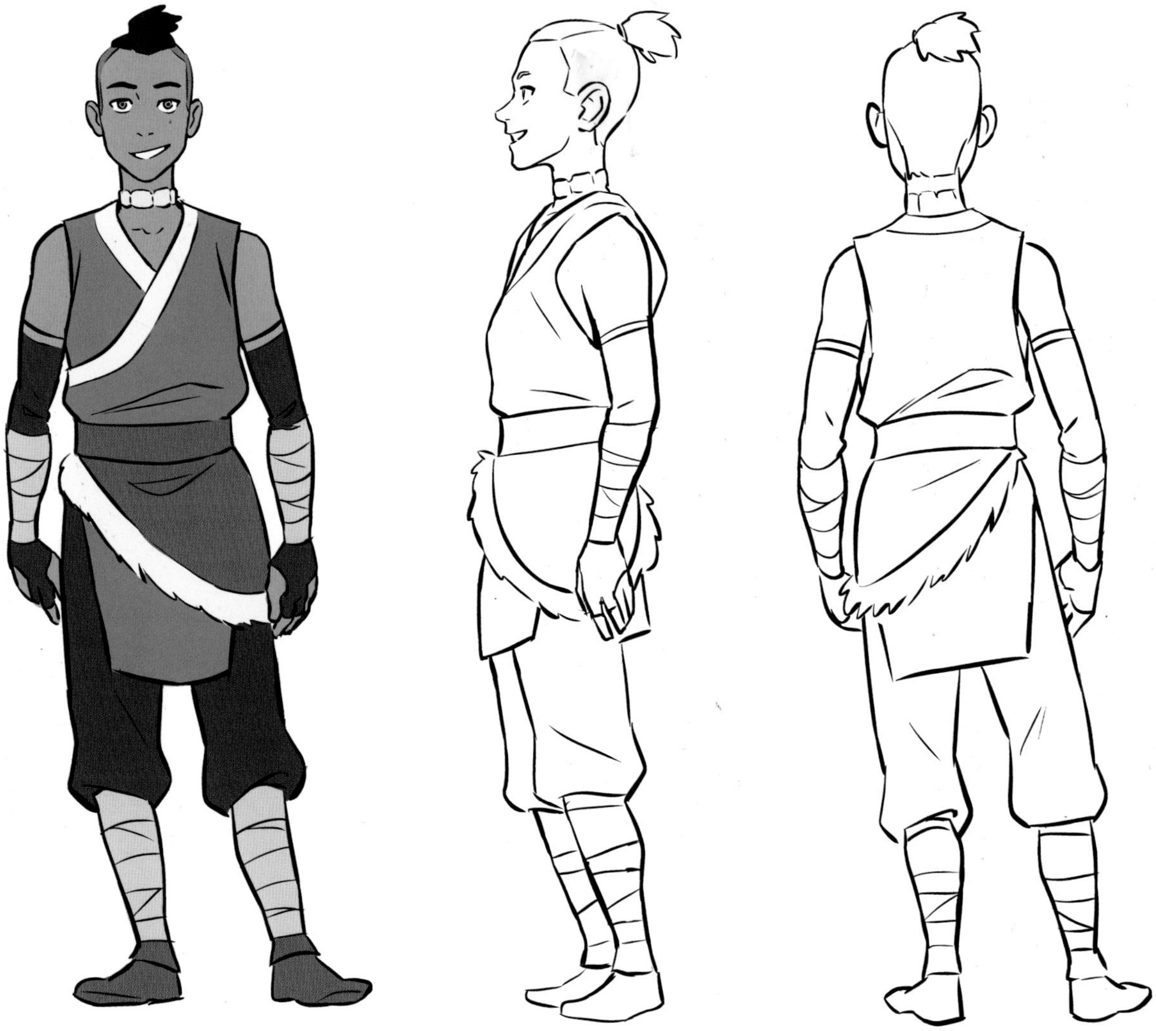

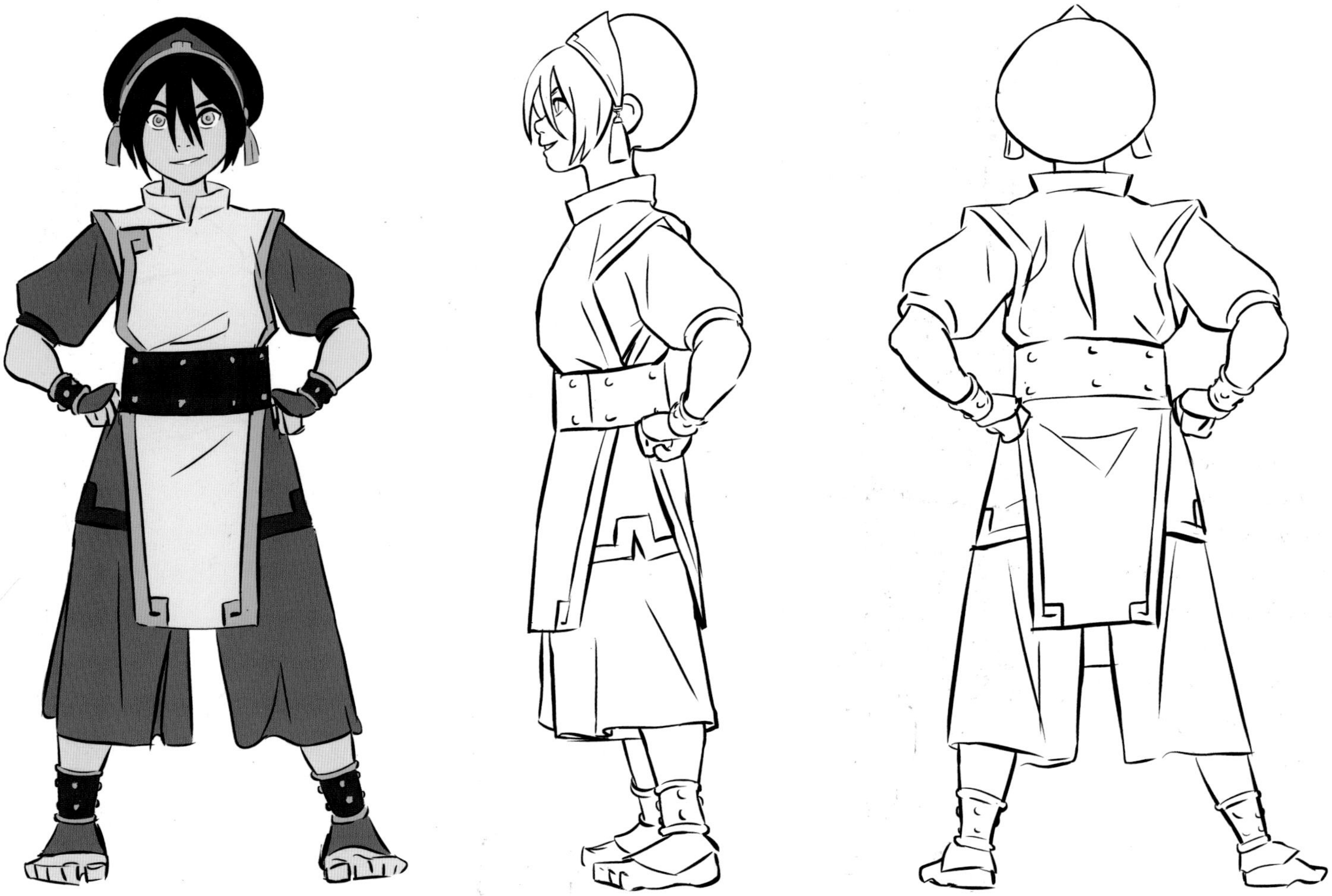

GENERAL CITY BUILDINGS?

(BUT TALLER THAN THIS)

Some initial explorations for rundown buildings in Cranefish Town.

CRANEFISH MARKET SQUARE

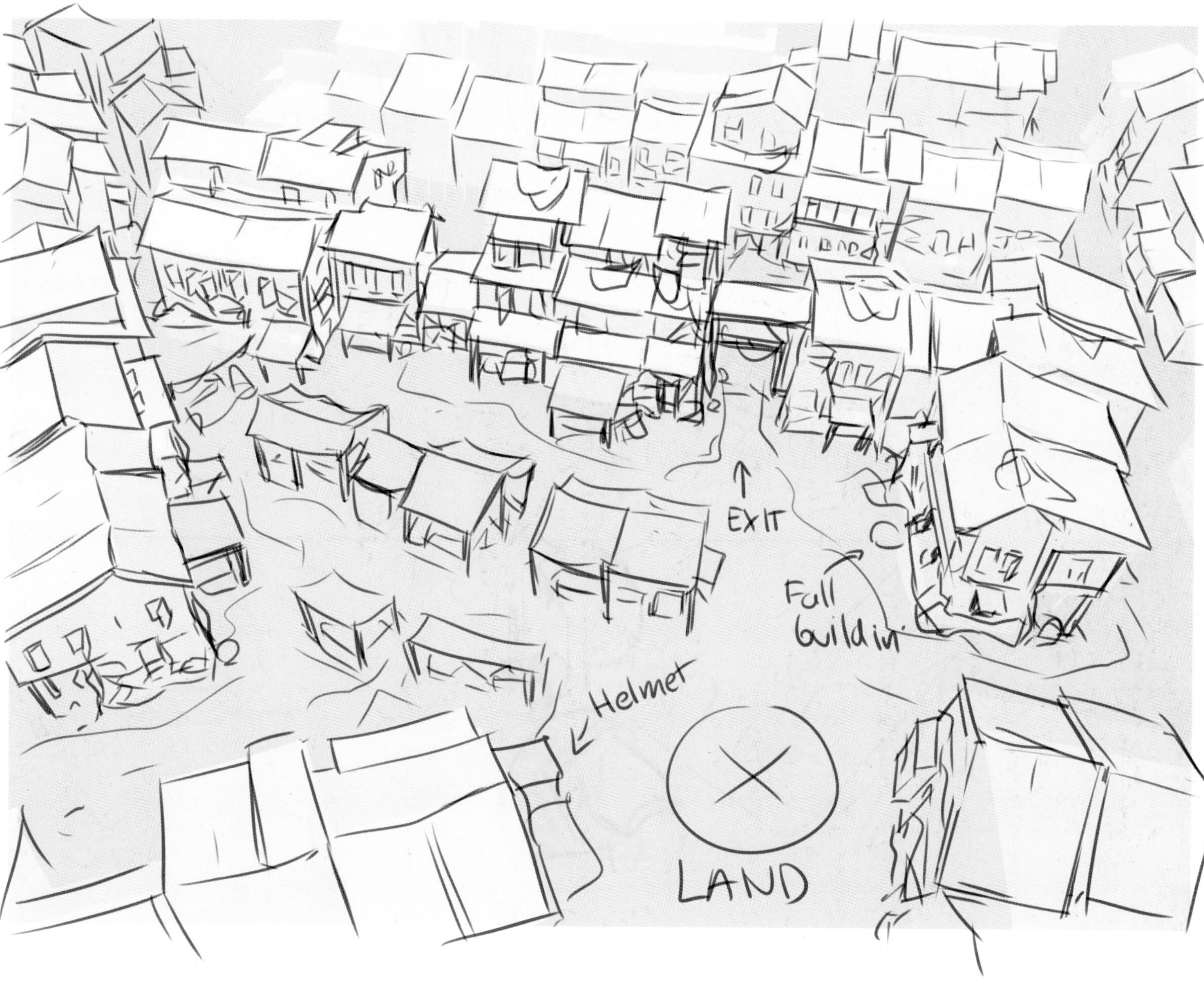
EXIT
Full buildin'
Helmet
LAND

A sketch of the market from early in the first book. I created simple 3D models in a program called Blender for most of the backgrounds in *Imbalance*, which I used as a base to draw over.

Design for Liling's house. You can see more clearly the 3D models I used in the background here. These models were especially handy for scenes we returned to several times (like Liling's house), as it ensured that buildings were placed consistently.

nickelodeon
降去神通
AVATAR
THE LAST AIRBENDER
THE PROMISE
BRYAN KONIETZKO
MICHAEL DANTE DIMARTINO
GENE LUEN YANG
GURIHIRU

AVATAR
THE LAST AIRBENDER
THE PROMISE · PART TWO
THE PROMISE · PART THREE

Avatar: The Last Airbender—The Promise Library Edition
978-1-61655-074-5 $39.99

Avatar: The Last Airbender—The Promise Part 1
978-1-59582-811-8 $12.99

Avatar: The Last Airbender—The Promise Part 2
978-1-59582-875-0 $12.99

Avatar: The Last Airbender—The Promise Part 3
978-1-59582-941-2 $12.99

Avatar: The Last Airbender—The Search Library Edition
978-1-61655-226-8 $39.99

Avatar: The Last Airbender—The Search Part 1
978-1-61655-054-7 $12.99

Avatar: The Last Airbender—The Search Part 2
978-1-61655-190-2 $12.99

Avatar: The Last Airbender—The Search Part 3
978-1-61655-184-1 $12.99

降去神通
AVATAR
THE LAST AIRBENDER
THE SEARCH
MICHAEL DANTE DIMARTINO

nickelodeon
AVATAR
THE LAST AIRBENDER
THE SEARCH · PART ONE
THE SEARCH · PART TWO
THE SEARCH · PART THREE

nickelodeon
降去神通
AVATAR
THE LAST AIRBENDER
THE RIFT

nickelodeon
AVATAR
THE LAST AIRBENDER
THE RIFT · PART ONE
THE RIFT · PART TWO
THE RIFT · PART THREE

Avatar: The Last Airbender—The Rift Library Edition
978-1-61655-550-4 $39.99

Avatar: The Last Airbender—The Rift Part 1
978-1-61655-295-4 $12.99

Avatar: The Last Airbender—The Rift Part 2
978-1-61655-296-1 $12.99

Avatar: The Last Airbender—The Rift Part 3
978-1-61655-297-8 $10.99

Avatar: The Last Airbender—Smoke and Shadow Library Edition
978-1-50670-013-7 $39.99

Avatar: The Last Airbender—Smoke and Shadow Part 1
978-1-61655-761-4 $12.99

Avatar: The Last Airbender—Smoke and Shadow Part 2
978-1-61655-790-4 $12.99

Avatar: The Last Airbender—Smoke and Shadow Part 3
978-1-61655-838-3 $12.99

nickelodeon
降去神通
AVATAR
THE LAST AIRBENDER
SMOKE AND SHADOW

nickelodeon
AVATAR
THE LAST AIRBENDER
SMOKE AND SHADOW · PART THREE

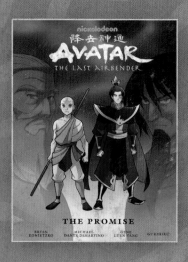

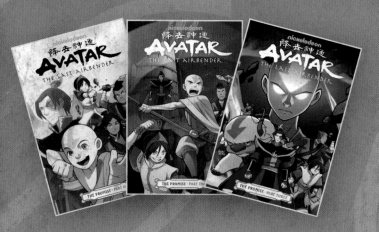

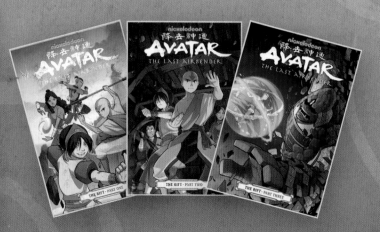

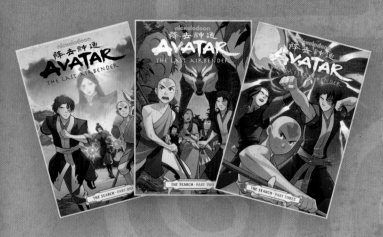

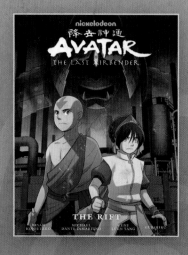

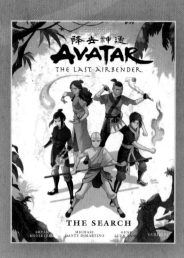

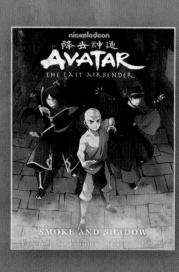

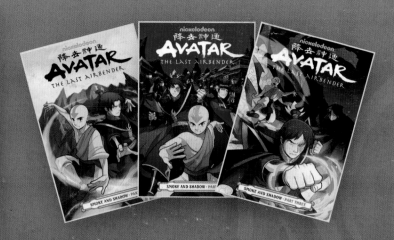

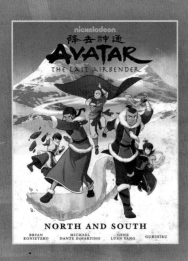

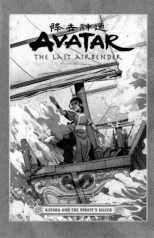
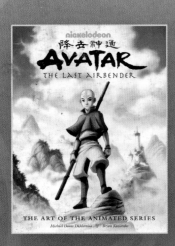

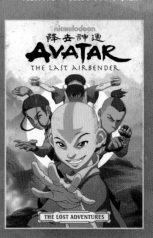

MIKE RICHARDSON
President and Publisher

NEIL HANKERSON
Executive Vice President

TOM WEDDLE
Chief Financial Officer

RANDY STRADLEY
Vice President of Publishing

NICK McWHORTER
Chief Business Development Officer

DALE LaFOUNTAIN
Chief Information Officer

MATT PARKINSON
Vice President of Marketing

VANESSA TODD-HOLMES
Vice President of Production and Scheduling

MARK BERNARDI
Vice President of Book Trade and Digital Sales

KEN LIZZI
General Counsel

DAVE MARSHALL
Editor in Chief

DAVEY ESTRADA
Editorial Director

CHRIS WARNER
Senior Books Editor

CARY GRAZZINI
Director of Specialty Projects

LIA RIBACCHI
Art Director

MATT DRYER
Director of Digital Art and Prepress

MICHAEL GOMBOS
Senior Director of Licensed Publications

KARI YADRO
Director of Custom Programs

KARI TORSON
Director of International Licensing

SEAN BRICE
Director of Trade Sales

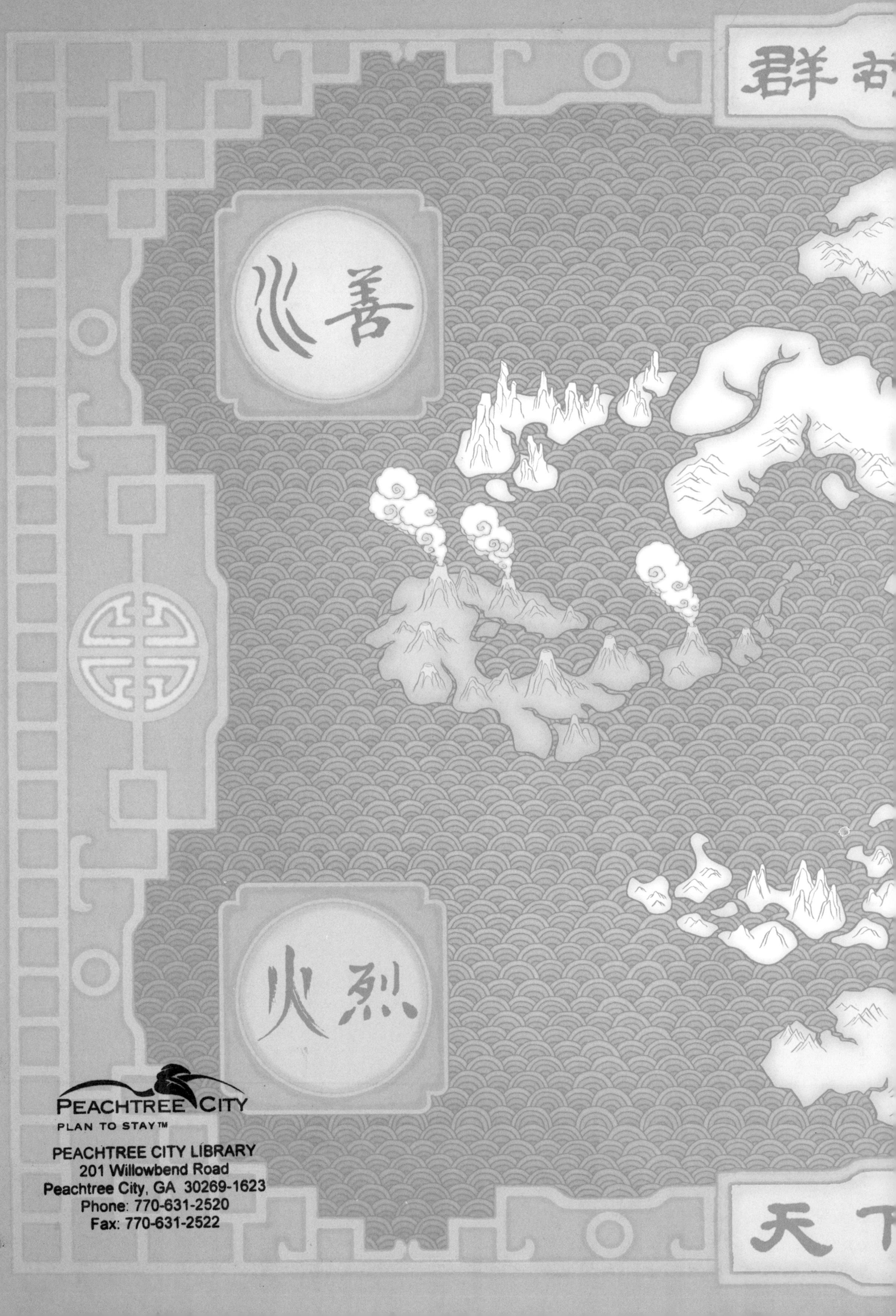
群
善
火烈
天下